FOLLOW THE NORTH STAR

. . . a story of passion and jealousy—and a lusty journey through the terrifying realities of the Old South, as thousands of slaves struggle against all odds to reach the Canadian border.

. . . the powerful sequel to an epic begun in *THE PASSION STONE.*

What the critics said about Harriette de Jarnette's first blockbuster:

. . . splendid, romanticized illustration of the pre-war South . . . colorful and consistent characterization . . .

—The Cincinnati Enquirer

. . . compelling reading.

—Santa Cruz Sentinel

Also by Harriette de Jarnette:

THE PASSION STONE
THE GOLDEN THRESHOLD

Follow the North Star

Harriette deJarnette

To my husband, Joseph Madison, who endured eight thousand miles and primitive campsites while I researched the background for this historical romance.

Book Margins, Inc.

A BMI Edition

Published by special arrangement with Dorchester Publishing

Printed in the United States of America.

FOREWORD

In the years immediately prior to the Civil War there were many freedmen, both of black and of mixed blood, in the United States.

From the earliest days of slavery, masters had freed slaves for various reasons. At the time of the Revolutionary War, to counter the British Army's offer of freedom to any slave refugee who joined their forces, the Continental Army retaliated with the same invitation.

These former slaves were freed at the end of the war, and the masters were never compensated, because it was assumed that had the runaway not joined the Continental Army, they'd have gone to the British and be lost to their owners in any event.

As the amount of free former slaves grew in number, so did the alarm of the white people in the Slave States. Insurrections had increased, and escapes were commonplace. Harriet Tubman, a former slave, became famous for the numbers she conducted to freedom, and so did a variety of other people. Some of these were white men, who, for one reason or another, found a challenge in the work.

The Refugee Slave Law of 1850 made it extremely difficult for a black man or person of color to exist in safety, even though their family had been free for generations back. In essence, the law gave permission for slave hunters to go into the Free States and bring out any person of black blood that they chose to consider a refugee. Providing there was no white man to stand witness for the

5

black, the hunter needed only to swear to the accusation. The profit in reselling these "refugees" to slave dealers was tremendous. No black man's word could be accepted as evidence, and, therefore, any protest on the part of the prisoner was meaningless. The only true safety lay in Canada.

Each state had its own law as to the degree of black blood that constituted whether a man or woman was legally black or white. In the Spanish possessions and the British colonies, anyone with less than a quarter of black blood was no longer considered negroid. However, in the United States, the qualifications were much more stringent. In most cases, anyone with less than one-eighth black blood was legally white. The law that anyone with a drop of black blood in him, no matter how much, was in fact *all* black did not come into effect until after the Civil War.

In Ohio, a Quaker, Levi Coffin, became famous for his work in smuggling to Canada the refugees brought to his house. He was the unchallenged "President of the Underground Railroad." His book, *Reminiscences,* can be found in most libraries today. The author is grateful for the information embodied in this work.

Many of the incidents in this novel are fictionalized accounts based on actual happenings to men and women who sought their freedom by following the north star. The Negro spirituals in this work are all traditional. Because it was the custom to change a word here and there in accordance with occasion or mood, the reader might find slight variations in the songs as they have heard them sung.

"You run away!" his master said.
"Ran away?" the slave answered. "Us follow the North Star."

"There was an old woman in Mississippi
    who heard of Canada.
She knew she had to go a long way up
    the Mississippi River, cross over
    and steer by the North Star."
            —from *Make Free* by W. Breyfogle

"That man must of got on a railroad that runs underground!"
—Attributed to a frustrated slave owner in pursuit of a slave.

PRELUDE
January 1859

They had cleaned the shack and even unrolled a carpet taken from the furniture wagon. It was stretched over the floor of pounded dirt to where the flames flickered and strained in the fireplace of mud-plastered timbers. Somebody had repaired the ropes that stretched over the abandoned bedframe. Her pallet and bedding were already in place.

She sat in the rocking chair, hoping to warm herself and the dying black baby she held. Earlier, she had seen that it was bathed and stripped of its wet, filthy garments. Now it lay in her arms wrapped in a scarf of white wool. At first it had given an occasional mewling cry, but now it was still, each breath an effort for the tiny lungs.

She tried not to think of its mother, whose thin garments were hardly more adequate than the infant's had been, and who probably by now had a chain on her ankle.

She knew she shouldn't have hidden the woman. That she'd endangered the entire venture in the doing. But that was over now. Past. The deputized slave hunters had what they sought, and later she'd pay the price.

She heard his footsteps. He came through the door without bothering to knock, glanced at the bedstead, and threw his sleeping roll into a far corner, still tied. His eyes swept over her, and through the anger she saw something else, the unleashing of a desire that up to now had been concealed.

She looked away, knowing she had broken her promise, so there was no holding him to his. That was part of their bargain. Tonight his bedroll would remain in the corner, tied. He would join her.

He crossed the floor and took the baby from her arms.

"You've already put every man and woman in this outfit under suspicion," he said. "Isn't that enough? Or do you intend to add child stealing to our credits?"

"The baby's sick," she protested.

"To death," he agreed. "At least permit its mother to share its last few hours."

"She's in chains."

"Should that make a difference?" He started to remove the scarf, but she caught his hand.

"Leave it."

"You'll need it later. Remember, the further north we get, the colder the weather."

"No!" Her voice had risen.

He shrugged. "I tell you, it's dying."

"Then let it die warm."

She had dressed for bed, and when she reached out to stop him from stripping the baby, her robe had fallen open. She was aware of the clinging quality of the thin muslin of her nightdress as his eyes lingered on the swell of her breasts.

"I promised to share a bottle or two of rum with the deputies," he told her. "I'll be away for awhile." His angry eyes met her defiant, dark ones. "Unbraid your hair while I'm gone."

She watched him leave, knowing there would be no escape. Then she took hold of the heavy, honey-colored braid of hair and threw it over her shoulder. No way. She wouldn't hasten to obey his orders like some meek private in a dictator's army!

She climbed into bed. The day had been a hard one, and she was tired as well as apprehensive. She thought of how it would be outside by the big fire. Their own men would have to spend the night shackled, as they must spend any night that strangers were near.

He would be sitting by the deputies, drinking and talking. And her love would be there, too.

10

Twenty-eight black former slaves, eleven of which were women and two were children. A bride's dowry, moving from New Orleans to "a place in Kentucky near the Ohio River," as the papers they carried put it. Yes, she thought ruefully, the papers. Everything in it right down to the dowry agreement and the marriage lines.

Hunted men. Outlaws with prices on their heads. Refugees, all of them. And she'd been stupid enough to attract the very attention they'd planned so carefully to avoid.

She fell asleep praying that the talk and the rum would last out the night.

A light awakened her, and then came the strong reek of rum. He was standing over her, holding a stubby candle. With exaggerated care, he tilted it until there was a sufficient splotch of wax on the shaky table to hold the base.

"The baby died," he said. "The woman won't let anyone take it from her."

She threw back the covers and reached for her robe.

"I'll go to her—" she started, but he threw her back onto the bed.

"Goddamn it!" he exclaimed. "Don't you ever learn? Isn't there anything resembling a brain in that head of yours?"

She glared at him and he returned the look, swaying slightly. Then slowly, methodically, he began to undress.

She squeezed her eyes shut and moved back as far as the wall permitted. The bed sank a little as he crawled in beside her, the warmth of his naked body a shock to every nerve end.

"Damn the room," he muttered. "It won't stand still . . . Those bastards were out to finish both bottles—and me with them . . ."

There was a long silence. Only the heavy sound of his breathing reached her ears. She opened her eyes and restrained an hysterical impulse to laugh. He had passed out in the middle of a sentence.

There remained nothing to do but to draw up the

11

covers. The night was cold. She averted her head so as not to look at his nakedness, thankful that the candle was guttering to an end.

She thought longingly of his bedroll in the corner, but there was no way she could climb over him without risking his awakening. He rolled in his sleep, pressing her even harder against the wall.

Gradually she found herself becoming aware of the fact that the feel of his warm, male body against her own was decidedly not unpleasant. A strange, aching heat passed over the parts closest to him. The parts from the waist down.

He stirred and flung out an arm. Now his hand rested on her belly, and a languid, quivering sensation brought with it a sudden desire to stretch. A shuddering stretch with every nerve tingling. She prayed he wouldn't awaken, but her body called out on a different note.

She experimentally reached out and touched the soft hair on his chest. Shocked at her own daring, she hastily started to withdraw her hand, but it was caught and held. Then his breath was warm against her ear as he turned to her. Again that incomprehensible urge to stretch. Like a cat being petted, she thought, disgusted at her inability to control what was happening to her.

He made a little sound of annoyance and pulled her nightdress up under her chin. His lips found the tips of her breasts and then moved across her belly. She drew up her legs in token protest, but he laughed and pushed them down. With both hands he cradled her buttocks, drawing her to him.

She was powerless to control her body as it moved against him bereft of all reason, possessed of responses that had nothing to do with herself. There was no escape, but had there been, she'd have turned from it.

Her breath came in little half-sobs as he readied her for himself. She cried out, and he muffled the sound by pressing his mouth over hers.

12

"A bride of a month isn't usually a virgin," he said after the tension had eased. "There are ears that might hear."

Again he was stroking her, firing her passion. "I'm sorry," he whispered suddenly, and she felt the urgency of him. "Bite my shoulder if you must. But quietly..."

This time there was no cry of pain, but she did bite into his flesh, clutching, gasping, whispering his name. When finally they lay still, clinging to each other, spent and breathless, he touched his arm.

"Next time I bed you," he said, his laughter tickling her neck, "remind me to wear a shoulder pad."

Then he slept again, but she remained imprisoned in his arms. She moved once, and in his sleep his grip tightened.

The end of virginity, she thought. And the end of innocence.

She could feel that though he slept, he'd soon awaken again.

She smiled, wondering how it was possible to smile. But she liked knowing these things about him, liked the intimate pressure of his maleness against her body.

To give the devil his due, she could hardly call what had happened a rape.

It was quiet outside. Everyone slept, but the fire burned high against the cold of the January night. She could see the flickering light through the thin cowhide of the window.

She thought back in a kind of wonder to that morning she first met him at Bijou. To the headstrong, willful girl who had been raised to believe she was the niece of Donna and Breel Luton. She'd have laughed, if anyone had told her that morning that within a week she'd learn she was not whom she supposed herself to be. That within a month she'd face a choice that ended with her throwing in her lot with this caravan of ten wagons, traveling in the direction of the North Star.

BOOK ONE

Fannette

BIJOU—1858

The day Fannette met Anton Verdier and Jared McLaury the usual early-morning quiet of Bijou had been disrupted by the sounds of pursuit. A party of angry plantation owners was out after a band of pilfering maroons, and the keening of their hounds echoed out of the swamplands.

It wasn't really the matter of men being hunted that bothered Fannette, it was the dismal baying of the hounds on the chase. Ever since she could remember, that had been enough to send chills racing down her spine.

Why? she wondered. What were maroons but runaways, outlaws and trouble-making freedmen? Thieves who'd been robbing every storehouse up and down the bayou, assisted in all probability by slaves in the quarters? No, she sincerely hoped they'd be caught. Then there'd be an end to the disturbance.

Besides, she had her own personal dilemma to occupy her thoughts. She set aside the sampler she'd been working on. She hated needlework anyway, and her Uncle Breel was standing outside on the balcony that encircled the second story of the house.

It's time, she decided, to have a talk with him.

He glanced up as she joined him. He had been leaning over the grilled iron railing, and Fannette noticed that the white hair which had recently appeared at his temples was making further inroads against the black of his sideburns. That his thoughts were in the past she knew by the abstracted manner in which he had been staring out at his empty kennels. Once his pack had yelped and cavorted there, but now the weeds grew lush and untrampled.

"There was the time," he remarked, "when I'd have

had my hounds out too."

"I suppose someone has to do it," she replied, her interest far from the subject. "They can't just be allowed to run free and live off our storehouses."

"At over fifteen hundred dollars for a prime hand, I'd think not." A half-smile was on his lips, but Fannette was too preoccupied with her own problems to notice it. "Guy DuBois claims that band of maroons is recruiting runaways faster than a man can replace them."

It really wasn't her concern. She shrugged. "I thought that was why folks around here hired a patrol."

"With a good start, who's going to catch them?" Breel glanced at the road outside the gates. A road that ended in swamps. "There isn't the hound that can track them through a marsh. Come cold weather, most of the runaways will sneak back anyway."

"Then why—"

Her uncle looked down into her upturned face. His stormy dark eyes so like her own were gentle for once.

"A chase brings out the atavistic in most men, Fannette."

She knew he understood how the keening of the hounds affected her, and that Aunt Donna knew also. When still a child she had often run to them screaming out her terror. More than once she'd seen them exchange knowing looks.

The baying faded into a distant place, and Fannette drew a deep, grateful breath. Her uncle put a protective arm around her shoulder and glanced up at the darkening sky.

"I'm glad we got the cane seed in early," he remarked. "From the look of things, we'll have to stop cutting and put all hands to carting wood for the mill while the roads hold."

Cane cutting! That concerned her even less than maroons.

Cane-cutting time. October. October 1858. She had been twenty years old for over a month now. Twenty and

18

not even betrothed, let alone married! Donna and Breel Luton had arranged a marriage contract for their son, Ted, before he was even out of short pants! Why hadn't they done their duty by her?

After all, she reflected, I am their ward and they're my only relatives. Yes, it was certainly time something was said. Past the time, in fact.

"Will Ted and Adelle have their wedding as soon as he's home from the university?" she ventured as an opener.

"I'll leave that up to them." Again her uncle's attention appeared captured and held by the past. "Sometimes it isn't wise for a young man to have too much freedom between school and settling down."

Well, if a hint didn't work, it was time to meet the issue without mincing words. She gripped the top bar of the railing and unconsciously tilted her chin at its most stubborn angle.

"Do you realize I'm twenty, Uncle Breel? Ted's almost a year younger than I am. It's ridiculous to be twenty and not married! And what's more, whenever a man's shown an interest in me, you send him packing. You know this has happened just about everytime I've been at a party."

He raised an eyebrow. "It has?"

"Yes!" she retorted, taking courage. "And to my knowledge, neither you nor Aunt Donna have ever given a thought to a marriage agreement for me. I know there was money left for my care. Isn't it enough for a dowry? Certainly it isn't the family background!"

A warning darkness flashed into her uncle's eyes. Breel Luton's temper was feared by everyone at Bijou from the lowliest of kitchen help to Aunt Donna and herself. She could still remember the last time one of his black moods took hold of him. How he had closed himself in the library with a bottle of brandy. That had been over a year ago. That bout had ended, as usual, with him riding into New Orleans.

"There are reasons, Fannette. Sound reasons. I don't

19

want to hear anything further about it."

He strode across the balcony, and she heard the door close as he went into the house. Merciful Mother! she thought, I hope I haven't set him off!

Nobody knew where he went on those wild rides into the city. It was certain it wasn't to the splendid town house on the Esplanade Publique, the mansion Aunt Donna's father, Theodor Moulton, had built when he first came to Louisiana. During her uncle's absence nothing was ever the same at Bijou. Time hung suspended, waiting for the morning when one of the field hands would come running to the house, shouting that the master was up the road.

Then he would ride into sight and draw up his horse near where Donna would be waiting. Terribly thin, unwashed, his still handsome face ravaged, and his flashing black eyes bloodshot, he would dismount and stand in front of his wife until she held out her hand.

Fannette frowned. Did everyone have a dark side? Something alien that fought to emerge? It was certain that she did. She dearly longed to be sweet and gentle and forgiving. Like Aunt Donna, in fact. Sometimes she even managed this phenomenon for days, then the other Fannette would surface. The stormy, passionate, wanting Fannette. The Fannette who knew when the slaves were holding forbidden voodoo gatherings out in the tumbled down shed at the edge of the cane fields . . .

This was the Fannette who wasn't afraid of the room at the end of the hall. Who would stand by the window in there, fascinated by the muted fireglow against the sky. Once she even stole out of the house and watched from the concealment of the cane brakes. But that was something she preferred not to remember. . .

"Fannette Randolph," she said softly, "you were never intended to be an old maid!" What use were lace-trimmed gowns in the latest fashion, or bonnets designed to protect the traditional magnolia whiteness of her skin, if there were no man to stand proudly at her side? And what advantage was her curling, honey-bright hair and dark eyes when her guardians permitted her no callers?

Randolph. That was another thing. She'd never understood why her name wasn't Luton until the head mistress at her school had commented on it.

"Randolph," Miss Mabelot had said in her precise, ladylike voice. "Madame Luton, I knew of the Shadney Randolphs. Madame was a Beauzart originally. They had no children."

Aunt Donna had smiled her sweetest, but she spoke in a tone that indicated she resented prying.

"Madame Randolph took Fannette to live with her just before her own death. Fannette's mother was a . . . relative. But in the terrible sickness of 1838 . . ." Donna's white gloved hands spread in a gesture of implied tragedy.

"So many orphaned during those dreadful times . . ." Miss Mabelot murmured. The matter ended there.

If Miss Mabelot knew of the Randolphs, then they must have been as important as the Lutons. So why the strange expression on Uncle Breel's face when she mentioned background? And the Randolphs certainly hadn't been poor.

"Nette, *chérie,*" Aunt Donna had said the day she finished school, "you'll never need to worry about money. There was a trust fund arranged for you when you were born. And it gives a very generous monthly allotment."

So it wasn't a dowry. And what good was money if it didn't serve a purpose? Her knowledge of such things was limited, but lately she'd become aware of a need, of a restlessness, of a certainty that there was more to life than the fit of a new gown.

It wasn't family. The Lutons were firmly entrenched in the society of New Orleans long before Donna's father had fled the slave revolt in Santo Domingo. Yet there were those who disapproved of Uncle Breel.

It had to do with that long-ago time when all but Bijou's cane fields had fallen into disrepair. When the white house had stood derelict on its high pillars, and the green shutters had flapped on broken hinges. When the overgrown gardens had been a jungle of neglect.

Now and then she heard stories that scarcely seemed believable. But even she could remember the time of replanting and rebuilding that old house. Shadowy figures moved in those memories, and it was difficult to separate reality from dream.

But that had no bearing on her problem. Those things were past. Forgotten. The present was what mattered.

Yes. Decidedly Aunt Donna was the one who should be confronted. While she held a deep love and respect for her uncle, his dark eyes had a way of penetrating beyond what she said to discover what she meant. As if he knew her better than she knew herself.

Her mind settled on the point, she moved to the stairway which, like most bayou houses, led from the second floor to the gardens.

She paused and glanced at the sloping lawns with none of her usual appreciation for the tropical garden beyond. Absently her eyes swept over the controlled, lush beauty of hibiscus, magnolia and scattered tiger lilies that reached out to the stand of live oak, their branches draped with Spanish moss. Her attention was held for a minute by the neat rows of cabins that were dimly visible, then passed on to the sugar house outlined clear and distinct against the sky.

Bijou, she mused. Set in the midst of the swampland like the jewel for which it was named. Even the turgid stream that flowed past its boundaries only led into deeper marsh. In season, the hogsheads of sugar had to be carted to the DuBois landing, so they could be floated downstream to the Mississippi.

She descended the stairs slowly and crossed the lawn to a bench under a shade tree. The leaves were dropping, bright-colored, rustling reminders that fall would soon replace winter.

She decided to walk to the edge of the garden and sit for awhile in the gazebo. She needed the quiet in order to plan how she'd approach Donna, and she was assured of privacy there. Through the years the columned pavilion had been considered her special place. Even her cousin, Ted, had been refused when he'd requested a second floor be added to make it a *garconniére*.

A horse neighed a warning. She looked up, startled, just in time to see someone dart from the shadows and run into the cover of mature cane.

Fannette hesitated between caution and curiosity. There was a live oak standing between her and the building, a screen of Spanish moss flowing downward, concealing the entrance . . . Someone is there! she thought.

A premonition of danger swept over her. Never had she been gripped by so intangible a fear. She gathered up her ruffled skirts, intending to run, to escape whatever threatened, but the sound of boots crushing the shell path caused her to hesitate.

A tall, fair-haired young man stepped out from the shadows of the white trelliswork. He stood very still. Watching. Interested and unabashed.

She had never seen him before, and she knew everyone up and down the bayou. A stranger. And what right had he there? Standing in her favorite place, as if he and not the Lutons owned Bijou?

He was fashionably dressed in a dark riding coat, a white cravat knotted at his throat. In one hand he held a crop, and with the other he swept off his high, beaver hat in a gesture of exaggerated courtesy.

"Good day, madame," he greeted her, his eyes laughing at her alarmed expression. "I didn't anticipate so charming a caller."

II

She stared at the stranger. His skin was bronzed darker than his thatch of fair hair, and his eyes were a bright blue. He continued to grin at her, as if he had every right in the world to trespass. She decided she definitely did not like him. She wasn't accustomed to men who treated her as if she were just anyone.

"Does my uncle know you're here?" she demanded.

"I haven't had the pleasure of meeting the gentleman," he replied. His eyes went toward the house. "However, I've heard considerable about him."

His accent was certainly not of Louisiana. Not of the South, for that matter. Nor was the steady way in which he regarded her, half mocking, half intrigued. None of the flash of admiration she'd come to expect. And not a trace of the protective courtesy she felt was her due.

"A man ran from the back of the gazebo just now," she said, watching for a change of expression. "He could be one of those they're after!"

"I hadn't explored that possibility, madame," he replied thoughtfully. "But then, with my back to the gazebo, it's extremely unlikely I'd have even seen him."

"Of course you saw him!" she exclaimed in exasperation.

"It's unfortunate, but I don't have eyes in the back of my head."

His smile dared her to say more.

Her eyes snapped with fury and frustration. Hadn't she enough to concern her without this impudent interloper?

"Just who are you?" Aunt Donna would never have approved of the tone she used. She bit her lip, annoyed that a total stranger could provoke her to such a degree.

24

He bowed from the waist, "Madame—"

"And I am not 'madame,' " Fannette interrupted. "I am Madame Luton's niece."

"Ah," he said softly.

"And what should that imply?" Was he deliberately trying to sidetrack her? Still, there was something in the inflection of his voice that had caught her interest.

"Nothing. Nothing at all." He paused. "You want to know what I'm doing here?"

She waited. A slight breeze blew between them, loosening more leaves. "Permit me," he said, and brushed a bright bit of autumn off her shoulder. Then he folded his arms across his chest, his eyes on the trees that fringed the end of the garden.

"I really don't enjoy a hunt—whether it's an animal or a man." He spoke with an air of resigned patience that made her feel just a little beneath the level of a half-wit. "Furthermore," he continued, "I didn't bring along enough clothes to relish getting what I'm wearing in a muddied condition."

"So you saw our gates and took it upon yourself to wait out the hunt in our gazebo?" Anyone who knew Fannette would have been warned by her voice.

He brightened. "Exactly."

"Then we'll go to the road together and wait. The hunt's over and they'll be coming back. I'm interested in learning whether any of them has ever seen you before."

The party was returning. The hounds were yelping rather than baying and the sounds were growing closer.

"Perhaps you'd better untie your horse," Fannette suggested. "And don't try racing away. I'll only send them after you."

"I believe you would," he acknowledged. He disappeared behind the trees, and a few minutes later he reappeared leading a big bay gelding.

"I've been giving the matter some thought," he said as they started down the path. "You're far too pretty to have

25

such a suspicious mind. Just what am I supposed to be up to?"

"As if you didn't know!" She stopped walking and turned on him. "Dealing with the maroons at first guess, or helping a slave to run off. We call men like you slave stealers!"

He laughed until the tears ran from his eyes.

"Good God! Good God almighty! Do I look like a pinch-nosed abolitionist? What you probably saw was one of your own hands who sneaked away from the cutting to snatch a little rest."

They reached the gate, and in the distance a band of men splattered up mud as their horses trotted down the road. The hounds were silent now, trailing in their wake.

They waited together, and Fannette began to feel less certain. The man beside her showed no inclination to bolt. His eyes were on her face rather than on the hunters.

"For your information," he said, "my name's Jared McLaury, and I'm a guest of Anton Verdier. At present the two of us have accepted the hospitality of the DuBois family. In fact, there's Giles DuBois up there in the lead."

It was indeed Giles DuBois, and Verdier was a familiar name. Jean Verdier was the agent who took care of Bijou's sugar shipments once the hogsheads reached New Orleans. Fannette knew the family, though she'd never met Anton. Dimly, she remembered something about a younger son who was away at school.

She thought of the aristrocratic little French speaking woman who often visited her Aunt Donna at the house on Esplanade Publique.

"*Bien,*" she replied, trying to sound like her aunt. "We shall see." Then she added triumphantly, "I happen to know Madame Verdier very well, so if you're lying it won't take long to get the truth!"

"I should have guessed you were unmarried," he murmured. "What man could stand such an obstinate female?"

26

Before she had time to vent her indignation at what was obviously an unjust statement, a rider pulled away from the party and put his horse to a gallop.

"Jared!" he shouted, waving his tall top hat. "And just when it seemed there was reason for hope! I thought you'd been left in the swamp!" He drew up on the reins, his elegant fawn-colored breeches and black boots plastered with mud, his wavy black hair ruffled by the rising wind.

His horse strained at the bit, but he checked it with a firm grip as his eyes flashed over Fannette. With a quick, graceful motion, he dismounted and took her hand. All the admiration she could desire was in his face.

"Mademoiselle Luton?" he asked hesitantly. "Permit me the introduction. I'm Anton Verdier."

She smiled up at him, almost forgetting the man at her side. Who would have expected the autocratic Madame Verdier to have so charming a son? And handsome. Not at all like his stodgy brother, Henri. The sky had darkened, and there were the first hesitant raindrops on the hand that still held hers, but suddenly the day was bright and she was glad she wasn't married or betrothed. At last it all made sense.

"My name is Randolph," she said softly. "But I live with the Lutons. I'm their niece." She glanced down at her hands, her cheeks warm. "I'm acquainted with Madame Verdier, your mother."

"I knew it was a mistake to stay away from New Orleans for so many years," he told her, looking into her eyes. "And on my return what do I find? My best friend in the company of the most beautiful girl in Louisiana while I'm out chasing the hounds!"

That brought about a return to reality and the matter at hand. She turned to McLaury to find he was regarding the two of them with open amusement.

"Then you do know this man?"

Anton gave an exaggerated sigh. "I wish I could say I

27

didn't, but unfortunately I'll have to confess to knowledge of him. We attended the university together."

"Would that be Mr. Luton?" Jared asked.

They all turned as Breel approached, the rain splattering on his bare head and shoulders. Anton stepped forward, hand extended.

"*Bonjour,* Monsieur Luton. I'm Anton Verdier."

Breel shook Anton's hand, but his eyes were on Fannette.

"Fannette," he said, "don't you realize the rain's coming down? God almighty, girl, get into the house before you're drenched!"

He turned then to the horsemen who had drawn up while he was talking. "They got away, gentlemen?" He smiled slightly. "I imagine you're ready for a warm drink and a hot fire." He nodded toward Giles DuBois. "Leave the horses at the stable. We'll be serving in the library."

"You'll join us?" Anton whispered as Fannette moved to leave.

She nodded and glanced nervously toward her uncle, but he hadn't heard. She smiled quickly at Anton, and then ran toward the house as the rain began to fall.

A fire crackled in the library, and the branches outside the window dripped sodden foliage onto the lawn. Occasionally there was the pounding of an increased onslaught from above.

Refreshed and warm, the men sat around the hearth, booted legs crossed, steaming mugs in their hands. Leticia, who was in charge of the house girls, helped André, the butler, to serve. There wasn't a mud splatter on the waxed wood or thick rug that missed her wrathful eyes. Leticia would find a speck of dirt on a gnat, Fannette decided.

Anton joined her where she stood in the doorway. He held a mug in his hand.

28

"Now I remember," he said. "A long time ago I heard Maman speak of a little girl who had come to stay with Madame Luton. At that time I was more interested in frogs."

"And now?" Fannette asked, looking down at her hands in the best tradition.

"Anything attractive and female. But frogs, also, if they're done to his liking." Jared spoke from behind Fannette, and a flash of annoyance crossed Anton's face.

"I don't consider that a joke," he said to his friend. "You had your chance for a *tête à tête* with Mademoiselle Randolph. Now go somewhere else and permit me my time."

"Oh, we had an interesting *tête à tête,*" McLaury agreed. "I was accused of trespassing and slave stealing or being an abolitionist. I'm not entirely clear which."

Donna Luton joined them. Her dark hair was swept back into a chignon, held in place by ribbon-bound lace. Her eyes sparkled with laughter. Only a faint tracing of what might someday become wrinkles betrayed her age. Even so, she could easily have been taken for less than her thirty-nine years, and Fannette saw admiration in McLaury's face as he bent over her hand. The admiration that she herself had expected but not received.

"I consider it an honor, Madame Luton," he said.

She turned to Anton. "And Anton! I haven't seen you since you were a very young boy!"

"Chasing frogs," McLaury mumbled into Fannette's ear.

Donna smiled at him, then returned her attention to Anton.

"Now that you're back, will you be entering your father's business? I understand your brother Henri's doing very well."

Anton shook his head. "Maman would have me on my way to France immediately if I hadn't protested. I said I must have a holiday between school and learning to

29

make wine."

France! Fannette stared at him in dismay. Had she found him only to lose him before there was even courting time? It was all very unfair!

"I remember when your mother came to New Orleans as a bride," Donna said. "Even then she told me that it was her duty to have two sons, one to help her husband in the family business, and the other to inherit her father's vineyard when he was old enough to join his uncle in France."

Anton made an unhappy sound, his eyes on Fannette. "Why couldn't my uncle's wife have had six sons instead of six daughters?" he asked.

"Good God, man!" McLaury exclaimed. "How can you be forced into doing something you don't want to do? It's your life!" He turned to Donna. "We've been arguing this point for the last two years."

Both Donna and Anton regarded him through shocked eyes.

"But it's a family thing!" Donna exclaimed. "There can be no question. Anything else, well, *c'est impossible*!"

Anton nodded in agreement. "I'm my uncle's heir. He's a deValois and I'll take his name. That's the way it is with the old families."

McLaury muttered something Fannette was certain hadn't been intended for her ears.

"And you, Monsieur?"

"May I do the honors?" Anton requested. "My friend, Jared McLaury. His brother, Andrew, captained the *Diana*, and my father did business with him for years. Until," he hesitated, "last year."

"When he was murdered." McLaury's voice was harsh, his eyes a hard, metallic blue. Deep lines appeared on either side of his firm mouth.

"I'm sorry," Donna murmured.

"I was told he'd drowned. It wasn't until later I learned it was with a weight attached to his feet."

30

There was a shocked silence, and DuBois's voice carried to them.

"I hear you've hired extra hands for the cutting and grinding, Luton."

"The cotton people are through with their harvesting, so it wasn't hard to come by twelve good workers," Breel replied. Fannette turned around and saw that his eyes were on her, just as they always seemed to be when she was enjoying the company of handsome young men. He sent a worried glance in Donna's direction.

"I thought you believed in the seven-year system," DuBois remarked, tapping out his pipe.

Breel turned his attention back to his guest, a scowl still on his face.

"You think wrong, then. I've never seen the economics of working slaves until they're worn out and drop dead. Nor of replacing them every seven years with fresh stock. Not with a prime hand going at close to two thousand dollars."

"Down river I hear they're using Irish and German immigrants to clear the swamps. A planter's not out of pocket if a hired hand sickens and dies. A man just can't afford to chance the loss of a prime black."

"That's the weakness of our entire system. We'd all be better off if we hired our hands. Instead, we're responsible for them as well as their families, but we're in too deep to climb out." Breel paused while André bent to refill his mug. "Right now I'm more concerned about getting wood to the mill before the roads are too cut up for the oxen."

DuBois sighed. "And I'm fretting about whether I've enough wood cut and seasoned. I never expected the crop that came in."

The fire crackled and several of the others nodded in agreement.

"I had to resort to green wood one year," Breel said. "It easily took twice as much to get the same heat."

Lord, Fannette thought, didn't they realize there were more important things in life than cane planting?

"It looks as if I'll have to windrow before I'm through." DuBois swirled the liquor in his mug unhappily. "There's sure to be a frost before we get all the cane in."

"Windrow?" McLaury whispered to Fannette. "What the devil is that?" Fannette realized his question was more for the purpose of dissipating the tension he'd created than for knowledge. But a planter standing near chose to inform him.

"It's cutting the cane as fast as possible and piling it in the middle of the rows so it'll be protected until it can be brought in, or there's enough wood for the boilers." He set down his steaming mug and held out a hand.

"I'm Clint Brown, and I knew your brother. Are you going to take over where he left off?"

For just a fraction of a second McLaury's eyes narrowed. Fannette wouldn't have noticed, except that Anton was regarding his friend quizzically, an amused tilt to his brow.

Then she decided it was all in her imagination, because McLaury smiled and held out his hand.

"If I captained a steamboat, it'd end on the first sandbar. The fact is, I found he had commitments when I went through his papers. I came south to attend to them."

DuBois's voice carried to them again.

"I always have held that a short holiday gets the grinding off to a better start. Specially as there's no way we'll be through until mid-January. Mrs. DuBois plans to open the house for company and a dance tomorrow night, Breel."

Breel nodded absently, his eyes again worrying over Fannette.

"We'd be honored to have you and Madame Luton—and Fannette, of course," DuBois continued. "It should be a welcome break before the work starts. We've already sent a shoat out to the quarters so they can have

32

a barbecue.''

Fannette ran to where her uncle sat.

"Please!" she begged. "You said we wouldn't be having Christmas until after the New Year. A dance would make the time go so much faster!"

And Anton would be there! So little time if he were being sent to France! she thought.

Her uncle shook his head.

"You'll be in New Orleans with your aunt during the holidays. I rather think you won't be deprived."

"Please," she entreated. "Do you know how long it's been since we were anywhere?"

"I would enjoy it." Donna spoke from the other side of the room.

Breel looked up, his eyes searching his wife's face.

"Do you think it wise, my dear?"

"Oh, it is! It is!" Fannette exclaimed.

Her uncle smiled, but she noticed his eyes were still troubled when they traveled to where Anton and Jared McLaury stood.

"We thank you for the invitation," he told DuBois. "We're already into the cane cutting and I hesitate to leave, but it seems the womenfolk outnumber me."

Fannette was aware of him watching her as she hurried back to Anton.

III

"*Vraiment, cherie,* a bayou party can hardly be considered a formal occasion," Donna protested. "The green velvet ballgown was made for the LaMotte's New Year's Eve reception. That was understood."

"Oh, a house full of old people! Who notices what anyone else wears? Everyone I know will be at the DuBois party," Fannette retorted.

Donna looked at the new gown through dubious eyes. "When I consented to a neckline low on your shoulder and draped *à la grecque,* I hadn't understood it would show quite so much bosom."

"Or that I had so much bosom to show?"

"Now you're being impertinent!" Donna laughed.

But in the end she had Donna's permission, even though her uncle set down a firm foot when she suggested that she wear her new cage of steel springs attached to vertical strips of muslin under the full skirts.

"We'll none of us fit into the carriage if you wear that contraption," he had stated bluntly. So, there was nothing to do but wear a *jupon de crinoline,* her familiar petticoat lined with stiff layers of horsehair.

Perhaps it was just as well. She really hadn't mastered every problem that came with wearing a cage. One must sit just so, or the front would pop up. Her new white silk evening boots were attractive, but it would hardly lend dignity to the occasion. Then there was the chance of moving too close to a stand and upsetting something. Well, it would all be perfected by New Year's Eve.

Meanwhile, the shimmering, deepening shades of emerald were caught and reflected by the lamplight. She liked the way the back overskirt flowed from waist to floor in

34

trailing ruffles, and the extra expense of black lace set low on her shoulders and draping down to the point of her boned bodice was certainly justified. Especially where it cascaded down over the straight front skirt, the emerald of the velvet gleaming through.

Her hair was pulled back from her face in the latest style, and she wove a wreath of satin rosebuds among the piled curls that fell to the nape of her neck. The same flowers were repeated in the little gathered tucks of lace down the front of her gown.

"Thank heavens those dreadful loops of hair in front of the ears are out," she told her aunt's maid, who was helping her dress. "They reminded me of a hound."

"Anyway you fix it, your hair look pretty," the maid assured her.

She studied her face, trying to see it as if for the first time. Her eyes were long and dark, the delicately etched line of brow and heavy lashes making them appear more narrow than they actually were. Her nose was straight and delicate, and high cheekbones slanted down to a firm chin. She wasn't certain about her mouth. Expressive? Yes. And willful. The full lips moved easily between a pout and laughter.

If Anton had found her interesting in the rain with her hair gathered back into a snood, he was certain to be pleased by her appearance now. There was no doubt about it, her gown would be the most elegant on the dance floor.

And she had the feeling that Anton had a taste for elegance . . .

She half closed her eyes, hearing his voice with all the special little nuances meant only for her. His gaze had never shifted from her face the day before, and even as he took his leave with the rest of the hunting party, he had looked back for a last glimpse of her standing at the head of the stairway.

And to think that he should have come into her life at

exactly the right time! There was no longer even the need of that discussion with her aunt. Unless, the thought was disenheartening, unless Anton was already betrothed.

She thought back to the conversations between Donna Luton and Madame Verdier. There had been much talk about the arrangements made for Henri, Anton's older brother, but nothing about Anton.

Donna entered the room with a jeweler's satin box in her hands. She was wearing chameleon silk, the shades changing from soft rose to burgandy as she moved, the full skirts standing out over the stiff crinoline, though not nearly with the fullness of Fannette's gown. The neckline was fashionably low over her shoulders, displaying her matched pearls to advantage. Her hair was simply arranged, gathered low on her neck with a wreath of tiny white flowers merging into the knot. Her toilette was simple and restrained. Yet Fannette knew that next to her, the other women would appear dowdy. Donna Luton had an inbred elegance that could not be assumed.

"Did Madame Verdier ever say whether there was a marriage contract for Anton?" Fannette asked.

"She said they weren't arranging a marriage until they were certain he'd go to her brother. A French marriage would be more satisfactory in that case." Donna frowned, her eyes troubled. "Nette, *cherie,* I hope you aren't setting your thoughts in that direction?"

The danger signs were there, so Fannette made an attempt at disinterest.

"Aunt Donna! I only met him yesterday!"

Donna's eyes continued to study her face, a little worry line between her brows.

"You're precious to me, Nette. I shouldn't want to see you hurt." She glanced down at the box she held and lifted the lid.

Fannette gasped as her aunt took out a perfect emerald set in heavy, filigreed gold. She realized the value must be in excess of Donna's pearls. Or, possibly, of the Moulton

36

diamond, for that matter.

"You'll let me wear that?" she exclaimed as her aunt fastened it to the point where the black lace *bretelle* met over her breast.

"It belonged to your mother. I intended to give it to you for the New Year's party, but it seems wrong to wear that gown without it."

She stood back, studying the girl. "I'm never certain whether you're really as beautiful as she. Sometimes you remind me of her, then other times I find nothing similar."

Suddenly she caught Fannette's hands, and there were tears in her eyes.

"I wish you were mine," she said softly, almost desperately. "Nette, I want you to know that. I wish you had been mine."

Her aunt's words continued to trouble Fannette as the carriage jolted over the rain-rutted road. There was so much she wanted to ask, but always there was a wall . . .

Her thoughts drifted to that long-ago time when she had hidden in the cane brakes.

It had been June. On St. John's Eve. All day there had been excitement among the slaves and whispering exchanges. Most of Bijou's fieldhands were blacks from Santo Domingo. Theodor Moulton had been among the few to escape with a fortune intact and slaves still faithful. Fannette became as familiar with the Haitian dialect as with the patois of the Creole negroes.

There was to be a meeting that night, and no doubt about it! Long after her aunt and uncle had retired to their room, she crept out into the hall and to her place by the window that overlooked the swamps. The room at the end of the hall which nobody cared to occupy—but where her mother had once stayed.

There was still the armoire full of dresses. Out of style, perhaps, but beautiful, the materials and colors still rich, kept fresh by heavy dust covers and regular airing. Almost as if she were momentarily expected back.

And maybe she had been. In the beginning.

This was one occasion when she did not stop to open the door of the armoire. She went directly to the window. Perhaps it was because St. John's Eve was reputed to hold special magic for voodoo worshipers, or maybe it was because she was at puberty, that restless, seeking time. Whatever it was, the pull of the distant fires drew her as never before.

In slippers and a white nightdress, she hurried down the outside staircase, across the path of crushed oyster shells, and into the young cane.

She hunched down, hiding, and a strange sensation ran through her body as she watched the shining black faces turned toward their *kanzo*, the voodoo priest, as he held a writhing serpent over their heads. In back of him a man waved a struggling white chicken, the sacrifice, and the cry went up for blood.

"*Damballa Wédo, C'est sang li mandé. Damballa Wédo, c'est sang li mandé pou allé!* It is blood he asks for. It is blood he wants before he leaves."

She shuddered and the chanting grew louder, until it seemed to surround her on all sides. The great flames leaped out of the fire, flames that reached to the sky and beyond.

"*Damballa Wédo!*"

The cry went up with the flames. Invoking . . . entreating . . . praying . . .

"*Damballa Wédo!*"

The snake straightened in the *kanzo's* hands and slithered out of his grip.

It looped and swirled over the dry earth until it found the place where she hid. It stopped at her feet and lifted its head, tongue flicking. Then it curled into a still, tight circle.

Even now she remembered the horror she felt. All sing-

38

ing and chanting—even the entreaties—ceased. There was a heavy, portentous silence, broken finally by one of the field women.

She leapt to a place in front of the fire, screaming out strange names. She whirled around and around, tearing off her frock. Finally she lay still, in a shuddering heap.

The *kanzo* parted the cane and stared down at Fannette, his eyes wild in the moonlight.

"A *mamaloi*!" he shouted. He turned back to the fire, still calling out in a Haitian dialect. "A *mamaloi*! Like her mother! Le Grand Zombi has selected her as he selected her mother!"

Mamaloi! A voodoo priestess. Was he saying that of Fannette Randolph? Fannette of the dainty hands and feet? Fannette who wore ruffled frocks?

The *kanzo's* eyes probed deeply into hers. Suddenly she was overcome with a compulsion to pick up the snake, to caress it, to hold it close. She moved slowly, not realizing she moved. With the snake cradled to her chest, she approached the fire.

Everyone fell back, leaving her a clear passage. Only the crackling of the fire broke the silence as it leaped even higher against the star-dusted June night.

In her mind, she heard the *kanzo's* commands. She raised the snake above her head and then—shattering and imperative—was another order, and it drowned out everything else. She turned her back to the silent audience, and with all the strength in her ten-year-old arms, she hurled their symbol of the Grand Zombi into the flames.

She was aware of shouting, screams, weeping, but darkness overcame her. A furious nightmare of images, maledictions, and, finally, of peace.

She awakened in her own bed in the morning. None of the house servants ever spoke of what had happened. Not even in a hint.

But Donna knew. Somehow she found out. She was in the bedroom when Fannette awakened. She sat on the

39

edge of the bed, her hands behind her neck as she undid the catch to the golden crucifix she always wore.

Fannette sat up and Donna brushed away the heavy, curly hair. Gently she fastened the clasp at the back of Fannette's neck.

"I want you to wear this," she said. "It's been mine since I was a little girl."

After she left the room, Fannette settled back into her pillow, fingering the chain and cross. Did Donna consider this a safeguard against voodoo? How could she, when everyone knew that Marie LaVeau, once queen of voodoo, had combined religious figures of the Catholic Church with the emblems of the Grand Zombi?

Besides, why should she need protection? Hadn't she thrown the snake into the fire? She'd repudiated any claim voodoo might have on her, past and present.

Strange, she so thoroughly understood this when no one had ever really explained voodoo worship or the Grand Zombi to her. All she knew was garnered from whispered talk among house servants. Still, she knew.

And she knew that whatever the heritage, she was freed of a part. She would never again be called a *mamaloi*, no matter what her mother might have been.

Her mother. There was the key to everything. Who had she been? More important, what had she been?

"I swear I've never known you to be quiet for so long," her Uncle Breel laughed.

"What was my mother like?" she asked. "What really happened to her?"

The laughter left her Uncle's eyes, and he turned to stare out of the window.

Her aunt took her hand and squeezed it.

"Someday maybe we'll discuss it. But not now, *cherie*."

IV

All thoughts of the past were swept away by the bright lights of the DuBois house beaming on the road ahead. As they drove up the avenue, they could hear the sounds of merry making in the quarters, and carriages were standing in line near the stables.

Anton had been waiting by the *porte cochere,* and he stepped forward.

"God almighty," Breel muttered to Donna. "All in formal black, and lace on his kid gloves. Does he think he's attending the opera?"

"Bien, he'll match our Fannette," Donna said. "Though I do remember at that age anything was an occasion."

Anton assisted Donna out of the door, and then took Fannette's arm as she stepped to the ground.

"Do you realize yours was the last carriage to arrive?" he chided. "I've been waiting since the first! How could you be so cruel?"

"You must forgive my impetuous friend." Jared McLaury elbowed Anton aside. He raised her hand and brushed it lightly with his lips.

Kaintuck! To kiss an unmarried girl's hand, it just wasn't done! Had he no manners, no knowlege of etiquette? And even had she been Donna and a married woman, she still could have taken offense. To touch her flesh with his lips! Kaintuck!

She drew her hand back quickly, letting him see her displeasure, but the glint in McLaury's eyes was undefinable, and for a second she wondered if his error hadn't been deliberate. A sort of mockery of the elaborate French decorum. In any event, she felt the warm blood rushing into

41

her cheeks at the unexpected sensation brought on by his touch. Kaintuck!

"You have a very beautiful mouth," he said quite unexpectedly.

She fingered the emerald at her neck and looked around for a distraction. Anton took her arm hastily.

"It's I who've been waiting for Miss Randolph," he said. "God knows where you've been, but I'd be pleased if you returned to wherever it might be."

He led Fannette up the steps and into the house. Madame DuBois was already greeting the Lutons, her plump, middle-aged face framed by a wreath of flowers. A style that had been passé for at least a decade. One might wonder if she still wore a cap indoors!

And there was Giles DuBois, equally resplendent—and outdated—in his parricide, the high, stiff collar that poked his chin with every turn of the head.

"Don't they ever go into New Orleans?" Anton whispered in awe.

"Only on business." The maid took Fannette's wrap, and she was aware of Anton's deep, admiring breath.

"I've heard that in the galleries of my Uncle Etienne's home there are portraits of the deValois ancestors, and a more aristocratic lot aren't to be found in all of France. But you, the tilt of your head, your beautiful, haughty face—you'd do them honor!"

Fannette smiled. "I understand the Randolphs weren't of Louisiana. Why, they might even have been Kaintucks!"

"Oh no!" he assured her. "I've made inquiries. Madame Randolph was a Beauzart. A fine family, both here and in France."

"But if I'm a Randolph—"

McLaury had followed them into the house, and he laughed. "There's no reasoning with a man in Anton's besotted condition."

"Go away," Anton muttered, then he turned his full at-

42

tention back to Fannette. "You must be chilled from the ride," he said. "I'll seat you here by the fire while I get a glass of hot punch."

Anton had no sooner left than McLaury took a place on the bench by her side.

"You've the look of a huntress," he told her. "And why have you settled on my poor friend?"

Because he's handsome, she thought. Because he's charming, and because I know I can learn to love him. Somehow, under Jared's steady scrutiny, she felt uneasy. Was it really because she was twenty and becoming apprehensive? That lately she'd begun to sense that something, somewhere, was not what it seemed?

"You can be certain," she replied, "that if I have that look, it isn't on your account."

He yawned. "I told you I dislike hunting. The only thing I like even less is being hunted."

Anton reappeared with two glasses.

"I've but two hands, Jared," he told his friend, his eyes flashing their meaning. "I'm desolated, but you'll have to go after your own."

McLaury bowed to Fannette.

"I'm also not fond of remaining in the proximity of a snare," he said softly. "You won't find me an encumbrance."

Anton moved closer.

"You were saying?"

"Nothing important." McLaury rose to his feet, brushed at the velvet lapel of his frockcoat, and smoothed his cravat. He sniffed at the glass Anton held. "Certainly they must have something stronger? Something worth the search?"

Anton watched his friend's retreat and took the vacant seat.

"It's not like him to be such a nuisance," he said, frowning. "Especially when he knows I've so much to say to you. There's really very little time. Maman is very upset that I've postponed sailing this long. But, I suppose, in January. . ."

Fannette felt a moment of panic. He would be going back to New Orleans within the next few days. It would be well into November before she and Donna left for their holiday. So much could happen in between.

"You understand why I had an interest? Why I inquired about the Randolphs?" His dark eyes were fixed on her face. His voice anxious, unsure.

"Perhaps," Fannette said guardedly, "I should resent it."

He caught her hands between his own. "I beg you not to! It's most important I present your family background to Maman. She places a great significance on such things."

In spite of her attraction to Anton, Fannette was aware of a slight irritation. Who was Madame Verdier that she should set herself up as a judge?

"Must she approve of my background before you dare dance with me? Must we have her permission for the next round of the ballroom floor?" she asked, her eyes flashing indignation.

"You don't understand—"

"Then let's set down our cups and dance! I can sit by the fire at Bijou!"

The fiddler was tuning his instrument, and the other musicians were taking their places. Anton rose to his feet and held his hand out to Fannette.

"We'll dance together for the rest of our lives if what I wish comes true," he told her. "Now is a time when there's need to talk."

This, Fannette decided, was the moment to pretend to misunderstand. "Before I commit myself to that," she laughed, "I really must know if our steps match!"

They matched, and matched well. Fannette drifted about the floor, content to have him lead her into each new movement. He hadn't learned to dance in the bayou,

44

that was for certain. One of New Orleans finest dance instructors, she'd guess. Just as Donna had taken pains she have the best of teachers.

"I could dance with you forever," he whispered, "but I must insist we talk."

She decided to consent. He started to lead her toward the hallway, and she glanced around hastily. Her Aunt Donna was dancing with Giles DuBois, and her Uncle Breel was gallantly trying to guide his panting hostess around the dance floor.

She followed Anton through the archway.

"I'll get you a wrap," he decided, looking around. "Then we can step out onto the balcony. It's not easy to say what I want to say above the screech of a fiddle."

He left, and she idly watched the dancers. Lenore, from down the bayou, was moving about the floor with her fiancé. She was wearing a gown that from the waist downward flounced out in tiers of pastel-tinted tulle. Like a rainbow left over from summer, Fannette thought. And Celine was in one of those new dresses with a round waistline, sash tied in the back. Thin as she was, there still seemed a distinct resemblance to a barrel. Maybe, if one lowered the top hoop . . .

How stupid! To stand here with a mind full of gowns and styles when the most important moment of her life was just ahead!

She moved out onto the balcony and leaned over the railing. Below, lanterns gave a muted light, encased in the misty air. She closed her eyes, savoring the fresh coolness after the heat of the crowded house. The sound of footsteps directly below carried upward. She glanced down at the path and dimly made out a figure disappearing in the direction of the quarters.

The barbecue out there was well under way, judging by the odors, she thought, and they were shouting about Lally and Jake jumping the broomstick backwards.

Très bien, Lally. Don't imagine you're the only one!

45

Only her broomstick would be the altar of the cathedral. Certainly Madame Verdier would insist upon New Orleans. And Aunt Donna would have her veil made of imported lace.

She drew herself up, her eyes straining to penetrate into the shadows.

Since when did an overseer wear a cutaway frockcoat? And what was a white man doing down there if he wasn't the overseer? She could make out a thatch of fair hair bared to the drizzle and white gloves.

It had to be Jared McLaury!

While she watched, a tall, powerfully-built black man came out of the darkness. He wore a bright-colored woolen stocking cap, and he took it off as he neared the other. The two of them conversed for a few minutes, then the one she suspected was Jared glanced toward the house and moved to the other side of a huge tree out of her sight.

She jumped as a hand touched her shoulder.

"I hope you haven't taken a chill?" Anton's voice was concerned. He covered her shoulders with her wrap. "I had no idea you'd come out here alone."

She decided not to mention what she'd seen. She took the chair Anton had pulled out for her, and he knelt beside it.

"I intend to present myself to your uncle tomorrow and ask permission to court you," he said. "But we have such a short time . . . You'll forgive me if I ask you if there's hope?"

"How could I say so soon?" Fannette murmured. Then, seeing his stricken expression, she relented. After all, there really wasn't that much time! She touched his shoulder lightly. "There's no one I'd rather have court me, Anton."

His face lit up. "It'll be no hardship to go to France if it's with you at my side! I'd go anywhere. Anywhere in the world! From that first moment out at the gate, I knew!"

"We've got to go back inside," Fannette said. "Every-

46

body watches what everyone else does at these dances, and Uncle Breel—"

"Then I'll tell him right here of my intentions!"

She shook her head. Perhaps she should warn him?

"Anton, my uncle has been most discouraging to anyone who called."

"But surely not to me?" Anton exclaimed. "A Verdier? You must realize he has known my father for a very long time!"

Just the same, Fannette thought uneasily. Just the same . . .

McLaury joined them as they came through the door. Somehow he seemed different than when he'd left them earlier. Quieter, serious. Worried, even.

"While you return Miss Randolph's wrap, I'll chance a round of the floor with her," he said to Anton.

She was about to refuse, but her curiosity was too great. She extended her hand to him, and she knew at once that she had been right in her suspicions. He had been on the path. His sleeve was damp, and moisture glistened in his hair.

"I presume you've snapped the trap?"

She glared at him. "I can't see where it's your concern."

"But it is!" he replied unexpectedly and with sincerity. "There's something I've just learned—" He paused. "If you go ahead with encouraging Anton, you'll end up regretting it. Believe me, I know what I'm saying."

"And Anton thinks you're a friend!"

"I am." He spoke quietly. "And yours, also. That's why I'm begging you to forget him. Tell him you feel kindly toward him, but there'd be nothing accomplished by calling on your uncle."

She stopped dancing, her eyes sparkling with anger.

"Of all the impudent, dictatorial demands!"

His mouth was grim, and for once his eyes were devoid of humor. "It's none of that. Your uncle won't give his consent, I can assure you of that. If you persist, you'll make it unpleasant all the way around."

"I really believe you're out of your mind."

"At the moment, Miss Randolph," he replied, "I wish that I were."

His words put a damper on the rest of the evening. Nothing could erase the cold fear she'd felt when she saw the pity in his eyes as he watched her return to Anton.

Pity? She was Fannette Randolph. Anton was in love with her, and she was the happiest girl in the world!

V

The next day Anton rode through Bijou's gates before noon. The sun was shining again, and the entire world seemed to glow, but still Fannette could not entirely dispel her apprehension. She had decided earlier that she would remain in her room until after he had seen her uncle. She moved out of sight down the hallway when André answered the door.

She hesitated on the threshold, wishing she had the courage to listen from outside the library. This time would be different, she thought. Uncle Breel couldn't refuse the son of his old friend, Jean Verdier.

Do I love Anton? she wondered. But did it really matter? She'd always heard that love came after marriage, and certainly it wouldn't be difficult to become very fond of him.

A loud voice carried down the hall. Uncle Breel shouting? He, who for all his quick temper, never raised his voice? He who could accomplish more with a lifted eyebrow than others with a roar?

The library door opened and closed, and Anton appeared in the hallway. André silently handed him his tall beaver hat and his riding crop before seeing him out.

Fannette stood very still, uncertain of whether to follow Anton or go to her uncle and demand to learn the reason for his anger. She heard the butler move toward the library as her uncle called for brandy. The door closed after him.

She came to life, then. She ran out onto the balcony and down the stairs. Anton was stalking toward the stables, his head high and his gloved hand snapping the crop against his boot as he walked.

"Anton!" she called, still running. The fallen brown leaves of the magnolia swirled up around her feet, and the brilliant foliage of a persimmon tree blew past her face and flying skirts.

He turned around, his lips white, and his eyes flashing black lights of fury.

"He had the presumption to refuse me permission to call!" Anton exclaimed as she drew up to him. "A Verdier. A de Valois! Do you understand, Fannette? He refused and he declined to offer a reason!"

How had Jared McLaury foreseen this?

She led him to the privacy of the gazebo. She sat down on the grecian bench, trying to think. Trying to understand.

Anton paced back and forth, hands clasped under the tails of his riding coat, his hat and crop resting on a marble-topped table.

"I know it's neither you nor your family," Fannette finally said. "You aren't the first to be sent away. Only I never minded it that much before."

He stopped in front of her, looking down into her upturned face.

"Is a courtship necessary? If you love me, I'll defy him! I'll make you my wife. There's nobody can take you from me!"

Fannette frowned. "We can hardly go to the cathedral and demand to be married. Or even to my own parish priest."

"I'd fight the world for you, don't you understand?" He paused. "At first I thought your uncle's reason had to do with dowry. I understand you're an orphan. But when I told him it didn't matter to me and I'd insist Maman accept you without a *dot*, he went insane. That's when he started to shout."

"I heard him," Fannette said quietly.

"He all but threw me out the door." Anton took to pacing again. Then he stopped, his forehead creased in thought.

"You and your aunt will be in New Orleans for the holidays? He'll stay at Bijou?"

"He has to," Fannette explained. "He'll be busy day and night seeing to the grinding."

Anton smiled unexpectedly. "It'll be simple," he said. "I'll make arrangements to sail right after the new year. I'll see that you get to the ship, and once we're out at sea, the captain can marry us. We'll have a priest bless the marriage when we get to France."

Fannette hesitated. An elopement took a bit of thought. It would cut her off from everything and everyone.

I'm twenty, she thought. Anton loves me. There might never be anyone who'll ever love me as much.

Did she love him? Yes, she decided, she must love him. Why else would she have been so upset at Breel's attitude?

"Yes," she said quietly.

He caught her into his arms and kissed her. It was the first time a man had ever held her, and she wasn't certain whether she like it.

"I love you so much," he whispered, his lips lingering near hers. "January seems so long a time to wait . . ." He kissed her again, hungrily.

She pulled away, her face flushed, and he was immediately contrite.

"I forget myself," he told her. "But how can I not? Every part of me reaches out to you, to hold you, to protect you . . ." He kept her hands between his own.

She glanced down at them, avoiding the ardor of his gaze.

"We'll have to plan carefully," she told him. "My uncle must have no suspicion."

He nodded in agreement. "When you're in New Orleans I'll arrange that Maman call on your aunt." His fingers tightened. "I want you to be present. I want her to see you, to get to know you."

"But she would never approve of an elopement."

"No," he smiled slightly. "But when she has my letter from France, she'll know I've chosen a wife who'll do no dishonor to the deValois."

"Is that so important?" Fannette asked. She hesitated. "Can you love me as much as you say and still be worried about your mother accepting me?"

I'm giving up Donna, she wanted to exclaim. And Uncle Breel. Maybe he is unreasonable, but I love him!

"It's very important, my darling," he said, and kissed her again.

Maybe a woman isn't really supposed to like being kissed, she thought. Just as she'd heard there were other things a woman didn't really care about but must accept.

After Anton rode out the gate, Fannette continued to sit in the pavilion. She looked around, appreciating the oaks, the flowering trees now almost stripped bare. Appreciating the sounds from the quarters, the distant slashing of cane. Everything that was Bijou.

Finally she stood up, straight and resolute. Uncle Breel must be faced, and this time she would not be put off by either a word or a look.

The library door was closed. A warning in itself. Ordinarily that was sufficient to send her away to await another time, but now she took the doorknob in a firm grip, turned it, and went into the room.

He looked up as she crossed the floor. He did not rise to his feet, but remained seated in his chair. An empty glass was on the table beside a decanter, but the brandy level was not noticeably reduced. Yet his eyes were on it, and she knew he was pulled between the necessity of his presence outdoors and the temptation offered by the liquor.

"I was expecting you," he said. "But I can't pretend it was with any elation."

A low fire burned in the grate, but it was dying now that the morning chill was out of the air. Fannette fixed her eyes on the coals.

"Anton Verdier called on you awhile ago."

"You can look at me, Fannette. Whatever either of your parents might have passed down to you, it wasn't being afraid to face an issue head up."

She heard Donna Luton's soft step, then the noise of the door being closed.

"Breel, maybe this can wait?"

Breel's eyes went past Fannette to his wife.

"We both know it's waited too long now."

"I realize I've been wrong. Wrong in many things. I promised to send her to France when she was old enough, and I failed to do it. I didn't do anything right, and it's Fannette who has to pay."

Breel got out of the chair and went to Donna. He put his arm around her shoulder.

"My dear," he said quietly, "you did your very best."

"Not when it came to the choice of leaving you alone while I took her to France. Breel, you've always been my great weakness."

"Thank God for that."

He faced Fannette, his mouth a thin, resolute line. "I had good reason to send Verdier away. That high-nosed bitch he calls Maman would have the truth about you in the time it'd take a dog to find a flea!"

Suddenly she didn't want to know. Didn't want to hear what he was about to say. Her heart began to pound in her chest and it was hard to breathe.

She found her voice. "The truth?"

It was Donna's turn, and she spoke gently but with determination. "I lied about your relationship to the Randolphs. Your mother was Shadney Randolph's *placee*."

Fannette stared at Donna, not believing, hoping for a smile to tell her it was a very bad joke. But Donna did not make jokes of that sort.

A *placee*. A mistress who was a *gens de couleur*! The existence of these women was known only too well to Creole wives and daughters, but rarely openly discussed. Everyone knew about the Quadroon Ball, and once she'd seen the rows of white cottages by the ramparts where most of them lived. Often at the theater she'd admired the beautiful, fashionable women who sat in their own section, resplendent with jewels that many a wife would dearly have loved to possess.

"Then I'm—" She couldn't finish. It was as if the knowledge only became a fact with the words.

"You're not a *gens de couleur*," Donna reassured her. "At least not in Louisiana. It's even doubtful that your mother was. Way back there was black blood. She claimed to be an octoroon—one-eighth black—but I doubt it very much. At most she was likely a sixteenth, which isn't even considered colored. As for you," Donna spread her hands, "there's no question. I broke no law in sending you to a white school. By law you're white."

"In Louisiana. What of the other states?"

"There are different rules, but you've passed beyond them. Can't you see? It's not only the question of blood, it's the circumstances that are bound to be uncovered when Madame Verdier makes her inquiries."

"And she will." Breel's voice was bitter. "She'll turn over every stone for her son's inspection."

Fannette looked at the two of them, her eyes sparkling and defiant.

"Do you imagine any of this will matter to Anton?"

"Especially to Anton, Nette, *cherie*."

"He loves me, Aunt Donna."

"You're asking too much of a man who's been taught to set so much importance on family."

"This Shadney Randolph. He's dead?"

"He was killed in a duel."

It all followed. More duels were fought under the Oaks over *placees* than over wives or daughters. Still, she had to know all there was to know. It was easier to accept these things while she was in a state of shock.

"Was my mother the cause of the duel?"

"You see," Donna evaded, "all of this would become known to Madame Verdier. Perhaps more."

"More! God in heaven, can there be more?" Fannette hardly recognized her voice. She had started to tremble and she looked down at her hands as Donna took them between her own. Donna's fingers were darker than the ones they held.

She forced herself to sound calm. There was so much she needed to know.

"Aunt Donna, are you really related to me at all?"

"I've always wished I were, Nette, *cherie*."

"And Uncle Breel?"

A faint color stained Donna's cheeks. She avoided looking at Fannette.

"It may as well all surface, Donna, my dear." Breel was back in his chair, his voice expressionless. "Fannette, I'm your father." Then he added, as if determined not to spare himself, "But don't blame your mother for that. She detested me. And rightly so."

Of all she'd learned, that was the most shattering knowledge. It was impossible to meet his eyes without a sense of shame for both of them. Breel whom she loved and respected more than anyone in the world.

Too much! And Anton. How could she tell him?

"I'd fight the world for you!" Anton had said. She had to believe it was true.

But she kept remembering how Jared McLaury had looked at her with pity in his eyes.

VI

It was Donna's custom to open the town house in New Orleans the first or second week of November, depending upon when the harvesting of the cane reached its peak.

As she explained to friends, it made very little difference whether she was in New Orleans or at Bijou during the time of cutting cane and sugar making. Breel only left the mill a few hours a day for necessary sleep. He even took his meals with the overseer. Watching, directing, encouraging.

On chilly nights it wasn't unusual for him to send word up to the house for rum to reward a willing worker.

"Enough for jubilation, but not enough to endanger," he would say. For there was danger. A boiler could explode. The belt could convey an unwary worker as well as the cane.

And it was also a time of jubilation. A good harvest benefited master and slave alike. The happy faces of the children in the quarters told everyone when the first drawing off of the molasses was. Everyone was busy. Men and women stripped the leaves from the cane and loaded it into carts. In the sugar house the juice was pressed out of the stalks and boiled, first to extract the impurities, and then to finally crystalize it into sugar. Meanwhile, ox-drawn wagons were loaded with wood for the boilers, and they rattled back and forth between the mill and the swamp's edge, where the lumber had been stacked to season during the summer.

The fires were never permitted to die unless a frost came. When this happened all hands had to be set to windrowing the cane to protect it from the elements. Hour after hour, throughout the day and night, operations

56

must continue. There was no time for either the slaves or the master to loiter.

Still, it was the most exciting part of the year. The slaves looked forward to it as they did a holiday. It was a matter of astonishment to Northern visitors that it was almost unknown for a slave to run away during this season.

For one thing, molasses, a by-product, was not rationed to the hardest workers at this time, and molasses was a treat usually reserved for holidays and Sundays. Also, once the hogsheads of sugar were ready for shipment, Christmas and New Year's would be combined into a week-long celebration. The extent of extra rations and gifts were often predicated by the number of hogsheads that floated downstream.

Fannette was grateful for the work that spared her the agony of having to face Breel over the dinner table. Whenever she heard him in the house she took refuge in her room. It was even difficult to look directly at Donna.

And Anton. What would he say? Whatever he said or did, one thing was certain. Once in New Orleans she would refuse to return to Bijou.

"Please, *cherie*," Donna entreated. "You mustn't feel the way you do. You're beautiful and you're not poor. Whether at the moment you believe it or choose not to, you're very fortunate."

"How would you feel if everything turned out to be a lie?" Fannette demanded.

"There was a time," Donna told her, "when I found life distasteful and a burden. When I wondered if I could continue to face what had to be faced." She moved over to a window and pulled aside a drape. The trees outside were bare, and the flowers dying. It didn't seem as if summer would ever come again.

For the first time, Fannette wondered about the young Donna. The woman who had received into her house a child her husband had by another woman. And, judging by the room at the end of the hall at Bijou, the woman herself.

"I never realized that Unc—" she stopped herself, "that he was a cruel man."

"Devil-ridden," Donna said quietly, "but not cruel." She paused. "Perhaps you'd like to know more of your mother?"

"No!" Fannette exclaimed quickly. "She's something that never really happened."

Donna moved across the room and held Fannette's face against her breast.

"Nette, *cherie*, your mother did the best she could for you. She planned you'd go to France where none of this scandal would be known. Blame me, if you must blame someone."

"It would have been better if I'd been told. And Anton—"

"You must prepare yourself, Fannette. Marriage to him is impossible. There are questions Madame Verdier has the right to ask. Where was your mother born? Who was your father? Where were they married? Your baptismal papers, where are they? Those things she'd demand to know regardless of anything else."

But not if Anton and I elope, she thought. Then it will be too late . . .

"Those things never stay hidden for long, Nette."

Finally the time came when they drove through the great iron gates with the "M" monogram for Moulton, past the two flowing fountains, to the *porte cochére* of the mansion on the Esplanade Publique.

The week before André, the butler, had headed a retinue of house servants sent to remove dust covers and to air out the rooms. Now everything sparkled, from the black Italian marble of the fireplaces to the crystal candelabrum. The polished wood of the floor was agleam, and all dust had been banished from drapes and rugs.

"I have a surprise for you," Donna said. She beckoned to a young, light-skinned girl. "This is Zette. Her mother's Aline, our caretaker here. You remember Zette, *cherie*?"

Fannette thought a minute. Aline always seemed to have a flock of growing children at her heels. They ranged in skin tones from deep Congo black to mulatto, like the girl in front of her.

Donna brushed back the curly hair and the girl smiled shyly.

"Zette wants to learn to be a maid and to be truthful. It's annoying to share my girl with you, so Zette will attend you in the future. She learns quickly."

Just a few weeks before, the idea of having her own maid would have thrilled Fannette, and she'd have enjoyed teaching the girl her duties. But now she acknowledged the gift with a shrug of her shoulders. Come January and she'd be leaving New Orleans and everything in it. There'd be a new life with Anton in France, and as mistress of his uncle's house, she'd choose her own maids.

Donna's eyes reflected her disappointment, and not for the first time, since that day in the library.

"Doesn't anything excite you anymore, Nette?"

"Should it?" Fannette asked. Her eyes darkened. "Yes, Donna, there is one thing. Promise me I never have to go back to Bijou."

"That's impossible," Donna said quietly. "Do you think it's easy for Breel? He loves you very much."

"And I hate him!" Fannette crossed to the window and stared out through tears that smarted and blurred her vision. She heard Donna leave, but she knew Zette was still in the room.

"You might as well go upstairs and start unpacking my clothes," she said. "Madame Luton's girl will show you what to do."

There was no merit in deceiving herself, she reflected. She panicked each time she thought of telling Anton what she had learned.

And was it really necessary? After all, an elopement meant she'd be on her way to another country before Madame Verdier had any opportunity to ask questions. It would be a *fait accompli*.

Outside, everything looked very much as it had looked when they'd left New Orleans for Bijou almost a year ago. The lawns were green and clipped, the hedges trimmed. The iron grillwork of the high fence stretched from the main gate down to the smaller gate that was used by the tradesmen. A splattering of rain had begun to fall.

Somewhere, in a distant part of the house, one of the maids was singing a song as she worked. Always before the words had amused her, but no longer.

> "*Yan pas savon qui assez bon*
> *Por blanchi vous la peau!*"

She thought of the words and translated them from the Creole patois of the singer.

> "*No soap has might to wash the blight*
> *And scrub you white all through!*"

She could no longer control the tears. They had started to roll down her cheeks. She opened the garden doors and ran outside into the increasing rain. Half blind and dabbing at her eyes, she almost knocked down a tall, lanky boy.

He snatched off his knitted cap, apologizing and grinning all at the same time.

"Aren't you supposed to be working in the garden?" she demanded.

He shook his head. The black hair kinked tightly to his scalp, and raindrops glistened in it.

"I a free man," he told her. "My girl, she live here."

"I don't think you're supposed to be wandering around the garden," Fannette said, feeling cross and embarrassed

60

at the same time. The tears refused to stop rolling down her cheeks.

The boy made no comment, but there was concern in his intelligent eyes. "My name's Jove, Miss Nette," he said. "Can I go fetch you someone?"

"Just leave!" she exclaimed. "Just leave me alone!" She wiped at her eyes with the flaring cloth of her wide sleeve. When she looked up again, he was gone.

He knew who I was, she thought. But then, why shouldn't he?

The next morning André brought Donna a note from Madame Verdier. They were at the breakfast table, and Donna excused herself to read the message. Fannette watched the frown form and eyes darken with annoyance.

"Madame wishes the pleasure of presenting her son to-morrow afternoon," Donna said. She tapped the note. "Nette, this must not be. How do I refuse madame without offending her?"

"Is there any reason why you should refuse her?"

"Oh Nette! It's impossible. How could he place me in this position? He knows Breel has forbidden him to call."

Fannette tried to control her own increasing apprehension. She forced herself to look away from the note.

"What am I to do, Nette?"

"Why shouldn't madame expect to present her son, Donna? You can hardly expect that Anton told her what happened at Bijou."

Donna was silent a minute. Then she nodded reluctantly.

"You're right, of course. But, *cherie*, you'll not press the situation? You'll be discreet?"

Fannette brushed at a crumb and laughed. "With both you and Madame Verdier present, what indiscretion could Anton and I possibly manage?"

The visit was very formal, as was always the case with

Madame Verdier. It was plain that the little Frenchwoman was proud of her tall, elegant son, but her manner remained unbending. Even when she reached out to touch his hand, it was with an aloof dignity. Fannette breathed a little prayer of gratitude that she'd be in a different country away from her prospective mother-in-law.

Nobody would be deserving of Anton in Madame Verdier's eyes, she thought. Henri's betrothed must be terrified!

Anton attended his mother, speaking only once to Fannette, and then in a reserved manner that seemed totally alien to the man who had begged her to marry him. It wasn't until the women began to discuss a shopping trip that they dared look at each other.

She watched as he tucked a folded note under his chair cushion. She nodded.

Finally the visit came to an end, and Donna walked into the hall with her guests. Fannette snatched the note from its hiding place. Anton wrote in a fine, slanting hand:

Maman intends to shop with Madame Luton tomorrow afternoon.

I'll wait by the lower gate and we can talk safely in the garden.

Until then, all my love,
your Anton.

She crumpled the note and threw it into the fire. Then she joined the others, but remained at a little distance, lingering in the doorway. Anton looked at her and she nodded.

Actually, she realized, she was breaking the tradition so strictly followed by unmarried girls of her class. It was unthinkable to meet a young man without a chaperon nearby. Had Breel given Anton permission to call, it would have been understood that on all visits either Donna or one of the older maids would be within a discreet distance, needlework or darning in their hands.

At Bijou life had been more relaxed. But even so, Breel would have stormed after her had he known that she'd followed Anton out the door that terrible morning when he'd declared his intentions. Certainly André would have reported her action, if he hadn't been called into the library.

But what did it matter? An elopement was hardly smiled upon, either. From now on, she decided, the stiff rules of etiquette no longer applied. In any event, not where Anton was concerned.

Still, she made certain that Donna and Madame Verdier were well on their way the next morning before she prepared herself to leave the house.

She tried on three different dresses and still could not arrive at a decision. Finally she settled on her new princess-styled gown. It fitted tightly at the waist where it came to a V in the front, gored so that the material flared out into a wide skirt. She liked the bayadére stripes of blue that were woven into the material, and the velvet bands of the same color that bordered her full pagoda sleeves and the hemline.

She ran a blue ribbon through her hair and Zette fastened her pardessus, a fitted, three-quarter-length wrap. Then she studied herself in the mirror. She looked no different than she had back at Bijou when Anton had declared his love. Her hair still fell in curls from the knot at the back of her head, her eyes were still dark and sparkling, and her lips as soft. If I have to tell him, she wondered, will I continue to look the same to him?

"I'm going to walk in the garden," she told Zette. She looked around for something to occupy the girl. "You can take the plume off my old riding hat and put it on the new velvet one."

André opened the door for her.

"A bit of air in the garden," she murmured. But she was sure they must all know. That her voice and face must certainly betray her excitement—and trepidation.

She approached the lower gate from a side path. Anton was waiting in the shadows of a huge oak. She hesitated, looking around to make certain there was no one near.

Winter had set its mark on everything. Maybe that was why she felt so despondent. In Louisiana most vegetation knew no season except after a frost, but there was still the dank, sealed-away look of November on all sides. She shivered, wishing she'd worn a heavier wrap.

Anton caught sight of her and he hurried to the gate. He swept off his hat. His black hair curled in front of his ears and above the collar, which turned outward over his neck cloth quite in the latest fashion. Surely no girl ever had a more handsome man court her!

She opened the gate, then led him quickly away from the path to a bench by the fountain. A place hidden from the rest of the garden by shrubbery and trees. The only servant she would risk meeting here was the old gardener.

He took her into his arms, lips on hers. Then he took her face between his hands and searched into her eyes.

"I could hardly endure being so close yesterday—and so far away. If you'd looked out your window last night, you'd have seen me under the tree there. I watched until the lamp went out and the room was dark."

"How did you know which window to watch?" she asked, unable to suppress a flush of pleasure at the flattery.

"I saw you looking out when Maman and I drove up. By the way, she commented that you were a pretty thing and knew enough to keep your mouth shut."

"I was petrified," Fannette responded truthfully.

He moved his chin in her hair. "Is there any chance your uncle will relent? I'm certain Maman will be happy with my choice."

Happy? Fannette felt an hysterical desire to laugh. She shook her head. "He'll not relent. Not ever."

"Did he give you a reason? *Qui diable!* What reason

could possibly exist? He was like a madman!"

She was silent.

"You may tell me. Mind, it doesn't matter, but I'm not without curiosity."

She could pretend she still did not know Breel's reason. She could pass it off as an eccentricity of an eccentric man. She could laugh and let him kiss her again. Only she kept hearing Donna's words. They rang through her head:

"Those things never stay hidden for long, Nette."

Nor would they. Anton would be justified in feeling she had lied. That she had deceived him. He might even come to hate her for it.

Still, the temptation was strong. "Why should it matter?" she asked. "We'll be married on the boat, so it won't really make a difference."

His eyes sharpened and he drew away from her.

"Then there is something!"

"Everything!" What was the use? Donna was right. "In the first place, Breel isn't my uncle. He's my father."

"My God! What will Maman think?" Anton bit his lip, his eyes thoughtful. "But your name's Randolph. Your mother was their relative? A young girl who was deceived? Those things happen—but what a terrible scandal! Maman will never—"

She understood then the pity she'd seen in McLaury's eyes. She wanted to stop there, but knew there was nothing left to lose. She may as well reveal the entire sordid truth.

"There's more, Anton. My mother was Shadney Randolph's *placee*."

His face lost all color. He swore softly and fervently. Words she'd never even heard before.

"How did they dare?" he finally asked her, his voice still choked with shock and rage. "How could they dare pass you as a lady of breeding and family?"

"They broke no law," Fannette replied with a desperate sort of calm. "My mother wasn't of New Orleans. Donna

65

says it's questionable that she was even *gens de couleur* under Louisiana's *code noir*. And I'm certainly not."

"Perhaps," he agreed. "But a deValois? It's not possible, Fannette." His voice softened. "In France there'd be no question of color—even if it were much more. It's the scandal that's important. The lack of family name."

"You said nothing mattered." It was impossible to keep bitterness out of her voice.

"My sons matter. The name and tradition they have a right to expect."

She turned to leave, but he caught her arm.

"Fannette, I do love you! I've never wanted another woman the way I want you. Give me a chance. Let my head clear so I can think."

"It won't change what I am."

"Please," he begged. "Please meet me here tomorrow. Find an excuse to walk in the garden the way you did today. I'll be waiting from noon on. Until midnight, if necessary!"

She hesitated. "I don't know," she said finally. "I won't promise."

VII

She lay awake throughout the night. It was impossible to wipe from her mind the bleak future she faced. The fact that now there was no way she could avoid returning to Bijou—and Breel. Strangely enough, that mattered more than losing Anton.

A hundred times she resolved not to let Anton in the gate. She might, at least, keep her pride. Besides, what was there to be gained? Everything that could be said had been said.

Still, directly after the noon meal and as soon as Donna retired to her room for the customary siesta, Fannette found herself on her way out the garden door.

Anton was waiting. That he was highly perturbed was beyond question. He led the way to the bench and fountain without a greeting.

"It's even worse than I imagined," he informed her abruptly. "I stopped by the coffee house and encouraged some of my father's old friends to talk of past scandals. I mentioned Luton's name. Then it all came out, like an infection from an ancient wound."

"Don't those old gossips ever forget anything?"

"Forget?" He laughed. "It's still as fresh as yesterday. You didn't tell me it was Luton who killed Randolph."

With her mother Randolph's mistress and Luton her father, how could it have been otherwise? she thought. Then she said to him, "There are duels everyday, and men are killed. Why should this be any different?"

He tapped his walking stick against his boot and moved uneasily on the bench. "Randolph was killed with a foul, Fannette. That's a thing that'll never be forgotten."

He got to his feet and stood looking at the fountain, his

67

back to her. "It happened just before the sickness in 1838. Your mother left after that. There was talk that she married a planter in Virginia. Another scandal, and she came back to New Orleans for awhile. Then she disappeared again. Later her daughter, a young baby then, was brought to live in her house by the ramparts."

Fannette moved to his side and caught his arm. "I've a sister?" she asked.

He nodded. "A half-sister more likely. I went by the place. It's a well-kept cottage, and she has house slaves. A cook, a maid—possibly more. She's educated, by the Ursulines, I should imagine. She's younger than you—and very pretty."

Fannette was aware of an irrational surge of jealousy.

"You saw her?"

"When she went to the market with her cook. Like the others down there, she dresses with elegance. She holds her head like a queen."

Again that jealousy. Of her own sister?

"She's darker than you. There's no resemblance."

Thank Lord for that, at least!

They were silent for a few minutes.

"I can't stop loving you," Anton said unexpectedly. He caught her to him and held her, kissing her as the fountain splashed behind them. His hands moved over her back, and his lips were on her ear, her cheek, her neck.

She pushed him away, but he refused to release her.

"You'll be my mistress, Fannette. We'll go to France together just as we planned. Eventually I'll have to take a wife, but you'll be my love."

"Mistress?" she repeated, her eyes wide and shocked.

He caught her hands and pulled her back against him. "What else is left for us? In France, a mistress can hold an honored place. You'll never want for anything."

"Except marriage."

"I couldn't hurt Maman."

"But you can take a mistress."

"Of course. But in my heart you'll always be my wife." He paused. "I'll arrange for a cabin for you on the boat. You'll not be embarrassed."

She snatched her hands free and ran for the house.

Donna met her in the hallway.

"I was afraid—" she started.

Fannette brushed past her and ran up the stairs to her room, but Donna followed.

"I tried to stop you, Nette, *cherie,*" she said.

"He was very gallant. He said I could be his mistress."

"Don't be so bitter, Nette. He really hasn't much choice."

"Hasn't he?" Fannette demanded. "Oh, hasn't he?"

"Nette, don't be a fool. There are other men who'll love you for what you are. He isn't the only one in the world."

"Donna," Fannette sobbed, "you don't understand what it's like to be in love!"

Donna smiled a wry ghost of a smile. "Don't I, *cherie*? Perhaps it's you who must learn."

VIII

Christmas was approaching, and Fannette knew there were few afternoons, rain or storm, when Anton failed to take up his vigil under the oak. At first he remained for the better part of an hour, but as the weather worsened and the holiday season progressed, he remained only long enough to be certain he was seen by her.

There was none of the usual joyful anticipation for the sparkle and gaiety of the season. Each day she hoped for a note. A note telling her that he could not live without her and that if it was marriage she demanded, then there would be marriage. But no such note arrived.

On the day before Christmas, Zette hurried into the room, black eyes aglow with excitement.

"Dey's a man in de hall!" she exclaimed, almost dancing. "He got a ca'age waitin' and he ask for you to ride with him. He say he want to talk."

Anton couldn't have timed it better. Donna was out finishing her long list of Christmas items that must be presented when the grinding was over, and André, the butler, was enjoying lunch which would be followed by his afternoon rest.

She brushed her hair and wished that she hadn't become so pale the last few weeks. Zette helped her with her wrap, and Fannette selected a new bonnet with a narrow rim that would not hide her profile, nor the small red roses nestling against her cheek. Anton! Anton, come to tell her his love for her overshadowed the fear of his mother's displeasure. Anton!

She hurried down the stairs and into the entrance hall. Then she stopped with an exclamation of annoyance.

The man who had been waiting, turned to her and

bowed. His bright blue eyes were concerned as they swept over her, but the old, amused smile was on his lips.

"It's hardly flattering to see you so disappointed," he told her. He took her hand and looked down into her face. "And so wan. You're not the type of a woman who can fall gracefully into a decline. I think someone should have told you that."

"Why are you here?" she demanded.

"To take you for a ride." He held open the door and waited for her to go out. "And hopefully to put some sense in your head."

Before she could refuse, he had caught her arm in a firm grip. She was forced to either put up a struggle or to follow him down the stairs to the *porte cochére*, where a carriage stood waiting. The curtains were pulled and the horses moved restlessly.

McLaury gave brief instructions to the driver, and then climbed inside.

"I rather think Anton would be unhappy if he knew I borrowed his father's carriage and driver to take you for a ride," he remarked. "But I find it rather satisfying."

"Then you didn't bring a message from Anton?"

"I came to talk about him. While it would have been improper for him to discuss a fiancée with another man, there's no such restriction concerning a mistress."

She clenched her hands together in her lap.

"I am not his mistress."

"But you are considering it. Strongly."

She turned on him and unleashed the fury only he seemed able to arouse in her. "What if I am?" she demanded. "I believe he'll make me his wife once we're away from his mother. Yes, I am considering it. He's even promised me a separate cabin on the boat. Between here and France—"

"You stupid little fool!" he shouted, cutting off her words. "You innocent, stupid female! I've seen Anton in love dozens of times, and always it's the end of the world—until he gets his way. Of course, in the past, none of those girls would have satisfied Madame Verdier, so there was no question of marriage. You must understand a satisfied Anton is a bored Anton."

She slapped him across the face.

He caught her hand in a grip that made her cry out. Even his mouth was white, but the mark of her fingers had begun to show on his jaw.

"Do you know what being a mistress implies?" he asked very softly. "Have you any idea what happens between a man and a woman?"

There was color in plenty in her cheeks as she read the intent in his eyes. He brushed back her bonnet, and one arm went around her, holding her helpless. His mouth pressed down on hers while his other hand moved over her back, slipping around to cup her breast. He raised his head and looked down at her, and she stared back, her lips slightly parted. When Anton had kissed her, it hadn't been like that!

With a muffled exclamation, he yanked the sloping shoulders of her dress down, and she heard the material rip. He moved her camisole aside, lips and tongue on her breasts, caressing, playing, his fingers finding places where she'd never been touched before. His weight carried her back onto the seat, and her breath caught, then came in sobs as she fought against him. His mouth traveled up to her neck, her ears, then closed again on her lips. It was no longer necessary to hold her still, but his fingers continued to stroke her.

Mother of Mercy. . . God . . . Oh God . . . The warming flood of heat quivered through her. She lay in his arms, wanting whatever it was a man did to a woman.

Suddenly he yanked her to a sitting position. He made an attempt to smooth the bodice of her dress, trying to pull up the shoulders and noticing the jagged tear for the first time. He pushed down her skirts and brought her cloak up around her neck.

72

His hand was unsteady as he gave her the ruffled bonnet. "You'll have to tie that," he told her. "I can't trust myself yet." His eyes lingered on her. "That was too close," he added, and she realized he intended the observation as an apology.

Her breath was still uneven, but she glared at him.

He smiled slightly. "I can assure you, Fannette, saying goodbye to Anton won't end your world."

"Anton never dared to touch me like that!"

"I hope not," he agreed, brushing back his hair. "But do you think Anton is the man to put a mistress on a pedestal and worship from afar?"

He reached across her and pulled up the curtain. She saw, then, that the carriage had been brought to a halt and the driver was waiting for instructions. Was that all that had saved her?

In an effort to avoid his eyes, she looked out the window. They were parked squarely in front of a white cottage. A much larger dwelling than those that bordered it.

Suddenly it looked very familiar. As familiar as the house on Esplanade Publique. Yet she was positive she'd never seen it before.

It was a second before she realized McLaury was instructing her.

"Twist your bonnet a little more to the right." His glance swept over her, critical and impersonal. "I'm sorry I tore your gown, but wear your wrap hooked at the neck and it won't show. Zette can be trusted to mend it and keep her mouth shut."

"You know my maid?"

"I've made it my business to know most things about you. About Bijou, for that matter."

He opened the door, and the driver jumped down, ready to assist them.

"Do you intend for me to get out here?" Fannette asked, incredulous. "Isn't this that place near the ramparts?"

"It's hardly Gallatin Street, though from the prissy tone of your voice, a person might think it was."

"Why have you taken me here?"

"Because it's time someone did. There's no one in that cottage who doesn't know of you. It might be said there's been a lifeline between this place and Bijou for a number of years. Madame Luton always calls here when she's in town. She's Poppy's guardian as well as yours."

"Poppy?"

Jared McLaury smiled, a different smile than he'd ever had for her. It hinted of affection and respect.

"Juliet. When she was little she was called Papillotes because her hair curled as if it had just come out of brown paper wrappers. It was Madame Luton who started calling her Poppy."

Inside that cottage were pages of her life that Fannette had no desire to turn. Once read, nothing would ever be the same again. She drew back, shaking her head.

"I won't go in there," she said. "I don't want to meet that woman."

"Girl," he corrected. He'd climbed out and was waiting to assist her. Unwillingly she permitted him to draw her out onto the banquette.

"I don't think you're a coward, Fannette?" It was a question, not a statement.

She moved slowly up the walk and short flight of stairs. He followed her closely and tapped on the door with his walking stick.

A stout black woman of middle years answered. Her face broke into a grin.

" 'Bout time you call," she scolded. "Miss Poppy thought you forgit us. My man, Trojan, he say you busy. I say you never too busy to see Miss Poppy!"

"Letty, you old nag!" McLaury laughed. "Now I know why Trojan spends so much time in the bayou country!"

"I cut them up both, you tell me him got another woman up there!" Her voice was ferocious, but her

74

eyes twinkled.

A girl came into the hallway. The full skirt of her cerise-colored taffeta gown rustled to her quick movements as she hastened to greet them.

"Jared!" she exclaimed. "I thought it was decided you shouldn't visit here until—" Her eyes rested on Fannette, and her words came to a sudden halt in midsentence.

Fannette returned the curious survey. The girl who stood by McLaury was smaller than she, of a build that managed to appear both delicate and voluptuous. Her great mass of black hair curled around a well-shaped head and was held in place at the nape of her neck by a snood the same color as her gown. Her eyes were large and golden in a heart-shaped face. Her features small and fine.

She extended a small, smooth hand. Fannette noticed there was the slightest suggestion of warm copper to her skin, but she was no darker than many a Creole of the old French-Spanish families.

"You're Fannette," Poppy said, delighted. "And you're so beautiful!"

But I'll never have your charm, Fannette thought rebelliously, nor as tiny a waist! And even Anton had never looked at her the way McLaury gazed down at Poppy. The respect and admiration. And, yes, the affection. There was no doubt about it, this was the sort of female who appealed to a man's protective instincts. And, *merci beaucoup*, it was Jared, not Anton who gazed down at the girl with that uncharacteristic devotion!

Poppy glanced apprehensively down the street.

"I think we should go inside," she suggested, and Jared nodded in agreement.

She led the way into a small, but beautifully appointed room. Letty disappeared into another part of the house, and a few minutes later a blue turbaned maid brought them a tray with coffee and cream. From under lowered lids she studied Fannette as she arranged the cups.

75

When she finally swept out of the room, Poppy turned her attention back to McLaury.

"Trojan was by a while ago. He says everything is going well. Isn't it chancing suspicion for you to be here?"

Jared shrugged. "Taking chances makes life worthwhile."

"Not when there are others to be endangered," Poppy disagreed.

He frowned. "As usual, you're right. But I wanted Fannette to meet you. Before she runs away, I think she should know what it is she's running from."

"I would thank you not to discuss me with strangers," Fannette said indignantly. "And I'm not running away."

He raised an eyebrow. "Then you're going back to Bijou when the time comes?"

"Following the man you love isn't running away."

"No," Poppy agreed. "It's far more dangerous."

Fannette lifted her cup and sipped at the beverage. She studied the girl over the rim. Poppy's wide, golden eyes returned the stare.

"I'm glad Jared brought you here. I've always wanted to meet you. We are related, you know."

"Yes," Fannette replied coolly, "I know." She turned to McLaury. "Now will you see me home? If Donna returns and finds I'm away—"

At the door she paused. "None of this was my idea," she told Poppy.

"That," Jared said when they were once again inside the carriage, "wasn't exactly my idea of a happy reunion."

"What did you expect? That I'd be happy to meet a sister who's a *gens de couleur*?" And such a beautiful one!

"Do you think she was that impressed with meeting a sister who proved an insufferable snob?"

And with no reason. No reason at all, Fannette thought. Reluctantly she had to admit that she no longer liked herself very much. And that she couldn't meet Jared's eyes without the color rushing into her face.

She forced the conversation onto another track.

"Just as we left, a big black man came to the back of the hall. I knew who he was right away. He even wore the same stocking cap."

"And who was he?" Jared's voice was very soft.

"The man who ran out of the gazebo that morning. The same negro I saw you talking to at the DuBois party!" she exclaimed triumphantly.

He looked sharply at her.

"Yes, I did see you. I was up on the balcony waiting for Anton to bring me a wrap. You were on the path to the quarters."

He was silent for a minute.

"Fannette," he finally said, "you've an amazing proclivity for appearing in unexpected places at the worst possible times. I wonder if I can trust you not to talk about what you saw?"

"Why?" she wanted to know.

"There are reasons I can't explain right now. The man you saw was Trojan. He's a free man, and he has a pass to visit Bijou anytime he wishes.

"And the DuBois plantation?"

"He was there to tell me something he thought was important. It was about you, as a matter of fact."

"Oh," she said quietly. At least that explained Jared's preknowledge.

She shrugged. "It really isn't my business. However, there is one thing I want to make very clear."

He waited. They had pulled through the iron gates and were stopped by the *porte cochere*.

"I never, never want to see you again!"

He nodded his acceptance of her statement and assisted her out of the carriage.

"And furthermore, you've a lot to learn about women, if you think taking me to that cottage can possibly have

77

any bearing on what I decide to do!"

At least she had the satisfaction of seeing a disturbed look come into his eyes as she left him.

IX

She couldn't help but be reminded of the DuBois party when Anton greeted her at the LaMott's formal New Year's Eve ball. She was again wearing her emerald gown, and he was in black, which was quite correct on this occasion.

They managed to escape to the conservatory that led out into the courtyard. It no longer mattered, Fannette reflected. What if they were seen? Her decision was going to evoke far greater scandal than the fact she permitted herself to talk to a man unchaperoned.

He took her into his arms and kissed her for long minutes. She surrendered passively, grateful that his lips brought none of the frightening sensations that had overcome her in the carriage with McLaury. Life with Anton would be serene, she told herself. She would be pampered and protected. It was completely understandable that she could never be his wife. It even pleased her a little that Jared had accomplished the direct opposite of his intentions when he'd brought her to the cottage and Poppy. He had forced her to throw aside her illusions and face facts. She was not Fannette of Bijou and Esplanade Publique. She was Fannette, the daughter of a *placee* and her lover. A product of Rampart Street.

"You will go with me?" he whispered.

She nodded.

His eyes searched into hers. "It isn't just an escape? I'd be without honor if I didn't give you the chance to consider. Is it to avoid Luton or because you love me? Think hard, because I promise there'll never be another opportunity."

"I have thought," she said truthfully. "I think I'll be

79

happy with you." And someday I'll love you, she promised herself.

He took her hand and held it to his lips. "I've arranged to sail on the fourth," he told her. "I've already reserved a cabin for you."

"You were so certain?" The thought disturbed her.

"We love each other, how can it be any other way?" He kissed her lightly on the forehead. "You see the faith I have in you?"

They moved back into the brightly illuminated ballroom, and Fannette found it slightly disconcerting that Anton should hold her arm with a proprietory air.

It was planned that they return to Bijou on the seventh of January, so it was not difficult for Fannette to pack her largest trunk with the things she thought she might need in France. Warm clothes, because certainly even sunny France must have winter. Her emerald velvet ballgown, because she wanted to do Anton proud. And her black velvet riding habit and new plumed hat with its broad, upturned brim. Zette was excellent with a needle, and she'd transferred the saucy feather from the old hat to the new as expertly as she'd mended the ripped bodice of the dress that Jared had torn.

Yet, Fannette had the feeling that Zette knew a great deal more than she revealed. That her eyes missed nothing and watched for more. Maybe it had been the fact that McLaury knew of her. Or maybe it was only that as the appointed day drew closer, Fannette felt a growing need to be secretive.

Even Donna raised an eyebrow when Fannette insisted that her packed trunk be taken down to the hall.

"Really, Nette," she remarked, "It would be better to keep it in your room than to clutter up the vestibule."

"It's in my way," Fannette replied. "But I'll keep the other one upstairs until André sends for it."

80

"At least I'm grateful you're reconciled to Bijou," Donna said, and Fannette felt a stab of guilt.

She and Anton had only dared one meeting, and that was two days before they were to leave.

"I encouraged Maman to have a going away party for me the evening I sail," he told her. "Of course Madame Luton will attend. That way I can send my carriage after you and the trunk. Will your butler have retired to the back of the house by ten?"

She nodded. "Unless someone comes to the door."

"You'll be waiting at that time?"

"Wouldn't it be expected that I attend the party?"

"But you're heartbroken. How could you possibly keep back the tears? Madame Luton won't press you."

She had to laugh at his doleful expression. "Conceited!"

"And with the best reason in the world." He kissed her lightly on the lips, but there was anticipation in his eyes and it made her feel uneasy. "I'll be good to you," he whispered as he took his leave.

Good to me, she thought, but not as my husband. But still there would be many days between sailing and disembarking in France. And she'd hold the key to her cabin. Who knew what might happen once he was away from Maman's influence? He did desire her, and desire had brought many a strong man to heel. Or so she'd heard.

But she had begun to feel unsure. Frightened. And she knew it was too late to turn back.

"You're certain you'll be all right, Nette, *cherie*?" Donna worried as her maid fastened her evening cloak. "You look feverish, and you're being so brave. It makes me feel uneasy."

"Not brave enough to go with you. Nor to wish Anton bon voyage."

André held open the door, but still Donna hesitated.

In a sudden burst of emotion, Fannette threw her arms around Donna. "I do love you!" she exclaimed. "If you really had been my mother, I couldn't love you more!"

"You're certain you're all right, *cherie*?" Donna asked anxiously for the second time.

Fannette forced a laugh. "Do you expect me to be happy?"

"Nette, maybe it'd be better if I stayed with you?"

Fannette kissed Donna's cheek. "And offend Madame Verdier? Just don't wake me up to tell me about the party!"

It was close to eleven o'clock when the carriage drew up outside the gate. Fannette watched from the porch, hoping there would be no sound that could cause André to leave the warmth of the kitchen.

Two men came up the walk, hardly discernible in the shadows. One she recognized as the Verdier coachman, but the other was lighter skinned and well dressed.

"I'm Louis, Monsieur Anton's valet," he told her. "You have a trunk?"

She opened the door and the two men each took an end handle. She caught up a cloak and her reticule and followed, first closing the door as quietly as possible. She paused for just a second to look about her. At the familiar house, the gardens, the trees and hedges. I'll never see it again, she thought. It's a part of me, but I'll never see it again.

The carriage moved down the street and turned the corner. A pulse beat explosively in Fannette's throat and she found she was twisting her hands in her lap. As they approached the wharf, traffic thickened even at that late hour. The cool winter air was heavy with the odor of exotic cargoes. Small crafts tugged at their mooring, and shadowy figures were storing last-minute freight on ships scheduled, like the one she would board, to sail with the dawn. Seamen lurched back to their berths, and occasionally there was the raucous bellow of flatboatmen, that vanishing species in a world of steam.

The valet hailed two men who had been lounging against a stack of bales. Money exchanged hands, and they took up the heavy trunk. Louis then helped her step down onto the planks of the dock.

He moved aside, permitting her to proceed him up the ramp. The ship rocked slightly in the mist of the January night, shadowlike and frightening. It was all a part of a dream. Nothing was real. Nothing was tangible. Everything was cloaked in unreality. Here and there a lantern glowed through a haze of fog. There were muffled curses, an occasional shout. Sometimes a face would emerge from the darkness, only to disappear.

Her feet on the deck, she paused to look back. Like Lot's wife, she thought. And maybe it would be better if she turned to a pillar of salt like her Biblical counterpart. Her thoughts fled over the tree-shadowed road that led to Bijou.

"Mademoiselle Randolph . . ." It was the soft voice of Anton's man, Louis. He spoke Creole French with an educated accent. "It's not good to linger, mademoiselle."

She turned to follow him, and caught her breath. Approaching her, heading in the direction of the ramp, was a broad-shouldered giant of a negro. He took off his stocking cap. His graying hair was clipped close to the scalp, and she saw he was an older man than she'd first thought.

Was she fated to encounter him in unexpected places? Would he be waiting in France when she left the boat? She quickly averted her eyes and followed Louis.

They moved through a dark passageway, descended stairs, and finally reached a cabin where the two roustabouts waited. Louis unlocked the door and waited until the men had deposited her trunk.

He motioned for Fannette to enter after the dockman departed, but she felt a reluctance to step over the high threshold.

"*S'il vous plait,* mademoiselle," Louis murmured.

A lamp swayed from a chain, illuminating what she realized must be the best possible accommodation. There was an armoire with its door open, and she saw Anton's clothes were already neatly hung inside. His night attire waited folded on a table by the bed and his brushes on a nearby stand.

She turned to Louis and saw that he was busy laying out her own night things.

"Monsieur has engaged a separate cabin for me," she told him. "My trunk doesn't belong in here."

The valet shrugged, continuing with his work.

"There were late passengers in need of a cabin and the captain appealed to Monsieur Anton. They agreed it wasn't necessary to retain space that would not be used."

He set out her dressing case and closed the trunk.

"There'll be a girl to attend you tomorrow. The captain has promised monsieur." He started for the door.

Fannette found her voice. "You're leaving?" she asked in a near panic.

"The carriage has to be back for Monsieur Anton."

When the port had closed behind him, her eyes darted over the intimate closeness of Anton's and her own clothing, at her trunk waiting to be unpacked in the morning. For the first time she understood that this was not to be a romantic adventure involving a chivalrous knight and a maiden whose virtue was, above all, to be protected. In truth, she couldn't blame Anton because with his provident French ancestry he saw fit to dispense with an unnecessary expenditure. He had made it plain enough she was to be his mistress, and certainly it had not been his intention to wait until France . . .

She thought of the carriage and where Jared's hands had touched her. Then she thought of Anton.

Oh God. Was she trapped? The dreamlike quality of her elopement had grown into a nightmare. Outside the porthole, warning horns blared through the thickening fog. Wharf noises increased as dawn and sailing times drew closer. Occasionally there were footsteps in the companionway, and she listened, terrified that they might stop outside.

I couldn't, she thought. I don't love him enough.

She considered the possibility of running out into the night, but set aside the temptation. Not with drunken rivermen lurching about the dock shouting bleared obscenities at each other. Nor was she anxious to chance the mercies of the burly roustabouts who waited in the shadows. She heard the shrill voice of a wharf harlot calling out to someone on a moored craft. No lone woman was safe out there at this hour.

The time to tell Anton she'd changed her mind was past. He would be coming to her soon, flushed from farewell toasts, anticipating her. If she tried to escape at this stage, the injury to his pride would be irreparable. He'd find himself a laughing stock from the captain down to his own valet. And pride, next to honor, was essential to Anton.

There were footsteps outside again, and this time they did stop by her door. She clenched her hands over her abdomen, feeling physically ill.

The door was flung open and she jumped to her feet, hand against her mouth.

"Goddamn you!" McLaury exclaimed, his face white with anger. "If it weren't for Trojan, I'd leave you here to become the whore you seem determined to be. And why the hell did you have to pick this ship, and tonight? As of now, just by being here I'm endangering the chances of two men who've earned their right to a new life!"

He motioned to Trojan, and the black man easily shouldered the trunk that had previously required two men to lift. McLaury caught up her cloak and threw it around her. He handed her the dressing case, and she snatched for her reticule. Then he took her arm and roughly yanked her into the companionway. He kicked out behind him, slamming the port with his heel.

An extension-top phaeton waited in the shadows. The mare hitched to it was pawing nervously, sending out columns of steam from her impatient nostrils. It was an imposing carriage, with triangular side quarters and curtains that could be rolled down.

Trojan heaved the trunk up onto the front end where he could straddle it with his legs while he drove. Jared opened the low door and assisted her up into the high-slung vehicle.

"My brother's," he said, as if his possession required an explanation. "He kept it at a livery stable for his use in town. I imagine the side curtains had their purpose besides holding out the weather."

"For the ladies?"

He gave a short laugh. "Hardly." He looked back at the ship, as Trojan took the reins and the carriage moved over the wharf planking. "I just hope to hell Anton doesn't raise an uproar and demand the decks be searched."

"What was Trojan doing there tonight? Did you send him to spy on me?"

"Do you really think you're worth it? Trojan was there for something much more important. There are two men signed on the roster as seamen. They've been hunted up and down the States. Their description is in the hands of every slave catcher in the South. That ship is their only way to leave here whole. And in Europe they'll be able to live out their lives without being hounded."

"Runaways?"

"One of them was a freedman. But that doesn't mean a damn if a slave catcher swears he's not. He had to kill to get away. The other was a slave. He ran away so many times he was sent to work in the swamps. He ran away from there, and Trojan found him half dead. If he's sent back to the swamps, he'll be dead in a month. We can't take the chance of sending him overland."

She drew herself up, outraged pride flashing in her eyes.

"Since you obviously consider them so much more important than I," she said, "I suppose I should be flattered that you bothered."

"You're hardly in a position to become uppity, not after pulling a damn fool stunt like tonight." He paused and drew a deep breath. "I'm going to tell you something. When fruit's ready to be eaten, it takes on a bloom. You send out a bloom that's near to overpowering."

"You're saying that I—"

"That you'll make someone a damn satisfying wife. The kind that isn't found in every bushel."

"But not a mistress?" There was bitterness in her voice.

"Not to Anton."

She decided to leave it at that.

He was silent for the rest of the trip. Finally the horse was drawn up in a quiet street, and Fannette realized it was the white cottage where she'd met Poppy.

Jared jumped out, spoke to Trojan, and then hurried forward to a covered spring wagon that was being loaded. He spoke briefly to one of the workers, and then returned to lead Fannette up the walk to the door.

Despite the lateness of the hour, lamps were burning in all the rooms. Trunks and furniture jammed the entrance hall, and Poppy threaded her way around the clutter, hurrying to greet them.

"You got there in time! Oh, Fannette, how could you be so stupid? I've been praying Jared would get there first!"

"You should have saved the effort for something more deserving," Jared muttered and brushed past the clutter.

"Letty!" he called. "Have Adena brew something hot!" He motioned for Fannette to follow him into the sitting room.

She looked around, puzzled. All the furniture was intact. Then where did the items in the hall originate?

Trojan had followed them, and McLaury pulled aside a curtain to look out the window.

"Tell them to get on with the loading. I want that wagon

on the way to the Settlement by daybreak. Thank God that's the last of them!"

Trojan nodded and left the room.

Poppy joined them, holding a tray with two cups and a pitcher of hot chocolate. She handed McLaury a mug filled with a fragrant, steaming beverage.

Jared sipped slowly at his drink, his eyes veiled in thought. Fannette looked from him to Poppy as things began to fall into a pattern.

"You're one of those people!" she announced suddenly. "I was right about you from the first. You're a slave stealer."

"We prefer to use other terms. You managed to fall right into the middle of a very important operation."

"Anyone who helps runaways escape is a slave stealer."

"Most of the people we're concerned with right now haven't been anyone's slave for a very long time. They've been living out in the swamps, hiding, knowing that even some of their own could turn them in for the reward."

"Why do you risk your life for them? You don't seem the sort of man who—"

"And I'm not!" he retorted. He set aside his cup and moved restlessly to where he could watch out the window.

"My brother captained a steamboat that took on cargo at New Orleans. Like a lot of other men raised in the North, he was opposed to slavery, and he wasn't averse to smuggling runaways when the opportunity arose. Two hundred dollars from New Orleans to Cincinnati was the standard fee. He took it when available, and it paid for the times when there was no money." He turned to face her. "And looking back, I imagine it helped to pay for my education as well."

He picked up his cup and stared down into it. "I was just getting a start in my law practice when I heard he was drowned. Drowned! A man who grew up swimming in the Atlantic. Drowned in a river? When I went through his papers I understood. It didn't take much probing to find

88

he'd been killed by planters who took the law into their own hands."

"And why shouldn't they?" Fannette demanded. "All my life I've heard how useless it is to wait for the courts!"

McLaury's eyes were veiled again, but his mouth was grim.

"It's been the joy of my life to aid every runaway I find. To set free men who've plagued the plantations. Who hide in the swamps while men hunt them. Every two thousand dollars worth of prime hand I can snatch from his owner and see safe with the Quakers in Ohio is another payment on the debt I'm collecting for my brother."

Poppy spoke up. "And this time so much is involved!" Her voice was low, but excited. "I'm going and so are Letty and Trojan. They've a lot to lose and they're taking a chance with their freedom."

Fannette looked at the girl with sudden interest.

"You want to go to Canada with them?"

Poppy shook her head, her large eyes very serious. "My place is here. I've had plans about my life since I can remember. But this once I can help."

She poured another cup for Fannette and set her own down to cool. "When a man or a woman runs away, he has nothing to guide him but the North Star," she continued. "He hides by day and follows the star by night. Most often he's captured, or he dies of the cold and hunger. These people we're helping are all folks who've earned their freedom by suffering, if nothing else."

Fannette frowned and shook her head. "You'll never get away with it. You'll be caught for sure. It's a fine and jail, isn't it? Or is it worse?"

"But that's it!" Poppy exclaimed eagerly. "Who is there to question movers? A man and his bride with her dowry of household goods and slaves, heading for his land in Kentucky near the Ohio River. There's no reason for it to fail, unless someone—"

Fannette felt the impact of Jared's and Poppy's eyes,

but her mind had raced ahead and found a solution to her own problem. She leaned toward them.

"I want to go with you," she said, her voice vibrant with excitement.

"You?" McLaury laughed. "Pampered, spoiled, Anton-stricken you? This is winter, it won't be a pleasure trip. The first bad storm will see you whimpering for home."

"If a bride, the daughter of a family able to afford a dowry of prime hands and their women, could travel those roads this time of year, then so can I. How would I be different from her?"

His eyes narrowed. "Still trying to escape? Haven't you the backbone to face up to what's real?"

"No," Fannette admitted. "I haven't. Maybe in time, but not yet."

Poppy had been watching both of them. She touched McLaury on the arm. "Neither of us can fully understand the shock she's had. Maybe in her place I might have done worse."

"Would it be possible?" he asked.

"We can use her, Jared. She'd fit the part much better than I would."

"You'd not go?"

"Oh, I'd go. She might need me. The kind of girl we're considering would have a maid. She told the truth when she said she was the part."

He continued to frown.

"Please!" Fannette begged. "I promise I won't fail you!"

He gave a short, ugly laugh. "You heard the price. Where's your two hundred dollars?"

Poppy gasped and Jared turned on her.

"Why should she be different? The money has to come from somewhere. She'll eat and she'll need a tent to share with you. She'll be an added expense."

Fannette opened her reticule and fished inside it until

90

her fingers closed over the case that held the emerald brooch. She threw it at his feet.

"That should pay and a bit more!" she exclaimed, her eyes flashing contempt.

He picked it up, read the jeweler's name, opened the case, and held the emerald to the light.

"So it will," he agreed.

X

"You realize," McLaury told Fannette, "that if we take you, it'll delay us by at least a day. The wagons are already waiting at the Settlement."

The Settlement, she learned, was a hidden village in the swamp country. A headquarters for the maroon bands. Meanwhile, Poppy showed her to a comfortable bed and brought her some night clothes to wear. Fannette's own had already been packed in the wagon.

She wondered if it were the end of a bad dream or the beginning of something worse, as she watched Trojan carry her trunk from the phaeton and place it beside the other pieces that had been crowded into the hallway. Jared was right, of course. She was running away, but surely the venture ahead couldn't be too bad if Poppy had consented to go.

The dawn light was already filtering through the jalousie at the window and she closed her eyes against it. Anton's ship would be sailing, she thought, and she was aware of a sense of loss. It was as though a part of her life had ended, and she would never again rise to those same heights of joy and anticipation she had experienced with Anton.

It was afternoon when Fannette awakened to the sound of voices in the sitting room. She lay in bed awhile, studying the unfamiliar surroundings. Trying to put in order the confusing events of the night before.

Finally she threw back her covers and dressed. She tied her hair with a ribbon, permitting it to fall in waves down her back. She felt sapped of all energy. Even the effort to arrange a coiffure was beyond her.

She went out into the hallway, and Poppy called to her.

92

There was a guest seated on the sofa, sipping at *cafe au lait*.

"Fannette," Poppy said, "Ferne has asked to meet you."

Ferne was past middle age, her coiled hair was quite white, her aquiline face gaunt. Her black eyes darted over Fannette's face, searching, probing . . .

"Ferne was a friend of our mother's."

A white eyebrow lifted over smoldering, scornful eyes. "Friend?"

"You were her sponsor when first she came to New Orleans."

"And I've been sorry for that a thousand times. Because of Naida."

"Naida! You're obsessed with Naida." Poppy's voice was still soft, but there was impatience in the tone.

"You can't deny that Naida died because your mother wanted this cottage? Naida who couldn't bear to harm a fly?"

"Naida killed herself because she couldn't face life. It was a sin."

"Naida?" Fannette looked from one woman to the other, puzzled.

"This cottage once belonged to Naida. It was the biggest of the cottages, and I'm certain more than our mother envied her it." Poppy paused. "Shadney Randolph bought it after Naida's suicide."

A stirring in the grave. Old wrongs. Old wounds.

"Why did she do such a thing?" Fannette crossed herself out of habit and glanced around, almost expecting to see a sad little ghost.

Poppy's eyes locked with Ferne's. "She cut her wrists in the kitchen down the hall. She did it because she was told her protector had married that day. And he had promised her he wouldn't."

Poppy went to the window and pulled aside the curtains so they could see outside. "I don't know if you understand how it is with a *placee*," she said.

Women moved down the street, followed by blue-turbaned maids who balanced baskets on their heads. Elegant women, tastefully, even lavishly dressed. Women who moved with grace and modesty.

"A *placee* accepts only the man she loves as her protector. It's not the way it is with the Creole families, where marriages are arranged between a man and a woman who might not even know each other. A *placee* takes her protector for life, knowing he must marry someday. Knowing that he might come to love his wife. Should this happen, or should he leave her—well, a suicide isn't uncommon."

"But Naida's was to no purpose," Ferne interrupted.

"What suicide is?" Poppy demanded.

Ferne directed her attention to Fannette. "A note was on its way. A note explaining that the marriage was a financial necessity that would change nothing."

"Our mother didn't know of this note when she told Naida of the wedding!" Poppy exclaimed.

"Would it have made any difference to her? She'd wanted this cottage for a long time."

Poppy's face had lost color and Letty paused in arranging the coffee tray. Trojan turned from a window at the other end of the room and silenced his wife with a warning scowl.

Fannette hadn't noticed him before, so quiet was he, his eyes watching the street through a slit in the blinds. So this was the man who carried messages between the maroon band and the cottage. The man who recruited runaways and guided refugees to the safety of the Settlement. Giles DuBois, for one, would have given much for this knowledge.

"Look at me," the woman called Ferne said in an authorative voice, and Fannette felt herself compelled to obey. "You were still in your mother's womb when we stood over Naida. Naida's blood was on the hems of our skirts, and I had only one thought, that you, the unborn, should not be like the mother. *Oui,* I did a bad thing. I used my power where it should never have been used. To change a soul."

Was the woman insane? Fannette forced herself to look away from those compelling eyes.

"There's no way anyone but God can change a soul," Poppy exclaimed. "There's no power in voodoo. The sisters of the Church teach there is only one power."

"Stupidities!" Ferne snapped. "There are many powers! I captured Naida's soul before it left her. But what of the soul that already lived within the unborn? Can the two entities dwell together without there being unhappiness? Did I create a battleground when I called her soul to enter the child your mother carried?"

"You created nothing!" Poppy retorted, eyes flashing. "Look at Fannette! There's your proof. It is all in your imagination. This thing that happened twenty years ago! And voodoo! The worship of voodoo is wicked, demeaning, destructive, and without any real power!"

"Do you really believe that?" Ferne asked.

Fannette picked up a tiny statuette and examined it without seeing it, trying to shut her ears to the conversation.

Voodoo. She'd put that behind her when she was ten. Voodoo and the frightening fascination it had once held for her. But Poppy was wrong. There was a power there. An evil power. And this woman, Ferne, could have used it. Could have thought she was doing a good thing, unmindful of the truth that good could not come from what was evil.

And then there was another thing to consider. The conflict between the meek Fannette and the willful Fannette. The two sides of her personality that had perplexed Donna and worried Breel. But the meek Fannette was capable of some very daring deeds. In her heart, she'd always felt it had been the meek Fannette who'd thrown the snake into the fire. That it had been the willful Fannette who had attracted and held it.

"See!" Ferne shrieked, pointing at what Fannette held. "See? There's your answer!"

Fannette looked at the carving, seeing it for the first time. It was a woman with a bent head. A woman who subjected herself to despair. The Blessed Mother? No, the inscription at the base said Persephone. Persephone mourning for the home she thought never to see again.

"That belonged to Naida!" Ferne exclaimed. "What more do you need than that? Of all the things in this room, Fannette selected what was Naida's!"

"It's been here as long as I can remember," Poppy said. "On the mantel."

"It was left. Many things were left."

McLaury appeared in the doorway, followed by an elderly man who looked about the room quizzically.

"I didn't realize you had company," Jared said to Poppy.

Ferne started for the door. "I was leaving." She paused, her eyes on Fannette once again. And on the tiny figure Fannette held. Then she went out into the hall, and Poppy, once again the hostess, followed her.

Fannette shivered, and without realizing it, dropped the figurine into a pocket. Jared regarded her with interested concern.

"I hardly recognize you," he told her. "A compliant Fannette. What did that witch say that could subdue you?"

Fannette shook herself free of the apathy. "She talked of the past, of something that happened here before I was born."

"If it has that effect, I'd advise you to forget whatever it was." Jared turned toward the man who stood near his elbow.

"Your honor," he said, "this is Fannette." He took Fannette by the hand and drew her closer. "My dear, this gentleman is a judge and an old friend of my brother's. He's prepared the papers necessary for our marriage."

The judge smiled warmly at her as he took a legal-appearing document out of a portmanteau. "We'll need the signatures," he told them, and placed the papers on the writing desk.

Fannette stared at the two men. Marriage? Necessary papers?

Jared laughed. "If you could see yourself!" he said as he dipped the quill into the inkpot.

Fannette backed away. "If this is a joke, it's in very bad taste." Her eyes searched his.

"I've already told you there can be no room for error." He dashed off his signature and turned to her. "Can't you understand that a document proving we are what we say could mean the difference between a successful mission and jail?'"

"I'll not do it." Her voice threatened to fail her. "That wasn't part of the agreement." Was this what life held for a woman alone? One trap following another? First the cabin on the boat engaged for two? Now this?

Jared threw down the pen in exasperation. "Hells bells, Fannette. Surely you can't believe I want a marriage to you? There'll be no trouble getting an annulment later. A marriage has to be consummated to remain legal."

He continued to regard Fannette, a frown drawing his brows together. Poppy rejoined them, and he glanced toward her.

"Would you mind if we stepped into the room across the hall? In fairness, there are a few things that should be made clear to Fannette before we go any further."

Poppy nodded in agreement.

"I'm sorry to delay you, your honor," Jared said to the judge. "If you'll be kind enough to take that seat for a few minutes. Poppy, maybe a cup of coffee?"

They crossed the hallway and went into a room that might once have been a nursery, but was now furnished as a classroom. Jared indicated a chair. After Fannette was seated, he leaned against a cabinet, looking down at her.

"To be frank," he said, "I feel I'm making a mistake. Still, it is true you'd be more convincing as a dowried bride than Poppy would be. But I can see there'll be problems."

"I swear I won't be any trouble," she promised. "I simply can't go back to Bijou! But marriage—" Fannette found she was tearing at her lace handkerchief. She made an effort to steady her hands.

"Perhaps you might find it a protection? I'm a man with a man's normal desires, and—"

She stared at him and he laughed.

"You hadn't thought of that?" The mockery was back. "I assure you your virtue won't be impaired. Not as long as you hold up your end of the bargain. I might add that there will be nights when it'll be necessary to share quarters."

"You didn't tell me that before."

"Oh, you'll be safe enough. It'll only be when there are others staying in our camp. A bridegroom could hardly be expected to leave his bride sleeping with her maid."

"Oh." She thought about that for a minute. And she thought of Breel and Bijou.

"I can't go back to Bijou," she repeated.

She signed the document, and a sudden premonition took hold of her. Her hand was trembling when she put the quill back into its holder.

Jared smiled down on her as they took their places in front of the judge.

"Now for the necessary words. I must apologize for not being able to find a priest for the occasion."

"Oh no!" she exclaimed. "Then it would be binding."

All of the time she felt his smile mocking her, daring her. And she had the disheartening feeling that he hadn't been entirely truthful.

98

XI

Jared McLaury came by with the phaeton late that afternoon. Trojan held the reins to the same spirited horse he'd used the evening before. It twitched its tail nervously while Poppy and Fannette were helped up the high step.

Jared glanced at the sleek animal, approving its dainty, pawing motions.

"She's trained to a sidesaddle as well as a harness," he remarked. "She'll do well."

"You mean we're to have the phaeton?" Poppy asked in astonishment.

He nodded. "I don't think the pampered bride we have in mind would take kindly to riding in the wagon with the stock."

She stared at him out of her large, golden eyes. Then, unexpectedly, she burst into laughter.

"Indeed not, Jared!" she agreed.

No one paid particular attention to the horse and rider that left the shadow of a tree to follow at a distance. Trojan sat up in the driver's seat, obviously delighted with the high-stepping filly and elegant conveyance, and Jared was silent, seeming, for some inexplicable reason, to be avoiding Poppy's amused gaze.

It was much later in the day, about the time darkness threatened to hide the dim trail, when the horse and rider drew into full view.

A sharp obscenity from Jared caused both girls to lean over the low door so they could look back on the trail.

Fannette gasped, her face whitening, and Poppy turned to her anxiously.

"Are you all right?" she asked.

"It's Anton." Fannette whispered in shocked disbelief.

"I thought he'd be at sea by now!"

Trojan pulled in the mare, and McLaury dismounted his bay. He stroke over to the interloper and seized the horse's bridle.

"How long have you been following?" he demanded.

Anton lounged back in his saddle, the reins loose in his hands.

"Since you left the cottage," he replied easily.

"How the hell—"

Anton smiled. His eyes had already found Fannette, who was leaning over the phaeton's door.

"It didn't take much acumen to recognize Trojan's description. I've seen you talking with him more than once. It was connecting him with the cottage that took time. And more time yet to get a horse from my father's stable without more than one groom being the wiser. At present I'd prefer it was thought that I was at sea."

"And what about that? The ship that sailed this morning?"

"Hopefully, Louis, my valet, is guarding the cabin. Everything I hold of value is stored there."

He paused, looking at the women.

"Everything except what I valued most, and that has already been stolen."

"Not stolen, but willingly rescued. It seems something was left to be desired on the value you set."

"That's what I intend to learn."

"Do you realize you're on a trail that'll be obliterated in the morning? Usually anyone so unfortunate as to stumble on it first ends up the same way."

Anton shrugged.

"You think to frighten me, Jared?"

"I was hoping to."

"I've known what it is you've been up to for a long time. I've found it not of the slightest importance. What are slaves to me? We've some that've been in the family for years, and they're more trouble than they're worth.

Our livelihood is shipping. It's not in crops."

"Do you expect me to believe you're not hoping to cause trouble?"

"The only thing that concerns me is Fannette. I'd hardly expect her to be a part of your work. Aside from all other things, it isn't in character."

McLaury grinned suddenly.

"And why shouldn't Mrs. McLaury be involved in her husband's work?"

Anton lifted his whip, and for one fearful second, Fannette thought he would bring it down across McLaury's face.

"Damn you! I've had enough of you and your jokes!"

Jared made no motion to sidestep the threatening crop. He continued to grin.

"I'm not joking, Anton. I've the papers to prove what I've said."

"My God, man, do you expect me to believe that? Less than twenty-four hours ago Fannette was waiting to leave for France with me!"

He looked directly at Fannette.

"Haven't you anything to say?"

Fannette found she was gripping Poppy's hand.

"I told you I couldn't go back to Bijou. Then I realized—"she groped for the right words, "that I couldn't go through with what you planned."

"But you'd marry him? Marry him when I'm the man you love?"

She opened the door and climbed down from the carriage. She ran to where he still sat his horse and looked up at him, her eyes begging him to understand.

"It isn't really a marriage. Mr. McLaury had a—"

"My dear," McLaury interrupted, "you really must start to call me Jared. I don't believe it's the custom in Louisiana for a wife to address her husband with such formality."

She bit her lip. "Jared had a judge he knew make out

101

the papers. In case of questions later. So we could prove we're what we say we are."

"I'd never realized he had such a talent for details."

"It doesn't mean anything, Anton. It doesn't mean anything at all!"

Her hand was on his knee, and he bent to raise it to his lips, his eyes still on her face.

"If for no other reason than to make certain of that, I intend to go with you. Surely your new husband can't object to his bride's brother traveling with you? To make certain his dear sister is safe?"

Unexpectedly Jared laughed. He loosened his hold on the bridle.

"I've always admired your nerve, Anton," he acknowledged. "And strangely enough, I trust you. If you really intend to throw in your chances with our little caravan you're welcome. You'll add authenticity to my Louisiana bride."

Trojan started to speak, but Jared shook his head.

"I'm certain it'll ease the bride's fears. Except," his eyes darkened slightly as he turned them on Fannette, "I hope you'll realize it would be quite improper to show an undue amount of affection for your brother? It'll be my pleasure to make certain the two of you will never be alone, and to supervise when you're together."

Anton scowled, the quick temper flashing in his eyes.

"I don't intend to put up with any insult to Fannette. You may as well learn right now that my full purpose is to protect her."

"Against whom?" Jared inquired gently. "Surely not against yourself?"

"If so much wasn't at stake, I'd call you out!" Anton exclaimed.

"But there is much at stake," Jared reminded him. "And don't you ever forget it!"

Anton threw aside his reins and dismounted, his face distorted with rage. Poppy ran to his side and caught him

102

by the arm.

"Stop it!" she stormed. "Both of you, stop it! Soon it'll be dark, and it won't help any of us to be caught out here!"

Trojan nodded emphatically. " 'Gators," he remarked gloomily, "dey likes black meat best. Ebrybody knows dat."

Anton moved to brush Poppy aside, but he paused and looked down into her anxious face. His frown disappeared, and he smiled at her, his earlier rage gone.

"You're right, mademoiselle," he agreed. "May I assist both of you into the carriage?"

The Settlement was a busy little village with small, easily removable dwellings that blended into the cypress knoll. Men and women moved around small cookfires, and children played under foot. The keynote was the quiet. Even the young had been taught to keep their voices low, just as their parents had learned to make fires with a minimum amount of smoke.

Barrels of meal, hams, smoked meats and cured pork were stacked by a wagon that was in the process of being loaded with kitchen equipment. Letty was watching, hands on hips, eyes dubious.

"I'se lady's maid, not cook," she was protesting to anyone who cared to listen.

"At least we won't starve," Fannette said to Poppy.

"I'm not that certain. Not if Letty's doing the cooking," Poppy replied.

Jared came up to them.

"You two will sleep in that hut over there tonight," he told them. "I'd suggest you go to bed right after supper. We'll leave before dawn."

He turned to Anton. "From here on we'll share a tent. That way I'll be able to keep an eye on you." He grinned with evident relish. "And as of now the only one who can look at Fannette with longing happens to be me."

"You enjoy this joke of yours, don't you?" Anton

103

asked grimly.

"As a matter of fact, my friend," Jared retorted, "I do!"

But Fannette hardly heard the exchange of words because of the wonder she felt of actually standing in the midst of that legendary place. The Settlement. The hidden village of hunted men and women, the refuge of the runaway, the fugitive. The place plantation owners for miles around had sought in vain.

She remembered when only the year before Giles DuBois had gathered together planters from up and down the bayou, determined to find this hideout.

"Why do they call it the Settlement?" Fannette had asked Breel.

He'd shrugged. "A name as good as any," he'd replied. "What else can you call a place where hunted men and women can come to live in peace? A place so well hidden and so deep in the swampland that no white man can find it?"

And they hadn't found it, either. On the way back from the unsuccessful search, a mud-splattered, weary Giles DuBois had stopped by Bijou.

"It's no use," he had told Breel, anger flashing in his eyes. "Those damn maroons know ways into the marshes that I swear even a 'gator couldn't find. How outlaws and runaways find their way to it defeats me!"

"I imagine it's like the Underground Railway," Breel surmised. "Word is sent, and they're conducted to the place." He grinned. "It's a pity you can't fly, maybe you'd come on it then."

"I wonder," DuBois muttered. "I wonder if even a bird could see down through that dense growth of cypress and oak. Halsey from up the river almost lost his life when he tried a side path. It was only luck we got him out. Lost his horse, though. No way we could pull it free in time."

Trojan took off his cap as he passed Fannette, bringing her back to the present. She knew he was on his way to obliterate any sign of their passage off the regular road.

For the first time she realized how deeply she was committed to the journey at hand.

XII

"Where am I? How did I get here?" Fannette asked herself as she balanced between sleep and awakening. The ground was hard under her pallet, and the chill of the damp January air cut through the thin material of her nightdress as she sat up.

Of course. The Settlement. That explained the little hut with its smoky fire and the dim light from a candle.

"Are you always this hard to awaken?" Poppy laughed.

"But it's still night!" Fannette protested. Then she saw that Poppy was already dressed, her abundant hair coiled around her head.

"Jared expects the wagons to be well out of the swamp before daylight. I hated to wake you, but there isn't much time to dress."

Fannette flexed her shoulders and moaned.

"Mine, too," Poppy sympathized. "But we'll have to get used to the ground. We can't expect a bed to be set up for us each night." She gestured toward some clothing that was heaped on a chair. "Jove brought me to your trunk and I took out everything that looked warm." She shivered. "We'll be heading north and we're certain to have frost and snow by the time we reach Cincinnati."

Cincinnati. Until Cincinnati she was Mrs. McLaury . . . And Anton—Anton was her brother. How had it happened so fast?

Fannette dressed with hands made clumsy by the cold.

"Why in January?" she wanted to know. "Couldn't he have done this thing in the spring or the fall? And wouldn't it have been easier to go by boat?"

"In the winter traffic's light overland," Poppy replied.

106

"And traveling by boat would be too much of a risk. There could very well be passengers who might recognize some of our people." She paused at the sound of a knock. "That'll be Letty and Trojan's boy, Jove. He was in earlier with warm water for me. It must be your turn now."

She opened the door and a tall black boy stood waiting with a bucket half full of warm water, a grin on his face.

Poppy turned to Fannette. "This is Jove," she said. "My best pupil. I'm really proud of him."

Fannette stared at Jove. "I've seen you before." She hesitated. "In the garden, wasn't it?"

He nodded. "You better hurry, Miz McLaury," he said. "Mr. Jared's yelling for everyone to get in the wagons."

"Miss Fannette," she corrected.

Jove shook his head. "He say it's Miz McLaury." The door closed behind him.

Fannette scrubbed at herself and regarded the stack of clothing with dismay. She hastily selected what looked warmest, for once paying no attention to style or color. She noticed that Poppy was wearing heavy, but plain garments. The sort that might be given a well-liked maid.

"Aren't we going to eat breakfast?" she protested. Like Poppy, she had wound her already braided hair around her head. Obviously time for brushing and combing was not permitted.

"We'll stop for food later. We have to be on the highway by daylight." Poppy was busy gathering up the excess clothing. "It'll probably be warmer then, anyway."

"I don't think I'll ever be warm again," Fannette grumbled.

Jove was waiting outside. He relieved Poppy of her burden and disappeared into the darkness. Torches flared in the area where the wagons waited, and Fannette saw that each was hitched to a team of two horses. From the muffled confusion of voices she assumed that the women and children were already inside under the canvas tops.

The men were standing around or pacing back and

107

forth in an effort to keep warm. Anton was already in the saddle and he waved to her. Jared rode by on the big bay gelding she'd seen that day by the gazebo at Bijou.

Had that morning ever existed? Was there really a place called Bijou and a Fannette whose entire world had revolved around finding a husband?

"Get into the buggy!" Jared shouted. "Damn it, women. We should be underway by now!"

They hurried to the dark outline of the phaeton. Jove waited to help them, his teeth gleaming in the flickering light.

"You be careful, Miss Poppy," he admonished, handing them a quilt. "Now tuck this around tight."

Fannette had climbed in first, and Poppy settled beside her.

"To listen to Jove, you'd swear I was made of glass!"

Well, at least she had someone who showed concern, Fannette thought resentfully. Aside from a casual wave, Anton had been too engrossed in watching the wagons to extend his usual gallantries. And Jared was riding back and forth on his bay, bellowing out orders. They might as well have stumbled and fallen on their faces, for all he cared.

"Jove's taken to numbers and books so fast that I expect he might end up a teacher himself," Poppy was saying. "I almost gave up on his grammar, but he's improving."

Fannette tried to make out Poppy's features in the darkness.

"You're teaching negroes? Aren't you afraid you'll be caught?"

Poppy shrugged. "The Ursuline sisters have taught them since they first came to New Orleans."

"But you're not an Ursuline!" Fannette smiled at the thought of beautiful, exotic Poppy in a long, drab habit, her luxuriant hair covered by a wimple, with only her golden eyes to hint at what was hidden within.

108

But Poppy's voice was serious, thoughtful. "I suppose you might say I inherited the desire to teach from both my father and my grandfather. Or maybe it was hearing about them that took my interest."

"I've been wondering if Breel was your father too."

"Oh never!" Poppy laughed. "When I was little, Trojan used to tell me about my father. They were very good friends. My father told him that my grandfather had been a professor up north, and he came south to teach the free *gens de couleur*. He fell in love with one of his pupils and married her, even though it was against the law."

"She was colored?" But of course, Poppy had never made a secret of that.

"A fourth. A quadroon." Fanette was silent for a few minutes, thinking. So that explained the faint hint of copper tinge to her complexion. Her father would have been an octoroon. That was so close to being white that it hardly mattered—but still close enough to have a legal designation. Poppy herself would be an octoroon or less. It would depend upon how much black blood their mother had. A trace, Donna had said. And she, Fannette—but did it really matter?

"My grandfather was jailed for teaching negroes," Poppy went on. "My father was under ten, so they sold him with his mother. You know, in Louisiana there's a law against taking a child from its mother if its under ten? Trojan said my grandmother taught my father all she knew and that when he grew up his one desire was to carry on the work my grandfather had started."

"And now you," Fannette said in wonder. Light-hearted, laughing Poppy a teacher? It was incredible.

"Yes," Poppy replied. "Only they won't be able to jail me."

"Only the nuns can teach safely," Fannette reminded her.

"I know," Poppy replied.

Fannette hesitated, unwilling to probe into Poppy's

reply, but still aware something should be said. She changed back to the original subject.

"And what happened to your father?" she asked.

"Trojan doesn't talk much about that, only that it was he who established the Settlement. I was still a baby when he ran away."

"And you've never heard of him since?"

"I like to think he's alive somewhere," Poppy said softly, "that he's still teaching, but maybe in Canada where they won't put him in jail or hang him."

Fannette hesitated, half tempted to ask about the woman who had been their mother, then found she could not. There was a place locked away in her mind, and it held Breel along with the shadowy figure of the one who'd borne her. She didn't dare to probe, to open it to light and air. There were too many ghosts that might be let loose.

They rode in silence for the rest of the morning. Jove whistled or hummed, as the mood took him, and by daylight they were on the main road through the bayou. The sun finally sent rays of warmth through the heavy screen of trees and moss.

"Aren't we ever going to stop for breakfast?" Fannette finally complained, breaking the silence inside the phaeton.

"I think that's the cook wagon drawn over up ahead," Poppy reassured her. "They left before we did."

Fannette craned her head over the side and saw that Jared was riding down the road, instructing the drivers to pull over. She gave a sigh of relief. Her stomach was grumbling in a most unladylike manner.

The air was colder outside the phaeton, and Fannette paced back and forth, pulling her fur-lined hood close to her head. She felt a stab of sympathy for the black women who climbed from the canvas-hooded wagons, their heads bound in turbans, and shawls clutched to their shivering shoulders.

There were ten wagons in all, she discovered. Some

110

were obviously used for transporting the women and children, the others, she surmised, for the furniture and household equipment she'd seen in the hall of the cottage by the ramparts.

Up ahead, the kitchen wagon waited, and smoke rose in puffs from the portable cookstove. She followed Poppy in the direction of promised warmth.

Letty was struggling with huge pots that bubbled, and as they drew near, Trojan stopped feeding wood into the back of the stove and snatched at the coffee pot as it boiled over and set the fire to sizzling.

"I tells him and I tells him, I ain't no cook. I'se lady's maid," Letty was complaining.

Trojan paused to grin at Fannette and Poppy.

"An' I tells her a body tryin' to eat her victuals won't have no doubts about dat!"

"Dat's when he tells me he'll find himself a nice plump girl to do his cooking. Dat's when I tells Adena to teach me what she knows."

McLaury rode up in time to hear the last. "Judging from what I've just eaten, I'd suggest Trojan keep on looking," he said.

Fannette turned around. Jared was sitting his horse a little behind her. He was handsome in the early light, his fair hair, shorter than Anton's, falling over his forehead, his blue eyes shining with *joie de vivre*. It would appear, she thought resentfully, the rougher the going, the more he thrived on it.

"Take gruel to the women with children first," he told Trojan as he dismounted. "They'll need more time than the rest." His grin faded as he watched Anton hurry to Fannette's side.

"I've looked everywhere for you!" Anton exclaimed. He pulled her to the side, his eyes anxious. "*Chérie*, can't you see this isn't for you? Do I have to insist you abandon this charade and ride back to New Orleans with me?"

Jared moved up beside them. "You're hardly in a position to insist upon anything. Nor to call my wife *chérie,* for that matter. Keep it up and you'll have us all in jail."

"And that's where you belong, if you haven't the eyes to see neither of these women are suited to this life. My God! You might at least have let them sleep until sunrise."

"I'm in charge here," McLaury told him. "You can still turn back if you don't like it. I'm warning you that my orders are to be obeyed, and the first order is to watch how you address Mrs. McLaury."

Anton glared angrily at him, then turned abruptly and went to where his horse was feeding.

"I'm not—" Fannette started, her eyes stormy.

Jared's grin was back. He took her left hand and gently straightened the clenched fingers. Then he stripped off her glove.

"For this trip you certainly are," he interrupted as he slid a ring on her finger. It was a heavy ring of braided gold. She had noticed McLaury wearing it when first they met, but now it fit her finger as if made for it.

He nodded in satisfaction. "Abe's a good goldsmith," he said. "He worked hard at sizing that. And Poppy was right, your fingers are about the same."

He turned to Poppy and kissed her lightly on the cheek.

"It was Poppy who remembered about a ring. A detail like that could mean the difference between life and death before we're through."

Poppy! Fannette looked at the unfamiliar band on her left ring finger. She could almost hate Poppy!

XIII

Letty stood by with a scowl on her face as great gobs of her cooking were scraped into the garbage hole.

"I'se lady's maid," she muttered to anyone who cared to listen.

"I can't understand how Jared could have made such a poor arrangement," Fannette complained to Poppy.

"*D'accord*," Poppy shrugged. "But there is this to say, Letty made such a fuss about Trojan going without her, that Jared finally agreed to take her as cook. Trojan tried to warn him. And truthfully, I don't believe even Trojan realized it would be quite this bad."

Fannette shuddered, remembering the lumps and scorched smell. And even by Creole standards the coffee was bitter. It was debatable that milk, had they any, could have helped.

Lunch, if anything, was even a worse disaster. Jared paced back and forth scowling when the allotted hour stretched to nearly two.

"I realized there would be risks," Anton moaned, "but not to my stomach."

The afternoon progressed and so did the sullen exchange of surmises regarding dinner. Fannette tried to distract herself by listening to and watching the bayou scenery. She saw a *cheniére* rising out of the swamp, covered by a live oak, and heard the distant roar of an alligator—a sure sign of rain, they'd say at Bijou. A red-winged black-bird darted in a thicket, a marsh wren and, occasionally, a colony of egrets were to be seen here or there. None of which could make her forget the hollowness of her stomach.

Beside her, Poppy's fingers moved nimbly over her rosary beads.

"If they take one's mind off food, then I regret I forgot mine," Fannette said.

Evening finally brought the wagons to a halt. Tents were pitched, two large ones for the men and women, and two smaller ones to be shared by Anton and Jared and by Poppy and Fannette. Her back ached at the thought of another night on a hard pallet.

Letty's face was grim as she struggled over the cookstove. Jared stood nearby, listening to complaints, suffering, Fannette was certain, from a mixture of hunger pangs and indigestion.

Even Jove was subdued.

Jove with his expressive eyes and his tremendous joy in life. Jove who had been in his glory all day, driving "his ladies" in the phaeton.

"Pa try to tell Mr. Jared," he told Fannette.

Old Chippers, the carpenter, was hammering on some sort of a contraption nearby. Jove's eyes rested on him. "Now Chippers there, he old man, an' food don't mean that much to him. But me, I near dying for some victuals."

He hitched out his chin and ran his finger along the neckband of his wool shirt, and Fannette realized he was approaching the real reason for singling her out.

"Miz McLaury," he started.

"Miss Fannette," Fannette corrected automatically.

"Miz McLaury, I been wantin' have a talk with you."

"With me?" Fannette looked at him, startled. "Whatever about?"

"Yore girl, Miz McLaury. That Zette."

Zette? So Zette was the girl Jove had been watching for that rainy day in the garden in New Orleans. Really, Fannette, she told herself, you might have realized that before. How else had Jared known the name of her maid? Still, it would take some looking into . . .

"I been takin' Zette out come Sunday and when there's a barbecue on Sat'day night. I been savin' my money so's I

114

can buy her free someday. I'm hopin' the price ain't so high I've got to wait till I a old man, like Chippers there."

"Zette belongs to Madame Luton," Fannette replied. "She isn't mine."

"Miss Donna, she say different. She say she give you Zette." He scowled. " 'Sides, she say I too young. Miz McLaury, I be near seventeen, and Zette, she be fifteen come March."

The suspicion deepened. "Did Mr. Jared have something to do with Zette becoming my maid?" But how could he? How possibly?

Jove nodded. "Mr. Jared see me with Zette, and he hear she belong to Miss Donna. He tells her to ask if she can be maid to you."

Had he really been keeping that close a tab on her? And why?

"Zette was 'fraid at first, but when she ast, Miss Donna say she thought it was a fine idea."

"Oh."

"Miz McLaury—"

"Jove, you call Poppy 'Miss Poppy.' You even call Madame Luton 'Miss Donna.' Why can't you call me Miss Fannette instead of Mrs. McLaury?"

"Because he say to call you Miz McLaury."

"Mr. Jared?"

"Mr. Jared."

"You're missing a show!" Poppy exclaimed coming up to them. "Come over by the stove!"

A large black woman was confronting Letty.

"You done ruin't enuf victuals!" she said, her voice loud enough to stop everyone in their work.

"Amen!" said a small, gentle-appearing man who stood close behind. He was holding the hand of a boy who watched with a grin, strong teeth white and startling against the black of his skin.

"Move aside, woman." The deep voice boded no argument.

Letty glowered back her defiance.

"Ain't no high-handed Gawgaw nigger gonna take dis wagon away from Trojan an' me. You go tend yore own bus'ness."

"You let me to that fire, ain't no one gonna starve or git sick," the other woman retorted. "Ain't got no notion to take yore wagon."

Letty regarded her with suspicion. "If I leave you cook, you don't bother the back where Trojan and me sleep?" She turned to Trojan. "You got sumpin' to say?"

"Between rumblin' an' grumblin', my stomach, he don' care. He just crave food he can eat."

Jared came up beside Fannette. "Emily's a good cook," he commented. "There was a large reward offered for her."

"*Ciel!* I should hope she can cook," Anton muttered. "I'd come to suspect Letty was the weapon you were using to send me on my way!"

Emily had brushed Letty aside and she sniffed at the pans on the stove. She called to the scholarly-looking little man.

"Wednesday, you dump dese pots. Mind, you take dem ober dere. Don' wanna git sick smellin' dem!"

Wednesday and the pans disappeared. "Now, Friday," she said to the boy, "when yore pa cums back, you scamper for wood? You heah?"

While the utensils were scrubbed to Emily's specifications, she rummaged through the sacks and barrels of provisions.

"How dat woman she can ruin good food, I don' know," she mumbled to anyone who cared to listen.

Well, at least there was hope of a dinner that night, Fannette decided. She moved away from the others, to the edge of the camp. Poppy, Jared and Anton had gone to the open fire where they were chattering as they watched Emily. Jove was helping with the horses, and for the first time since leaving the cottage by the ramparts, she found

116

herself alone to think.

So much to consider. Donna. Donna must be frantic by now. She felt guilty at the thought, but what else had been left to her? And Jared. Was revenge for his brother the only reason for this dangerous venture? He seemed to glory in it. She'd heard of men who lived with danger for the very joy of it. Was he one of those?

And Anton. Anton who was putting up with discomfort for her sake. Anton who obviously hated discomfort! That, at least, was flattering. But he hasn't flattered you with an offer of marriage, she reminded herself.

It was then she had the feeling that she was not alone. That she was being watched, that her mind was being probed. Ridiculous! she thought.

She looked around, but the only person anywhere near was a bent old woman. Wiry strands of white hair straggled from the confinement of a red kerchief that the old woman wore. She was wearing clothes that hung loosely over her slack, withered frame, and she had tightly pressed lips that suggested toothlessness.

The old woman moved closer until her eyes were peering up at Fannette. Incredible greenish eyes in a wrinkled black face.

Mother of Mercy! If ever there were a witch! And the strange obsession that her very thoughts were being tapped. Not since the afternoon she'd met Ferne had she felt anything like this.

Flickering images and transient concepts flashed like snatches of lightning through her brain. The woman reached out her hand and touched Fannette. A part of her being welcomed the touch, but another part shrank back, fear-stricken.

Then the old woman moved away.

Poppy passed by, slate in hand. "There you are!" she exclaimed. "Anton's been looking everywhere for you." She tapped the slate. "And I'm looking for Jove. I've got his lesson prepared."

117

Fannette was only dimly aware of her. She continued to stare after the bent figure.

"Who is that?"

Poppy glanced down the path. "Oh, that's Glory. Letty claims that no matter the ailment, Glory'll brew a cure. Herbs, I imagine."

Those eyes, Fannette thought. Those penetrating, light eyes in that face of darkness. Those wrinkled lips that moved to words without sound. She felt a wave of dizziness.

And she was reminded of Ferne staring at her in the front room of Poppy's cottage.

Still, there was a difference. A very great difference. Ferne wore her power like a cloak that could be put on or taken off. But the power in the old woman's eyes came from deep inside. A healing power with none of the malignancy of voodoo.

"I felt as if she were trying to warn me of something." Fannette realized that she was trembling.

Poppy's eyes flickered over the encampment. "Considering everything, a warning's hardly out of place."

"No!" Fannette's voice was impatient. "It had nothing to do with any of this. It concerned me. She stared beyond me, the way Ferne did. As if she saw more than me . . ."

Poppy laughed. "Ferne! She's obsessed with that pathetic suicide—and voodoo. She never comes to my cottage without some mention of it."

"She did a wrong thing and it haunts her."

Poppy gestured scornfully. "Voodoo! A combination of hysteria and superstition!" She frowned, remembering, and when she continued, there was less assurance in her voice. "To be truthful, there was the time when Ferne was held to be even more powerful than Madame Dede. By the ignorant, of course!"

Madame Dede. Like Marie LaVeau, a high priestess of voodoo. For the second time that night, Fannette felt a chill of warning. She moved her foot in the soft earth,

118

concentrating on a small insect she'd uncovered.

"At Bijou—out by the old sugar house—sometimes there were meetings. I always knew when there was one, even though Breel and Donna didn't. I'd get out of bed at night and watch the fires. Once, when I was very young, I felt myself drawn to the place. I hid in the cane to watch." Fannette looked up into Poppy's eyes. "The snake came to where I was hiding."

"It came to you?" Poppy's very evident horror set strangely against her professed disbelief.

Hesitant and reluctant, Fannette continued. "I felt as if this wasn't the first time. That it had happened before— and I accepted it. I carried it to where the fire burned . . ."

The memory took hold. She was ten years old again, and she felt the pull of something alien.

"Suddenly I hated it, despised it! I threw it into the flames!"

"*Sacre Coeur*!" Poppy whispered. "It's a marvel they didn't kill you!"

"They were afraid of me. I saw it in their faces."

"*Oui*! If Le Grand Zombi came to you, yes, they'd be afraid." She looked more closely at Fannette. "You're shivering. Are you cold—or has it to do with Glory?"

"Both," Fannette admitted. "I should be wearing something warmer than this pardessus." She touched her light wrap. "I'll go get my hooded cloak."

But they both knew it wasn't the January dampness that chilled her. She left Poppy and hurried to the tent. She'd said too much, she knew that. There were some things better left untold.

She raised the canvas flap and almost fell over Letty. Letty was squatting on the ground in front of her trunk, stacks of neatly folded clothing beside her.

Clearly an invasion of privacy! For the moment, at least, it was a welcome diversion.

"Why are you going through my trunk?" Fannette demanded.

Letty had been humming a Gullah spiritual. She stopped and grinned.

"Miz McLaury—"

"Miss Fannette."

"Miz McLaury, I neber see such a mess! You got dis trunk lak a cat been scratchin' a hole to pee."

Completely unjust! Poppy had taken out warm garments the night before, and Jove had replaced them.

"I did not!" she retorted.

"Neber you mind. Miss Poppy, her trunk near as bad. Dat Emily, she can do the cookin'. I'se lady's maid and the two of you is 'nough to keep me busy!" She continued to shake out items, fold them and set them in piles, humming and smiling.

Poppy burst in, her eyes bright with laughter, and Fannette realized with relief that the previous conversation was completely forgotten.

"Nette, you must come and see what they've made for us!"

She led Fannette out into the dimming evening light, ignoring the longing glances Fannette directed toward the line that was forming around the stove.

"Poppy, the food's ready!"

"Are you always hungry? This is of much more importance!" Poppy continued leading toward a fringe of trees. Just out of sight of the camp, she came to a halt in front of the fruit of Chippers's hammer and saw.

Four sturdy posts rested in the ground forming an ample square. Canvas was strung from post to post, screening the interior from view. Poppy moved aside the canvas flap and Fannette saw that a box was set in the center of the enclosure. A hole was cut into the top, and closer investigation revealed a shallow pit dug underneath.

"Just who thought up this?" Fannette asked, delighted.

"Jared, of course. Letty said he saw us disappear into the bushes this afternoon, and he figured no bridegroom

120

was going to have his bride squat on the ground and maybe put herself out of business with poison ivy."

"Poppy!"

"Well, that's what Letty said."

"This is just for the two of us?"

"They've marked off the place for the women. And the men, well, they just sort of wander into the woods. Trojan warned Letty that if she lowered her big black rear part on it, it'd collapse for sure."

It was embarrassing that Jared should notice such things, but, still, one had to be grateful.

"What elegance!" Poppy chortled. "A portable privy!" She looked at Fannette thoughtfully and then giggled again. "Really, Nette, I feel slighted Jared never worried about me riding in a spring wagon, or gave a thought about where I might get poison ivy, for that matter."

"He would have. Once you were on the road."

"Nette, are you really blind?"

Flattering, of course, to imagine a man cared enough for her comfort to show special consideration. But Jared? Never! Anton, yes. But not Jared.

Anton was waiting with three well-filled plates.

"I was afraid the food would be gone," he said. "So—*voila*!"

They sat on a fallen tree and ate with relish. When finally his plate was empty, Anton sighed and brushed his waistcoat.

"Do you realize that I left New Orleans without a change of clothing? It'll be Baton Rouge before I can get something, and even then there'll be no time for a proper tailor."

Jared was standing near, watching the foodline.

"I don't see anyone forcing you to stay with us," he remarked.

Anton regarded him through cold eyes. "And neither is anyone going to force me to leave."

The men glowered at each other, and Poppy picked at

121

what little food was left on her plate in obvious distress. Donna would have approved, Fannette told herself. But she was frankly too hungry for ladylike performances.

"Maybe you can borrow something of Jared's?" Poppy suggested.

"I'll go in rags first!" He turned to Fannette. "Hasn't this one day been enough? How can I make you reconsider?"

Marry me, possibly, Fannette thought. She paused with a fork in midair. Was that really what she wanted?

What had happened to her thinking? Of course it was what she wanted! Hadn't marriage been her principle goal, and wasn't Anton the ideal husband?

Who am I? she asked herself. Then, firmly, I'm Fannette Randolph, who cannot face Bijou and Breel. I am Fannette Randolph, who could not become a mistress to Anton . . .

And for the time, at least, I'm Mrs. McLaury.

The full impact of her position struck her with the shattering force of a wave. Everything depended on her carrying out her part in the charade, to use Anton's word. Should, by some miracle, Anton ask her to marry him, she wasn't in a situation to accept.

Not until Cincinnati.

And even then, how long did it take to annul a marriage? Why hadn't she thought of that before?

She looked about her, marveling at the trust that had been placed in her. She looked at each of the men and the women, seeing them for the first time as individuals. Watching them as they laughed, joked and praised Emily's cooking.

What had their life been? From what were they running, and to where were they going?

Anton gathered the plates. He paused as he took Fannette's from her lap.

"Consider," he said softly, "is this what you want?"

She turned her head away from him, her mind not really on his question.

These joyous people. These laughing people. She couldn't fail them, not even for Anton. Especially not for Anton . . .

There, then, was the truth. She no longer imagined she loved him. She liked him, yes. And was flattered by his attention. But nothing more.

Anton shrugged and moved away with the dishes. Poppy took her slate and looked around for Jove. Jared was conferring with Trojan, but Fannette found that again she was not alone.

A slight man of medium years stood at a respectful distance. He had taken off his woolen cap, and Fannette saw that he was light of skin, that he had the bronze shade of mixed blood.

Poppy paused to acknowledge him. "I haven't seen you all day, Abe," she said.

"Mr. Jared has us all busy," he replied. "I just now finished seeing to the saddle horses. I still haven't eaten."

"Well," Poppy advised as she moved away, "you'd better hurry. Everyone's after seconds."

Abe twirled his cap nervously. He had a large, hooked nose, and Fannette wished he'd put his cap back on his shiny bald head. The weather had turned decidedly chilly. His eyes, large and liquid under graying brows, were on Fannette's left hand.

"About the ring, Mrs. McLaury. Does it feel right?"

Feel right? How could it? It brought constant awareness of Jared's claim on her, temporary, though it might be.

Until Cincinnati . . .

"Do you mean, does it fit?"

He nodded.

"It fits well enough," she admitted, feeling ungracious.

"Mr. McLaury was most particular about it. It's a fine ring, you know. I like to work with material of that sort, but I was sorry to have to take out such a big piece."

He took it out of his pocket to show her. "There's certainly a difference in the size of your finger and his," he went on. "But he says that when we're where we can get the proper material, he'll have me work it into a ring. Like a setting."

Why? Jared could keep his ring. Could have it any day he chose!

Still, she enjoyed the little man's eagerness. There certainly was no call to hurt his feelings.

"I do fair enough work with gold and silver," he was saying. "I like to work with them. But not that shoddy stuff my owner used to give me."

"You worked for a jeweler?"

Abe's eyes had a faraway look in them. Fannette realized he no longer saw her.

Who were they? she wondered. Who were these people she was helping to escape? What did they ask of life? Why were they staking everything on the chance to reach Canada? What had been so terrible that they must run from it?

Nearby, Emily's husband, Wednesday, sang softly as he helped his wife clean the cooking pots:

"Oh, I'm gonna sing along de way
We'll shout o'er all our sorrows
An' I'm gonna sing along de way
For I'll be free tomorrow."

BOOK TWO

These Joyous People

"Good mornin', brother Pilgrim,
   Pray tell me where you bound . . ."

—from "Joshua Fit the Battle of Jericho,"
   an old negro spiritual

I

Had he worked for a jeweler? Yes, he had once. But that had been a long time ago.

Abe thought of the quiet shop in a side street in Atlanta, Georgia. Of the window offering rings and brooches of exquisite workmanship. Of the kindly, clever artisan whom he knew to be his father, though it was forbidden to call him that. Of the delicate, light-skinned lady who was his mother and his father's wife, though she could never be called that, either.

He thought of the long hours he worked beside this man, his father, learning to design beautiful fantasies in gold and silver. He remembered setting the precious stones, knowing they would adorn the finger or neck of some rich white lady. Or set in her hair like a crown on a queen's head.

Sometimes, when they were alone, the man he couldn't call his father, would deck his mother with the most precious, the most rare gems in his shop. She would wear the silk gown he'd bought for her when he'd visited cousins somewhere in a place called New York. They'd sip tea, just like in the big houses. Or, if it were Saturday, they'd drink his special wine from ceremonial glasses. The man he couldn't call father would lay a shawl over his shoulders and chant in the light of a seven-pronged candelabrum. The shop would be locked and the shades drawn. It was a scene from a different world.

Once his mother had told him about how she'd come to meet this man. She'd been a maid, a house slave, in one of the big, beautiful houses along one of the most exclusive streets. His father, Abraham, had been called in to repair rings and restring the necklaces that had been in the family through the years. His mother had been the maid trusted to take the pieces to Abraham in the room set aside for his use.

His work must have been more than satisfactory. He was commissioned to create a fanciful ruby and diamond brooch for the mistress of the house.

Abe's mother often talked of that brooch. Of how she and the bearded jeweler, Abraham, discussed it. How they discovered that she, too, had the gift of design, and of how he had used some of her ideas.

When the time finally came for Abraham to leave the house, he knew he could not go without the woman he had come to love. He could not marry her, but perhaps he could buy her.

The master had been delighted with Abraham's work, and he understood that a man alone, an artisan who was about to set up his own shop, would need a housekeeper. So it was arranged.

Often as a boy, Abe had heard Abraham lament the fact that the state laws had made it very difficult to liberate a slave, just as they had forbidden marriage between a white man and a person of color. To liberate a slave, one must appear before magistrates and place a bond. One must swear to things that were not true. Everything was designed to make emancipation almost impossible by a society that wanted no more freed blacks to stir discontent among their own slaves.

And Abraham was terrified of anything that had to do with courts and the awesome authority vested in the judges. He murmured about the terrible times he'd known in the country where he'd spent his youth.

"Never you mind," his mother would say in her gentle voice. "I'm here with you, and what does it matter whether I'm freed or a slave? Why bother with what makes no difference?"

"But the boy. The child follows the state of the mother, Ellie. I cannot see my own flesh and blood a slave."

128

"You'll be here to see that he isn't," she had replied with her usual faith. Nothing could happen to change this great happiness that was hers. How could it? And her son, young though he was, already showed talent. Some of his designs even surpassed those of his father.

Abe was fifteen when a terrible thing happened. The man he could not call his father was attacked in the street on his way to deliver a very valuable necklace of matched pearls. He'd been left in a gutter to bleed out his life.

The client was sympathetic, but unwilling to take the loss of the necklace's worth. While Abraham had designed many valuable pieces, it had always been on commission. His own stock, and even the small building that housed his home and shop, did not meet the amount of his indebtedness.

But the sale of Abraham's two slaves, mother and son, evened the balance.

Abe closed his eyes tightly. He could still see his mother's face when they were handed over to the slave dealers. They were put on the block together, to be sold as a pair.

Then—he shuddered at the memory—the fat, swarthy man with shoe-button eyes that fed on his mother's body appeared. She'd been stripped of her customary, respectable house frocks and clad for the block in a thin shift that did nothing to disguise her delicate curves. Her abundant hair had been freed of the braids she'd wrapped around her head. It hung in glossy curls over her shoulders, framing the beauty of her dusky, sensitive face.

Tanus was a traveling dry goods and novelties merchant. He made good money and had recently come into more, left by an uncle who'd never known him. He had reached a time in his life when he felt the need of a steady woman to please his appetites, both sensual and domestic. Here, he decided, was the right woman. Not too young. A young woman was only trouble. And not too old. An older woman might cook well enough, but he wanted more than a cook.

"The price on the woman is fair enough," he told the dealer. "But I don't want the boy. And you're crazy, the price you ask!"

The dealer shook his head. "He's a craftsman. A jeweler. He could take that there old piece of brass and with the right equipment make you a geegaw that'd charm the pants off most any young filly."

Tanus ran his not too clean finger over his long, sharp chin, and narrowed his tiny eyes until only little black slits were visible. Adding jewelry to his wares might not be a bad idea. Most folks didn't know the difference between what was genuine and what was fake, anyway. Just as long as it was pretty and it sparkled. He'd have to inquire about the equipment he'd need. Maybe a burner of sorts for melting, shaping. . . .

The dealer had been watching closely. "It'd be a profitable line," he coaxed, "And you can get the essentials cheap. The shop that this boy comes from is for sale and so are the tools."

Tanus took the day to make inquiries, and toward evening he returned to buy the pair. His two horses and the large, suprisingly comfortable house wagon waited outside.

That night Abe slept under the wagon and heard his mother's screams. He burrowed under his covers trying to drown out Tanus's delighted laughter. Later he was to find that the ultimate horror was the nights he heard the crack of a whip. This always happened when Tanus had been drinking heavily. But his mother no longer screamed. She just grew thinner, more drawn, and barely touched her food, though the bulge under her loose dress proclaimed that she should be eating for two.

They were near a little Alabama town the night her time came. Even then she didn't scream. Just closed her eyes tightly, and, as if the last of her strength was devoured by the first pain, she died. The baby still in her.

130

Tanus became a madman then. He disappeared, leaving the frail body still lying on the blood-soaked bed in the heat of summer. He was gone for a week, and when he returned he was fit for nothing for days after.

Abe had buried his mother, cleaned the linens, and set things to rights. But nothing could set right the hatred that had been growing but was now matured inside his heart.

Day and night he lived with the hate. He cooked, cleaned and created intricate designs out of the most dross of materials. He cringed inside at the prices charged to folks who couldn't afford the money, even had a fair sum been asked. His honesty suffered over the knowledge that it was the beauty of his craftmanship that brought about these ill-afforded purchases in the first place.

The years passed. The horses died and were replaced. The wagon was repaired many times. They drove from state to state and to the territories. Sometimes they even went westward to where families waited for the spring before setting out across the plains.

Tanus turned gray and then white. His gross body lost flesh and his jowls hung on either side of his sharp chin with its billy-goat beard. But he had the appearance of one who would endure beyond time.

Abe himself had lost his hair early, as had Abraham. He noted with pride that his nose was long and arched high at the bridge. He clung to memories of old Abraham, happy to see the proof of relationship in himself. But to be free. That was a hopeless dream. Until that day! That glorious day!

If Tanus had truthfully represented his wares, told folks that in one day's wearing his rings would turn a finger green, it wouldn't have happened. But no. According to him, he sold only gold of the highest quality. The sparkly pieces of glass were diamonds (with the slightest flaw, you understand, that's why he was able to offer them so cheaply). His paste beads were pearls.

Why, he carried a fortune in rare jewels! Look at those

131

sapphires,he would say.They were obtained only at great difficulty. That they were only glass, he never mentioned.

So it was, that one night in a lonely camp outside a fair-sized town, Abe returned from the spring with a bucket of water in time to see two roughly-dressed men ride up to the campfire.

Tanus stepped out of the wagon at the sound of their voices, and before he came down the steps, a shot rang out.

The two men dismounted. A quick examination was all that was needed. A disgusted nudge with a mud-encrusted boot, and they stepped over him, to strip the wagon of its treasures.

Abe watched from the screen of trees, ready to run, but they'd been intent only on the shining, glittering hoard. They filled their saddlebags and were out of sight before the sun had moved down on the horizon.

Abe waited a very long time, his mind busy with the possibilities. He was free! Only, not really. Who would believe he hadn't been the one who killed and robbed his master? There was no hiding the wagon and horses. They were a familiar sight. No. He had to put as much country as possible between himself and what had been Tanus.

First, he dragged the body inside where it wouldn't be seen by a passing traveler. Then he gathered his belongings together and wrapped them in a blanket. He put all the food he could carry into a hamper and set off for the woods.

Those first summers of hiding weren't too unpleasant. Living in woods and swamps, going into fields at night for peas and corn. Finding fruits and berries in the orchards and forest. Fishing a quiet stream. When winter came he went to a cave he'd discovered. He made a crude bow and learned to shoot it at deer and possum. He smoked the meat and cut it into strips. He had a stone and sling, equally accurate for squirrel and bird.

Yes, at first he'd enjoyed the life. Then, as the second

year came to an end, he realized he was lonely for the sound of a human voice. Realized that man needed his own kind.

This yearning drew him dangerously close to towns. He drifted southward, and one August he found himself in the cypress swamps outside of New Orleans.

All day he watched from the brush as folks left the city. Some in fine carriages, some in wagons, and still others with their scanty belongings strapped to their backs. They camped by the roadside at night, and one morning, in his search for food, he came on a campsite from which the people had fled in terror. A man lay dead, still in his bed-roll, covered with the filth of the sickness that had taken him.

It was then that Abe realized he had come on the city at a time of plague, and he knew he must leave. He shouldered his pack and started northward, but within a day he knew he had waited too long. The sickness was on him.

He was fortunate. He was near a fresh stream, and in his pack there were strips of jerked meat and loaves of dried persimmon. He covered himself as well as he could, knowing he most likely wouldn't last the night out.

"Let death leave me dignity," he prayed. But where did one find dignity in the terrible death of yellow fever?

The mosquitoes swarmed around him, but he no longer cared. He was drenched in sweat. He vomited vile smelling messes. Sometimes he was aware enough to take water from the jug he had left at hand. But he would die. He knew that. Daily he marveled at the fact that he had not already died.

Then, one afternoon, he opened his eyes and mind to the fact that it hadn't been ordained for him to die. He was too weak to more than gulp at his water jug. It was warm and brackish. He wished he could drink of the cool water in the stream below. Wished he could cleanse himself. The smell of the illness on him was almost more than he could bear.

"Be thankful," he told himself. "Be thankful you have water and you can drink."

By evening he could reach into a pocket for a bit of jerky, and he was able to break a piece of the persimmon loaf. Strength was returning, he thought.

Then there was darkness . . .

He awakened to voices. Two black men were bending over him. He was stripped of his filthy clothing, and his body had been slushed clean with water.

"How long you been hidin'?" one of the men asked when he saw that Abe was awake.

"Two years. Maybe close to three," Abe replied.

He was alive! Alive and clean! That such a miracle should happen to him! That God should be so good!

The second man left his small fire, and the two of them lifted Abe so he could drink the broth they'd brewed from dried venison. At first the liquid was too hot for more than a sip. Then swallowing came easier.

"What you do?" the first man asked.

Abe spread his hands. "The man who owned me was robbed and killed. I knew better than to stay and be blamed. There's a price on my head. But maybe folks have forgotten."

"Slave hunters never forgit," the second man said. "Sometimes they catch a man, mebbe ten years after."

"We takes him to Trojan?" the first man asked.

The second nodded. "Can't no ways take him to the Settlement less Trojan say so."

And that, Abe thought, was how he came to resize a ring for this white lady. The best of wedding rings, because it was made from one the man himself had worn and cherished. Abraham, whom he couldn't call father, would have approved and been happy.

He looked at the ring with pride.

"I can't even see where it joins," Fannette said. "You must be a very good jeweler."

McLaury left Trojan and came up to where they talked.

His eyes took on a quizzical expression when he saw that Fannette was examining her ring.

"Checking on your work?" he asked Abe.

"Maybe looking back into the past," Abe said. "I'm proud you asked me to size this wedding ring for Mrs. McLaury. I hope she'll wear it in happiness for many years."

Fannette lowered her eyes, feeling a shame at deceiving the earnest little man. But the shame was quickly replaced by anger at Jared's hypocrisy.

Jared shook the little man's hand, and his voice was so sincere that Fannette thought she'd either scream or laugh right out.

"Thank you, Abe," Jared said. "I hope so, too."

II

After two days of following the bayou through marsh country, the wagons finally turned onto the River Road, heading north. They rattled past shacks, cabins and an occasional great house that was set well back of lush stretches of lawn and tree-lined avenue. In those places there would be high levees fronting the river. A futile endeavor on the part of the plantation owner. Nothing restrained the restless brown waters that moved with the seasons, relentlessly carving away great stretches of lawn and field.

The crops had been gathered, but it would still be several months before the stubble could be burned and plowed under for the new planting. Fannette decided that Jared had chosen his time well. There was almost no activity. Only an occasional passing cart or smoke curling out of a chimney.

But on the surface of the river, steamboats churned up the water, and passengers called out to them as they passed on their way upstream.

"Donna promised that someday we'd take a trip on a riverboat," Fannette said enviously. "Those folks out there don't look a bit cold!"

"Just be glad we're not traveling in the spring or summer," Poppy replied. "Jared says the Natchez Trace has a fearsome reputation for bugs and mosquitoes once the weather warms. Then the streams swell with the rain and runoff, and the bottomlands are bogs."

But it was difficult to be grateful when, in the evening, sitting by their campfire, they could see the warm glow of bright lights in the chilly night, knowing that folks were dancing and laughing in sparkling ballrooms.

It was a long, hard journey they had undertaken. Sixteen or twenty days by boat. Close to three months by River Road. Then over the all but abandoned Trace. Finally came the back roads of Kentucky.

Till Cincinnati.

And a hard bed under canvas. True, Jove saw that they had pitchers of hot water in the mornings and that everything was done for their comfort. Still . . .

"We could stop over at most of the big houses," Poppy remarked, her mind apparently plowing the same channel. "They always welcome ready cash in exchange for room and board."

"Then why don't we?" It was bad enough to know that there would be few if any inns left on the Trace, and it was insufferable to realize they were knowingly passing up comfort when it might be had.

"People ask questions, and it's easy to forget. Easy to give the wrong answers. Besides, most the places would expect us to shackle our people."

So it was a surprise to both of them when Jared made arrangements to spend the night at a small plantation. It was the same day that the road crossed the Mississippi.

It had been a tiresome afternoon of loading wagons and horses onto a flatboat. Tempers were short, and the two children, Emma's nine-year-old boy, Friday, and Abby's seven-year-old Tressa, were shouting insults at each other. This had spread to the parents, and it was with difficulty that Poppy led Tressa's mother, Abby, away from an indignant Emily.

"Her man Wednesday might be a preacher," Abby muttered, "but that no way make her a saint! And that chile! He gotta debil in him fo' shore!"

"Oh Christ!" Jared muttered. "Why couldn't we have left the women and children behind?" He had been helping the men dislodge a wheel that had embedded in a crevice. He threw down the wedge he'd been holding, jumped on his horse, and disappeared up the road.

When he returned he had Jove hitch the phaeton, and

137

he rode beside it until they turned up an avenue and came into sight of a white house with stubbled fields behind a new lawn and barn.

"Imagine!" Fannette gloated. "A roof and a floor. Maybe even a hot tub of water!"

Poppy looked at her strangely. Under any other circumstances Fannette might have imagined there was mischief in her wide eyes.

"And the best possible room for Mrs. McLaury . . ." Poppy added.

Merciful Mother in heaven! She had forgotten. He had warned her they'd be expected to share the same room!

The phaeton stopped under the *porte cochere,* Jared had already dismounted to help them down. It seemed to Fannette that he held her hand a fraction of a second too long. Touched her waist when he needn't. She moved away from him, her eyes on his face.

He lifted an eyebrow. "God almighty, Fannette," he muttered, "Stop looking like a startled virgin! The Lemmons will think I'm a monster. By this time a bride is expected to be reconciled to her state. And no matter what you might hope, I've no intention of rape!"

She gasped and Poppy laughed.

He moved closer, tilted her face up to his, and unexpectedly touched her lips with his.

"When I made the arrangements, I informed Bart Lemmon that Anton and I would stay in the barn with our stock."

"But Poppy said they'd have to be shackled, if—"

"That would defeat my reason for staying here."

So it hadn't been for her sake, after all?

"You most likely would never give it a thought, my dear Mrs. McLaury, but there are eight men and women who've been separated from each other since the trip began. They've started to grumble."

And they're sneaking into the woods in the evening, she thought, but refrained from mentioning it.

138

"It might not have occurred to you," he continued, "but there are women who look forward to spending a night with their husbands. So I arranged for the use of the barn."

"I still don't see where that—"

"They'll have a party tonight. Just like a Saturday night in the quarters. Of course, it'll be necessary that Anton and I stay with them to keep order."

"And," his eyes were disconcertingly on her face again, "there are all sorts of places where two people might find privacy in a big barn."

She flushed and he grinned. He caught her hand and pulled her back again.

"Perhaps you might consider—"

She yanked her hand free, and his laughter followed her as she moved closer to Poppy.

"I hate him!" she said fervently, lowering her voice as the Lemmons came out to greet them.

The interior of the house was far from spacious by Bijou's standards, but Fannette was delighted with the room Madeline Lemmon gave her. Already a fire was burning under a marble mantel, and there was a deep piled rug on the floor.

Madeline looked around, checking to see that all was in order. "I'll have a tub brought up for you," she said. "When we travel, that's the first thing I want when we stop."

A comfortable bed with a feather mattress. Crisp white linen and a mosquitoe *baire*. An inlaid table and two comfortable chairs. Why had she never before truly appreciated such things?

"Bart's having a fire built in a drum in the barn," Madeline Lemmon went on. "So Mr. McLaury and your brother will find it comfortable there. And I'll send out cots for them. And, oh, they're coming up with your trunk. Just send your maid down for anything you might need."

139

Poppy and Fannette exchanged glances. Blessed Mother! Fannette thought. Poppy'll be expected to eat in the kitchen house with the slaves and share a bed with one of the maids!

"If it's not too inconvenient, Mrs. Lemmon, could you arrange a pallet for my maid? She always sleeps near the door when my husband can't be with me."

"Certainly. But, my dear, you're quite safe here."

"Oh, of course!" Fannette smiled. "But Mr. McLaury feels easier when he knows she's there to tend my needs."

"Naturally." Obviously Madeline Lemmon was happy with one less arrangement to be made. Not that she wouldn't charge for it, anyway. With all the great sums of money coming and going on paper, it was a rare pleasure to see cash.

And that Mrs. McLaury must certainly be a pampered bride! And such a strong, handsome husband. And imagine! Twenty-eight slaves as part of her dowry. Twenty-eight! A fortune!

After the door closed, Fannette went to her trunk. All Letty's efforts toward organization were disregarded as she dug into it, searching for her flounced frock of striped Peking silk. She held it up in dismay.

"It's crushed beyond hope!" she said.

"And they'll expect me to press it." Poppy looked at it dismally. "I'm no better with a flatiron that you."

"Then you'd scorch it for sure."

But there was always a way, if one gave the matter sufficient thought. Fannette's eyes rested on her reticule, and she dug out some coins. "Find the girl who does their ironing and give her these." She frowned, thinking. "And you can tell her I need you upstairs to help with my bath."

When Poppy returned from the kitchen house, the tub was already in the center of the room, surrounded by steaming pots of water. Poppy threw herself onto the bed, bouncing happily.

"A real bed! A floor and a rug!" she gloated, kicking

140

off her slippers.

Fannette was sitting in the easy chair, taking down her hair. Had it ever been so long between washings? And a pitcher of hot water in the morning was hardly a substitute for a steaming tub!

"You can take the first bath," Poppy offered. "I just want to lie here and enjoy this bed for awhile." She sobered. "It was good of you to consider me, Nette. I was regretting I'd gone as the maid instead of the bride!" She laughed. "Of course, being from the North, Jared doesn't understand that some folks might wonder if it weren't more than a cross of French and Spanish that gave my skin a touch of copper."

Fannette eyed her appraisingly. "You could pass," she said. "Some of Donna's friends were darker."

There was a light tap on the door, and Fannette paused in the act of undoing hooks. She moved around the tub and turned the knob. A brown young woman stood in the hall holding her dress.

"I'm Tansy," she announced. "This is a mighty pretty thing, Miz McLaury."

Fannette smiled and accepted the gown.

Thinking back on that afternoon, Fannette was to wonder why lightning hadn't flashed and thunder hadn't pealed in warning.

Tansy, a pert brown young woman with inquisitive eyes. Tansy, who was to be her undoing.

III

When Tansy carried the freshly ironed gown up the stairs and knocked on the bedroom door, she expected it would be the maid who took it from her.

And such a fancy maid! Those McLaury folks sure must be quality, Tansy thought. She knew that a girl who could have passed for white and who was as pretty as Poppy just had to cost a cartload of money. And such high manners! Like a real white lady. And she knew about ladies, because her man, Bates, was the butler who brought tea and such into the sitting room when Mrs. Lemmon entertained.

And then, instead of the maid, that Miz McLaury herself answered the door. Such a nice mannered woman. More like a girl than a married woman, come to think of it.

"Oh, but you've done beautiful work!" she exclaimed. Then she caught up her purse and took out still more coins. Lordy, money must be fair to dripping through her hands! Then, when she turned to look around, Tansy had to remember to shut her mouth. The maid was sitting on the bed!

"Poppy," Miz McLaury said, "I swear I thought it would never be right again! Letty said my trunk looked as if a cat had been digging in it."

"I never could fold things," the maid laughed. Then she saw that Tansy was still in the doorway, and Tansy knew her eyes must have been big, round circles by then. The girl, Poppy, jumped down onto the floor.

"I was after a mosquito," she explained.

A mosquito in January? Everyone knew they died with winter. And besides, she wasn't after anything. She'd been

142

lying there and chattering—laughing, even. And not paying any mind to the bath that steamed in the tub anymore than she was helping her mistress. Why, it even looked as if Miz McLaury had been undoing her own frock!

What a story to tell them in the kitchen house!

Miz McLaury took on dignity then, like Tansy'd seen Mrs. Lemmon do when she didn't want something noticed.

"Thank you," Miz McLaury said. "If I need anything further, I'll have my maid ask for you."

Tansy knew when she was being dismissed. She bobbed her head, gave the expected giggles, and rattling the coins in her apron pocket, she closed the door.

But, as she moved on down the hall, she began to wonder if the time she'd watched for might not have come. True, she'd intended to wait out the winter, but that Miz McLaury appeared mighty easy going . . .

Besides, the longer she held back, the greater the chance the same thing might happen to her that happened to Miz Tubman.

Only backwards.

She wished that she'd been able to go along when that Harriet Tubman sneaked into a cabin and told folks that wanted to follow her she'd lead them to a place called Canada. The place where no one could turn anyone in, even if they had run away.

Her man, Bates, had been the first to say he'd go, and Tansy had felt hurt inside, because he knew she'd have to stay, big as she was with their child.

"Don't you worry, honey," he'd told her, looking handsome and proud in his butler uniform. He spoke proud, too, and she didn't do so bad herself. The Lemmons made the house servants talk like white folks. No quarters talk was permitted, not even in the kitchen where Tansy was the first assistant to the cook. If she stayed, someday she might be cook herself, and that was a mighty fine job. And how could her Bates do better than butler?

But it was no use. He left, and so did three others. That week there must have been close to fifteen niggers running off into the woods. And not one of them was ever caught.

And now the baby was four months old. And there'd never been a word from Bates . . .

She thought of what had happened to that Harriet Tubman. Miz Tubman, she still called herself. She ran away and got to Canada. Then she came back for her husband. But no ways would he go with her. The master had married him to another woman, and he just wasn't figuring on leaving his new wife for the old one.

She never stopped calling herself Miz Tubman, though. And she never took another man. She just spent all her years helping folks to get to Canada.

By the time she reached the kitchen house, Tansy's mind was made up. She had heard that most anyone believed you if you followed movers close and said you were part of them. The thing was to stay just out of sight.

Then, maybe, when they were far enough away, she might ask that Miz McLaury for help. A white lady who let her maid act so free and sit on a bed, just might be willing to listen.

She'd wrap the baby up warm. At night, maybe, she could steal food from the camp. And she'd heard that the free colored people were mightly helpful to runaways.

And so Tansy sang to herself as she went into the kitchen. She took her baby from his corner and settled herself to feed him.

It was January, but look at that sun! Looked as if it might be through with raining, she told herself, though deep inside she knew that to be unlikely.

Meanwhile, in the bedroom upstairs Fannette dried herself and Poppy bathed. Fannette hummed as she brushed her hair in front of the mirror.

Hummed with no realization that back in the kitchen a second cook called Tansy had sealed the fate of the caravan.

144

IV

Anton was in the very best of humors when he joined them at dinner. The son of the family was of his size, and Anton had managed the purchase of shirts and trousers. For a price, it was true. *Merde!* The best tailor in New Orleans would hardly have charged more. But still, they were new, having been purchased after the cotton crop had put credit on the Lemmons' books. And better, still, his own clothes were being laundered by one of the maids.

His eyes rested on Fannette with appreciation. Her tawny hair swung back into curls that cascaded down her back with interwoven flowers. Certainly the neckline of her lavender-striped silk frock was even lower than the emerald velvet. Not quite right for winter, but let her once again enjoy warmth and happiness.

Let her enjoy what should be hers.

He pondered the question of offering marriage to her as he filled his plate. The food was ample, and more steamed on the buffet, but he had to admit the Lemmons' cook didn't hold a candle to Emily.

Sacre Coeur! What was he doing with this convoy of cutthroats? Fugitives! Maroons! Outlaws! Name it, and there'd be one in the group. He, Anton, who dearly loved his comfort and his elegant clothes.

But it was an adventure. And what adventure could there be in France with a winery to attend? There he would be expected to forget the joy of being young, rich and without responsibilities. In short, to settle down.

And with Fannette, that might not be such a bad fate.

But *maman*? *Diable*! That would be a scene. Hopefully by letter only. And if the letters became too much, one might always burn them and pretend they

145

hadn't arrived.

"Your sister looks simply beautiful," Mrs. Lemmon said. "What wonders a bath and fresh clothes can do for a woman."

Sister? It was a moment before Anton had fully recovered his poise. He nodded in appreciation.

"Fannette is always beautiful," he agreed. "Even in camp and bundled up in warm coats. But here, in your handsome dining room, and with such a lavish meal—"

"Oh, not really lavish!" Madeline Lemmon protested, pleased. But it was the best she could manage. She recognized quality when she saw it. And twenty-eight slaves! Why, when their Macey married, she doubted they could even spare her a maid.

But then, Bart was doing well. Weren't they taking on new land? Someday, maybe, she'd be able to afford to dress her daughter the way Mrs. McLaury dressed. And no doubt about it, young Kirk had made a good profit out of selling those new things of his to that Monsieur Verdier.

And just how did a young dandy like that happen to be on the road without even a change of underwear?

"I hope Kirk's things fit comfortably, Mr. Verdier."

"Oh, splendid. Splendid!" Anton realized there was a question in her eyes. "My trunk fell off one of the wagons. We sent back for it when we saw the damage, but someone had picked it up."

"Thieves everywhere," she murmured. "But wouldn't it have been simpler to have sent everything by water and travel to Kentucky by riverboat?" She paused. "I do believe Mr. McLaury did mention his home was near the Ohio River, didn't he? The trip all the way from New Orleans to Cincinnati doesn't take much more than three weeks!"

Fannette moved her fork on her plate without actually spearing her meat. That was what Poppy meant by embarrassing questions! Anton was dabbing at his mouth with a napkin as if he hadn't heard. So it was up to her.

"*C'est en vain!* " she murmured, as she imagined Donna might under the same circumstances. "It is so embarrassing to admit, but I'm terrified of steamboats. I won't even go near where one's docked."

"My goodness," Mrs. Lemmon said. "They're such fun."

"Not if you've seen one explode." Fannette dabbed at her eyes, pleased with herself. "Not if one's younger brother. . ." She let her words drift.

"Oh." Madeline paled. "Oh, my dear. . ."

And so that finished that.

"Jared expects you to join him at the barn and watch the dancing with him after dinner," Anton said when he'd recovered. He looked at Fannette with new respect. *Absolument!* She might prove a match for *maman* at that.

Poppy was waiting in their room with a heavy wrap for Fannette.

"I had them dish me up a plate downstairs," she said. "I told them I was so busy getting your things in order that there wasn't time to sit in the kitchen house."

So Poppy was too proud to eat with the house slaves.

"They'll think I'm a heartless mistress."

Poppy shook her head. "Those people in the kitchen are much harder to deceive than their owners," she explained. "They see things white folks are too busy to notice. For instance, that girl Tansy. . ."

Fannette nodded in agreement. She'd been aware of Tansy throughout the dinner. As second cook in a small household, Tansy had helped to serve the food, bringing in hot dishes. Always her eyes followed Fannette. There was something speculative about the way she watched.

"Oh, Nette," Poppy wailed, "Jared would have a fit if he knew that girl caught me lazing on the bed."

"No one pays attention to kitchen talk," Fannette replied, wishing she could believe what she said.

147

They went out the side door and started toward the barn.

"Do I smell hog roasting?" Fannette asked. "I swear I wish I hadn't eaten!"

They found Jared standing near the fire, watching Jove turn the improvised spit. Young hog it was.

"God alone knows how they came by it," Jared muttered, seeing Poppy look at it with raised eyebrows.

Jove grinned and gave over to young Friday.

"They say it's not from the Lemmons' sty," Jared went on. "Wild pig, they told me. They claim Juba was in the pine woods back there and found it walking around."

Anton had come down the path in time to hear the explanation. "Wild pig? *Zut!* I'm happy I won't be here to listen to complaints from the cabin people."

Jared shrugged. "I'll ask Bart Lemmon the value. He can handle it when the protest gets to him." He glanced toward the barn. "Trouble is, they've lived by pilfering for so long that it comes natural to them."

Jove laughed. "There a song 'bout how a nigger never go into the wood without corn in his pocket."

Abe came up holding a fiddle. "Made it myself," he told Fannette. "When Jove gets going on his mouth organ and me on this, we get out something worth dancing to."

Jove pulled a harmonica out of a pocket and followed Abe into the barn. Already their people were grouping around the side, leaving the center open for the dancers. They called out to the musicians.

Jared took Poppy by the hand. "We'll start them off!" he told her and whisked her away, leaving Anton and Fannette alone.

"A girl may dance with her brother," Anton decided, bowing as formally as at the LaMotte's ball. "You must excuse my lack of gloves."

How long since she'd danced? She who loved to dance? Since that New Year's ball—or had it been forever?

She was aware of Poppy and Jared nearby, and the

148

rhythmical clapping to the time of the music. She couldn't remember when she'd ever so enjoyed a dance.

Laughing and flushed, they finally collapsed on the sideline. Jove blew out his harmonica and Abe wiped his forehead.

"Now that you've started the dancing off," Jared said, "it might be as well if you two women went back to the house."

"Why?" Fannette demanded.

"Because this is their night to jubilate, and they might find the two of you an inhibiting influence."

"And what about you and Anton?"

Jared's eyes took on a thinly veiled meaning. "We're men. They won't mind us."

"Oh." The embarrassing color was warm in her cheeks again.

"However," he continued, his eyes still on her face, "since you seem determined to make a night of it, I think we could get away with one more dance. They'd expect me to dance with my bride."

Fannette started to back away, but Jared caught her hand and signaled to Abe and Jove.

He danced well, not with the practised grace of Anton, but with authority and evident enjoyment. She looked up at him, flustered and very much aware of the strength in the arm that encircled her waist. Her dark eyes sought into the deep blue of his, but she saw his attention was caught and held by her mouth. A bit of fair hair had fallen over his forehead, and he tossed it back without changing the direction of his gaze. Then she realized that they were alone in the center of the floor. Poppy and Anton were watching from the sidelines. Anton was glowering, but Poppy had a smile on her face.

"I was thinking about the afternoon we went for a ride in that closed carriage," Jared said.

Still more color rushed to Fannette's cheeks.

"And I feel bound to mention that I don't approve of

149

my wife wearing so low a neckline."

She expected to see the familiar mocking smile, but instead his arm tightened, drawing her against him, and his other arm closed around her shoulders. She threw her head back, but not before his lips were on hers.

Then there was the warmth of his mouth searching hungrily, finding what it sought, as her own lips parted and her arms went around his neck. When he finally raised his head, there was a gleam of triumph in his eyes.

It was then that she became aware of the hooting, shouting and cheering. Still pink of cheek, she realized they'd been the central performers to a very enthusiastic audience. Anger and embarrassment mingled, and Jared held her wrist firmly.

"I've experienced the power in that hand," he whispered, grinning. "My face had welts for days after."

Poppy was laughing, but Anton made no attempt to conceal his fury.

"Such an eye-catching act!" Poppy exclaimed. "I haven't seen better at the Orleans Theater!"

Anton swore in mixed French and English, only pausing because Bart Lemmon joined them, holding a decanter of brandy and three glasses.

"Reckoned I'd like to share my evening libation with you gentlemen," he said.

"The ladies were about to leave," Jared told him as he watched his host pour the amber liquor. "But first permit me to toast my bride."

Anton had taken up a glass, and for one fearful minute, Fannette thought he'd smash it rather than drink, but Jared's warning glance brought him back to sanity.

Jared drank down his toast, then he turned to Fannette.

"My dear, Trojan and Anton could see to our people. Perhaps you'd prefer to have me join you later?"

Of a certainty it was for Bart Lemmon's benefit. But still she was conscious of a growing sense of disquiet. Jared's eyes were searching into hers, and she realized this

150

was not one of his jokes. He was asking a question knowing that she still felt the effect of his kiss.

"It's up to you." His meaning was abundantly clear.

She managed an easy smile, knowing that Bart Lemmon was watching with interest.

"I've arranged for Poppy to sleep in my room," Fannette said. "So you needn't worry." Then, her eyes daring him to object, she stood on tiptoes to kiss Anton on the lips.

"Goodnight, brother," she smiled up into his eyes. "I do hope the two of you will be able to get some sleep tonight."

"Nette!" Poppy chided as they started up the path. "Why do you bait them?"

"You saw him!" Fannette exclaimed, no longer able to control her anger. "And right in front of everybody!"

"Of course it would have been better if you'd been alone. But even so, I didn't notice that you pushed him away."

"Poppy, you're absolutely disgusting."

"Disgusting? Oh, Nette!"

Fannette hurried up the path, but Poppy ran after her.

"Why should this man and woman thing be such an embarrassment to you?" she teased. "I dread to think what it would have been had you really run off with Anton!"

The thought was beyond considering.

Then why was it so different with Jared? When he kissed her she might just as well have been back in the carriage. Her body had shown the same traitorous reactions. And what was worse, he knew it. It had been in his eyes when she left him.

She drew a deep breath of resolution.

Let Jared talk of fruit ready for the picking. This fruit would rather wither on the vine!

V

"Come, my lub, an' go wid me,
I'm gwine away to Tennessee."

Jove looked back into the phaeton and grinned at them, ending his song abruptly. It wasn't one of his usual songs, but a minstrel show tune that had come down from New York.

"Reckon I the only one with enough get up and go to sing today," he told the girls.

It was true. They had started late, men and women emerging from different parts of the barn, stretching and yawning. And there had been no harmonizing the usual morning spiritual as they went on their way. Still, tempers were no longer as short as before their stop, even though there were several who looked as if they might not have slept the night before.

"Sure wish that Zette go with us," Jove continued. "That Zette frivolous for sure, but I miss her something bad."

"What are you going to do about Zette?" Poppy asked Fannette.

Fannette shrugged. "First I have to find out if she's actually mine."

"I've a notion the sooner they marry the better."

"Why Donna's right, they're just children, Poppy."

"I don't think Jove has dancing on his mind . . ."

Jove heard them and turned again, grinning. "I shore don't," he admitted, "but ain't no one but Zette for me. Why that Sassie girl near asked for it, but I don't want no Sassie. I wants Zette."

"Isn't Sassie Juba's girl?" Poppy asked.

"She any girl to any man that'll bring her somethin' pretty. Juba's 'bout out of his mind."

Poppy frowned. "I'll have a talk with her."

"I can't see that it's our business," Fannette said.

Poppy shook her head. "Anything that might bring on trouble is our business."

Fannette shrugged and looked out at the scenery. Some birds flushed at the sound of the wagons and flew south. Too early to go north, she reflected, wondering that birds should be wiser than men.

The clouds were gathering up ahead, Well, it was to be expected. They'd had fine weather for January, and no one could presume they'd finish the journey without rain.

They took their evening stop in a field across from a levee. The plantation house was out of their sight, hidden by trees and shrubs. The rain was moving in fast, she decided, as she climbed the slope of the embankment and sat on top where she could watch the river. The air was warmer than had been the last few days. A thunder shower. The humidity could only mean that.

The river stretched out below her. Brown and placid on the surface, giving lie to the currents that flowed underneath. Currents that recognized neither wealthy planter or poor farmer in its depredations. Taking where it wanted to take, and bestowing where it was not wanted.

Jared came up beside her. He pointed up stream to where a pair of torches flared against the darkening sky. "That's a wood yard where the riverboats take on fuel." He settled down, resting on his heels.

Together they watched the progress of a brightly illuminated side wheeler moving toward the shore and the beacons.

"Yes," Anton said, joining them. "Watch and you'll see them put down two planks. One for the men carrying wood onto the boat, and the other for those leaving to get another load."

"And, if you count real well," Jared went on, unper-

153

turbed by the interruption, "you might find that where fifteen men went up, twelve came off."

Anton chuckled softly. "So that's one of the ways!"

"Then there's the locked cabin."

"We know that one," Anton agreed. "A white man books a cabin—both berths—all of the way from New Orleans to Cincinnati."

Jared nodded. "He pays in full, gets the keys. Once he's paid and has the keys, even the captain has no right to enter the cabin he's taken."

"Why should it matter?" Fannette asked, trying to count the distant figures scurrying up and down the planks.

"No one pays attention to three or four black men carrying trunks. No one notices that those trunks aren't any heavier than if they had contained food and water for maybe three weeks."

"And who is there to notice that they never come out of the cabin after they go in?" Anton concluded.

"No more than anyone pays much attention to three or four black men carrying trunks out of a cabin once the boat docks in Cincinnati."

"Breel Luton should hear you!" Fannette exclaimed, looking at the two of them.

"Oh, he's aware of that game. I know for a fact that at least once he was the white man who booked a cabin." Jared studied her face in the dim light. "Don't you know that Bijou has been a focal point of activity for many years?"

"Hogs and corn were stolen from us just like the other bayou plantations," Fannette informed them indignantly.

"Perhaps contributed," Jared suggested, "would be the better word."

"I'd rather not learn too much about such activities," Anton said, moving to leave. "Someday I might accidently reveal more than I should to the wrong person."

Jared's eyes were back on the river. Below them, on the

bank, two quiet figures walked hand in hand toward a clump of trees.

Jared smiled and turned to Fannette. "They stir thoughts," he said. "We share a tent tonight, you know."

She stared at him. "You promised—"

He shrugged. "No need to worry. We've company. A party on horseback are traveling to Natchez. They'll stay at our camp until tomorrow."

Fannette was aware of faint voices below, and Jared's smile took on meaning.

"You are my bride, you know."

She looked away, back to the pair by the river bank, but they had disappeared into the trees.

VI

The moonless night was growing more chilly, but neither Pearl nor George Washington minded. The main thing was that they were together, away from the camp. They had found a place near the river, but hidden by brush and trees. They could look out through the foliage when the bank came alive with the light of a steamboat moving upstream, water thrashing in its wake.

They sat very close on the bedroll George Washington had remembered to bring.

" 'Cept for that boat, we alone," Pearl said. George Washington put his arms around her and they kissed again.

"Man, he wasn't meant to be kept from his woman," he said with feeling.

"Can't expect they goin' put up a tent for each couple," Pearl observed with her usual practical assessment.

George Washington's arms tightened and they swayed backwards. His hands had started to move over her, and Pearl unbuttoned her blouse so he could nuzzle into the hollow between her full, taut breasts.

"Glad I got me a woman with plenty up there," George Washington murmured as he usually did at such times.

She felt his increasing ardor, and it matched her own.

"You suppose someone might come by?" she asked.

"Don't care if the whole Revulushonary Army cum by," he replied. "Ain' nothin' gonna stop me now, girl."

And not me, either, Pearl thought as she reached for him in the dark. She was ready. Had been ready since first they'd looked into each other's eyes back at camp, and by mutual consent had moved away, to where they could be alone.

She held to him, her strong hips moving in rhythm with his. Holding tightly to each other. Giving, receiving and clinging, until breath and reality returned.

"That was good," he finally said, lips against her ear. "But it always good with you."

But it hadn't been, once . . .

That terrible time which she tried to forget, but which lived with her still, even now, as she lay content in her man's arms. Even now when she knew they were heading for Canada and freedom. Where a white man couldn't swear away their liberty, where a black driver couldn't—

"See here, you stop that 'membering," George Washington told her harshly. "Ain' no way to treat yore man after he been good to you."

She laughed at his joke, trying to sound as if he really could drive away those memories. "Who's been good to who?" she demanded. "Seems to me you got what you wants."

"Neber gets all of you I wants," he demurred. "Ain' that much in the whole worl'." And he bent over her again, to show her what he meant.

But still the memories persisted as they lay still and exhausted. She knew that he was back there, too. Always their minds marched together. Maybe it was because they'd known each other since either of them could remember.

They'd grown up living next door to each other in a little town in Virginia. Had played together on the hillsides, and attended the Baptist Church where old Preacher Watkins warned them against old brother devil, twice on Sundays and continuously on Wednesdays at the evening prayer meetings.

Once when they were sixteen and walking hand in hand, the old preacher had stopped them on the street, his kind black eyes concerned as they probed into their young faces.

"You ain' sinnin', are you uns?" he asked.

They had been considering it, but hadn't yet. So they both became very righteous.

"You start thinkin' 'bout it, you sees me. I marry you right. No jumpin over that broomstick like some I hears 'bout."

They thought about that later. The old preacher was respected by the white folks as well as the black. It had been a long time since the rule had been heeded about a white man having to be there when he gave his sermons, even though this law was strictly enforced. But there was no one who needed to fear Preacher Watkins. He was on the side of peace. Talk of black insurrection and the fact they were led by preachers more times than not was enough to make his kinky white hair stand up straight.

"Mebbe we better do what he say," George Washington said to Pearl as they watched the preacher go on his way. And Pearl, thinking of how she'd felt just a while ago when George Washington kissed her behind the trees, nodded her head.

She glanced down at him and blushed. It was plain to see why the preacher had stopped them. George Washington wasn't settled back again.

He saw where her eyes had gone. "Mebbe it's de ole debil in der," he said, mimicking the preacher. "He ain' gonna lay down, seems lak."

So they told their parents, and that Sunday Preacher Watkins said the words.

"Ain' you feelin' good cus you wait?" he asked them afterwards. They both avoided his eyes, because they hadn't. They'd gone right back to those trees and did what made de ole debil lay down again. Still, it was close enough so they felt virtuous.

George Washington and Pearl Deboney were special, and they both knew it. Hardly any of their friends and neighbors could boast they'd been free folks back as far as two generations. George Washington's great-great-grandfather had fought in the Revolution, and after the war all

158

the black men who'd fought for their country were made free.

"Who paid the owners?" she'd asked George Washington once, but he only shook his head.

"Don' know," he admitted, "but every man he fight, he git free."

So, after that, every first boy born in the family was called George Washington.

With the Deboney family it was different. Pearl heard the story often. How her grandpa saved his young master when robbers came at them with guns and tomahawks on the old Natchez Trace Trail, the road Mr. Jared said that they would soon be following.

Only in those days it had been different. Rivermen rode their cargo-laden flatboats down the Ohio and Mississippi to New Orleans. Broke up their crafts for lumber, sold it, and started the long trip back by foot or horseback. A riotous, brawling procession of them retracing their way to the north where they'd again take on cargo on newly built rafts. Wealthy men traveled the road as well, and so did express riders with the mail. And bandits preyed on all alike.

Young Mr. Deboney wanted adventure at seventeen, and his pa, the old master, let him ride down to New Orleans with a keelboatman. But it was only with the provision his body servant, Delfus, go with him. Young Deboney and Delfus were of the same age, but from all Pearl had heard, Delfus was a giant of a boy. Big and strong like her own George Washington. Like herself, for that matter. It ran in the family to be near six feet tall if you were a woman, and more if you were a man.

Coming back, over the Trace Road, young Deboney and Delfus, who was later to become her grandfather, were attacked by the most fearsome of the outlaws. How Delfus did what he did was a story that varied. But it ended with the two highwaymen being tied to a tree, half dead, Delfus guarding while young Deboney went

159

for the law.

So when old Master Deboney got the story, he made Delfus a free man and allowed him to take the name of Deboney.

Delfus Deboney soon found a job in a stable. He worked hard, but it was near three years before he had enough money to buy his girl, Molly, free. And then only because young Deboney was the new master and had made a special price.

Yes, she and George Washington were different, and they sure enough had reason to hold up their heads.

When first they were married they lived for awhile with George Washington's folks. Then he got apprenticed to a blacksmith. His wages weren't much to boast of, but he was young and he was strong. Even more important, he learned fast. When the old smith died and the shop was put up for sale, George Washington could outsmith anyone around.

"We go to a free state," he announced to her. "Virginny don' like free niggers anymore'n we like to see black men slavin' for white. How we hold up our heads when we see that?"

Anything he said was right with her. They took their savings, cried something furious over leaving folks and friends, and started out.

They decided on Indiana. Maybe because by the time they reached there, they were tired of walking and winter was coming fast.

It didn't take much time for George Washington to find himself an old smith who needed young help. He gave them a warm place to sleep in a sectioned-off part of the barn, and Pearl never minded the smell of horse manure too much, even though the forge fires made it mighty hot in the summer. Her man was doing well, and that was what mattered. She did miss Virginia and her folks, though.

Pretty soon George Washington was doing all the work;

160

the old smith was puny and ailing. So Pearl, proud of her strong, beautiful body, took over working side by side with her man. Sometimes the old smith would talk about fixing them up with the shop when Jesus took him, but they didn't get up too much hope. White people made lots of talk with promises that never came true. But it was something to talk about at night after they'd slushed each other with cool water at the pump and walked in the cool evening to enjoy all those stars up there in heaven.

Then, just when it looked as if life would keep going on the same way, day after day, they got the word. It was a traveling preacher that brought it to them, just like it was a traveling preacher who had taken word back home of where they'd come to live.

"Yore pa's 'bout ready to go to Glory," the preacher told George Washington. "He gittin' more puny each day. Preacher Watkins knowed I was comin' this way, and he say I tell you iff'en you wants to see yore pa, you best come home quick 'fore Jesus takes him."

They packed what they'd need. The old man closed down the forge, but said he'd open it when they got back. He even gave them an old mule that had been left by some movers. It wasn't much, but it could carry their bedrolls and provisions. Even though Pearl was hoping by then that she might have started another George Washington, she didn't dare ride the poor, swaybacked creature.

The best days they ever had were those days on the road. No worries. A blacksmith shop waiting for them to return, spring warming the air and greening the grass. If it wasn't for George Washington's misery for his pa, it might have been as if they were just married.

Hunting was good. Rabbits seemed to wait for their snares, and possum were everywhere. Pearl got real good with a sling shot.

Then one night when they were sitting over their cookfire a little back from the road those white men rode up . . .

"As I live and breathe, Luke, we got us a pair of runaways!" the dirtier of the two said. He scratched at his whiskers.

"Sure have!" His partner agreed. "Bet someone's askin' a fair heap of money for them. Strapping buck and wench if ever I see any."

George Washington stood and took off his cap, standing with his head a little sideways, the way folks had to do when talking to a white man.

"Massa," he said in his quiet voice, "we ain't runnin' away. We free. I been free since my great-great-gran'daddy fight the Revolushon."

They howled with laughter, jabbing at each other.

"You all heah that?" the one with whiskers shouted. "What you say, girl? You gran'mammy fight the revolution too?"

"My gran'mammy get bought free," Pearl replied with dignity.

"An' who gonna believe the two of you?" the one called Luke jeered as he pulled out a gun and pointed it at them.

"I got my papers," George Washington said, pulling them from his pocket. He handed them to Whiskers, who gave them to his partner.

"This what I think of papers," the man said, and threw them into the fire.

George Washington started to jump for them, but Whiskers turned his gun on Pearl's head.

"You move, we shoots her," Luke said. "She'd fetch a good price, but you're prime, man. We shoot her first."

It was all a sick dream. Shackles on their ankles, and her man's wrists chained together. One night the man called Luke tried to pull up her skirts and do it to her, but she ripped his face to bleeding shreds while Whiskers laughed.

"Christ! She's got a strong man's muscle in those arms," her would-be assailant whimpered.

162

"Ain't you a man? You got it up, you gonna be put off?" Whiskers howled, doubling over with laughing. Pearl decided he was one of those who got theirs out of watching.

The little man, Luke, put his foot behind her legs and tipped her back before she knew what was up. He freed her ankles so he could get where he wanted to get, and she lay very still as he bent over her.

Then she shot her knees up. He folded into a weeping, cursing heap.

He didn't try for anything after that. She wondered, as he limped around the fire next morning, if he'd ever be able to try again.

She and George Washington looked at each other, and they were able to grin.

They were luckier than most. The slave dealer sold them as a pair and they were sent down river to the deep South. But together, that was the important thing. Pearl figured she might even endure hell fire if George Washington was with her.

It wasn't a bad plantation where they found themselves. They had a cabin, but the food was all cooked in the kitchen house and it was plain. The owner wasn't a big landowner, just sort of middle, but with enough pickers to need an overseer and a black driver. He was taking on new lands and working toward being big someday.

At first it was hard, out in the sun, and her hands got sore from picking. Both she and George Washington ended each day bent double. Then they got the swing of it.

It would have been easier if she hadn't been certain by now that another George Washington—or maybe a sister—was growing in her belly.

Her man swore like never before. He who had been asking her each month, back in Indiana, if she thought there might be someone on the way.

"He ain' gonna be born a slave!" he shouted. And from that day they started to hoard food that could be carried.

163

Dried meats, strips of smoked pork. Anything they could save or steal when the cook wasn't looking. They hid everything in a corner under some old junk that had been in the cabin when they first came.

Then one day, Big Ervin, the black driver, sent George Washington to the gatehouse with a message for the overseer. It was during the noon rest time, and the gatehouse was at the far end of the land, so it meant George Washington would be gone a good spell. Pearl felt a shaking inside, like her innards knew something terrible was going to happen. She'd seen it in Big Ervin's eyes every time he looked at her lately.

"Follow me, girl," he said after George Washington was out of earshot. "I got sumpin' special for you."

She followed him because there was no choice. She had already felt the slash of his whip those first few days before she'd learned to pick right. George Washington's back looked as if a snake had tracked back and forth on it with a razor on its belly.

He took her to the far field where there was a clump of concealing trees by a little stream.

"Now take off dem clothes," he said.

She shook her head. But it wasn't any use. He was on her like a bull, and no amount of fighting could stop him. He raked at her, tore into her, panting and shouting. She felt as if she'd been ripped open, but he laughed when he saw what he'd done, and went at her again.

When he finally stopped, she could hardly move for the pain. She lay with her head twisted to the side, moaning even though she tried not to.

"You stay here today," he told her, looking down at her sprawled body. "But come mornin' you gets the whip if you ain't in the field."

She never knew how George Washington guessed where they'd be. It was certain that when he got back and found them missing, he'd figured why he had been sent away.

She was too dazed to see him when he came up behind

164

Big Ervin and caught him around the throat with his strong right arm. Big Ervin struggled to free himself, that was for sure, but years at the forge were in George Washington's favor.

Somehow she pulled herself to her feet. By then the driver lay still, his face a bluish-black, and his thick tongue hanging out. She caught the big whip up in her hand and slashed and slashed and slashed. . . .

"You stop now, girl," George Washington said, catching her arm. "Important thing is to git away."

They crept through the line of trees to their cabin. The field hands were still resting, waiting for the noon sun to lessen and their driver to return. Pearl gathered together what was at hand, while George Washington packed everything into two bundles. They made it back to where the trees edged the land. Then they ran until they came to where the swamps started. They splashed through the green top scum of the water, felt mud ooze and pull at their feet, and rested against cypress trees. They fought their way through tree limbs heavy with moss, and rested again when they found firm ground. They ran. Always they ran.

For two days they broke their way through the wild greenery. Then it was too much for Pearl. Pains gripped her, and she fell on a knoll as she felt her baby slip from her in blinding, tearing flashes.

She was sick for a long time. Later, George Washington told her he'd almost given up hope. Then some men found them.

One of them was as black as either George Washington or Pearl, the other a light brown. They had mules laden with supplies, and a quick glance was all they needed.

"Glory will take care of her," one of them told George Washington.

George Washington's eyes widened. "She ain't agoin' to Glory if us can help it!" he exclaimed.

The two men laughed, and later Pearl found out why

165

when withered, bent Glory fed her brews and broth and dragged her back from the arms of Jesus to her own George Washington.

Then had come the bad time. The time when she couldn't abide the touch of a man. Not even her own gentle, loving George Washington.

"Honey," he pleaded, "I ain't gonna hurt you. You knows I love you."

"An' I loves you, too," she told him over and over. But still, the minute his hands touched her skin, she stiffened with remembered terror.

"Go to another woman," she finally begged him. "I ain't no good for no man."

"You the only woman," he insisted.

It took nearly two months before she could even lie beside him at night, and she knew that even her George Washington was beginning to lose patience.

Then, just when she'd about given herself up, the miracle happened.

They had been lying in bed close, but not in a way that brought back bad memories of violation. Drowsily they talked, and her mind went back to that first time, when after the encounter with Preacher Watkins, they'd gone back to the hidden spot in the trees.

As usual, George Washington's thoughts marched alongside her own.

"You near fainted when you saw what I had," he chuckled.

"What you talkin' 'bout?" she demanded. "You didn't even know what to do with it."

"Oh, I knew that, all right. I just wasn't rightly certain of 'zakly where."

"I wasn't sure myself," she admitted. And they both rocked with laughter at the memory of that wonderful, fumbling experience.

"You tell me," he asked when finally they were quiet again, "did or didn't I disflower you?"

166

"Deflower," she corrected. "Least, that what Preacher Watkins call it when he reads it."

"You figure a word like that oughta be in the Holy Book?" he asked.

Pearl thought a minute. "Well, I reckon as it has to. If it wasn't for the deflowering there couldn't no way be all that begattin' and begettin'."

She smiled at the memory of that long-ago afternoon when the old debil went back where he ought to be. But neither of them was exactly certain that their sinning had been consummated.

"I was half deflowered, anyway," she decided.

But two days later when the preacher married them, she found her George Washington had worked hard at gathering information. It was a certain fact he knew what he was about on their wedding night. Just thinking of it started her woman juices flowing again, and the warming ache made her body quiver. She put her arms around her man and pulled him up against her.

"I know where it goes now," she whispered.

"Pearl, honey?"

And it was all right after that. It was all right! He was afraid at first, expecting her to stiffen up, but instead he found her eager and joyful. She held to him with tears flowing down her cheeks, as she thanked her Lord that he'd given her back her womanhood. He was crying too, and they knew the two of them had come through a bad time for good.

"Mebbe we have a new George Washington, after all," he said.

"Or a sister to him." It didn't really matter as long as they had one or the other.

Only now it had been two years since that time. Each month her hopes died and crawled into a deeper grave. Maybe now there'd never be another quickening, she thought, looking up at the clouds that were again gathering in the sky.

Another riverboat churned past. She could smell the smoke from the great stacks. What was wrong with her, questioning what had been given? It was a time to be joyful. Weren't they on their way to Canada? The Lord had granted her so much that was good, she couldn't rightly complain.

Beside her, George Washington stirred.

"Getting mighty cold out here, girl," he said. "Best we git ourselfs back to the tents 'fore the rain start in."

VII

Fannette had no idea when he came into the tent. She only knew that she awakened in the night to hear him breathing in his sleep, somewhere in the darkness.

She thought about him and about Anton. How different they both were from what they'd seemed in New Orleans. Suppose she'd left on the ship with Anton. Would she have found happiness of a sort? They'd be far out at sea now, and the thought of journeying to France excited her.

Then her mind went back to the dance in the barn that night. She smiled in the dark, remembering the hooting, clapping approval of their people.

Their people. These happy, carefree men and women. These hunted fugitives. That man and woman whispering in their shadowy shelter near the river.

And Jared looking down at her in the light of evening . . .

What did he really feel toward her? How much was a mockery of her own arrogance? How much was actual? Or was he one of those men who felt more manly for taking a woman down a peg or two?

And what were her feelings toward him? She drew her thoughts to a halt. That was territory better left unexplored. But decidedly she was thankful that she hadn't run off with Anton. And, yes, thankful that their wedding plans had been thwarted.

And their people. What did they think? Their people. Yes. That was the way she thought of them now. Their people.

She awakened in the morning to find the blankets across the tent neatly rolled and a steaming jug of water

169

on the stand. Rain was drumming down on the canvas.

She paused to look at the bedroll as she dressed. Suppose he hadn't kept his promise? Suppose he had come to her in the night. She remembered the carriage and his kiss on the dance floor. She remembered aching in parts of herself. Parts a decent girl never thought about.

The bloom on the fruit. Fruit ripe for the picking. Why had he ever used that term?

VIII

Both Anton and Jared decided to let their beards grow.

"It's damn uncomfortable to try for a clean shave on a cold morning," Jared had grunted apologetically when Poppy raised her eyebrows at the beginning of a blond fuzz on his chin.

"It is becoming *de rigueur,*" Anton explained, but Fannette wondered if Jared's excuse hadn't been the more honest.

Now, one day's journey from Baton Rouge, she found herself comparing the two. It gave Jared somewhat the appearance of a young Norse god, but Anton was affecting a pointed, carefully trimmed beard. She found it difficult to decide whether it would result in his hoped for air of sophistication, or merely give him the look of a scholar—which he certainly was not.

After two days of steady rain, there were indications that clear weather might be returning. They stayed over in camp so that long lines of wash might be hung out to dry.

"If more bad weather moves in," Jared said, "we'll have to stay at a plantation again and rent the barn." His eyes were worried as they studied a new formation of dark clouds. "The things will dry fast enough by a fire, but . . ."

Questions. Always that fear of questions. Too many had been asked by the Lemmons. And there would be more at any place where they might stay.

Anton left the camp in the morning. He had friends in Baton Rouge, he announced. Hopefully, he might be able to find a place that sold suitable men's clothing.

It was the afternoon of that same day when Trojan made the announcement that was the change the fate of the caravan—and of the people who journeyed with it.

"Der's someone followin' us," he told Jared.

Jared glanced back on the road, as if expecting to see the person.

"You figure?"

Trojan nodded. "He a runaway, else he come up an' walk with us."

Jared shrugged.

"Most movers sooner or later pick up a fugitive. You think we've reason to worry?"

Trojan looked down at his feet, his eyes gloomy.

"A runaway bring the law or a slave catcher mighty fast. Mebbe they say we help him."

"Why should they?"

"Becuz he followin' since the Lemmon place. Emily, she say victuals be missin', and at night sumbody be goin' through the garbage hole we digs."

Jared whistled softly. "Can't be very pleasant to follow us in this rain. Whoever it is must be desperate."

"Dat's what I thinkin'."

Jared drew a deep breath and turned back to the road they'd just traveled.

"I guess we both know what has to be done."

"I got to go catch him 'fore we in trouble."

Fannette paused on her way past them. "Trouble?" she repeated as Trojan left.

"Trouble," Jared agreed. "Just what we don't need, a slave catcher nosing around. There's hardly a person here who could bear a close scrutiny."

Fannette looked out at the people. The women were bent over wash tubs while their men cheerfully hung the wet garments on the lines.

"You keep saying that, and I keep finding it hard to believe. Certainly not Wednesday over there. Sunday evening I listened to him preach about brotherhood and love."

"He does a fine job of that." Jared smiled faintly as he watched the man scrub down a pot. "And that's only one of the reasons he's wanted in three states. For preaching without a white man present. And for his little sideline."

"Sideline?"

"He's incited at least two insurrections. Maybe more."

"Oh." Impossible to picture the meek little man urging his people to set out with a pitch fork or ax.

One of their joyous people . . .

The next afternoon Anton returned at about the same time as the rain started to fall. He had a new portmanteau secured to his saddle, and he was wearing a Prince Albert cape. The velvet collar lent an air of elegance, but Fannette stifled a giggle when she saw he sported a Wide Awake, the wide-brimmed, flat-crowned felt hat that Prince Albert had made popular for country wear. It didn't appear it was going to take very kindly to the damp weather. Already it had begun to sag.

The full impact of Anton's new raiment was marred by Trojan's appearance with a rain-sodden figure trailing him.

"The poor thing!" Fannette exclaimed as she realized the fugitive was a woman clutching a bundle to her breast.

Her hair was streaming water, and the thin clothes she wore clung to her body. She was barely recognizable as the pert brown maid at the Lemmon plantation.

"Tansy!" Fannette said, and Jared turned to look at her.

"She belongs to the Lemmons," Fannette explained.

The baby set up a series of short, gasping cries.

"He's hungry," the woman said with surprising dignity.

Emily paused in her cooking and glanced at them. She picked up some empty sacks and took them to the woman, but Jared waved her back.

"Being wet a few more minutes can't hurt her now," he said coldly. "I need to ask a few questions before you take her to the women's tent."

Thumbs hooked in his belt, he studied Tansy.

"Why the hell did you decide to follow us in this foul

173

weather? The baby sounds sick and you don't look much better."

"The sun shining when we leaves," she replied sullenly.

"It damn well hasn't the last few days."

Had he no feeling for the poor thing? Impossible to stand by and watch the woman shiver while he asked unimportant questions!

"Jared, you've got to stop abusing her long enough for her to get into something dry!" Fannette interrupted.

He turned on her angrily, but then, unexpectedly, he shrugged and called Emily back.

"Take her to the women's tent and see if you can find something dry. Those sacks should do for the baby."

He watched them leave, still scowling. "I'll have to ride into town with her and turn her over to the authorities."

His voice had carried to Tansy. She gave a scream of rage and ran back to him.

"You can't do that, Mr. McLaury! I goin' to find my man in Canada. I hear talk your folks go to Canada. I wants to go with you."

Jared's eyes narrowed and he caught her by the arm.

"Where'd you hear talk of Canada?" he demanded.

Something sly crept into her face. Something knowing.

"I stay close in the wood at night, and I hear them talk."

"Christ almighty! You know how niggers gossip. There's none of these people who maybe don't think wishful about Canada, but we're only going as far as the Ohio River. I've land in Kentucky. You'd have a long, cold trip from here and you'd be caught sure."

"My man, Bates, he go to Canada."

"You think you can find one black man in Canada? It's a big place. For God's sake, woman, you're damned lucky to have owners like the Lemmons. I'm going to see you get back to them."

Tansy appealed to Fannette, her eyes pleading. She held out the baby.

"We got to find my man, Bates," she said. "I saw at the

174

house that you a kind lady. I know then you help us."

How could anyone turn away from such trust? Could anyone fault the poor creature for wanting to be with her husband?

"Please," Fannette said to Jared. "What difference could one more make?"

"You damn well know the difference it could make." There was no compassion in his voice. No relenting.

Fannette's eyes locked with his, her chin up. She made a little contemptuous sound.

"Didn't my emerald bring enough money to pay her way as well as mine?" she demanded.

For a moment she thought he'd strike her. His eyes were a blue blaze and his lips were white with fury. Then, abruptly, he turned his back on her and beckoned to Trojan.

"We'll stay in this camp till you find some free colored people who'll take her in," he said. "I'll leave word at a station ahead. Hopefully, they'll have her on the way before she's caught up with."

"You think that smart, Mr. Jared?" Trojan asked doubtfully.

"We both damn well know it isn't."

"Station?" Fannette asked as Trojan led the woman away.

"Station," he repeated. "There are folks along the way who help refugees. We call their places stations."

"Then why haven't we gotten help from them? Maybe a place to spend the night when the weather's bad?"

"Because I planned so we wouldn't be in need of them, not until the Quakers take over in Ohio. These folks are taking a big risk as it is, and it wouldn't be easy to make a party of twenty-eight fugitives disappear."

"Disappear?"

"That's why they call their organization an underground railroad. But if it comes to where we have to ask their help, I know how to contact them along the way."

She still couldn't feel easy in her mind about Tansy. True, he'd changed his plan to send her back to the Lemmons. Still . . .

"If free people take Tansy in, wouldn't they have to turn her out at the first sign of trouble?"

His eyes were cold and his voice devoid of emotion.

"I'm afraid, madame, that's the risk she took when she ran away."

"But the baby?"

"Trojan's gone for Glory. She'll have something to help it—if it can be helped." He spread his hands in a gesture of futility. "How could that woman be so stupid?"

"She loves her husband," Fannette replied. "She doesn't want to lose him."

She watched as Glory hobbled up to the women's tent, her kerchief-wrapped bundle clutched as tightly as Tansy had clutched her baby.

Glory.

The least of their people. But one of the most important.

IX

Glory gave the baby back to its mother, but her thoughts were on Miz McLaury and the stormy, black looks she was giving her man. She nodded to herself. While the storm was there, they were safe. It was the other one, the soft one, that was to be feared.

It was many years since Glory had dwelt on the confusions and contradictions that were part of being young and having a man on one's mind. Much of her own youth had been bound and burned up in the fires that had gradually brought her body to the dryness of old ashes and old age.

But there were parts that she'd never forget. Such as the day when the slavers came to her village and chained men, women and children into long kaffles.

But there were good things too. There was the old grandmother who'd taught her about herbs and berries, the ones that, used properly, might restore health, and the others that were certain to do away with an enemy. These were important things, and not to be forgotten.

There was also that bad time in the stinking black hold of a slave ship. Her mind refused to retain any but brief, fleeting pictures of that. A mind was a good thing. It knew when to hold memories. And when to erase them.

And then there were those bright days when she'd been a young girl with men following after her. Sooner or later they'd find out about her powers and her knowledge, then they shied away and turned to some simple, frivolous-minded female . . .

All except Penry. He hadn't cared about what she knew and what she could do. He only cared that when he talked to her, she listened and understood. Penry was a thinking man. Maybe if that hadn't been so, he'd be alive today.

It wasn't permitted for them to marry like the white folks. The old master was set against black people doing anything that might give them the suspicion that they were above the barnyard animals.

But she and Penry got married in their own minds, and they had a fine, strong daughter. They might have had sons as well, if Penry hadn't gotten himself mixed up with a rebellion on the next holding. They took him away, and they both knew he would never return.

She'd tried. So often she'd tried to explain to him that if it was freedom he wanted, they need only run away and live in the woods. With all she knew about plants and trapping, they could have had a good life.

But no, not Penry. He just kept listening to the men who came to the quarters at night and told folks how there were enough black people in the South to run out the white man. No use arguing that just more white men would come, that only here in the South did the black men outnumber the white.

No. He was smart enough. Smart in the wrong way.

If her daughter hadn't given birth to Bethany, she might have gone into the woods by herself after they took Penry. Her daughter had a fine, strapping man. Good-natured and strong, but not a thinker. And that wasn't bad. Most women were better off without a thinking man, life being what it was. A man who would bend to an overseer's orders, who didn't question the black driver. A man who never thought different of a master who kept them working even on Saturday and Sunday and didn't give them something extra for it. No, it was better to have a man who didn't think.

Little Bethany. Now that was a different story. At ten years of age, little Bethany was still puny and had a mind that darted about like a butterfly that couldn't find a flower. Sometimes she finished what she started, but more often, she just drifted into something else. Her mind simply wasn't able to hold a thought. Not even a simple one.

At fifteen she was no better.

Glory loved her pretty, vacant granddaughter as she'd never loved anyone else. It was only her special brews and her constant watching that kept the girl alive, for Bethany's kind didn't often live past puberty. Nature had left off too soon on her body, as well as her mind.

But Bethany was a loving child, with laughter sparkling in her eyes, taking joy in everything that came her way. At fifteen, the children followed her, begging her to play with them. Even the overseer agreed that she'd never last out in the sun picking cotton or digging out weeds, and so Glory showed him how useful Bethany could be if they put her to watching the little ones during the day.

Except—and Glory worked hard to keep anyone from learning this—there were times when Bethany would just wander away, leaving the children to their own devices. The good thing was that it never happened except when it was near time for the workers to come back from the fields. And Glory always made sure she was the first to go to the fenced place where the children played.

At such times, after their mothers had fetched their children, Glory would leave the quarters and go back into the trees that stood nearby. Go to the stream and the hidden place where she knew she'd find her granddaughter.

The girl would be sitting on a rise, her wide eyes watching the water bounce and splash over the rocks. Never a motion. Never a twitch. Even her mind was still. Glory had a power that she learned way back in that other land, taught to her by the old grandmother of the village. She could reach out and feel the waves of a mind. But there were no waves around Bethany. Only quiet. Deathly quiet, as if what should be a mind was wrapped tight against the outside.

Glory knew the shock that would come if she disrupted Bethany at these times. That the wavering hold on life could be snapped that easily. So she would just squat nearby and wait till the girl's spirit decided to come back. When it did, Bethany would sigh, as if resigned to the renewal of life. And stretch.

Then she would see her grandmother and run to her, throwing her arms around her, making happy sounds.

Yes, mindless though Bethany might be, Glory had never felt such a love for her own self-reliant daughter as she did for her granddaughter. And Glory's daughter only felt shame for having mothered this strange child. She neglected Bethany for the noisy, healthy children which had soon followed.

Yes, Bethany belonged to Glory as no one else had ever belonged.

Then came the day when Glory had been called back to the field by the driver. His woman ailed and he wanted her to take a brew to his cabin.

When she got to the place where the children should be, her worst fears met with reality. The overseer had stopped by the quarters to inspect a faulty chimney, and he'd found the children running around outside the place of confinement. Bethany was nowhere in sight.

There was no denying where Bethany had gone. She was dragged back, still stunned. She stared at the red-faced, shouting man with no understanding.

"I'll have you whipped to your senses, you lazy slut!" he roared.

Glory caught her granddaughter and pushed her into the background.

"Leave her be!" she exclaimed. "She ain't got right senses, but she don't never leave till we here."

"She was gone tonight and we wasn't here!" he shouted and snatched the girl back.

"Take her to the shed," he called to one of the men. "Tie her wrists to the posts and get the whip ready."

Glory felt the cold nausea of fear in her middle. The overseer was free with his whip. She saw in his mind the glee and perversion of natural desires that could only be satisfied by the feel of the whip handle as it lashed across a bare back. She knew, too, that Bethany would never last through the ordeal.

Like a madwoman, she went after the overseer. But he only laughed and called for the driver to hold her.

Arms clamped behind her back, she was forced to watch while they stripped the thin frock off Bethany's back, bearing her budding breasts and frail body.

Glory screamed when the whip cracked across the girl's shoulders, but Bethany made no sound. Her head fell forward, and Glory was reminded of the figure she'd once seen hanging from a cross.

Like the one that Miz McLaury wore.

Another crack, and still no sound. This time there was no sound from Glory, either. The girl's heart, never strong, had refused to hold out against this outrage. Glory knew the girl had gone back to whatever strange place it was that had sent her unprepared into a world where only the strong survived.

She had no word for anyone when they brought her the girl's body to lay out, only a look of contempt for her own daughter, who moaned and wailed over the child she'd never cared to love.

That night she stopped by the new grave at the edge of the land, and she told Bethany what she intended to do. Then she went into the woods, glad that the full moon made it almost as light as day. She found what she sought, and well after midnight she carried it in triumph to the cabin that now belonged to her alone.

Throughout the remainder of the night, she pounded and brewed. By dawn, she had what was necessary.

She worked silently in the field through the morning hours. She spoke not a word with anyone. Only her eyes were alert. At noon, her chance came. The overseer's meal was always sent down from the cook house, and she maneuvered to be the one to take it from the kitchen helper's hand and carry it to a stump under the shade of a tree. The

181

overseer always made certain he didn't have to take his noon meal out under the sun like the rest of them.

She had planned a slow working poison, and so the overseer was still hale and hearty when the time to quit came. But she knew it would start its work right after the evening meal.

Slow work.

He wouldn't die easily. But he would die. Bethany, out in her burying place, could rest easily now.

She gathered together what she had needed before leaving her cabin, her hoards of dried herbs, berries and leaves. Her cache of dried beans and strips of jerked meats.

And there was so much the land itself would provide. She went over her litany.

The husks of black walnuts dropped into a stream would stun the fish so that they were easy to catch.

If she were taken with a fever or the shakes, she had the bitter mixture from the boiled bark of a dogwood.

In the spring she could creep into the quarters and beg flour. The redbud flowers and young pods made better fritters than they had in the big house. Or she could make her own flour when the acorns fell. She'd boil them and leach out the bitterness with ashes, then grind them.

She needn't be without coffee. Ground persimmon seeds were just fine brewed in hot water. And when persimmon time came, she could dry the fruit and pound them into loaves.

The meat of the hickory nut could be used as butter or made into flour. The sap was as good as syrup or sugar.

It went on, endlessly. And there were the wild turkeys, so stupid one almost didn't need a snare. Rabbits, possums, coons—

She found a deep cave near a fresh running brook. A hiding place in the summer and a warm den in the winter. She regretted that she'd waited so long for her freedom. But then, Bethany had needed her. Bethany could never

182

have survived the changing seasons away from a warm cabin fire.

Sometimes, at night, she crept into the quarters carrying freshly caught game in exchange for material to make a dress or a warm blanket. She gathered news of her daughter and grandchildren. Learned they'd followed a black woman to a place called Canada.

As the years passed, she found she needed less from the quarters. Everything was at hand in the woods that surrounded her. No longer was there even news of those she'd known. Most of them lay near Bethany in the burying place. One day she saw her own reflection in a still pond.

Old. Bent. Withered. She tried to count the years, but there were too many.

She knew that she did love that strong daughter of hers. Not as she'd loved Bethany, but as kin. Her time to die would come soon, if years were the way one reckoned such things. And she wanted to be with kin when that time came. Where she'd be put down in a burial hole, not lie beside the path in a lone place where animals could tear at her dry old flesh.

She knew of the Settlement. Had even, upon occasion, stolen blankets or garments from the washlines. From the edge of the swamp she had often watched the folks who lived there, knowing that someday she'd go to them.

And now the time had come. In the past it had taken her only two days to reach the place, but now it was nearer to four.

They welcomed her, as she'd known they would. But when she told them she wanted to go to the place known as Canada, they shook their heads.

She was too old. It was a long way, that path to the North Star. Too long and too hard a path for an old, bent woman.

But she showed them that she could heal, that they needed her. It wasn't with words that she showed them. Only on a few, very necessary occasions had Glory used

183

words since when her cries had failed to save Bethany. Words had failed to save the one she loved, so now she despised them. Besides, living alone had strengthened her ability to reach a mind. Thinking hard sometimes even carried to an animal's brain. Thinking out in pictures, the way the village grandmother had taught her . . .

So they finally agreed to take her. And so, here she was. Riding in a wagon by day, brewing what was needed when others sickened.

And finding herself fearful of the conflict she saw inside Miz McLaury. Knowing that she could help, but that first she must be asked.

And, before that, the need must be realized.

X

The rain that had been spasmodic all morning suddenly lashed down on tent and wagon alike, but Fannette stood out in the open watching as Trojan loaded Tansy and her baby into a wagon. Oblivious to the discomfort, she remained outside her tent until they disappeared down the road.

Trojan returned in the evening. Alone.

Fannette still felt a sense of disquiet when they started back on the road early the next morning. As if a part of herself were protesting. Telling her she should have fought harder for Tansy. Insisted. And the weather was no help to her mood. There was a ceaseless downpour, and the horses' hoofs spumed up muck and water.

"We'll camp this side of Baton Rouge tonight," Poppy told Fannette. "Just out of the town, in fact. But tomorrow we'll be under a real roof again. Jared said we'd stay at a station until we dry out."

"Did he say what the folks would be like?" Fannette asked. She didn't feel up to laughing or even to enjoying food served at a table. Not when she thought of Tansy and her baby hiding in a shack somewhere—or maybe already in the hands of some slave catchers.

"There won't be any people. The place is deserted. The kind of cabin folks leave when they take out for the West. But it's solid and there's a good barn, so everyone'll be under cover."

"Except, perhaps, Tansy."

"Forget that woman, Fannette. Jared did right."

"It might have been different if she'd had the two hundred dollars."

"Fannette!"

Up ahead, Fannette could see him riding his big horse. He wore a sealskin slicker and a wide-brimmed hat of the same material. He gave more the appearance of an Atlantic fisherman than a lawyer. For some contrary reason, he seemed to be in high spirits as he nudged his bay and galloped on ahead.

"You'd think he was a duck or a fish," Fannette complained to Anton who was humped into the seat beside Jove.

Poor Anton! For all its fashionable appearance, his new Prince Albert cape wasn't nearly as waterproof as purported.

"They must have intended this for a London fog," he muttered, touching the sodden material. "*Parbleu!* It most certainly was never intended for a downpour!"

"Why didn't I think to wear heavy clothes and pack a blanket?" Tansy asked her baby as she trudged through the mud and water.

But it was certain there'd been a limit to what she could carry. The baby had grown so heavy. Not that he was anymore. Each day he was lighter—and more silent.

And the sun shining when I leaves, she remembered. Shining just like summer was due to start.

And that Miz McLaury would hide her. She knew that. If she'd gone to Miz McLaury in secret, she'd never have been caught, and she'd never have been sent to those free black folks who were most scared out of their skin that she'd be found with them.

And what reason did she have to believe Mr. McLaury when he told her some white men would come for her in a wagon? What white men had ever done that for a poor brown woman? Not unless it was to sell her right back to her owners!

No. She knew better then that. Lordy, yes she did!

She watched from a safe distance as they made camp

186

for the night. She waited for them to set up that canvas place for Miz McLaury and her maid. Lordy! What kind of maid was that who could do her things right in the same pot as a white lady?

The big worry was not to be caught by that fancy girl. For all her soft, silklike ways, she was hard underneath. Not soft like Miz McLaury. Tansy knew enough about women to see that.

Finally they'd set the poles firm in the soggy ground and wrapped the canvas around. They even slung canvas over the top to keep out the rain, Tansy was glad to observe. She waited, hidden in the brush, knowing Miz McLaury and her maid would soon come out to use it.

It wasn't long before she saw them heading for it, chattering and laughing, with good, heavy-hooded coats to protect them from the weather. Most likely nothing on their minds but the good food that was cooking. The smell of it twisted Tansy's stomach into new hunger pains.

And the baby. He'd hardly made a sound all day. She'd opened his mouth and fitted it around her nipple, but he wouldn't suckle. He just lay there making heavy noises with each breath.

When the women left, heading back to the campfire, Tansy crept inside the shelter. She tried to count on her fingers how many times she'd hidden out the night under that canvas, grateful for it, but afraid to sleep for fear someone might lift the door flap and look inside.

She tried to clean the baby, but what she needed was rags and warm water. And she didn't dare throw the soiled things down the hole in the stool, because she knew that after the canvas was taken away each morning, the woman, Letty, would come to throw in ashes and slush the wood with a bucket of water. She was sure to notice the things off the baby. And they smelled pretty strong, anyway.

The rain began to ease off, and she peeked out. The folks had finished eating. Some sat by the fire and some

187

went to the tents. The maid, Poppy, was heading toward the opening in the trees, and Tansy drew into the shadows of the brush.

She waited until the maid came out and went back to the tent she shared with Miz McLaury. Lordy, that was another funny thing. What kind of a man never slept with his woman, especially when she was such a pretty thing that most any husband in his right senses would be after regular?

Anyway, she'd hoped the maid might make her night visit separate from her mistress's. This way she was sure to catch Miz McLaury alone.

With the rain gone, the cold started to creep up on her. She wondered if her wet clothing would freeze by morning, and she began to worry that Miz McLaury might wait till it was too late to get any victuals for her. The cook was still serving some of the men who'd been taking care of the horses.

But no, Miz McLaury just stayed there by the fire talking to that Mr. Anton, her brother. Talking and giggling like a young courting girl.

Tansy curled her lip. Brother! A mighty funny brother that could look at his sister that way!

Then, finally, Miz McLaury stood up and took a candle to light her way where the trees darkened the clearing.

Tansy stepped out of the darkness.

"Miz McLaury," she whispered.

Miz McLaury almost dropped the candle, and her other hand went up to that cross she always wore.

"It's me. Tansy. You remember me?"

"But Trojan took you to some folks who were to hide you until—"

"They throw me out," Tansy lied. "They scared." That part was the truth, anyway.

"If Mr. McLaury finds you—"

"Please. Please, Miz McLaury. Please, my baby sick and I wet and hungry. Please help us." By that time Tansy

188

was on her knees in the mud, holding on to Miz McLaury's skirt like she'd planned. And it wasn't hard to make the tears roll down her face. It was easy to cry when you were that miserable.

"But there's no way I can help you."

Tansy was quiet, knowing from the softened tone that she'd won.

"There is the big furniture wagon," Miz McLaury said, half talking to herself. "No one ever goes to it, and it's pulled off to the side. At least you'd be out of the cold . . ."

"We hungry," Tansy said tearfully.

"I can still dish up another plate. Everyone knows I've a disgraceful appetite. But what about tomorrow? You can't let that baby get any more wet, and if you stay in the wagon, the driver will hear it when it cries."

Tansy was ready and hoping for exactly those words. "You bring me par'goric and he sleep all day. I heard talk that's what folks do when they hide with a baby."

"Paregoric?"

"Nobody travel with as many as here without they take par'goric for loose bowels," Tansy said firmly.

"Then it'd be in the medicine chest, and that's in the small furniture wagon." Again Miz McLaury fiddled with the cross that hung on a chain, and Tansy knew she was growing more nervous. Tansy pinched the baby, and it began its pathetic gasping little sobs. She held it out to the white woman.

"I don't get victuals I got nothing to feed him."

"Oh, I can't! I can't!" Miz McLaury cried, and when Tansy saw the tears in her eyes, she knew the words didn't mean anything.

"Now mind," Miz McLaury's voice was softer, different, "you'll leave the wagon when we're passing Baton Rouge tomorrow. Or when we have the noon stop. You'll find someone to help you in a place that large."

"I get out," Tansy promised, having no such intention. Lordy! If she worked it right, she might hide in the furniture wagon for weeks till they got to a big town far away. Much closer to Canada.

She really didn't know how long it took to get to Canada, but that's where Bates had gone. And now, with Miz McLaury getting her the victuals she needed, with no longer having to sneak to the garbage hole in the night—oh, it was going to be good!

And, maybe, given time, the baby might get dry again . . .

Sure enough, it was almost warm inside the big wagon, and there were lots of places to hide. Miz McLaury brought her a heaping plate of food that steamed in the cold and a jug of water. Later she came back with a cup of something that she pushed into the opening at the back.

"The paregoric. I hope you know how much is safe to use."

XI

Fannette moved up to the crackling, popping fire and tried to warm her hands, wondering if they'd ever stop trembling.

Whatever had possessed her? If Jared found out, he'd be furious. And rightly so. No one had the right to jeopardize the safety of the caravan for the sake of one runaway.

Anton looked up from the card game he was playing with Jared.

"Poppy went to bed, but why don't you stay up for awhile and keep us company?"

Fannette shook her head. Still not trusting her own voice. She left them and went to the tent.

Poppy was curled up under her covers, and Fannette put the candle behind the basin so it wouldn't shine too brightly. As she undressed, she could hear the click of Poppy's beads, and she felt a pang of guilt. The last thing she'd ever have thought of bringing was her rosary. When she was small and Father Pierre asked whether she remembered to count her beads daily, it was a matter for embarrassment. Truth to tell, she usually either forgot all about it or fell asleep in the middle of the first ten.

She touched the crucifix at her neck. At least she had that, and she'd try to do better in the future . . .

And what more appropriate time to resort to prayers? She shivered. Would even the warmth of her blankets ease the chill? She wished she could talk about what she'd done. But aside from interrupting Poppy's nightly devotions, it would be extremely foolish to confide in Poppy. No, there wasn't a person in the entire group who could be told. She was alone in her sympathy for the poor woman.

Poor, miserable creature, clutching a sick baby and searching for a lost husband.

She touched her crucifix again.

Why couldn't they understand?

In the morning she took Tansy a breakfast plate and returned with the empty one. She set it aside and picked up clean utensils. Even with her healthy appetite, this might seem a bit hoggish.To compensate she took half of what she'd ordinarily have taken. Then she found she needn't have bothered. All desire for food had left her. She was far too nervous to eat.

Only till they passed Baton Rouge. Then, at least, it would be over. Tonight the empty plate and water jug could be taken from the wagon, and she'd leave them near a log, the way a careless person might have done. They'd be discovered and gathered by the evening's appointed dishwashers.

Such a short distance to help the poor woman.

Anton rode ahead to look for game, and he came back dragging a buck behind his horse. The diversion was timely. During the noon rest no one paid attention to anything other than Emily, as she skinned the deer, covered it with a cloth against flies, and hung it to cure at the front of the cook wagon.

Fannette went to the back of the furniture wagon and called softly. There was no sound.

Oh thank you, Blessed Mother. Thank you, Mary and Joseph! Never, never, never again would she do such a foolish thing. Never!

It was close to evening when they reached the station. A deserted shack set among trees near a brook. A barn with a roof that Chippers easily made watertight. Letty and Jove went into the shack with broom and mop, and Chippers followed with his tool carrier.

Despite everything, Fannette still did not feel easy.

Something was wrong. And why did that old witch, Glory, keep looking at her? Shaking her head, clucking toothlessly, staring with those strange, light eyes shining out of her black face?

Of course, it was nothing more than the knowledge of her own guilt. It made her fanciful.

When dinner was ready, still holding her plate, Fannette moved toward the furniture wagon as if looking for a quiet place to sit. Now would be the best time to take the empty dishes and scatter them around the camp.

She set her food on the tailgate. The wagon didn't feel empty. Blessed Mother! Tansy had promised!

"I'm hungry!" It was a pathetic wail that caught Fannette in its grip. "But I tell my baby you won't forget." Tansy scooped up the food and began to eat greedily.

"Oh God!" Fannette gasped. "When I came by at noon, I could have sworn you weren't here!"

"Got to get out sometimes, just like everybody else," Tansy said complacently in between bites.

"But you were to leave at Baton Rouge."

"That the place Trojan took me. There no where in that place to hide."

Fannette picked up the empty dishes, leaving Tansy to finish her own food. Sick with apprehension, she moved back to where the others sat gossiping over their supper.

"Wonder who that is?" Jared said, coming up beside her. He stared down the road, and she made out two mud-splattered horsemen approaching.

That terrible trapped feeling worsened. It was cold standing in the clearing, but she felt as if she were about to suffocate.

"Looks like company," he added, frowning. The men had turned in the path. They stopped just short of the campfire and tied their horses to a tree. Jared moved toward them.

"I'm Sam Simmons," one of the men said, holding out his hand. "This here's my partner, Tom Harkins. Reckon you're the McLaury party from down Louisiana way?"

"I'm Jared McLaury," Jared acknowledged. He narrowed his eyes as he studied the men.

Sam reached into a pocket and brought out a legal-appearing paper.

"Tom and me are deputized to search out this female kitchen slave, Tansy. She run away from Bart Lemmon 'bout the time you folks stayed there."

Jared glanced carelessly at the document.

"We found a woman trailing us," he admitted. "But my men scared her off. We figured she might be a runaway, and I don't want traffic with that sort. My own stock gives me enough trouble."

"You don't mind if we search a little? Look in the wagons and suchlike?"

Jared shrugged. "Go ahead. There's nothing to find."

He moved away to check on the shack and to supervise the cleaning of the barn. Fannette fought the urge to run after him. To tell him everything before it was too late.

But it was already too late. Better he didn't know. Didn't have to pretend surprise. And they might not even bother with the big furniture wagon . . .

The deputies sauntered over to the women, looking them over one by one. Asking questions that were answered by monosyllables.

Perhaps she could warn Tansy. Get her out of the wagon before it was too late.

Sam turned back to her before she could edge away. He swept off his hat.

"Miz McLaury, I reckon?"

She nodded.

"Maybe you'd do us the kindness of asking the cook if she could spare us some victuals?"

"Oh, of course!" Fannette tried to sound hospitable. But Sam's eyes stayed on her as she went to Emily with the request.

Then they started to search the wagons, poking their

heads into the ones that were obviously empty.

Maybe Tansy had already gotten away. Maybe she'd had enough sense to take her plate and utensils. But Fannette knew that Tansy wouldn't care about such things. She'd only care to get herself and the baby to safety.

They were at the small furniture wagon now.

"Reckon that about finishes it," Tom said.

Sam pointed to the big wagon where it had been pulled well out of the way.

"We got that one yet."

Tom aimed a juicy mixture of brown liquid at a flat-topped rock.

"Furniture. Don't look like there'd be much place to hide in it with a squalling brat."

They studied the wagon, standing side by side, thumbs hooked into their belts. Then, as of one accord, they strode over to where it stood.

Sam jumped up onto the tailgate, and they could hear him pushing aside obstacles.

"Stinks like something rotten or shitty in here," he called to his partner.

Then—the sound Fannette had been dreading. A shrill scream.

Jared stopped what he'd been doing, and for one frightening minute, Fannette felt his eyes on her face. Then he went up to the wagon.

"What the hell have you got there?" he demanded.

Sam appeared, dragging a shrieking Tansy. She clutched her baby to her breast and continued to scream in high-pitched spurts as they pulled her to the ground.

Jared's mouth was a thin, white line, and again Fannette felt his eyes flash over her.

"She must have hidden when we stopped last night," he said calmly. "Nobody ever pays much attention to that wagon."

"Someone hid her," Sam said, and Tom's hand dropped to a point near his holster. "They'se dishes in there like those in that stack, and a jug of water like those by the stove. And the youngun's had a dose of paregoric."

He tore the baby from its mother's arms. It was filthy and it stunk, so he hastily set it down on a rock. Fannette shuddered when she saw he'd put the infant over the splotch of tobacco spittal.

"I told you we was sure to find her here!" Tom gloated.

Jared's eyes glinted with frustration. "We don't post a guard. It wouldn't have been difficult for her to hide and steal what food she might need while we were alseep."

"Like hell she did."

"Gentlemen, are you accusing me of hiding this woman?"

"You talk mighty queer for a Southerner."

"I never claimed to be one. My land's right across the Ohio from Cincinnati, and my folks came to Kentucky from the East. Talk to Mrs. McLaury, or her brother, Monsieur Verdier, if you want Southern talk."

"Oh, those Frenchies from N'Orleans way! Can't rightly call that talkin' Southern, either."

"Why the hell don't you just take this woman and get on your way?"

"Well now," Sam drawled. "It's near dark and gettin' as cold as a whore's ass. Reckon we'll put bracelets on this Tansy and camp along with you folks." He looked around. "We like company, and there's a bit more askin' I'd like to do."

"If one of my wife's slaves hid this woman, they're not going to tell you about it. And if I find out one of them did, that damn fool had better wish he hadn't been born."

Fannette held a plate of food in each hand, and it was all she could do not to drop them. Sam reached out for his, and Fannette managed to get the other to Tom. Even in the chill of oncoming darkness, she felt perspiration form on her upper lip and forehead. She kept her eyes on the ground. Afraid to look at Jared.

Suddenly he was the cordial host. "They've a good fire

196

going over there," he told the deputies. "Why not take your food to it? You can let the runaway bed down with our women tonight. They'll keep a watch on her."

"Time we get her shackled, we might do that, friend."

Jared started to move away.

"And mind," Sam called after him, "we've the right to see the papers on your stock. I reckon they're handy?"

"Would you like to see my marriage lines, too? And the dowry agreement?"

Sarcasm was lost on them. Sam nodded. "Wouldn't hurt a mite."

Jared went to the small furniture wagon and took out the tin box where he kept his papers. When he brought them over to the fireside he had the look of a man who'd become reconciled to a necessary annoyance.

"Here," he said. "You'll find everything in order. When you finish with your food, I'll be out with a bottle or two of rum. Before leaving New Orleans, I set up a fair stock that was right off the boat."

Fannette had stepped into the shadows, her back to a tree, her hands pressed against the cool, damp bark.

She was aware of Tansy staring at her. The men were busy with the papers, and for the moment the two of them were unobserved.

There was no supplication on the brown woman's face. It was sly and knowing.

"You git me free, Miz McLaury," she demanded.

"I can't!" Fannette said helplessly, her own fears making her voice almost incoherent. "Tansy, you know I did what I could."

"You git me free," Tansy repeated. "Else I tell things I see. I tell things I hear. Like why don't Mr. McLaury sleep in the tent with his new wife?"

"He will tonight," Fannette said dully. "Oh, yes, he will tonight . . ."

" 'Cause those men here, that's why. And what about what I hear when I hide in the trees? 'Bout Canada. That's what I hear. These folks ain't going to Kentucky, they going to Canada."

"Oh, you're wrong! You're wrong!"

"What 'bout that maid, Poppy? Why is she treated better'n most white girls? Why she sit on the bed and let you do your own things?"

"Tansy, I tried to help you. I tried my best."

"You git me free, or you be sorry."

Fannette turned away. Jared was closing the box, still talking to the deputies.

"Make yourself comfortable," he said. "I'll be back after I see to things."

He passed by her in the darkness, and Fannette wondered if he really didn't see her there. The men called to Tansy, one of them holding a shackle. Nearby Fannette heard a whimpering sound, and she remembered the baby.

It was lying motionless on the rock. Except for the whimper, she'd have thought it lifeless. She picked it up, and when she moved the wet cover from its face, she saw that mucus blocked its nose and its eyes were stuck closed.

Poppy came up to her.

"Leave it," she advised. "I've sent for Glory."

Fannette shook her head. How could they be so unsymphathetic to this poor fragment of humanity in its wet, sitnking rags? What had happened to them? To all of them?

She moved up the overgrown path to the shack carrying the baby against her.

"Tell Jove to bring me some warm water," she called back to Poppy. It was all she could do to keep from gagging. The smell was overpowering. "It needs a bath," she added unnecessarily.

"Have you ever bathed a baby?" Poppy asked, coming up to her.

Bathed a baby? She could hardly even remember holding one. But the sight of Glory limping toward her lent courage, and Fannette beckoned for the woman to follow her into the shack.

Glory clucked in disapproval as she stripped away the wrappings. She shook her head.

"At least clean the poor thing," Fannette said.

Glory poured the water into a basin, and gave Jove back the empty pitcher. Then she set to work.

Letty had finished putting things in order, and Jove came back with more warm water. He stood by, ready to help.

Fannette glanced around for the first time. Seen from inside, the shack was surprisingly comfortable. The pounded earth floor was covered with a rug from the small furniture wagon. A fire was crackling in a fireplace of mud-plastered timbers, and a rickety table held a lamp. There was even a newly mended rocking chair by the hearth.

Letty went out the door, and Poppy moved to follow her.

"Please don't go, Poppy," Fannette begged. She looked around, desperate for some excuse. "It smells awful in here, but with the door open it'll air out." She motioned to Jove. "If you'll take away those dirty rags . . ."

Jove set down the pitcher and gingerly filled the scrub pail with the disgarded garments. After he left with them, the air began to clear.

"It wasn't the smell," Poppy said. "It's that I can't stay tonight. Not even as your maid."

"But—"

Poppy avoided her eyes. "Jared said you weren't going to need me."

Blessed Virgin! She couldn't face him alone! Poppy's golden eyes, steady and candid, lifted to meet Fannette's dark ones.

"We're all depending on you, Nette. It's your fault this happened, and now it's up to you to remember your part. You're his bride, you know. And you really are. Try to

199

smile, even laugh a little."

"Laugh?" Fannette whispered.

"Nothing will undo what you've done. But try, at least. Act out your part."

Try? Pay the price of breaking a promise? *Give up your virtue quietly?* Was that what Poppy meant? Do what it is a woman does with a man? *And, for God's sake, don't run screaming out of the shack!*

Fannette caught Poppy by the arm. "You can't leave me! Please stay—"

Poppy shook her head and went to the door. "Stand here where they can see you. Remember to laugh, and call out that you won't need me tonight."

Fannette moved to the doorway and forced a smile. Somehow her voice said the words.

"By the way, Poppy, *chérie,* see to yourself before coming back. You must be very tired."

"*Merci,* Madame. I feel unwell."

Fannette hesitated, rebelling at the part assigned her.

"Stay, then. Letty can bring you supper in your tent. I can care for myself this once."

She closed the door and went to where Glory was drying the infant. Her trunk was nearby, and she rummaged through it until she came on a white wool scarf.

"Wrap him in this," she said to Glory.

The old woman plainly considered it a waste. She shook her head, but Fannette continued to hold it out. Finally, Glory shrugged, and taking it, swaddled the bare black body in it.

Fannette picked up the still bundle and carried it to the rocking chair. She sat down, cradling it. She was aware that for a moment the old woman stood very still, watching her. Then she took the basin of dirty water and left the shack.

Jove brought her a supper plate. His normal happy grin was replaced by a frown of deep concern.

"Mr. Jared, he sure mad," he announced unreas-

200

suringly. "I told him I did it. I tell him I hid that Tansy. But he only got madder."

"You shouldn't have!" Fannette said, touched. "Why did you?"

"Because I think you try to do a good thing. And because Zette belong to you. Zette say you're good to her." Jove shook his head. "He sure was mad. Said you have to face up to what you done, and I tell him it ain't you, it me." He set down the plate. "You shouldn't of, Miz McLaury."

"Miss Fannette." Even now the automatic correction came to her lips.

She picked at the food, then left the plate on the table. Finally she put the baby on the bed while she got into her night things. Maybe her fears were for nothing. Surely, he wouldn't dare . . .

The door opened without the preliminary of a knock. She snatched up the baby, alarmed. Jared stood on the threshold, framed by the glow of the outside fires. He glanced at her, at what she held, and tossed his sleeping roll into a far corner. It was still tied, and he made no move to unroll it.

After the first few words, she knew it was futile to argue about the baby. He was right, it did belong to its mother now that it was dry and clean.

On his way out he paused, and his eyes swept over her in a way that brought the blood to her cheeks.

"I've got to drink those bastards under the table," he said. "Be ready for me when I come back. And unbraid your hair."

She watched the door close. There had been a brief view of Trojan standing outside holding two bottles. Maybe Jared would stay out by the fire all night. Maybe he just wanted to alarm her.

She climbed into bed and pulled the covers over her head. Like an ostrich. She closed her eyes, realizing that she was very tired. The outside noises became a steady drone, and finally she slept.

When he came into the shack, awakening her with the light of his candle, she knew she must go to Tansy.

"The baby died. The woman's screaming like a banshee."

But it was no use. He had other plans . . .

He got undressed and climbed into bed beside her. But before she knew it, the rum must have taken its toll, and he fell fast alseep, not once having even touched her.

XII

He woke up to the realization that he was not alone. The warmth of her body, pressed as it was between him and the wall, was a definite shock. He lay still, trying to remember.

Earlier, when he had joined the slave catchers—or deputies, as they called themselves—his mind had still been inside the shack, not on the bottles that Trojan held.

He felt a little ashamed of the implied threat. But she had stood there, looking as if she expected instant rape, and the temptation had been irresistible. Not that he had any intention of carrying it through. Hell, he'd never taken a woman against her will, and he certainly wasn't going to start with the woman he intended should someday be his wife.

Changeable, defiant, arrogant Fannette. Fannette who risked his anger to help a runaway. A woman worth the winning, even if he had to fight the damned Creole to get her. It seemed long ago, in a dim past, when he and Anton had been inseparable friends. And they still were, somewhere under their rivalry for Fannette.

He tried to remember when he'd come back to the shack. Damn those slave catchers to hell! Anton had excused himself much earlier, about the time Trojan brought out another bottle. But it was past midnight before the two deputies became incoherent and finally passed out.

He told her about the baby. He remembered that much. And he remembered pushing her back on the bed when she tried to go to the woman, Tansy.

Two weeks on the road. Two weeks into a trip that might well take three months, and already there'd been trouble. Why, for the love of God, did that woman have to choose their wagons?

He felt Fannette stir. Christ! He was naked. Naked and under the covers with her beside him . . .

Oh, my God, had I? he thought. Obviously he hadn't. But if he didn't get the hell out of that bed and away from the warmth of her body damn soon . . .

Something tickled his chest and he reached to brush it away. He heard her gasp and realize he held her fingers.

He let them go, but his hand had started to move over her, over the yielding softness of her curves. He felt her flesh quiver under the light linen of her nightdress, then a shudder. And he knew it wasn't a shudder brought on by fear.

He never could remember the exact minute their mouths found each other, but he knew when he pulled the nightgown up away from her body. He knew when his lips found the round mounds of her breasts, brushed the nipples, and moved slowly over warm flesh, down to the flatness of her abdomen. He felt it draw in as she caught her breath and stirred to his caresses.

Stop! Right now, he must stop! But it was impossible. It was too late. Too late for both of them. She was waiting, ready. She made a little moaning sound that could have been his name, and her hands had gone behind his neck, her body moving in a sensuous rhythm of need under his.

He reached out, each hand cupping a side of her firm, rounded bottom, and he pulled her hard against him, glorying in her compliancy.

She whispered soft little words of desire, of a need she didn't understand, but was powerless to subdue. "Please . . ." she was murmuring. "Oh, please . . . please . . ."

He covered her, his desire thundering and crashing, but her sharp cry brought him back to the realization of her virginity. Even in his urgency, how could he have forgotten?

204

"I'm sorry... sorry..." he mumbled, knowing he must continue, that he was incapable of letting her go. Still, he managed to hold back, stroking her trembling body, soothing her fear, then his need was beyond all control.

"It's all right now," she whispered. "Only . . . please, gently. . ."

Gently? She might as well as ask for heaven or hell at that moment, but he tried. And when he held her sobbing against him, he stayed with her, knowing the importance of this first experience. That it should be brought to fulfillment for her, as well as for himself.

Knowing she was still wanting, needing, he stroked and caressed her, until at last she lay still against him.

"Nette," he grinned, "whatever your bloodline, it certainly isn't cold."

They lay together in blissful content. He kissed her. Her lips had fulfilled their promise. Those lips . . . They had been his undoing from the first. Sensuous, inviting lips in an innocent face.

He remembered telling her how beautiful he thought her mouth when he greeted her at the DuBois party, and he winced. He had resolved beforehand to remain cool, indifferent to the charms she so obviously knew she possessed. And then to come out with that idiotic remark. As smitten as Anton at his worst!

And then when they'd danced in the Lemmons' barn. Again her mouth had compelled him. He smiled, remembering her indignation when he'd taken her into his arms right in the middle of the floor.

It had been a long time since he'd had a woman, but that still didn't explain the ultimate completeness, the joy of possession. She lay in his arms as if designed to fit the curve of his body, the warmth of their flesh blending.

He felt the feather touch of her fingers as they explored, stroked. He caught her wrist, laughing.

"Keep that up," he warned, "and you'll be sorry." Then he added, "My poor shoulder. . ."

205

He knew the color would be in her cheeks. He could visualize the lowering of those long, curly eyelashes. There was nothing about her that he hadn't memorized.

He slept, then, only to awaken to renewed desire. He poked at the nightdress that was still crumpled under her arms.

"Raise up," he whispered.

She obeyed, and he slid the nightgown over her head. He made a bundle of it and threw it across the floor. He heard her soft laugh, and she sat up. He reached to pull her back to him, then realized that she was unbraiding her hair, tossing it free about her shoulders.

She lay down again, on her back, and he bent over her, running his fingers through the curly softness. Then his hands moved over her again, but this time with the certainty of possession.

"I don't want to hurt you," he whispered, "but do you think . . ."

Her arms went up to circle his shoulders, and this time he was able to use restraint until her passion matched his. This time her nails dug into his bare back as she pulled him close, closer . . .

"What a wildcat!" he gasped. "Your claws are worse than your teeth!"

"I couldn't stop myself." Her face was buried in his chest.

The scent of her hair was in his nose, the strands against his face.

"So ashamed . . ." she whispered. "And happy. So happy, Jared . . ."

"Ashamed? We've a marriage license. Have you forgotten?"

"But a girl shouldn't—It was like in the carriage. I didn't know exactly—but whatever it was, I wanted you to do it. Please don't think I'm something terrible—"

"You're mine. And you may as well learn right now at the start that I'm a very possessive man."

206

She giggled. "The neckline of my dress!"

"I also have a very quick temper." He paused. "That day you were going to sail with Anton, Poppy said she prayed I'd get there in time. Poppy realized that if I found you and Anton like we are now, I'd have killed him."

His voice was soft, but Fannette understood he meant his words as a warning, and she felt a sense of disquiet.

Then he was kissing her again, and all was joy.

After awhile they slept, not moving, but holding to each other. They slept, oblivious to the sounds of an ax splitting wood, to the rattling of kitchen utensils. The call for breakfast rang out, but still they slept.

Until Anton flung open the door, bringing the morning light with him into the shack.

XIII

"Oh, my God!" Anton exclaimed. He looked as if he might be sick right there on the carpet. His eyes found the crumpled heap of Fannette's nightdress, then moved to Jared's arm and shoulder, naked and encircling Fannette.

He muttered something undistinguishable and started for the bed, but Jared sat up and waved him back.

"At least have the decency to let a man pull on his drawers."

Fannette snatched at the bedcovers, but not soon enough to hide her own nakedness. Anton averted his face and turned away.

"You can wait for me outside," Jared said calmly as he buckled his belt.

"I came in here to tell you those men left with the woman," Anton's voice was muffled. "It was your place to face them, not mine."

He went out, slamming the door after him.

Jared reached for his shirt, and then decided against it. He turned to follow.

Fannette threw back the covers and ran to him.

"Please don't get in a fight!" she begged. "Stay here and he'll calm down."

"Are you that naive?" he asked, disengaging her arm. He paused by the door, his eyes sweeping over her nakedness. "And I don't want you out there."

As soon as she was alone, she snatched up her clothing. Trembling fingers fumbled at buttons, and her loose hair kept whipping at her face. Outside she heard Anton's voice, bitter and harsh, speaking a mixture of French and English. There was no sound from Jared.

She threw her hair back over her shoulder and looked at

the tumbled bed. Her face grew warm as she remembered. Oh, I love you . . . love you . . . love you . . . she thought, her body tingling at the memory of him caressing it till he brought her to the fullness of her womanhood. Then, later, moving to the peak of ecstasy, this time in unison with him. The glorious awareness of love that followed the mounting rapture. The final burst of completion.

The not wanting him to move, the wanting him to stay forever, holding her in the embrace that began in Eden. The feeling that now she was a part of him. Glorying in belonging to him . . .

She became aware of the sounds of scuffling outside. The sound of a smashing blow of flesh on flesh. The shack shook as a body fell against it. She heard muffled curses, then a resumption of the terrible pounding and grunting.

Stay inside? Impossible! She had to stop the fight before someone was killed!

Oh, I love you . . . love you . . .

The shack shook again, and there was the sound of voices as people ran to the scene. She threw open the door.

"Get back inside!" Jared shouted at her, but she was unable to move. Anton was trying to get to his feet, his face bloody, eyes already puffing. Jared stood over him, swaying, his breath coming fast. A cut bled from his lip, and there was the mark of a knuckle high on his cheek. A gash on his chin.

Trojan took his arm, pulling him away.

"That enough, Mr. Jared. You near kill Mr. Anton."

The blood continued to drip from Jared's lip, and Fannette rushed back into the shack for the water pitcher and a cloth. She started back out the door, then came to an abrupt halt.

Poppy was standing on tiptoes, tenderly cleansing Jared's wounds. She whispered something into his ear, and he grinned. Suddenly he had his arms around her, kissing her. Then he picked her up and whirled her around, while she struggled and laughed until he set her back on the ground.

How was it possible to hate someone the way she hated Poppy at that moment? And Jared? Her love? He had drawn out her passions, let her lie in his arms thinking herself loved. Willing to give without shame. Thinking he'd carry the memory in his heart just as she did. Thinking it was special.

And it was forgotten with the daylight. A release of pressures for which he'd been grateful. Nothing more.

He looked at her over Poppy's head, and Poppy moved away, her face flushed.

"I see you don't need my help," Fannette said, trying to sound unconcerned. He reached and took her arm, but she shook it free.

She hurried down the steps to where Anton sat leaning against the shack. Letty was holding a cup of water, and he'd just rinsed the blood out of his mouth.

Anton who loved her because she was Fannette. Anton who loved her enough to fight for her.

"You go back where you belongs," Letty protested as Fannette knelt down beside Anton. "You got no call to come here."

"I'll take care of him," she said, her voice cold. Just as cold as she felt inside. She poured water over the cloth and rinsed away the blood on Anton's cheek, hardly aware of what she was doing.

Anton glared at her out of half-closed eyes.

"Bitch!" he whispered. "You even stink of him!"

She shook back her hair. I'm sorry, she wanted to say. Sorry for being a trusting fool. Sorry for being a stupid, lovesick idiot! Sorry Jared had saved her from becoming Anton's mistress, only to make her his own.

Jared's fingers closed around her arm and he jerked her to her feet.

"I've sent for Glory to attend Anton. You're not needed here. Get back into the shack!"

210

She tried to pull away, but his grip was hard and firm, his eyes a cold blue.

"Haven't you embarrassed me enough?" he demanded. "Running to Anton like a lovesick schoolgirl? Are you going back to the shack, or do I have to drag you there?"

She had never seen him so angry before. And good! So he was embarrassed? Well, good again!

"I'll go," she told him, her eyes sullen.

Inside the single room, he closed the door, and then pulled her over to the window. He brushed aside the rotting hide and gave her the hand mirror she had kept on the table.

"Look at yourself!" His bruised lips quirked. "Like a whore from a dockside brothel!"

Her hair was in wild disarray, the bodice of her dress buttoned into the wrong holes, and her eyes . . . No wonder Anton had looked away. No one seeing her flushed face could possibly believe she'd been had against her will.

Jared set the mirror aside.

"For Christ's sake, fix yourself up! Everyone'll be staring at you." He paused. "And I expect you to stare right back." He started to leave, but turned to her again.

"I'm asking you to remember you're my wife. You're here to help our people to Canada. There's no place in this plan for you to take a lover. Even if he is Anton."

"But there's a place for a mistress!" Even to save her life, she couldn't have held back the angry accusation.

"If you're referring to Poppy, you're badly mistaken."

"You were hugging her. Kissing her."

"So I was," he agreed, and left.

She brushed her hair with quick, furious strokes, remembering the pleasure he'd found in it. Then she braided it into submission and coiled it into a large, severe knot at the nape of her neck. She selected her most drab gown, and wished she'd packed a plainer one. Though it already had a modest neckline, she added a collared inset.

She looked around the room, and her eyes rested on the

disordered bed. For the first time since the trip had begun, she smoothed out the covers and made it into a tight roll. A job that had been taken on by Letty.

She had barely finished tying it when Letty came through the door. She broke into a giggle.

"Mr. Jared a lot of man," she commented. "But no need you do that, I'se a married woman."

Absolutely the last straw! Tears of mortification splashed onto her cheeks.

"Time like this, do a girl good, she cry some," Letty approved. "But Mr. Jared, he worth it." She put down her burden, and Fannette saw that it was fresh bedding.

"Mr. Jared say it time to change the bed," she elaborated. "Besides, we stay here another night. You forgit?" She stripped down the bed after untying it. "My," she said approvingly, "you sure was a virgin. Sure was."

Wasn't a shred of self-respect to be left her? She went to the window and looked out, sick with humiliation.

"Mebbe us black women could teach you white ladies more'n you think about men folk," Letty prattled on. "It was a bad thing you go to Mr. Anton when yore man, he hurt."

She was interrupted by a knock on the door. It was Jove with the pitcher she'd left outside.

"Got you fresh water," he said with all his old cheer. Then he added reprovingly, "Now, you went and got Mr. Jared mad all over again."

Letty clucked in agreement, and Fannette caught up her shawl and hurried outdoors. She avoided the concerned glances that followed her as she made her way to a quiet place by the creek.

When she returned to the shack, she saw that Jared's bedroll had been removed and Poppy's sleeping things were beside her own. Poppy was sitting in the rocking chair, combing her hair, her feet stretched out to catch the heat of a new fire that burned beyond the hearth.

For a moment Fannette was tempted to go back outside, but a cold wind was blowing, and the sun had disappeared behind a new mass of clouds.

Poppy put aside her comb and looked at Fannette.

"Jared's concerned about what Anton might do. He's staying with him tonight."

So that was the explanation. Or was it?

"Do you think I care?" she asked, setting aside her shawl.

"Yes," Poppy said. "Yes, I do."

Fannette watched the flames catch onto a dry piece of wood.

"I guess you know," she said dully. "About last night."

"After the fight this morning, I doubt anything's much of a secret."

"And now he's after you."

"What?" Poppy exclaimed. "Oh, Nette, are you jealous?"

"He kissed you." She knew it would be better to leave the thing unsaid. To keep some dignity. But she couldn't. It was all there, ready to rush out. She had to learn what they meant to each other.

"Of course he kissed me. I said something he enjoyed hearing." Suddenly her laughter rang out. "So that's why you went to Anton?"

"Jared held you."

"Nette, shouldn't you grow up a little? Don't you know Jared could as easily have forged your marriage paper?"

"Why should he when he expects to annul the whole thing when we reach Cincinnati?"

Poppy regarded Fannette thoughtfully.

"Nette, I wonder if you realize the harm you've done?"

"They've got Tansy and her baby's dead. What more can you folks ask?"

"That we be left alone. And I think it's too late to ask that. I didn't trust Tansy. Didn't from first I saw her. She's a troublemaker."

"And you think the slave catchers will be back?"

"Yes."

"They won't find anything. I don't intend to repeat my crime."

"Mother of God!" Poppy exclaimed in exasperation, rising to her feet. "How many times have I told you that descriptions of most everyone out there are in the hands of professional slave catchers? Even Glory!"

"That bent old woman?" Fannette shook her head in disbelief.

"And Abe, and Pearl, and George Washington, and Chippers—you name them." Poppy was silent a minute. "Jared has asked me to pay special attention to Anton."

"Oh?" she said, surprised it should matter so little.

"Jared feels Anton respects me, that he'll listen to reason when I talk to him."

"And I'm soiled."

"You must put yourself in Anton's place. I'm sure he couldn't imagine what he saw this morning had anything to do with rape." She put her arm around Fannette's shoulder, her voice suddenly soft.

"Nette, where I was raised wasn't Gallatin Street, the place of the prostitutes. But it was a place where what goes on between a man and a woman is the most important conversation. One grows up protected in those cottages. But not innocent."

"And what is that supposed to mean?"

"That you've much to learn. You must put yourself in Jared's position. All our folks look up to him. But how will he keep their respect if they think he can't hold his own woman?"

"I'm not his woman."

Poppy raised an eyebrow. "Mrs. McLaury," she said, "you'd do well to rethink your role."

Rethink her role? How was it possible to do otherwise? Last night had been the beginning and the end of everything, as far as she was concerned. Even thinking about it, she felt a bodily reaction.

214

But what had it been to him?

Thank you, Miz McLaury. Real nice, Miz McLaury. When I feel the need, I'll be back, Miz McLaury. Might make a little more trouble for the annulment when we reach Cincinnati. But think of the fun it'll be when the nights grow dull . . .

Was that what it meant to him? If he felt the way she did, he'd be here, beside her, right this moment. After last night, how could he be anywhere else?

"Nette . . ." It was Poppy's voice in the darkness. "Nette, don't you understand? He *has* to be with Anton. Anton could ruin everything, if Tansy hasn't already. They'd believe a white man where they might not a runaway slave."

"I don't care," Fannette said. "I don't care!"

But she *did* care. He could come to her any place, any time, and she'd be waiting. Hating her own weakness, perhaps.

But waiting.

She thought of Anton. So easy to be strong and virtuous—when you didn't love the man!

XIV

Could this bruised and battered face belong to the elegant young man who had ridden up to Bijou's gates? Even Anton's hair showed signs of neglect. He made no attempt to brush it into the usual fashionable side part, and his pointed beard needed clipping.

He watched the morning activities through puffed, sullen eyes, but he managed a pained smile when Poppy came up to him with two filled plates.

Well, Fannette thought, she's carrying out her duties and seems to enjoy them. Let her. She could have Anton. Only please, please, leave Jared alone . . .

When the dishes were cleared away, Glory brought out her kerchief of medications and studied Anton's face from all angles. Finally she nodded, apparently pleased that it showed signs of healing. She and Poppy set to work cleaning the cuts and smearing the deeper slashes with a dark ointment.

"I'm afraid you'll be left with a scar up here on your cheekbone," Poppy said. "But then, folks will think it's from a duel and the women will find it romantic."

Jared came up to the circle and stood behind Fannette. He scowled when he saw that she was watching Anton.

"Letty's bringing water and a towel." he said. "I'd like you to wash my cuts and then get Glory over here with her ointment."

"Yesterday you did very well without help from me."

Thumbs hooked into his belt, he looked down at her.

"I did?"

"Why not call Poppy?" she added spitefully. "She's almost through."

His eyes continued to regard her. Steady, and without

216

anger. "Are you really that stupid? Don't you realize we might be under observation? Tansy talked. Don't think otherwise."

She glanced at the basin with disdain. "And what has that to do with me?"

"You, my dear, are my devoted bride. You couldn't bear not to tend my wounds."

Gingerly, Fannette squeezed out the cloth.

"If you jab me," he warned, "you'll be sorry later." His eyes projected a meaning that had her blushing. She dabbed at his cuts, cleansing them.

Suddenly he was laughing. He placed a hand on each of her shoulders and pulled her close, looking down at her. She could feel his reaction to her nearness, and she wondered if that were his purpose.

"You see what you do to me?" he asked softly.

She tried to push away.

"My dear," he said, "I think we need to have a talk." His fingers caught the snood she wore and he pulled it free. Her hair tumbled loose, spilling over her shoulders. "I've heard it's improper for a married woman to wear one of these," he added.

"You don't shave your beard on the road, maybe you might consider it's easier to wear a snood than to bother doing my hair up."

"Wear it loose, then."

"What!" she exclaimed indignantly.

He buried his face in the mass of curls at the curve of her neck and moved up her cheek to her ear and eyes, then, finally, his mouth was parting her lips, drawing, caressing . . . They stood locked together, swaying slightly. Finally, he loosened his hold. She staggered back against a tree, palms against the trunk. She stared at him out of half-veiled eyes, smoky with the passion he had stirred. Knowing she would never be free of him.

"Later," he said unsteadily, seeming to gain control of himself only with an effort. "Later. My God, you're beautiful!" Then he smiled wryly and glanced toward the fringe of forest.

"Whatever Tansy might have said about us, I think we've now effectively cleared away any doubts about or relationship."

So that was the reason for his embrace! Everything planned for effect. It wasn't she he had been thinking about, it'd been the caravan.

Damn him! She found herself thinking names she'd heard Breel use. Yes. All of those. And damn him! Damn him, as well!

He moved away, whistling. He paused by Tressa where she played near a wagon. He dropped the snood in her lap.

"Gift," he said. "*Lagniappe.*"

Later, standing in the doorway of the shack, hairpins between her teeth, Fannette saw Tressa parading around. The silken snood was over her kinked hair like a bonnet, the ribbons tied under her chin.

"Donna would have a fit," Fannette said. "She ordered it specially made for me."

Poppy laughed. "You can't blame Jared; Tressa was the only one near."

Fannette jabbed the last pin in her hair and tried to ignore the picture of the circle of people. Poppy and Glory near Anton, Letty holding a basin and Jove a pitcher. When Jared finally freed her from his embrace, they were standing alone, except for Tressa playing an imaginary game with a heap of pebbles.

"How two people can so completely forget there's anyone else in the world!" Poppy was still laughing.

Fannette grabbed up her wrap and went outside. She glanced around the camp. Obviously Jared had no intention of moving that day. A matter of bravado, she decided. His way of telling anyone who might be watching that he had nothing to fear.

The women were sitting together enjoying the thin sun

218

of late morning. Sassie, Juba's girl, was in the act of disappearing into the woods. From the corner of her eye, Fannette saw one of the younger men heading in the same direction.

So, Sassie! While Juba hunts and fishes, you find amusements of your own? She remembered what Poppy and Jove had said earlier. Did everyone, then, know about Sassie except Juba?

She looked around for something to do. Poppy and Anton were talking and laughing on the stoop of the shack, and she wondered briefly how they found so much to discuss.

She watched with disinterest as Crane, a squat, heavy-set man with a livid knife scar on one cheek, mended the canvas of a wagon. Abby, his wife, stood by, adding to his problem with a steady stream of advice.

Between the rising wind, his wife, and their little girl, Tressa, Fannette doubted he'd ever get the job done.

"Look!" Tressa tugged at his arm with one hand, and with the other pointed at Fannette's snood, still tangled in her hair. "Pa, look!"

Crane threw down his tools. "Woman," he shouted at his wife, "shut yore mouth and git that chile off me!"

Fannette moved away hastily. The last thing she needed to hear was a family argument. She walked down to the brook where she'd sat the evening before and found a place where the sun touched a rock. It was a cold sun, and she pulled up her fur-trimmed hood as she settled down to watch the water splash over pebbles and fallen branches.

"You mind I talk?"

Fannette looked up. A tall, very black, young woman stood near. She wasn't slim, but she was beautifully proportioned, and there was about her the hint of extraordinary physical strength. Standing behind her was a man, lighter of skin, but even taller. Again broad shoulders proclaimed well-developed muscles.

"We all knows Mr. Jared was mad when he find that

219

Tansy," the girl said. "But I watch, and I think mebbe I do the same as you. A lot of us ain't mad at you, no matter what happen. My George Washington feel the same as me."

"George Washington?"

The man grinned. "Pearl say it right. Way back, time of the Revolushon, we help fight and Gen'ral Washington say nigger who fight, gits free. Every woman in my fambly call her first boy George Washington."

"If your family was freed, what are you doing here with these runaways and fugitives?" Fannette asked.

His eyes darkened with remembered troubles. "Mebbe, someday, when we got lots of time, we tell you. Pearl, here, her fambly free too."

Poppy and Anton came walking toward them. Pearl smiled at them, and George Washington bobbed his head, then, hand in hand, the pair wandered on down the bank, following the stream.

"We lookin' for crawdads," George Washington called back over his shoulder. "Got some rabbit liver on a string."

"Venus in ebony. . ." Anton murmured, his eyes following the sway of Pearl's hips.

Fannette was frowning. "If they are freed folks, what are they doing here?"

"What an innocent!" Poppy shook her head. "How safe do you imagine a freed pair like that are when prime hands go at two thousand dollars each? Don't you realize that the Fugitive Slave Law they passed in 1850 requires no proof that a runaway is really a runaway beyond the slave catcher's word? A negro can't give evidence, not even for himself."

"Are you telling me that a freed person could be sold just that easy?"

"Unless there's a white person to swear he's free. And where does a black man find that white person when he's picked up away from the folks who know him?"

220

Fannette looked at Anton for confirmation, and he nodded his head.

Poppy glanced away from the couple, now far down stream.

"Jared sent me for you. He's riding into Baton Rouge for supplies and wants you to go with him."

If this was his attempt at a "talk," well he could come for her himself. She wasn't going to rush to him at his bidding, and he might as well learn this!

Poppy shrugged when Fannette made no attempt to move. "I'll let him know I told you," she said, and went away.

Anton remained. His eyes were puffed and discolored, but she was still aware that he was regarding her with a new sort of interest.

The gash on his cheek was deep and puckered. Poppy could well have been right. It did look as if he'd go through the remainder of his life carrying the mark of Jared's knuckles.

"And you held yourself above accepting an honorable offer," he murmured. There was something intimate, something knowing in his voice. As though it had been he who'd been with her that night.

"Since when has it been considered honorable to ask a woman to be your mistress?" she asked.

"In your circumstances, how could you have expected more? And permit me to observe, you seem to have settled for less."

"Have you forgotten Jared and I were married? That he has the paper to prove it?"

"Forged. Just as every paper he carries is forged."

"Issued by a respected judge with his seal."

He smiled unpleasantly. "And the priest who blessed this happy union?"

"That'll come later."

"Do you really believe that? You yourself said it was only to last until Cincinnati. Though, to be truthful, I

221

never thought he'd actually gone to the trouble to secure a legal document."

He knelt beside her, taking her hands into his own. "You didn't know it, but I was planning to ask you to marry me . . . in spite of everything. My mind has undergone changes since we left New Orleans—and Maman. I thought we could take a ship from the Atlantic and sail for France as man and wife." He shrugged. "Of course that's out of the question now."

"Was it ever really a question?" Her eyes were scornful. "Did you intend to dangle that promise in front of me the same way you swore you'd engage a separate cabin for me on that boat in New Orleans?"

He frowned. "Didn't Louis make that clear?" There was a truthful ring in his voice. "You know how hard it is to get a sailing out of New Orleans. How a person has to wait for an announcement in the paper. I engaged the last two cabins, and the captain appealed to me with a story about a woman who'd been visiting in New Orleans. She received word her husband had been injured, possibly dying, and she had to get to France. It would have been ungallant to refuse her the cabin. I didn't expect you'd spend much time in it, anyway."

"You were so sure of yourself?"

He shook his head. "As a matter of truth, there seemed the possibility that you might prove to be a cold woman. You must admit your responses to me were hardly ardent. Now I'm no longer troubled by that fear. That's why I'm renewing my offer."

"Have you forgotten that I'm tarnished?"

"A mistress needn't be a virgin. In fact, it's to be preferred."

"And so you've again honored me?"

"I'd give you security. And I can make you very happy."

She flushed, realizing the meaning behind the words.

"I doubt that," she said.

"Fannette, my innocent! Do you think he is the only

man who can stir you? Let me make love to you, and you'll learn it's not the man but what he knows! I've been told I'm quite expert."

"By women paid to say that, in all probability." Her eyes went down to their clasped hands. "Do you think I could sit here with Jared's hands holding mine and still stay at this distance?" She pulled her fingers free. "I wasn't able to become your mistress before, and I certainly couldn't now."

His smile turned cynical. "So you're above that? Truthfully, can you think you could go to a priest and expect him to believe that you haven't fornicated with Jared? As a Catholic, can you regard yourself as his wife because of a civil ceremony and a document?"

"So I should fornicate with you as a mistress, rather than with Jared as a wife?"

"As his mistress. Never anything more."

She stood, chin up, eyes flashing and defiant.

"As his mistress, then. As his mistress as long as he wants me."

"And then? After Cincinnati?"

"Until Cincinnati, at any rate and at any cost."

Jared was coming toward them with quick, impatient strides. "I sent for you," he said. "I've been waiting."

Anton bowed slightly. "Your mistress and I have been discussing the merits of fornication," he said.

Jared's eyes narrowed. "My wife, you mean. And am I certain that I heard right?"

"Ask Fannette what she is. Ask her if a civil marriage can make her your wife in her faith." He laughed. "An excellent question for a lawyer. You're her husband, I grant that. But she's not your wife."

Jared's face had darkened. "God and hell blast you! I came close to killing you yesterday, and I'm ready to finish the job!"

"The question of weapons belongs to the challenged," Anton reminded him. "Unfortunately, I left without my

223

sword, so we can hardly duel in the honorable manner."

"You know I'm not a swordsman."

"No more than I'm a pugilist. However, we both have pistols."

Fannette caught Anton by the arm. "Stop it!" she exclaimed. "Both of you! Stop it!"

Poppy came running over the damp, brown grass.

"*Sacre Maria!* Must you keep up this squabble? Like a pair of roosters in a barnyard with only one hen? There's more important things to concern us than this war between the two of you!"

Some of the stiffness left Jared, but his eyes were still angry when he turned to Fannette.

"Should you be entirely through with this discussion, might I prevail upon you to come up to the camp?" he requested with mock formality. "The horses are harnessed and waiting." He bowed slightly and took Poppy by the arm, leading her away.

"I want you to go with us," he told her when they were out of hearing.

Poppy looked up at him. "Why?" she asked.

"If I'm alone with Fannette right now, I might say things I'll regret later."

"This jealousy, it's insane! On both your parts."

"What he said about Fannette and me. Was it true?"

"Fundamentally," she admitted with reluctance. "Yes. I'm afraid Anton spoke the truth."

"And I'm supposed to stand by while superstitious mummery robs me of my wife?"

"It isn't mummery to Fannette. No more than it is to Anton."

"But you saw the ceremony and we've . . . been together." He looked back at Fannette and Anton, who were slowly walking toward the camp. "Why does she go to him, Poppy? She gave me every reason to believe she was over him, then I find them holding hands." He drew a deep, infuriated breath. "Christ, I don't know which of

224

them infuriates me most!"

His eyes flickered past her to Sassie, who was emerging from a strip of woods, a new bracelet on her wrist.

"And there's more trouble. Trojan warned me, but Juba said they were getting married. God almighty, what's wrong with women, Poppy?"

"Maybe they need more attention from their men."

"Juba knows we rely on him for fresh meat. He's our best hunter, and as for me I've got every man, woman and child in this caravan to worry about."

"And Fannette?"

"Oh Christ! Let her go to Anton, if that's what she wants!"

XV

Junie forced back a coughing fit, but it stayed with her, choking and gagging. Finally, she knew she had to give in to it or stop breathing. She wondered how much more her ribs could stand. Surely each one must be shattered by these spasms.

Just so Lem—she must remember to think of him as Willie—didn't hear her. He'd take on about how they should have stayed at the Settlement until she was better.

But she knew. Lord, yes, she knew. Wasn't anything going to make her better. And Lem—that is, Willie—they'd be coming after him unless he got to that Canada place. They wanted him too bad to give him up.

She thought of the wide, red scar on his neck. He hid it with high, buttoned-up shirts, even in the hot weather. And the "K" branded on his buttocks. Wouldn't be any trouble proving he was Yellar Lem if they caught up with him.

Ten white folks dead after that rebellion. Willie said he didn't do any of the killing, and she believed him. But it made no difference. Any man who took a hand in it was just as much to blame, they said.

If it wasn't for Willie, the little Renfrew girl would have had it too. But when he saw what was happening, he hid the white girl in a little cave by the creek. He didn't want any part of killing, not her Willie. He just wanted to break free for the both of them. When he saw what was happening, he tried to get away and come for her.

That's how they caught him. One of the men, who'd done such big talk about breaking free, saw that Willie was backing off. He reached out with that sickle, he did, and drew him back. Lord above, what a cut! Why, she thought for sure Willie's head would roll off when she saw them put him into a wagon.

Preacher said he was too tough to die. They threw him into the jail with the others, and somehow he got well.

So they could hang him.

"But I didn't do nothin'," Willie told her. "I didn't do nothin' 'tall. I hides little Miss Jenn, and I goes to get away when I sees all that blood and what they doin'."

"But you were with them," the white man said. "You were with them, and that's enough."

But he got away. He and the other ones. In the night the rest of the band sneaked up to the little jail. They killed the guard, and all of them got away.

Willie didn't kill the guard, but that didn't matter. He was with them. Same as before.

Junie leaned against a tree until the coughing eased a bit. She wiped her mouth. It made the cloth red, and that wasn't a good sign.

Just so Willie didn't know.

If the Lord permitted her to stay on her feet until Canada where he'd be safe, then she'd go to Jesus and not care. Just so she saw Willie where he was safe. Safe, what a sealing word that was . . .

It would have been better if he'd left the Settlement without her. But no matter how much she begged him to, he wouldn't. So she had to pretend the healing preacher healed her with that "laying on of the hands." It hadn't been easy, but she'd done it. With Glory's help. Glory had given her some black stuff to chew when the cough started to tickle her throat deep inside, warning her it was on its way. It had fooled Willie, all right. Just yesterday he'd talked about how she was getting better. How her eyes were bright again, and her cheeks were pink through the brown.

Of course she and Glory knew differently.

"How'd you get that *K* burned into you like that," she'd asked when first they were together after the old

227

master said it was all right for them to share a cabin. She knew it was a *K* because she heard the overseer call it that one day.

"Burned it on me when they puts me on a boat when I a boy," he told her. "Burn same on ebry man, woman and chile. I hear it's for the name of the boat brung us here."

Oh, they'd know he was Yellar Lem, for sure. No way to hide that brand and that scar. No way he could say he was any different.

She started to cough again, and wished Glory would hurry with a new poke of that black stuff.

She watched Miz McLaury come up the path with Mr. Anton. Mr. Jared looked mighty mad as he plunked Miss Poppy right onto the middle of the wagon seat.

White folks sure was peculiar. Everyone was happy when Mr. Jared went into that cabin like a man should. Everyone thought Mr. Anton got what he deserved, busting in like he did. And what was the matter with Miz McLaury, going to Mr. Anton like she did?

But she had her own load of worries. No need to fuss over the white folks's troubles. Each day she was a little weaker and it was harder to breathe, especially at night. At least, Willie didn't know about that. It was the Lord's blessing that he was over in the men's tent where he couldn't hear her gasping and choking.

If the weather had been warmer and drier, maybe things might not have been so bad. But getting wet in that rain, sure hadn't helped . . .

Mr. Jared said he was getting warm, heavy cloth so folks wouldn't feel the cold so much. But, maybe, for her it was too late.

At least Willie would be on his way to Canada. No matter what happened to her, he'd make it now.

Her breath was easier in her lungs, and she straightened up as she saw Willie come for her.

"You feelin' pore?" he asked anxiously.

She smiled and hid the reddened rag.

"Jus' fine," she said. "Jus' fine, ever since that healin' man touch me . . ."

They watched the spring wagon with Mr. Jared and the two ladies rock over the rough path.

If only a bad spell didn't come to her. Until that place— what was the name?

Until Cincinnati . . .

She thought of the spiritual Preacher Wednesday liked to bellow out in his big voice when the wagon wheels were miring:

Jesus is comin' bye an bye,
Keep a inchin' along
Like a po' inch worm, Massa,
Jesus is comin' bye an bye.

XVI

Jared watched as Fannette left the shack still fastening her hair. She came to the wagon—and a sudden halt.

"I thought I was to go with you," she said, staring at Poppy.

"You are," Jared said. He realized that his temper had again tricked him into doing everything wrong. Pride. Just a matter of pride.

And he had wanted to be alone with her. To try to straighten out the ridiculous misconceptions that had separated them. And he'd permitted pride to pay the devil with his good resolutions.

Poppy had returned Fannette's cold stare with a look of utter misery.

"Jared thought I'd be helpful in selecting some bolts of heavy cloth, so we can make warm clothes." She paused, but when only silence greeted her, she prattled on, self-consciously. "No one seemed to realize how cold it can get further north, and they've nothing that's really adequate."

Fannette turned to move away. "I don't think I'm needed," she said.

Inadvertently, Jared's eyes rested on Anton.

"Your place is here. Beside me."

"Oh yes," Fannette agreed. "I'm Mrs. McLaury. For the time, at least. But then," she looked Poppy full in the face, "it's understandable that I should find it hard to remember that."

Jove held her up onto the seat, and she arranged her skirts carefully, head averted.

Poppy started to chatter nervously in an attempt to ease the tension, and Jared made an effort to respond, but in his mind he was busy drafting the letter he planned to write after laying in the supplies.

He'd find a quiet tavern and have them draw him some beer. There'd be paper and pen to borrow from the lady's parlor, and the letter should be, yes, certainly it should be to Breel. By this time they'd be frantic with worry about Fannette. Especially Donna, who'd known of Anton's proposition.

"Dear sir," he thought, setting it down in his mind. "Your daughter is in good health and happy." He glanced surreptitiously at Fannette's stormy profile. "We were married just before leaving New Orleans, and are now en route to Cincinnati via the Natchez Trace and Kentucky. We should reach our destination in late March. The address where your messages may be held is . . ."

Well, something like that, anyway. The main thing was to relieve their minds—and to inform them of the marriage. He considered discussing the matter with Fannette, but a second glance at the angry angle of her chin dissuaded him.

He reached into a pocket and felt the letter Anton had given him. It would be entrusted to the same captain on a boat headed downstream.

"I wrote that I'd departed the ship at the very last minute because of a matter of honor," Anton had told him pointedly. "Also that I planned to sail from an Atlantic port."

Well, so much for that, anyway. . .

Jared left the women at a general merchandise store and went on to purchase supplies. Amazing how much food could be consumed in less than three weeks. He'd have to set in more provisions before leaving Natchez. There weren't many places left on the old Trace Road where food could be bought.

The Natchez Trace. Once the artery between the North and South, it was built over the age-old Indian trail by order of the United States Government. Once heavily

231

traveled with inns and trading posts every twenty miles, in those days anything could be purchased, from whiskey to flour.

Where were they all now? The Indians had left for somewhere in Oklahoma after the charter was signed by Dancing Rabbit. The highwaymen were gone, now that there was only an occasional trickling of farm carts or movers' wagons. And gone were the post express riders who made fantastic records, riding with the mail day and night. All of them gone with the boasting, cursing, frolicking rivermen. All banished by the advent of a boat that used steam to ply upstream on the Mississippi.

Jared finished loading the wagon, had his beer, and wrote his letter. He left the letters with a captain his brother had known and went to get Poppy and Fannette.

Poppy had bolts of heavy material set aside, and he pulled out his purse to settle the bill. Then he noticed another stack of purchases on the counter in front of Fannette. He picked up the accounting on that and saw it was marked: "Paid." He looked quizzically at Fannette.

"They are things I need," she told him defensively. "I didn't expect when I left Bijou that I'd be going north."

He pointed to Poppy's selections. "They should have been included with those things."

"I'm quite capable of paying for what I want," she replied. "I don't ask that my fare go toward the purchase of intimate items."

He swore softly, aware of the shopkeeper's interested eyes. Thank God he hadn't introduced her as his wife or there would have been talk. He picked up the accounting and placed it in his pocket.

He drove them back to where he'd had his beer, and the innkeeper's wife directed them to a room where they could refresh themselves. Fannette still haughty and indifferent, and Poppy plainly miserable.

After what seemed to him an unnecessarily long passage of time, they rejoined him. Their hair was smooth

232

and their dresses brushed free of road dust.

As handsome a pair as you'd find anywhere, he thought, and he helped them to their chairs. Now, he decided, would be a good time to make up for the morning. He leaned toward Fannette.

"I didn't order any food," he told her, "because I thought there might be something special you'd like. Something you've missed since Bijou. I'll even have them send out for it if necessary."

"It really doesn't matter," she replied, her voice icy. "Just anything. I'm really not hungry."

Poppy started to giggle uncontrollably. "Oh, Nette!" she said, "that's too much! You know you're always hungry."

Jared grinned in spite of all his good resolutions.

"I don't think either of you are very amusing!" Fannette exclaimed, indignant. "But I do feel it's a shame Jared insisted I come along. I'm certain you two could really enjoy being together today if I'd stayed back at camp."

Jared felt all good intentions melt away. "With Anton, no doubt."

"Stop it!" Poppy exclaimed. "Stop it, both of you!"

The rest of the meal passed in silence. Poppy was right. This trip should have been made by Fannette and himself alone. Pride and jealousy. Pride and jealousy, when important things were at stake.

On the way back, Fannette insisted on taking the outer seat. They rode in silence. Goddamn it, wasn't she his wife? And goddamn Anton doubly. Anton who'd spoiled what was between Fannette and himself. And Poppy. Poor, unhappy Poppy who was blamed where there should be no blame.

He glanced over at Fannette. We're too much alike, he decided. That was where part of the trouble lay.

Anton was waiting by the shack. "The men were back," he announced. "Back with posters and descriptions. They had each of our men parade in front of them."

"The women?" Jared asked.

Anton shrugged. "They didn't seem to interest them. But, *mon Dieu!* Did they want to know what happened to my face! I told them I tripped and fell into a thornbush, but, *eh bien,* they showed very little belief."

Jared had jumped down from the seat, and he reached up to help Poppy who was nearest. Jove had come running and stood below Fannette, but she smiled at Anton.

"Would you, *s'il vous plaît?*" she asked, and Anton's eyes gleamed with triumph.

"*Avec plaisir!*" he replied, reaching for her elbow. Instead, she placed her hands on his shoulders and swung down against him. He held her that way for a minute, and she laughed up into his face. Fannette of Bijou. Fannette the coquette.

"My skirt caught," she exclaimed demurely.

Like hell it did! Jared knew his face had reddened with the rage that made him tighten his fist. So, she thought she'd repay him for Poppy! There was an answer to that, too. It was time she learned where she belonged. Time to remove all doubt.

"Give Jove your packages to take up to the shack." His voice permitted no dissent. "Wait for me there."

She paused just a minute before stepping out of Anton's arms. She looked at Jared, her eyes daring him. Then she turned and went up the path. Poppy moved to follow, but Jared shook his head.

Jove had set down the parcels and was leaving as Jared came through the door. He closed it behind him, his eyes on Fannette.

She removed her head cloak, defiance in the tilt of her chin. Beautiful and imperious. And she stirred something savage in him, a part of his nature that he'd never known existed.

He crossed to where she stood and picked her up. She made no resistance, not even when he tossed her onto the

234

bed. He didn't bother with preliminaries. He stripped down her underthings and took her without tenderness. It wasn't an act of love, and he knew it. It was putting his brand on her, claiming her beyond question.

When he pulled himself off her, she made no sound, only turned her head. Somehow he was reminded of that statue she'd held back at the cottage by the ramparts. It was the day when that witch of a woman had said things that had left her so strangely subdued.

He belted his trousers, fighting a wave of shame.

"Act the whore and that's how I'll treat you," he told her.

She lay still, making no move to rearrange her skirts.

"Goddamn it!" he went on. "Can't you see I've enough worries without you playing up to Anton? Without you setting the two of us at each other's throat? I've my hands full just to keep us out of jail. Just to keep our people out of the slave catcher's hands. Doesn't that enter your self-centered little brain?"

"Why do you—do this to me, when it's Poppy you want?" Her voice was dull, calm and defeated.

"For God's sake, cover yourself!" he exclaimed in disgust.

He went to the table, and taking both the slip of her purchases and his purse out of his pocket, he carefully counted out the exact amount of the total.

"You may treat me like a harlot," she said, "but you don't have to pay me for the service."

He opened her reticule and saw that she had only a few coins left. He tossed in the money.

"I pay for what you buy. Get it through your head that you're my wife. As for intimate items, that's my pleasure."

He slammed the door behind him, and then leaned against it. Hating himself. Hating her for bringing him to what he'd done. Wanting to apologize, but too ashamed.

Pride. Pride and jealousy. And she was as guilty as he.

235

He had to get control of himself before the entire venture was destroyed by the two of them.

He owed the others that much.

At least until Cincinnati.

XVII

From the time Jared had tossed her on the bed until the door closed after him, Fannette's memory was hazy. She lost all account of the time that passed before Poppy knocked for permission to enter.

She came to full awareness when Poppy gave up knocking and came into the shack. Poppy shivered and went directly to the fire that had burned low. She tossed in some dry wood. Then she turned her attention to Fannette, who sat very still in the dimness, a small object cradled in her hands.

Without speaking, Poppy crossed the room, took the statuette from Fannette, and tossed it into the fire.

Fannette cried out. Her fingers went up to her crucifix and remained there while her eyes darted around the room. She looked at her cloak still on the floor, at the rumpled bed, at her reticule with money dumped from it onto the carpet. She went to the table and picked up the small jeweler's box. Her fingers touched the catch, and she stared down at the emerald brooch. She had only a faint memory of dumping the contents of her purse onto the floor, but there was the awareness of the sudden rage that had taken hold of her. Of the small statue tumbling into her hands, of how it had suddenly become something precious, something familiar . . .

"I think you know you acted very foolishly today," Poppy remarked, as she took the pins from her hair. She picked up her brush and paused a minute to look over at Fannette. "It wasn't very subtle, was it? Falling into Anton's arms as if he were your lover? There's so much you need to learn. You'll never excite Jared's love by such an action. Anger, maybe. Undoubtedly jealousy.

237

But not love."

"What do you know about love?" Fannette demanded. She closed the jeweler's box and dropped it into her purse. "What do you know about—" She glanced toward the bed.

"Enough. Enough to know a woman should not shame her man in front of others. Twice in two days you've made it seem Jared can't hold his own woman. I've already told you the harm this could do."

"If I went away tomorrow he'd hardly know I was gone. All that matters to him are those maroons."

"Remember that, then, and act accordingly."

"At least Anton thinks of me as a woman. Even now."

"Especially now." Poppy frowned and started to brush her hair with vigorous strokes that sent dust flying. "Between you and Juba's Sassie, we'll have every man here set against another."

"Sassie!" Fannette said contemptuously. "That's Juba's worry."

"It's all of our worry. Just as this feud you've caused between Jared and Anton. I'm not only concerned about Juba finding what she's up to, but I'm also concerned about the women. They're all ready to tear her apart."

It was a welcome relief to take her mind away from her own problems and divert them with another's.

Juba, that happy, laughing young man. Thick-set and broad-featured. Juba who brought in the biggest catch of fish, and whose snares never failed to catch a rabbit or a coon. Now that she thought back, he had been wearing a sullen, puzzled look ever since their stay at the Lemmons'.

And Sassie. Sassie sneaking into the brush, soon to be followed by a cautious, moving man who kept looking back over his shoulder . . .

And hardly ever the same man.

"We all like Juba," Poppy said, pausing to rest her arm. "But he's capable of terrible rages. Once when he was picking cotton, he wrenched the whip out of the driver's hand and almost beat him to death. Jared's worried, and so is Trojan."

Sassie—named Sarah by her mother, but called Sassie since she'd first learned to talk—hugged her knees tight against her small breasts. She had settled herself just beyond the fringe of woods and waited with half-closed eyes. She reflected on the look Hiram got when she told him where he could find her.

For a fact, she wasn't going to be able to hold him off much longer. She ran her fingers over the madras scarf he'd given her just the evening before. She suspected it belonged to his wife, because he'd warned her not to wear it until they reached that Canada place. She smiled. It was mighty pretty, all those colors.

And there was Juba reminding her that she'd promised to marry him. She supposed she might have to before long. Once a girl got herself married, that was the end of all the sweet talk and presents. Then a man got for nothing what he gave gifts and favors for before.

No doubts about it. There was reason to worry a little. And she'd done everything her ma had warned her to do, that first time she'd gone with a man.

"If I ain't gonna stop you frum sneakin' off, then mebbe I better tell you sum sense. You git him out of there when he 'bout to do it. You git it out 'fore it happen an' you ain't gonna have a parcel of younguns crawlin' 'round."

"How come you got five, den? And how come you look like you gonna have six?"

Her mother had smiled, her eyes lighting up, happy. "I gits to where I forgits to remember," she admitted. "But you git yore steady man 'fore you does that."

Well, Sassie thought, she'd never really liked doing it that much. Just the pretty talk and the good things they brought her while they waited for her to let them do more

239

than to put their hands in places. It beat her why a man always wanted to be feeling around a girl.

She heard Hiram come through the brush. She looked up at him with a wide smile.

"Why jus' look who here!" she said. "How you find me?"

"Jus' so my woman, Anabel, don' find me," he grinned.

He threw himself down beside her. "Sassie, girl, tonight I ain' gonna be put off. Tonight you ain' gonna git away like you do last night."

"I ain't?" She laughed, moving his hand to where she knew he liked to put it. "Juba, he out with a fishin' line. Reckon now's as good a time as any . . ."

XVIII

Fannette put her head out over the side of the phaeton and watched the shack disappear from sight. She knew there wasn't a crevice or corner of it that she'd ever forget. If there was anything left of Fannette Randolph of Bijou and the Esplanade Publique, it was in that room.

And what lay ahead? It was better not to think about it. She watched through unseeing eyes while they passed the stand of timber that had concealed the place.

Then, once again, they were back on the River Road. The three-day rest had done much toward lifting the spirit of the company. No one even remembers Tansy and her baby, Fannette mused, marveling that such a thing could be forgotten so soon.

And her own innocence. That lay back there in the shack, too. Jared rode ahead, and her eyes dwelt on him, unclothing him, remembering what it had been to lie in his smoothly muscled arms. Remembering his anger when he'd thrown her on the bed in the shack.

And the emerald brooch back in her reticule. Who was Jared? What was he? Quixotic, and then practical. Tight-fisted, and then generous. A tender, considerate lover who was capable of using her as if she were a whore. He was all of those things. And none.

And who am I? she wondered, realizing that she no longer knew. Only that she had changed, and was still changing.

The following days they passed by a cluster of rich plantation homes around St. Francisville. Finally they left Louisiana behind as they crossed the border into Mississippi.

Three more days and they'd be in Natchez. Three more days and the familiar river with its splendid boats would be left behind. Her last connection with New Orleans. No more watching the bright torches and flaming smoke-stacks from the river bank. No more imagining she was one of those extravagantly crinolined ladies dressing for a ball in a sparkling grand salon.

Did she regret what she was leaving? She wasn't certain. It could all be hers again, should she change her mind.

So could Bijou. So could Breel . . .

If she went back, would they know she was different when they looked at her? See in her eyes what had happened in the shack? Know that when she thought of Jared in the night she felt an ache that was almost a physical pain in places a lady shouldn't even think about?

No. She could never again be Fannette of Bijou. Not anymore than she could remain the girl Anton had courted.

She looked over at Anton who had paced his horse with the phaeton. He rode alongside, chattering with Poppy. Poppy had said something witty because they both broke into laughter. How could he have once meant everything to her? How could she now not feel even a tinge of envy? Envy was reserved for those times Jared paused to talk with Poppy. Jared who'd avoided looking in her own direction since—since what had happened when they came back from Baton Rouge.

She turned away from them and saw Juba plodding along near the edge of the road. Well, she wasn't alone. Juba had changed, too. No longer a laughing, happy young man with a joke for every difficulty. He was watching Sassie who'd gotten out of the spring wagon to walk alongside Nate Lack. And where was Lillie, Nate's wife? Probably watching through lowered, suspicious lids.

Anton rode on ahead and Poppy followed the direction

242

of Fannette's eyes.

"I tried talking to Sassie," she said. "But she just bobbed her head and giggled."

Jove turned to look back at them.

"You talk about Sassie? She after me, but she let me alone when I tell her I ain't gonna give her something pretty. I tell her anything pretty I get go to Zette."

Poppy spread her hands. "I don't suppose she's ever had much that was her own, and all this attention is bound to have gone to her head."

"Her head?" Jove chuckled. "Wherever it go, that ain't gonna be nothing to what'll happen if Lillie catch her with Nate. She been goin' with him last one, two nights. That Lillie, she mighty jealous woman."

That night Sassie was caught *en flagrant*. Not by Lillie, but by Juba.

From inside her tent, Fannette heard Sassie's sudden protesting shrieks. She and Poppy looked at each other in quick comprehension, and then they ran outside. Sassie was standing near a clump of trees, her kinky hair in disarray and her frock still tumbled. Juba was steadily pounding Nate with his fists, hauling him up to resume pounding everytime the slightly-built man fell to the ground.

It took three of them, Jared, George Washington and Trojan, to pull Juba away. Meanwhile Sassie kept up a steady scream.

George Washington wrenched a bloody knife out of Juba's fingers, and Pearl caught Sassie by the shoulders, shaking her.

"Shut yore mouth 'fore we have every man in the county here!" she exclaimed. Sassie shut up suddenly, her wide eyes on the knife George Washington held. It was dripping blood.

"You don' wanna cut Nate no more," George Washington told Juba gently. "Ain't gonna fix nothing."

Crane was helping Nate to sit up. The lobe was missing

243

from his left ear, and Glory hurried forward to stop the bleeding.

"Ain't nothin' gonna be set right 'less I kills him," Juba said.

"Then you gonna have to kill most every man in dis camp," Trojan reasoned. "Ain't many can say they ain't been foolin' 'round with her."

Sassie's scream cut through the air again. Fannette pulled her skirts back as Lillie lurched at the girl, and the two of them rolled across the ground. Lillie was obviously getting the best of the battle, and no one showed an inclination to break it up except Pearl.

Well, Fannette thought, she's probably about the only woman who didn't have anything to worry about.

Pearl called to Emily, and between them they finally stopped the fight. Lillie triumphantly held up a handful of Sassie's hair and a madras scarf she'd ripped from the bodice of Sassie's dress.

Sassie wrung her hands, wailing. "Us done nothin' bad. Jus' sum playin', mebbe. But swear to de Lord, we done nothin' bad!"

There was another screech, as Hiram's buxom wife, Anabel, snatched the scarf from Lillie's hand.

"Where you git that?" she demanded of Sassie.

"Where you think?" Sassie asked, suddenly impudent. "Woman can't keep her man, she ain't got nobody but her to blame."

Juba's eyes darted wildly from Nate back to Hiram. He tugged and wrenched, trying to free himself.

"Pack your things and leave," Jared said to him. "Pack your belongings and find your way by yourself."

"It ain't right!" Sassie shrieked in sudden defense of her would-be husband. "He pay his way like everybody else!"

Jared looked at her in disgust.

"I'd send you on your way too," he said. "Except it's against my principles to turn a woman out alone. Especially when I think what I'd do to you in Juba's place."

244

Trojan started to move forward to speak, but Anton touched him lightly on the arm. "I know Jared from the past," he said. "It's best to leave him until he quiets."

"He not mad," Trojan replied. "He worried. That Juba a good man, and I don' like to see him go. That Sassie, now . . ." Trojan made a noise deep in his throat.

George Washington gave Juba back his knife. Without a word, Juba wiped it clean and stuck it back into his belt. Then he went to the men's tent to get his pack.

The next morning Sassie was gone.

"He's killed her!" Fannette exclaimed, remembering Jared's words. "He hid at the edge of camp until he found his chance, and he killed her!"

"Nonsense," Poppy replied calmly. "Her clothes and bedding are gone. He came for her, and she sneaked out of the tent while the others slept. He didn't have killing in his mind."

They had passed Natchez and were camped near a vast Indian mound, when Fannette found that Poppy had correctly assessed the matter.

"*Nom de chien!*" Anton exclaimed as they sat in a circle, waiting for dinner. "Is that not the *femme fatale?* That Sassie bitch?"

It was Sassie. A very subdued Sassie trailing after Juba. They had been gone for three days, but she went straight to the women's tent where she left her belongings. Tossing them inside as freely as if she'd just taken them from the wagon.

Juba made his way through the others and stopped when he found Wednesday.

"Preacher," Juba said, "you git that Holy Book and say the words. Sassie ain' goin' hoppin' anymore."

Dinner preparations came to a standstill. Ever mindful of his wife's wrath where her cooking might suffer, Wednesday hurried through the passages.

"And now," he announced, "we all sing a song praising the Lord . . ." His eyes met his wife's warning glare. "After our supper, that is."

"Juba still has to go," Jared said.

Trojan shook his head. "Mr. Jared," he said, "when you goes after Mr. Anton for yore woman, ain't no one says you gotta go."

Jared looked at him for a long minute, then, unexpectedly, he started to laugh.

"Damned if you haven't a point!" he agreed. He made his way to the new bridegroom and shook his hand.

"Welcome to the brotherhood," he said. Then he added, his eyes on Fannette, "And may you be as confused as the rest of us!"

After supper, he brought out some rum. Long after the usual bedding-down time, Fannette and Poppy could hear joking and singing by the big open fire.

"Poor Juba," Poppy murmured.

"I don't know," Fannette replied enviously. "Sassie looked mighty content." Then she added, "What do you think happened?"

Poppy giggled.

They passed close to the Indian mound the next day, a broad mesa where once the Creek, Choctaw and Natchez tribes had played their games of competition. They looked up at the man-created heights above. Earth-filled basket by basket, a tribe too ancient to have a remembered name had constructed the huge hill in the center of the natural mound. But now, Fannette reflected, there was no longer anyone left to engage in sports events on the lower level, nor anyone to erect the ceremonial canopy on the upper. No one was left to worship whatever had been worshiped from the high place.

The country was winter bare. In some places, where the Trace had sunk down due to loess earth, packed hard by

246

thousands of feet through the years, it was like riding through a topless tunnel. Twisting brown tree roots lined the high banks on either side, and the branches and limbs of growth above stretched to meet in a barren embrace.

In the spring, Fannette told herself, everything would be a filmy haze of greenery, and bright scarlet tanagers would flit through the leaves. There would be the white beauty of blossoming dogwood and the purple hues of the redbud. But now there were only grim ghosts stretching out gnarled arms. She felt a strange sensation that she was trespassing into the past. That what lay ahead was a warning of the future.

I'm becoming fanciful, she chided herself. Yet she was seldom without a sense of unease. A feeling that something was waiting around the corner. And Jared . . . Jared who laughed with Poppy, conversed with Anton, conferred with Trojan—and who averted his eyes when ever she was near . . .

The rains started again, but the stands and inns that had once offered travelers shelter of a sort were now abandoned. Or, like Mount Locust, no longer open to the public.

The creeks were narrow and not yet swollen by the runoff of spring rains, but the banks were too high for wagon wheels. There were constant delays while trees were felled for bridges, and lashing the logs together was time consuming. Jared fussed and fumed, but Old Chippers, the carpenter, refused to be rushed.

"Ain't no way to make the work go fast," he said.

The phaeton was always the first to cross the makeshift bridges, then the furniture and cook wagons. The spring wagons with the women were last, though Fannette noticed that more and more of the women were choosing to walk across the planks, rather than to ride inside the swaying, bumping conveyances.

Fannette was sitting in the phaeton waiting for the last vehicles to cross a creek when the accident happened. She

247

had been watching the stately progress of a flock of snowy egrets and half listening to Wednesday leading a spiritual to urge on the last crossing.

"Roll de old chariot along, yes,
Roll de old chariot along, yes,
Ef yo don' hang on behin',
O, Christians, roll de old chariot along.

Devil's in de way,
Jus' roll right over,
If de devil's in de way,
Jus' roll right over,
An yo mus hang on behin', O Christians . . ."

Screams and the crashing of a heavy vehicle sent the egrets into the air, a fast moving white cloud. Both Fannette and Poppy jumped down from the phaeton and ran to the creek. A wheel in the last of the wagons had lodged in a crevice, toppling the canvas-covered cart into the water.

The fall was not a matter of a great distance, but the women inside were thrown into a heap. The icy water rushed through the front opening and out the back, soaking their clothing.

No one was badly hurt, and when the wagon was righted, Old Chippers decided it could be repaired. The women stood by shivering, water streaming from their heavy skirts.

Jared ordered a fire built and the women's tent set up. The drenched women went inside to strip off their garments, and gradually they emerged, wrapped in blankets and toweling their hair. Meantime the men strung up lines, and those who had crossed on foot, or gone in the first wagons, wrung out the wet articles and hung them to dry.

"Thanks to Our Lady, it isn't raining, anyway," Poppy said. She looked around. "Wasn't Willie's wife, Junie, in that wagon?"

"She ask to stay inside," Lillie offered. "She coughin'

248

pretty bad."

Pearl stood up. "She need the fire," she said, and went into the tent. She came out with Junie's wasted body cradled in her arms. She carried the frail woman as easily as she'd have carried a child, and she set her down near the fire.

"You jus' set here and git warm," she instructed Junie, but Junie slumped over.

Jared paused in his work and went to her.

"Get Glory!" he called to Trojan.

Junie tried to straighten up and gave a strangled cry. She tried to jam some black, chewy substance into her mouth, but still she coughed.

Fannette knelt beside her, pulling up the blanket that had slipped away from the hunched shoulders.

"Don' tell Lem . . ." Junie sobbed to Pearl. "Lem ain' to know I sick till . . . that place . . . Cincinnati."

Till Cincinnati. Fannette felt a chill, and she tightened the drawstrings on her warm furred hood.

XIX

"I've never felt so useless in all my life," Fannette protested to Poppy. "There must be something I can do!"

Junie, barely conscious, lay in the back of the cook wagon. Throughout the afternoon and evening Glory and Poppy had worked over her, and Letty had long since carried her bedding to the women's tent. Trojan was kept busy feeding the cookfire, while Emily had broth simmering. Kettles of water were at a constant boil to provide the steam Glory used to infiltrate the air around the pallet.

And still Junie gasped and coughed. It seemed to Fannette that no one's lungs could stand the punishment much longer.

Poppy poured boiling water into a basin and dropped in a liquid Glory had given her.

"It smells awful," Fannette added.

"It eases her breathing," Poppy replied, wrinkling her nose. "But it's only a matter of time . . ."

"Can't you make Wednesday stop leading everyone in those mournful spirituals?" Fannette asked, glancing toward the group gathered around the little preacher. "If I were dying, that would really upset me."

"You don't understand," Poppy said. "That's their way of praying. It gives Junie comfort."

Willie, a squat, yellow-skinned man, broke free of the group and came up to Poppy.

"How Junie?" He asked anxiously. "She still cough?"

"Glory's helping her," Poppy evaded.

Willie lowered his head and went back to the prayer meeting. Mellow voices rose in harmony:

"Oh, who is that acomin'?
Don't you grieve after me.

Oh, who is that acomin'?
Don't you grieve after me.
It looks like Gabriel,
Don't you grieve after me.
Lord, I don't want you to grieve after me."

Later, when Poppy came back to the cookfire to dip a cloth into steaming water, Fannette was still waiting, sometimes refilling a pot, sometimes adding a piece of wood.

"There's no use for you to stay up," Poppy said. "It's getting cold, and I promise I'll call you if I'm tired and need help. Why don't you try to rest?"

Poppy took the steaming cloth from the pot with a stick and went back to the wagon. Fannette stood up, realizing for the first time that it had turned cold and she felt stiff.

Then she realized Jared was watching her. He took a step in her direction, hesitated, then turned aside to go to Willie who sat nearby, face buried in his hands.

She had no right to be disappointed, she told herself. Blessed Virgin, didn't Jared have enough on his mind? Nothing but delays. Time had been lost removing fallen logs from across unused portions of the Trace and felling trees for new bridges. Then there was that three day wait while the bottomlands dried out after a torrential rain. Now a wagon had to be repaired and a woman was too sick for them to go on, even if the equipment were ready to roll.

She undressed and shivered as she pulled the covers up under her chin. She missed Poppy, and she felt depressed, lonely. And Jared . . . She must face the truth. He had pulled himself away from her as far as possible. Whatever he had felt was gone now. And it had been her own stupidity, her own pride, that had pushed him from her.

Why can't I be the one in there dying? she thought rebelliously. Junie had a man who loved her and would miss her. And what did she, Fannette, have? The memory of

251

one night spent in the arms of her lover. Could one night last out a lifetime?

She thought of the statuette. Of the comfort it had given her.

Why had Poppy thrown the doleful little figurine into the flames?

Outside, the fire blazed up, and shadows flickered against the tent walls. There were muffled voices and the constant rending sound of Junie coughing. There were footsteps that drew near. Poppy?

There was the darkening outline of someone standing near the entrance of her tent. Then it moved away.

Perhaps she was needed outside? She sat up, listening.

The footsteps returned. The shadow remained on the canvas for several minutes. Then the tent flooded with light as Jared stepped inside holding a lantern.

Fannette clutched the covers to her breasts. "Do they need me out there?" she asked.

"No." His voice sounded strange. "Glory's steam pots seem to have eased Junie's breathing, and Poppy says the poultices are beginning to do some good."

"Oh."

They regarded each other in silence. Jared's curly beard was clipped short and merged with his sideburns, contrasting with his deeply tanned skin and the startling blue of his eyes. He stood above her, a young buccaneer, a soldier of fortune from some previous century.

"I've come to apologize," he said. "I've never before mistreated a woman. Not even a whore."

"Thank you for the comparison," she replied coldly. "But why now? And why here?"

"You're alone."

"I've been alone a number of times."

He set the lantern on the stand and dropped to his knees beside the pallet.

"It was inexcusable," he said, all arrogance gone.

She didn't trust her voice. She was too aware of his

252

nearness. Of the tumult of her own emotions.

"When you smiled up at Anton, I went crazy. I had to prove you belonged to me."

"You'd given Poppy all your attention the entire day. I'm surprised you even noticed. I might just as well have been a door post."

"I was teaching you a lesson."

"Thank you again."

"Christ!" he exploded. "You all but invited Anton to—"

She stared at him, furious.

"That's what you think of me? When you know you're the only man who—"

"But it was Anton you wanted. Any man would recognize the invitation in your smile."

Her palm cracked against his jaw, and he caught her wrist.

"That's the second time you've done that," he told her, his voice like ice. "There'd better not be a third."

She tried to turn her head, but he took hold of her chin, forcing her to meet his eyes.

"You've made everything sordid and dirty," she whispered, ashamed of the tears rolling down her cheeks.

"Fannette . . ." he pleaded, humble once again.

"I thought what happened with us was special." She tried to control her voice. "Then you turned to Poppy as if it was something to be forgotten in the morning."

"Like hell it was," he said. "Like hell it was!"

He pulled her against him, pressing her to his chest, kissing her hair, whispering, comforting.

She lifted her face to his and found his lips. His hands moved over her shoulders, drawing her closer.

"Send me away," he pleaded. "Send me away, Fannette . . ."

"No."

"I made myself a promise . . ."

"Whenever anyone passed near the tent, I prayed it was

253

you . . ." Her arms still around his neck, she fell back on the pillow, taking him with her. "I need you. Oh, Jared I can hardly stand it, I need you so!"

He lay next to her, their mouths locked in a kiss while his hands traveled from her breasts to her thigh and then into intimate places.

"See?" she whispered, and shuddered to his touch. She murmured softly, pleasurably, urging him, unable to restrain her hunger for him.

He moved away, and she heard the thud of his boots, then the rustle of material as he took off his clothing. He put out the lantern, and then he was back beside her, their bodies pressed together.

"You're certain, Nette?" His tongue flicked the inside of her ear. His breath quickened with his desire, and when she moved against him, she could feel his arousal. "My darling, you're certain?"

"Yes . . ." she whispered. "Now . . . please, now!"

"Oh, I've wanted you . . . wanted you . . ."

And I love you . . . love you, she thought. Tell me you love me . . . She spoke to him. "Hurry. . . oh, hurry!"

And they were climbing again. Climbing in a glorious burst of color, of light, of almost unendurable pleasure. Reaching the pinnacle. Then lying close in the after-rapture of their union.

He pulled back the covers. Though the night was frosty, they both were misted with perspiration. He deliberately set about kissing every inch of her. His beard scratched her abdomen, and she quivered as his breath played over her skin, lips touching, fondling, until she was trembling and stretching, calling out to him again.

"I told you to send me away," he reminded her, laughing softly. "My beautiful, beautiful Nette, I warned you to send me away."

"You knew I couldn't. Jared, I've no shame at all!"

Later, when they lay quiet in the darkness, still close, still entwined, she tried to put what she felt into words.

254

"I think of it as climbing a hill with you right beside me. Each step brings a new, wonderful sensation, until we've come together in a blinding blaze of joy and oneness. I know that then I'm you and you're me."

"I wonder if you realize that it's not every man and woman who reach what we reach together," he said.

"I know." She hesitated. "At Donna's teas her guests talked about women things and forgot I was sitting in a corner."

"An education, Fannette!"

"No. They never came out and explained the things I really wanted to know." She cuddled closer. "It took you to show me that. Mostly they talked about their husbands. How now that they had provided children, they were glad their husbands took a mistress. Jared, I've heard some of them say that they were glad not to be bothered with . . . unpleasant duties. That's how they described it."

His arm tightened around her.

"That's why I didn't worry when Anton's lovemaking—"

"What!"

"Shh. They'll hear you outside." She nibbled his ear. "Anton's kisses, you idiot. You must know he kissed me? But I was glad when he stopped. I thought that was how it was with a woman. Until the afternoon when you took me for a ride in that closed carriage."

"The carriage." He chuckled. "That, my dear, was when I learned I had no control where you were concerned."

"Nor I with you." She giggled. "Zette looked at me with real respect when I gave her my dress to mend."

She lay with her head on his shoulder, enjoying the nearness as much as what had gone on before. The protective shelter of his arms.

"My wonderful, obstinate wife . . ." he murmured.

The words cut into her contentment. Above all, it was necessary that they be honest with each other. Maybe, that

255

way, the hurt that was bound to eventually come might be lessened. She was his mistress, used when there was the need, and set aside when the need was satisfied. It was a fact she was now willing to face and to accept. Anton had said she could expect no more, considering who her mother was. And certainly there was nothing in Jared's manner toward her that bore any resemblance to the relationship of a man with his wife.

"We both know what I am to you," she reminded him gently. "And it's not a wife."

His body grew rigid, and she felt him draw away. His voice was harsh when he spoke.

"You are my wife. No matter what Anton or anyone else may say, there's nothing can change the fact. Can you deny we stood before a judge and a wedding was performed?"

It was a temptation. He must realize how great a temptation, but she knew she could not let the truth be altered. Not even for what brief happiness the altering might buy for her.

The words weren't easy to say, but they must be said.

"And can you deny that we both realized it was just a form? Something to be annulled once the reason for it was past? Don't you remember saying that frankly you had no desire to marry me?"

"That isn't what I said at all!" he replied angrily. "I didn't make a statement, I asked a question. I asked if you thought I wanted a marriage to you. Ask me now, and I'll give you the answer."

He paused. "Besides, those grounds don't exist anymore. That's what Poppy informed me when she washed my cuts after the fight with Anton. She said I'd have to find grounds other than nonconsummation if I really wanted an annulment. That's why I kissed her."

"Kissing Poppy seems to be one of your habits." The bitterness was back in her voice, along with the return of jealousy. "And what grounds do you intend to use when the time comes?"

"Fannette!" he exclaimed, leaning on his elbow. "For the love of God! Must you make this a rut in the hay?"

"I want it understood that there's no reason to lie to me. To make promises you know you can't keep."

He sat up and threw back the covers.

"Until there's absolutely no question as to the validity of our relationship, I'll stay clear of you," he told her. "God help me, Fannette, I'll find another woman before I'll come to you!"

She caught his arm. "No," she begged, "please. Don't go away, Jared. Please don't go away. . ."

He spoke quietly, in self-disgust. "I told you that I came to apologize—and we both knew it was only an excuse. You were alone, and I couldn't stay away from you." He gathered up his clothing while he talked, and then he got to his feet. "Now I need to apologize again."

"Why?" She reached out for him, but he moved. "I came to you willingly. Even that first time, in the shack."

He looked down at her, as though trying to see her face in the dim light from outside.

"And I bore the marks of my conquest for nearly a week," he reminded her, his voice softening.

"And I bear them now." She lowered her eyes, remembering. "I'll need to wear a scarf tomorrow."

He knelt down beside her and touched her throat with light fingers. "My darling, I didn't realize . . ."

She caught and held his hand, and hope filled her when he kissed her lips.

"No," he said as he drew back. "It's no use. Not this way."

Sudden light washed over them, and the sound of Poppy's startled gasp.

"I'm sorry!" she exclaimed, embarrassed, and she started to retreat, but Jared called after her.

"I'll be out in a few minutes. Don't go away."

She paused. "I'd never have intruded if I'd known. I'll

stay with Junie. Glory needs to rest more than I do."

She dropped the tent flap back into place, and Jared swore as he finished pulling on his clothing.

"This time," he said, "I hope I've the guts to stick by my promise. Stop crying, damn it!"

"But there's no need to make promises!" she sobbed. "I don't want you to go! I'll be anything you want me to be . . ."

"Except my wife."

"Except to pretend."

He started to leave, and Fannette lifted herself up.

"Go, then," she stormed after him. "Go find a whore the next time you need a woman! Just do that!"

He paused. "Nette . . . Nette, I don't think that you understand—"

"Oh, but I do!" She tossed back her tousled hair, hating herself. Hating every word she said. "I do! And I hate you! Do your hear? I hate you!"

With her words still ringing in his ears, Jared ducked through the opening and out into the night. Poppy stood a little distance away, near the log fire.

"Jared," she said as he came up to her, "I cannot understand how a reasonably intelligent man can be such a stupendous fool."

"The first minute I know she's alone," he muttered bitterly, "I sneak into her bed like a dog with its tail between its legs."

Poppy smiled slightly, some of the mischief glinting in her eyes. "Not exactly," she corrected.

Jared felt a warmth creep into his face.

"For a young girl," he remarked, "you're damnably sophisticated."

"How could I be otherwise?" She sat on a stump, and he realized how tired she was. She stretched her hands out to the warmth of the flames.

"What's the matter?" she asked.

Jared scowled and shoved at a burning ember, prodding

258

it with the toe of his boot.

"It would seem the idea of being my wife is distasteful. She prefers the title of mistress."

Poppy remained silent.

"Goddamn it! The next time we pass near a town that has a church, I'll settle it once and for all. I'll take her to a priest even if I have to drag her to the altar. Certainly a man who's sworn to secrecy for confessions can keep his mouth shut about—what was Anton's term?—blessing the marriage."

"I wish I could tell you it could be as easy as that," Poppy said. "It isn't, you know. There's too many things standing in the way. Things that take time. And someone would be bound to find out."

"So?"

"Where would your story be? She's your dowried bride, you must remember. What's between you and Fannette cannot become more important than what might happen to our people."

"Hells bells! What more is required? We've proof of a civil marriage. And we . . . have been together. Isn't that enough?"

"You may be a lawyer, but you're not a Roman Catholic. Have you ever even been baptized?"

He shook his head. "My parents were principled folks. Firm and honest, direct from Scotland. But they weren't religious."

"You'd have to be baptized. No priest would marry Fannette to a pagan. Then there are other things. If you were Anton, it'd be simple. But not for you."

"Christ!" he exploded. "I'll become a Catholic, then! I'll do anything that has to be done!"

"There are things you'll have to learn. Promises to make—and keep. A confirmation." She shook her head. "It can all be done with time, and I can teach you. But meanwhile, she is your wife, and you do have rights."

He made an unpleasant noise.

"Show her the respect she deserves," Poppy said, her eyes beseeching him in the firelight. "Share the tent with her. I really wouldn't mind taking my things to the women's tent, and it would look more convincing."

He shook his head.

"Treat her as a wife instead of as a woman you visit when you've a need. Prove you love her."

"How can I when she thinks the way she does?"

"Do you imagine it's a secret that you were with her tonight? I'd have known even if I hadn't been with Junie. Have you ever thought about how Fannette will feel to know everyone's whispering that she was bedded last night?"

"It won't happen again," he promised grimly. Then, in a humbler vein, "I hope to God it won't, anyway."

Poppy shrugged. "*Je m'en lave les mains!*" she murmured. "I've told you what needs to be told."

His eyes searched into hers. "All of this is very hard for a 'pagan' to understand. You tell me that Fannette—who I doubt ever remembers to even say a prayer—feels she's sinning when we make love. Yet, you who carry a rosary in your pocket and never eat a meal without saying a blessing tell me I should take her to me as wife even though we don't have the sanction of a priest."

"The sanction will come later, and perhaps it's not as important to me because of where I was raised. For a *placee* there can be no question of marriage. *C'est impossible!* A priest's blessing? Also impossible. Yet they are the most faithful of women. And they are the most married. Perhaps this matter means less to me than to Fannette, who was raised to believe anything else is unthinkable."

"I see." He nodded his head.

"We are of the same mother, but we were raised in such a different manner. For instance, French is the language I first learned and is more natural to me. While Fannette thinks of English first, though Donna's family was of Santo Domingo and Breel's mother was French." Poppy rose and pulled her jacket tight. "It's cold, even by the fire."

She moved quietly across the clearing and went into the tent. At the sound of a muffled sob, she knelt by Fannette.

"Don't," she whispered. "Nette, *chérie,* don't!"

But there was nothing further she could say or do.

XX

"Junie's better, but not well enough for the road," Poppy told Jared the next morning.

"We'll stay over." He scowled. "Chippers's still got work to do on the damaged wagon anyway."

He moved away, kicking at a rock, and Poppy watched, knowing his ugly mood wasn't caused by the delay.

She poked at her breakfast. Did staying over really make any difference? Junie was dying, and Junie knew it. She'd be the last person to ask for special consideration. And why did she keep calling Lem? Willie was her husband. Was Lem a former lover that came to her mind in her sickness? Somehow that didn't fit with her concern for her husband. No, there was more to it than that.

Fannette came out of the tent, and Poppy noticed that she was paler, thinner. She bit her lip in exasperation. Between the two of them, Fannette and Jared were doing more to hurt the unity of the caravan than any fight Juba might have had over Sassie.

She looked over at Sassie and watched her bring Juba his breakfast. At least that was settled.

She made room beside her for Fannette.

"I don't feel up to breakfast," Fannette said. "Is Junie . . ."

"She's still alive. If Letty agrees to let her ride in the back of the wagon, we could start out again tomorrow."

"I heard Junie call Willie by a different name. Do you think Willie might not be his real name?"

"It's to be considered," Poppy said thoughtfully. "Yes. You could be right."

Fannette looked at the line forming by the cookstove. "How many of them are going by different names?" she

262

wondered aloud. "How many. . ."

"It's better not even to talk about it. Much better not to know."

Poppy took her dish to the stack of dirty plates and moved to the wagon where Junie lay. Junie would never make it to Canada. But how many of their people would? The venture had started to crumble with Tansy. How long before everything fell apart?

And did Fannette realize it had been she who'd brought on this damage? But that was unfair. Fannette had done what she thought was right to do. And had it really been Fannette? Glory had startled her by talking during the long nightwatch over Junie.

"A good thing you take that *obeah*. Good you give him to the fire."

Strange, had Glory really spoken or had it been her imagination?

And was it the statue of the grieving Persephone that she meant? *Obeah*. A fetish, a charm. A talisman. Something connected with another world.

"I must not let myself become imaginative," Poppy told herself.

XXI

The next night they camped near the busy little town of Rocky Springs, and the following morning Fannette watched Jared and Trojan leave in the wagon to purchase supplies. It was impossible not to remember that other supply trip to Baton Rouge nearly a month ago.

She moved over to the fireside where the women sat sewing the warm clothing they'd cut from the bolts of cloth purchased on that occasion. Even Sassie was busy with a needle.

What a different Sassie! Never a glance toward any man other than Juba. A word from him, and she'd drop everything to tend to his wants. Each morning she brought him his filled bowl, and each evening his plate. Now she was intent on hemming what could only be a scarf for him to wear.

"She jus' need to find out who boss," Juba had explained to Anton.

"A veritable miracle," Anton had acknowledged. "*Bien*. For you it works, for me it does not."

Jared and Trojan returned in time for lunch, and afterwards he and Poppy sat at a little distance from the others, deeply involved in a discussion. Fannette watched them with growing resentment.

She buried her pride and drew Poppy aside later.

"What is it that you and Jared find so interesting? You talked with him for nearly an hour."

"I'm teaching him," Poppy told her. "There are things he must know." Then, without warning, she kissed Fannette on the cheek.

"*Chérie,* we both love you very much."

Fannette said a word she'd never expect to ever use and

264

turned away.

Junie was wrapped in a blanket and propped near the fire. She held a needle and cloth cut to the pattern of a shirt, but her head was on her chest, her eyes closed.

At least, Fannette thought, that was something she could do. She took the material from the limp fingers and started to work. Junie opened her eyes to watch.

"I neber finish that," she said. "I knows when I starts that mebbe I neber finish."

"Oh Junie!" Fannette chided. "You're so much better!"

Junie shook her head and closed her eyes again.

In the early morning they left the camp by the springs, and the wagons rolled over the sunken Trace again. Only earthen banks twined with bare roots were visible on either side. Brown, Fannette thought. Bare. Dismal. She looked back. Of the thriving town they had just left, only the steeple of the little church on the hill could still be seen.

Jared had mentioned stopping at Dean's Stand the next night, but when they drew near to the old inn, it was obviously abandoned.

"We'll get in a few more miles," Jared decided. He rode next to the phaeton. His eyes lingered on Fannette.

"Maybe you'd rather stop now? You look tired."

She shook her head.

Tired? Yes, she had never felt so tired in all her life. Riding in the phaeton. Wondering how long it would hold up under the punishment of rough roads. Eating. Sleeping. Waking in the night to a loneliness she'd never known before. Eating again, riding, eating. Not enjoying her food, finding that everything irritated her. She, Fannette, whose sunny disposition had always delighted Donna. Irritated at everyone and everything. Wondering if it was because certain things hadn't happened when they should have. Travel, she'd often heard at Donna's teas, was almost certain to throw a woman off her natural course.

And looking up to find that Glory was watching her . . .

265

She was tired of hearing Junie cough in the night. Of hearing Jared swear when another creek had to be bridged. Of barren trees that looked as if never again would they grow leaves to soften the outlines of a grim winter forest and the steel-gray of a bleak sky.

Avoiding well-used roads, one night they camped near the town of Jackson. Again Trojan and Jared rode into town for supplies. Sitting around the fire, trying to get warm, she waited for a dinner she didn't want. She watched Pearl and George Washington stroll past, hand in hand. Married seven years, and it was as if they'd just discovered each other.

Seven years. And she and Jared couldn't spend one night of lovemaking without it ending in a fight.

Sassie and Juba were pressed close together by the open fire. Poppy was talking seriously with Jared. Poppy was laughing with Anton. Willie—or was it Lem?—was watching over Junie. Sometimes she thought only she and Jove were alone. And Jove knew Zette was waiting for him back in Louisiana.

There were bright moments when Jared paused in what he was doing, to talk to her, to worry because she was pale. But it was as if they were strangers—except for his obvious desire not to touch her. When their eyes met, she felt a warming glow, as if they were in actual physical contact. And she knew it was the same with him. Once she looked at him in a way that told him she knew he was stirred, and he turned away, angry.

At night she lay awake, imagining she heard his footsteps outside the tent. Damn Anton! she thought. If it weren't for Anton sleeping in the same tent with Jared, nothing could have kept her from going to him. Like a harlot, she told herself. Yes, like the whore he'd called her. But it didn't matter. Nothing could take away the deep hurt inside her chest. An actual, physical, choking pain.

Why couldn't he be as impulsive as Anton? Why did she have to love a stubborn Scotsman? And had he found other women? And, today, when he'd gone into Jackson, was it really for supplies?

Then she'd hear Junie coughing, moaning between spasms, and she'd feel shame.

The next day they passed another Indian mound, a burial place, but Jared pressed them onward.

"There's bottomland and a cypress swamp on ahead," he said. "The weather's been fair, and with good luck, we'll pass the marshy places without too much trouble. Providing the rain holds off."

And it was there, by the Cypress Swamps, that what Tansy had started bore fruit.

They'd only begun to pitch the tents when Juba came running out of the woods. He was still holding his snares, and a fishing line was tucked under his arm.

"It de slave men!" he shouted to Jared. "I see dem way down de road, roun' dat bend. And dey leadin' anuder horse like dey 'spect to catch sumpin'!"

Jared moved quickly to the smaller furniture wagon and took his gun from a trunk. He strapped it around his hips, and then he continued calmly with the work of setting up camp.

Junie, wrapped in a blanket, had already been led to a place by the newly-built fire. Fannette saw the anxious look she darted toward Willie.

"Las' time they comes," she said to Fannette, "they make Willie show the place on his neck. They keep askin' him things."

Two men rode into the clearing. Even in the growing dimness of the winter evening, Fannette recognized them. She glanced quickly at Jared, but he continued to supervise the laying out of the encampment.

The men tied up the horses and then stood by, watching.

"I want the women's tent put over there," Jared said to Chippers. Then he glanced at the two slave catchers.

"And to what do I owe this honor?"

"We missed you seeing us off back at Baton Rouge."

"Yes," Jared agreed. "That rum was potent."

Sam nodded. "Had a head for two days. But let's see, that was near a month ago. I'm ready to take on more now."

"Mighty good likker," his partner agreed.

"Am I to believe you gentlemen have followed me all this way just to get a snootful of my rum?"

"Well, now that you mention it, not exactly," Sam said. "For a fact, we come to get Yellar Lem."

Fannette was still standing by Junie, and she heard the stifled cry. Willie shot a warning glance in their direction.

Sam took a poster from his saddlebag.

"This here's a description of a nigger name of Lemuel. Yellar Lem, they called him."

Jared's body was tense, his eyes alert.

"No one here by that name," he said easily.

Sam pointed to the men driving tent stakes. "Time we came back to see you when you was in Baton Rouge, I thought I'd seen a notice that reminded me of that short, yellow-skinned nigger over there. Now, I'll bet that if he takes off that coat he's wearing, there'll be a big slash on his neck, like he near lost his head. Get him to drop his pants, and I'll bet you another bottle of rum you'll see he's got a *K* branded on the left side of his ass."

"I haven't the habit of looking to see what a man might have on his ass," Jared replied. "As for his neck, everyone knows it was an accident in a grinding mill."

"Grinding mill, shit!" Tom said. "He was never out of a cotton field till he took up with a murderin' band of cut-throat niggers. Killed near eleven white folks, it says here."

He pulled his gun and motioned with it to Willie.

"Get over here, nigger!" he shouted.

Willie took a quick look around, then with a sudden motion, he threw his hammer at Tom and sprinted for the cover of cypress.

Tom jumped aside and leveled his gun. Junie gave a

268

sharp cry and threw herself at him. The gun went off, making a muffled explosion, and Junie fell to the ground, a crumpled, lifeless heap of old blankets.

On the edge of the clearing, Willie stopped and spun around. He ran back to where Junie lay and turned her face upward. Then he eased her head gently back to the ground.

Slowly he came at Tom. Crouched, shoulders humped, his two hands hanging at his sides balled into fists. His eyes were murderous slits with tears in them. His lips were curled back, baring his teeth.

Tom fired another shot, but still Willie came on, a bright red splotch spreading on his shirt. Another shot, and still another. Still he came on. Tom leaped backwards.

Willie fell, then. Fell face downward and lay still.

Fannette watched, shocked. Jared approached the body, nudged it with the toe of his boot and shrugged.

"Those damn dealers will sell a man anything. My father-in-law would have apoplexy if he knew he'd bought an insurrectionist. Take the carrion away with you. I suppose the reward goes whether he's dead or alive?"

"Either way."

"After you strap him on the horse, take a few seconds for a bit of rum. Guess you won your bet, square enough."

"Got to get him to a judge who can swear to the identification."

Jared drew in the clear, frosty air.

"Well, the weather's with you, anyway," he said.

It seemed an interminable time to Fannette before the corpse was strapped across the empty saddle. The slave hunters stopped to down the rum, and only after three full mugs did they set about leaving.

Meanwhile, Junie remained where she'd fallen. No one dared go near her. No one dared to touch her.

They all know it could have been any one of them, Fannette thought. Each and everyone of her joyous people stood silent and stunned.

And frightened.

Her joyous people. Would any of them ever reach Cincinnati now?

She knew the slave hunters had caught the scent. They'd get their reward.

And they'd be back.

BOOK THREE

Till Cincinnati

"Jordan deep, Jordan wide . . ."

—From old negro spiritual

1

"Wonder where my brother an' sister gone,
Wonder where my brother an' sister gone,
They is gone to the wilderness,
Ain't comin' no more.

Wonder where we will lie down,
Wonder where we will lie down,
In some lonesome place, Lord,
Down on the ground.

Didn't you hear them angels moan?
Yes, I heard them angels moan,
Angels moanin' in my soul!
Didn't you hear the heaven bell ring?
Yes, I heard the heaven bell ring,
The angel moanin' in my soul."

Wednesday had finished the funeral reading over the new grave, and with tears streaking down his face, his strong, rich voice led in singing the final tribute. A tribute to the one they buried and to the one whose body had been taken.

Two lives, Fannette thought. Two lives, just like that!

The memory of the song, words altered here and there to fit the occasion, stayed with her as she tried to eat what was on her supper plate. She gave up, finally, setting the food aside.

Poppy and Anton talked quietly a little distance away, but there was none of the customary light repartee that ordinarily marked their conversation. Yet they both had cleaned their plates, Fannette observed a little bitterly. And so had the others. Was hers the only stomach left

273

queasy by what had happened that afternoon?

But there was no laughing, no joking among their people. The promise of frost earlier in the day was swept away by a southerly wind, and the evening was clear and warmer than most. Here and there couples wandered off to the shadows offered by a stand of timber. But Fannette had the feeling that this night it was to talk seriously of their fears. Of the premonitions that stalked all of them. Tonight was a time to discuss and to consider. Even Sassie seemed weighed with foreboding.

And where was Jared? Fannette's eyes swept over the camp, but he was nowhere in sight. Careful not to intrude on anyone, she moved to the edge of the woods, and by the dimming light she distinguished a lone figure sitting on a log. He was slumped forward, hands covering his face.

She hesitated. It was a shock to see him like this. She felt a sudden, overwhelming compassion.

She touched him lightly on the shoulder, and his head jerked up.

"Oh," he said. "Fannette. I expected it would be Trojan. We're having a council later tonight."

"There are folks in the woods."

"They'll be back. There are decisions to be made, and they have a right to their say."

He drew a deep, despondent breath. "This is the finish," he said. "Those bastards were studying every face in the camp while they swilled my rum. They'll come back with more posters and more descriptions."

She sat beside him and pulled him against her. With a little exclamation, he buried his face in her shoulder. She held him, rocking slightly. As she would have comforted a dejected child.

"We all trust you," she said softly. "I know they'll be willing to follow any plan you suggest."

"Plan!" His voice was muffled, but she could still hear the bitterness. "What plan but to scatter and run when the time comes?"

274

"It wasn't your fault."

But wasn't it? He had taken her into the venture. And it had been she who had brought on the pursuit when she'd hidden Tansy.

"Harriet Tubman led hundreds of refugees out of the South, and she never lost a man. I heard that once someone threatened to turn back and she pulled that gun she carried. She told him that a dead nigger didn't talk. He decided to go along after that."

"Junie was dying," Fannette said. "But did they have to kill Willie?"

"If he'd lived, it would only be to hang." Jared raised his head and looked into her eyes. "I had to act the way I did. As if none of it mattered. You understand that, don't you?"

"Of course." Hesitantly, she took his face between her hands and kissed him. With a muffled sigh, he put his arms around her, holding her as if she were all that was left.

"There's nothing in me that feels alive," he said. "Not even when I hold you. I think I died with Willie when they shot him."

"Only for awhile."

"Of the twenty-eight people I contracted to lead to the Quakers and Canada at least seventeen have records posted through the South. And those sons of bitches will find each and every one of them!"

She remained silent, realizing his need to talk.

"There's only the faintest chance they'll leave us alone. That they'll be content with the reward for Willie. We could keep on the way we've been traveling, or we could play it safe and break up. Continue on foot and horseback, and over back roads in the night. But then we'd look guilty as hell."

"How far do we still have to go? How many days?"

She held her breath, dreading the answer. How far to Cincinnati, Mrs. McLaury? How far, before you're Miss

275

Randolph again? How far to Banbury Cross? The old nursery rhyme incongruously flashed through her mind.

"It'll be late March if we're permitted to continue the way we are now. The wagons should average twenty miles a day. Of course we have to allow for stopovers. But if we leave the wagons and go on foot—God knows how long."

"We've been on the road a good month. And we aren't even halfway?"

"Hardly a third of the distance."

It could take forever, she thought, as long as she could be near him. She pushed away the thought, realizing it was life and death to their people.

As if sensing what was in her mind, his lips found hers again. The kiss was gentle. Understanding. There was none of the usual rushing desire, but rather she felt a security. As if her fears were being taken onto his shoulders. As if he were absorbing them.

There was a sound behind them, and Jared lifted his head with her still in his arms.

Anton was waiting. He cleared his throat again.

"They want me?" Jared asked. He showed neither impatience nor annoyance at the interruption. Only a sort of capitulation.

"Everyone's waiting. Trojan hesitated to disturb you, but I had no such reluctance."

Jared helped Fannette to rise. He took in a deep breath and moved toward the bright beacon of the fire.

Anton lingered in the shadows beside Fannette.

"That was a pretty scene," he remarked.

"Jared's discouraged," she said, watching as he was surrounded by the waiting people.

"Maybe I am too," he replied. "I've gone through a great deal to stay near you." He put his arms around her and drew her to him.

She made no move to resist. She remained motionless, hands at her sides.

"Diable!" he exclaimed. "I might just as well embrace a

276

rag doll! What has happened to the girl I kissed in a garden in New Orleans?"

"She never really existed," Fannette told him, and walked out into the clearing after Jared.

II

"You sure do make mighty fine stitches," Sassie said. Her round eyes followed Fannette's needle with admiration.

Fannette glanced up. As much as she detested sewing, stitching the shirt she'd taken from Junie's hands did keep her mind from fretting over the present. She looked critically at the collar she'd just finished. Donna had taken great pains to teach her the art of delicate needlework. What would she say if she saw that skill put to making a shirt for a maroon? A refugee wanted for insurrection?

Only he was dead.

"That 'bout fit my Juba," Sassie observed, appraising the broad cut.

Impulsively, Fannette thrust the work into Sassie's hands.

"Take it and finish it for Juba."

Sassie's face lit up. "Oh, he like that!"

Fannette studied her with curious eyes. "When you disappeared, I was afraid Juba had killed you," she confessed.

Sassie laughed, threw back her head, and laughed still more. Finally, with tears streaming down her cheeks, she shook her head.

"Dead woman don' do Juba no good," she said. "He tell me he watch time he found me with Nate. He say I don't git nothin' but mebbe a pretty bracelet. He tell me when he finish what he goin' do, I know I got somethin'."

"Oh?" Fannette had the feeling it would be better to leave it there.

"When I goes to make him take it out, he grab me, and he say, 'This time, girl, you git it good! And you likes it.'"

278

Fannette hastily got to her feet, but there was no stopping Sassie.

"So he keep on goin' till I starts to pleasure. Den he pleasure and pleasure me till us can hardly breathe, but I don' want for him to stop. He say, 'That better'n a gewgaw, girl?' And I says, 'It shore am.' "

"Take care with those stitches," Fannette interrupted faintly.

"Don' want no other man now," Sassie finished triumphantly. "Ain't no one know how to pleasure me like my Juba."

Bien. That should teach her not to ask questions! And now, somehow, it was difficult to get her mind off Jared.

Free of her self-imposed labor, Fannette moved restlessly across the camp. She stood a side, watching the activity around her, and thought back on the past two weeks.

When they'd left the area near the cypress swamp after what had happened to Junie and Willie, they were a discouraged, silent procession. She wasn't the only one who kept looking back up the road to see if the slave hunters were in pursuit.

They crossed the Robinson Road to Columbus, Mississippi, and camped near Red Dog Road. Rain started to fall that night, proving Jared's wisdom in pushing them past the bottomlands, leaving them no time to mourn the dead.

Rain followed them through the week, obliterating landmarks and causing delays. She saw what had been an Indian mission through flashes of lightning, and they camped that night near a place called French Camp, which seemed to be a school of some sort.

Each day, Jared pushed them harder. Each day he got every possible mile out of the lengthening hours of daylight.

January gone. February about to give way to March.

They stopped for a day of rest near a hill called Buzzard's Roost. Levi Colbert, a half-breed Scotsman, had lived close by, Jared told her. But he left when a treaty took the land from the Indians.

"It was George Colbert, Levi's father, who made history," he went on. "All the Indians loved that old Scotsman. I've heard it was because he never refused them whiskey. They protected his right to ferry travelers across the Tennessee, and he made a fortune with his monopoly. A rich man was apt to find himself poorer by the time he climbed the opposite bank."

"And how do we cross?" she asked. She knew he planned to ride ahead to make the arrangements. The Tennessee crossing was wide and deep.

"I'll arrange for a flatboat," he said. "There's not a chance of fording at this point. That's where old Colbert got travelers. Even Andrew Jackson."

"Nobody ever got Andrew Jackson," she maintained, remembering the legends she'd heard.

"Except that gouging Scotsman. The story is that in 1814 Old Hickory was rushing to New Orleans with his army to drive out the British. When he came to this point, Colbert charged him seventy-five thousand dollars to ferry his men across."

"Seventy-five thousand!" she repeated in disbelief. "But, at least, the Tennessee will be between us and those slave hunters!"

He looked at her quizzically. "And you think that'll make a difference?" Then he added more slowly. "This time we'll be ready for them."

With the passing of the rain, frost lay thick on the ground in the morning. Shivering groups huddled around the three big fires that burned through the night. The people walked up and down, stamping and clapping, trying to chase numbness from their feet and hands. In the afternoon the weather would warm a little, and it wasn't too unpleasant where the sun struck. But once the sun passed overhead, the cold penetrated even the heaviest sheepskin jacket.

Was it the cold that caused her to feel unwell? Caused her temper to grow increasingly short? She who had hardly known a sick day in her life?

It was finally Letty who faced her with the facts.

They were just out of Nashville, the Tennessee River four days behind them. The end of the Trace. Fannette felt rested and content for the first time in nearly a week. Jared had arranged for Poppy and her to stay at a farmhouse. A room with a real bed! And there was a tub the farmer's wife promised to have taken to their room and filled with warm water. It seemed nothing short of miraculous! A real wood floor with a braided circle of carpet.

To think, she mused, that she'd considered the Lemmon place adequate, but quite plain. What a different world she now inhabited.

Outside, she caught the bright flash of a scarlet tanager. She pointed it out to Poppy, who was taking her turn in the tub, knees almost touching her chin as she scrubbed under an arm.

"It's so beautiful today, I can almost believe in spring again," Fannette said, gathering together their soiled clothing. "I'll take these out to Letty," she added.

A place had been provided outside where the women could build fires and boil clothes. For weeks the only laundry facilities had been those offered by the icy creeks.

Letty was occupied with stirring a load of heavy washing. She looked up as Fannette stopped by her. It was chilly in the shade, but Letty's broad forehead dripped sweat.

"Miz McLaury," she said, looking at the bundle Fannette had dropped, "is that all?"

"Everything," Fannette assured her.

"You been holdin' back yore wash?"

"Why ever should I?"

Letty removed the stick from the boiling water. She set it on the bench where it made a fog in the sharp air.

"Dis the second time I have Miss Poppy's cloth." Letty tapped the boiler. "She say she jus' finish this morning. You ain't never give me none."

Fannette avoided the accusing eyes, knowing it was true. The night she'd dismissed Poppy at the shack by Baton Rouge, Poppy had told the truth when she'd claimed to be unwell. She'd been plagued with cramps all through the day. And hadn't she, herself, expected to be in the same state by the next week?

But it wasn't even a matter of two months yet. Surely it was too early to think about possibilities of . . .

"All of this travel's bound to have changed my cycle," she replied, resenting Letty's intrusion into what she didn't even discuss with Donna.

Letty sniffed. " 'All dis trabel!' " she mocked. "All dis sumpin' else, I'se thinkin'."

"Letty!" Fannette exclaimed. Then, realizing what the woman had in mind, she tried a gentler tack. "Please don't go talking around. Especially not to Mr. McLaury."

"Ain't he got the right to know?" Letty planted her wet hands on her hips and thrust her jaw forward at a righteous angle. "You a virgin when you went to him. Ain't it his doing?"

Fannette bit back a sharp rebuke. She must bring Letty to see the reasonableness of her request.

"I can't be sure so early," she said. "I don't want Mr. McLaury to be disappointed."

They seemed the right words, because Letty bobbed her head and grinned.

"I keeps my mouth shut, but he ain't gonna be dis'pointed. Glory, she the one tell me there ain't gonna be no cloth from you."

It can't be! Fannette assured herself, as she started back to the farmhouse. It just can't! But suppose it were true? Then the important thing was to keep Jared from know-

282

ing. Whatever decision he might make in Cincinnati must not be influenced by the fact she was pregnant.

Pride? Yes, certainly. But necessary pride.

III

From Nashville on, Jared was prepared for another visit by the slave hunters. Before the tents were dragged out of the wagons, three armed sentries were sent to hide in the woods. Fannette found the thought of guards watching over the camp comforting. But daily Jared grew noticeably more apprehensive.

But nothing happened. The people they encountered were friendly, and the evenings became a time of relaxation, of singing to the accompaniment of Jove's mouth organ or Abe's fiddle. Wednesday's great voice led them in rollicking spirituals to the rhythm of clapping hands and shouts of, "Amen!"

"We'll avoid Louisville, Kentucky," Jared told the company one night. "Louisville is a hangout for slave dealers and the men who bring them in."

George Washington and Pearl nodded. They'd been delivered into the hands of Louisville slave dealers. How long back was that? How many years, how many months? On the road, days, months and years were all one.

No. They'd go by way of Lexington.

"Sometimes I think you must lie awake all night, Nette," Poppy said accusingly. "You look dreadful."

Did she lie awake all night? No, only most of it. Listening to the footsteps outside. Wondering if they belonged to Jared. Every man, except Old Chipper and Anton, put in time for sentry duty, but no one as much time as Jared. Was it because he, too, found sleep difficult? Or was that wishful thinking on her part?

What would happen to her after Cincinnati? It was certain she couldn't return to Bijou. She touched her abdomen with light fingers. Almost unquestionably she was pregnant. Each morning it was harder to pretend to eat breakfast. Each morning the appetite inducing odors became more nauseating. And today her breasts hurt.

But she couldn't be unhappy. She wanted the baby. Wanted it whether or not she had its father. Thank the Merciful Mother money would never be a problem. She'd have Donna transfer her allotment to a Northern bank. She'd find a little house in a small town. Oh, she'd manage. But it took thinking.

How could it have happened? But of course, it most certainly should not be a surprise that it had happened . . .

"Fannette, where's that splendid appetite you used to have?" Poppy's voice was beginning to take on a suspicious note.

"How can I think of food when those terrible men might come at any time?"

And they did come when they were least expected. The slave hunters rode into the camp at the nooning. Had Jared even thought to post sentries? Fannette glanced anxiously toward the trees. Who would have expected this visit in broad daylight? Sam and Tom belonged to the evening. To the time of staking out tents.

Jared watched their approach. There might even have been relief in the way he got to his feet, carefully setting down his coffee cup.

"Gentlemen," he said, "you must have a thirst again. I warn you, travelers tell me there's a fury of a storm ahead. If you intend to continue following us, I hope you've provided yourself with warm clothes."

"Nope." Sam looked around and licked his lips in anticipation. "Reckon this'll put an end to our gallivanting. We got what we want now."

Jared raised an eyebrow, but remained silent.

Tom said, "We knew something was wrong right from the first. Now we got the proof that half yore niggers are wanted men."

"We figure any others to be runaways," Sam added.

"We're taking the lot of you in."

"Just the two of you, alone?" Jared smiled. "Such courage." He glanced at the gun Tom had trained on him, and then to Sam who was pulling his from its holster.

"Why doesn't he do something?" Fannette whispered to Poppy. "How can he stand there smiling?"

"Anybody in this camp make a move and we pull the trigger," Sam warned. "First on the women, but no one ain't going to get far. A posse's right behind us. Every man of them is deputized to shoot what he can't catch."

It was then Fannette saw the flash of sun on metal at the edge of the woods. Poppy, too, was watching. There was a sudden explosion, sending a flock of wild turkeys into the air.

In numb fascination, Fannette watched a red splotch spread from a hole in Sam's side. He dropped his revolver and doubled over, screaming. The second sentry's bullet caught Tom high in the right arm. Then the three guards appeared at the edge of the clearing, their guns ready.

A nod from Jared, and Trojan gathered up the two revolvers and handed one to Anton, the other to Jove.

Tom was clutching his right arm, blood seeping through his fingers, and Sam was on the ground, moaning.

Jared stood over them. "I haven't the desire to add your murder to my other honors," he told them. "We'll tie the two of you to a tree in sight of the road, and for your own sakes, I hope you told the truth about that posse."

George Washington and Jove dragged the two men to a tree. Meanwhile, food was dumped onto the ground, the soiled dishes heaped into the kitchen wagon. Catching up their belongings, the men and women piled into the spring wagons. The cookstove was still hot, and they left it where it was, the fire burning.

Jared saw Fannette glance toward it.

"We'll have no further need of it," he said. "And after tonight, we won't have a place to carry it."

286

The wagons started up at a speed that made Fannette catch her breath in anticipation of disaster, and she wondered how long the phaeton's wheels could take such punishment. Thank the Blessed Mother they were at least on a dry road!

Jared went on ahead, directing the line of wagons onto a side trail, turning down farm lanes and into the back country byways, threading in a northeasterly direction, looping and twisting.

He came back to them and rode for a minute beside the phaeton.

"Enjoy your comforts today," he called out. "After tonight, you'll be on horseback."

"What's to keep the posse from spreading out and catching us?" Fannette asked Poppy.

"Greed," Poppy replied. "Neither of those men were the sort to share in a reward. There is no posse."

"But someone will find them."

"And they'll have to rush them to a physician. Then they'll have to gather together a group to pursue us. By then we should be well under way."

Anton trotted alongside.

"*Allons enfants!*" He called out, above the clattering of wagons and the pounding of horse hoofs. He sounded almost jubilant. "*Nous allons!* I asked for adventure. But prison?"

Fannette leaned out, calling after him. "And Maman, Anton? What will Maman say?"

Poppy laughed. "Poor Anton," she said.

IV

It seemed they would never reach the destination Jared had set. That the sound of wheels creaking and horses snorting would continue forever.

"This is the first time in weeks that I really feel hungry," Fannette complained to Poppy. "Surely Jared could permit a long enough stop for us to eat!"

Poppy looked at her curiously in the dim interior of the phaeton. "It's heartening to hear you sound a little more like your old self," she said. Then she added in a more succinct vein, "But it was bound to happen after the first disturbance was past."

"Disturbance?" Fannette repeated.

"*Mais oui*," Poppy replied easily. "But as I understand it, your problem will now mainly be confined to the morning."

"Poppy. . ."

Poppy kissed Fannette's cheek lightly. "Even if Letty hadn't hinted—and you know Letty's hints—I'd have guessed."

"But I'm not certain."

"Of course you are! Don't worry, I'll keep your secret. For as long as I think wise."

"It's not for you to decide. This is my concern, and I'll not welcome any interference."

"And Jared?"

"Jared is my business. I especially don't want him to know."

"Aren't you being foolish?"

"I don't want to talk about it. I don't even want to think about it."

They rode in silence after that. Occasionally the moon

288

lit the way, but more often deepening clouds drifted across the sky, sending them into nearly complete darkness. Jared urged them on, permitting only brief stops to water and rest the horses.

Fannette finally closed her eyes and leaned her head back on the cushions. Would they continue forever? Surely humans and horses could be expected to endure only so much . . .

She awakened to find her cheek was resting on Poppy's shoulder. It was a lack of motion that had broken through her uneasy dreams. She was wrapped in a warm quilt, but still she shivered.

"Where are we?" she mumbled, raising her head. "What time is it?"

"Well past midnight, and at a station out of Bowling Green. We're in a stable, and Jared's making arrangements." Poppy was wide awake, excitement in her eyes.

"A stable?" The strong odor of fresh manure was almost overpowering.

"We made it!" Poppy exulted. "Jared was right, they did lie about a posse! And now we have a good start. Our Lady will be with us. Oh, I know she will be!"

Lanterns seemed to dart in all directions, the people carrying them mere shadows. There was the sound of voices. She could see Jared standing under the main lamp and he seemed to be striking a bargain with an old man in a night shirt. There was the sound of coins changing hands, the neighing of horses, and the clatter of wagon traces dropping to the ground.

Jared came up to the phaeton and leaned over the side. His eyes were dark and shining with the excitement and turmoil that filled the place. He enjoys the chase, Fannette thought resentfully. This is a game! Even Anton stood near with a half-smile on his lips.

Men! Did they never grow up?

"We've only one sidesaddle," Jared said. "The mare will take it, and they're trying to find another."

"Don't bother," Poppy told him. "When I was little, I used to go with Trojan and Letty out to Trojan's brother's farm. One summer I learned to ride bareback." She laughed, remembering. "Letty nearly had a fit when she caught me!"

"It won't have to be bareback. We'll have plenty of saddles, but they're all astride."

"Then I'll dress like a boy. I always thought that would be fun!"

Poppy, too? Were they all out of their minds? Or were they playing a game to keep up lagging spirits? Her own, perhaps?

Jared assisted them down from the phaeton. Fannette was last, and his hand lingered on her elbow.

"You're shivering," he said. She felt his fingers tighten.

She shook her head. It was fear and excitement rather than the cold, but he pulled the blanket closer around her shoulders.

She looked about at the frenzied activity. Bedrolls and provisions were strapped onto stomping horses and saddles cinched into place. Each person was selecting necessities and rolling them into a "budget." Wasn't that what Jared said the rivermen used to call their packs? A budget?

Ten wagons. Twenty horses. But there was the mare for her, the bay for Jared, and Anton's gelding. And Jared had arranged for Poppy to ride a gentle roan.

"We're lucky Jared refused to accept any horses that weren't trained to a saddle or pack," Poppy said. "And I thought he was being overly cautious!"

The stableman's wife took Poppy into the house, and when they returned, Poppy was rakishly attired in the clothing of a boy.

"My son outgrew them," the woman explained. "They fit her well enough, but who'd ever take her for a boy with that hair?"

"Oh no!" Fannette exclaimed. "Poppy, you mustn't

let them!"

But they sat her on a barrel, and Letty took over with a pair of shears.

"Really, it makes very little difference," Poppy murmured. But Fannette noticed that she kept her eyes tightly closed against the ruthless snipping of the scissors.

Jared surveyed the results and frowned. "Have you a straw hat with a wide brim?" he asked.

The hat was found. A tattered, well used one, and Fannette took her turn inside the house so she could change into a riding habit.

She tilted her velvet hat with its curved brim and saucy plume and laughed at her reflection. She began to feel some of the excitement of the chase.

That hat! The last time she'd worn it was on a morning ride over a bridle path in New Orleans. She wondered at the wisdom of wearing her best outfit this first night and saving the other for later. But then, again, why not?

She glanced down at her jacket and noticed it was much tighter across her breasts.

When she reentered the stable, she saw that the men had set up a trestle table. Emily, followed by the stableman's wife, brought out a steaming pot of soup and loaves of freshly baked bread from the kitchen and set it on the table.

And how could she possibly eat with the stench of manure all around her? But she could. And she did. She caught Poppy's amused smile as she helped herself to a second bowl of fragrant vegetables and meat simmered in a thick broth.

Jared leaned forward and explained his plans.

"We'll continue by backroads tonight," he told them, "and rest over tomorrow. After that, we'll divide into groups. I'll make out directions so we'll know where we're to meet each evening."

He paused. "Should we learn they're looking for us in this part of the counrty, we'll have to start hiding by day and traveling by night. I think you all know that if you lose track of the rest of us, just keep going north. Follow the North Star."

"And where will we sleep?" Anton asked. "Surely it's not your intention that the women sleep out in the rain and snow?"

"There are stations," Jared replied. "There are also barns and abandoned cabins. From here on we're in well-settled country, but a lot of folks have left their places to go wcst."

Anton looked skeptical. "Will we always have shelter?"

"We'll face that problem when and if it comes. We wouldn't be the first to pass a night without shelter."

They left after eating, a silent procession. Fannette tested her stirrups, settling more comfortably in the saddle. The mare had a pleasing stride, as gentle as her own chestnut back at Bijou. And thanks to Our Lady, Breel had insisted that she be an accomplished horsewoman!

The moon had finally won clear of the clouds and beamed unobstructedly down on the path they followed along the fringe of forest. It was nearing dawn, and the air was very cold. How long? she thought. How long before he permits us rest?

Then she thought of the women and children plodding in the rear, of the many miles they would cover on foot before reaching the Ohio River. Suddenly everything seemed to be devoid of hope. Easy tears rolled down her cheeks, and she dabbed at them in disgust.

Poppy drew alongside.

"Are you certain you're all right?" she asked.

"I'm fine. But those women. Walking. And the children."

"The children and Glory will ride with Jove and Letty on the regular road. Jared traded for an old cart to carry extra provisions."

Why should Poppy always know so much more of Jared's plans? She felt a return of jealousy.

"Nette, this is foolish. You must tell Jared so he can find a place for you to stay until this is over."

"No!" Fannette didn't realize how adamant she sounded until Anton, who was riding ahead, checked his mount and glanced back.

"You're all right?" he asked.

"Of course I'm all right!" she snapped. Why wouldn't they leave her alone?

"*Tres bien. Tres bien, ma cherie*! Must you cut off my head because I show concern?"

"I'm sorry," Fannette said, feeling ashamed.

But it was now such a short time she had until Cincinnati. Such a short time against the rest of her life.

V

Distant roosters were saluting the dawn when they stopped by a deserted cabin on a lonely hillside. It wasn't a disguised station shack, such as the one outside of Baton Rouge, but an abandoned structure. The floor was covered with rubble, and as soon as the rain started, the roof began to leak.

"It just can't rain!" Fannette exclaimed in dismay. The idea of riding horseback in a downpour was completely unsettling.

"We're staying here until evening," Jared said. "With luck it's a shower and will pass by then."

The men had built a fire, and the women worked at clearing away the litter. Even with puddles forming under the roof tree, the place began to take on the air of a habitation. Where there was room, and where the floor was dry, bedrolls were spread, and the weary group climbed into them without even eating. Fannette had only a faint memory of pulling her covers around her, right over her clothing. But she went to sleep knowing Poppy was nearby and that both Anton and Jared slept close to the door, guns at hand.

They left in the early evening, dividing into three sections.

"Trojan, you keep the cart on the regular road, and your folks'll follow along the tree line above," Jared said. "Poppy, you, Anton and Jove will lead the second group, and Fannette and I will follow with the third."

It was a fair enough division, Trojan decided. He was glad they'd abandoned the cookstove, because that left room for little Tressa to ride in the back. Friday, Emily's nine-year-old, let it be known he wasn't about to ride in the wagon like a little child, and it appeared he was doing better than most of the grown folks.

Ten, maybe twelve miles a day. That's what Mr. Jared said they should cover. Trojan shook his head. Not if the weather worsened. And not on the second day, when folks started to discover they had swollen feet and aching muscles.

He nudged Letty. She sat beside him, Glory on the outside. Glory hardly took any room. Now Letty, that was a different story. He chuckled. Letty had been a fancy-dressing, pert thing when first he saw her in Congo Square that long-ago Sunday. Come to think of it, his hair had been black then, too. And there hadn't been those wrinkles around his eyes. And he didn't let maybe a week go by, like he did now. Those days he was ready every night, and sometimes in the morning as well.

"What you think wrong between Mr. Jared and Miss Fannette?"

"Don't you let him catch you call her that!"

"She Miss Fannette to me since first I see her in cradle. And that a long time ago, woman."

Letty nodded in agreement.

"You reckons they jus' don' know what they wants?"

"Oh, they knows what they wants all right," Letty replied. "They jus' peacock proud. Rekon Miz McLaury, she cum 'round when her belly gits big."

Trojan stared at her. "You ain't tell me!" he said. Then he laughed. "Nothin' like that to bring folks 'round."

"It's Miss Poppy I worried 'bout. You see the way Mr. Anton been lookin' at her las' few days?"

They both contemplated that development in silence.

In his mind, Trojan ran over the division of the people again. Twenty-six in all now, counting the two young ones. Nine were with Mr. Jared, the same number with Jove and Miss Poppy. And six grown-ups were with him, in addition to Emily's boy and Tressa, who belonged to Crane, and that yammering wife of his, Abby. Wonder a man could put up with a woman likes of that!

Keep away snow. Keep away rain. And you, too. You keep away, wind. It was a chant that went through Trojan's mind in time to the beat of the horse's hoofs.

At midnight, he pulled off the road by a clump of trees and waited for the walkers. He built a fire so they could see it from above and come down for hot boiled coffee and the food Glory was putting together over the fire. It was a good thing they'd found those cabbages back in a neglected field. Nothing like cabbage leaves wrapped around food and left to bake in the ashes.

One by one, the walkers appeared. No two were supposed to walk together. Likewise, each of the three groups held their midnight rest at different locations.

Trojan studied his people through narrowed eyes. Abe was doing just fine, but Old Chippers was limping already.

"Sumpin' in dat shoe," Chippers said. He took it off and shook his head. "Jus' a foot," he decided.

Glory opened her bag and made a poultice for the blister.

"Climb in back of the cart," Trojan said, but the carpenter shook his head.

"I tells you what," Trojan went on, "I gittin' tard of staying up there. You take this here cart for a spell."

So once again they started out. Chippers on the cart seat, and Trojan afoot. Trouble was, Chippers forgot to halt every few hours so the people could rest. Trojan had to walk fast, to even run, in order to catch up and remind him.

"You wait here!" he panted. "Us got to rest our feet."

No one was really ready when it was time to start walking again, but that was the way it had to be. It was getting on toward dawn.

Trojan looked around for landmarks, his mind pondering on the time last fall when he and Mr. Jared, along with Jove, had made this trip. Like a picnic, it'd been. Deer, turkey, all sorts of game just anywhere you put your eyes. Fine, mild autumn weather. Well, what could he expect? This wasn't even spring as yet. Not this far north.

And, of course, they hadn't expected to be on foot. They'd marked down the good stopping places, figuring on daytime travel with wagons that could make at least twenty miles a day.

Streaks of light were brightening the horizon, and Trojan figured they maybe had another mile or so to go before they came to an old barn Jared had marked down for a sleeping place. They'd have made about twelve miles by then, and that wasn't bad for the first night. Only one blister so far. Up ahead, he could see the cart where Chippers had pulled it off the road. The last rest for the night.

One by one the walkers appeared from the hillside and threw themselves on the ground. Abby went over to the cart and looked inside.

That was when she let out a screech that had everyone jumping to their feet, looking for the slave hunters.

"My chile! My Tressa!" she screamed, waving her hands in the air. "Tressa! She ain' in de wagon!"

Trojan pushed aside the food sacks and canvas. Tressa wasn't in the cart, that was certain. And she wasn't any place else around, either.

Trojan looked at Chippers.

"When we leaves from the las' stop, was the girl in the wagon?"

"He sleep when I sees him. I didn't look, time we leaves."

"She have to pee!" Abby shouted. "Dat what happen. You leave her when she goes to pee!"

Trojan put his hands over his face, trying to shut out the woman's wails so he could think. He'd have to go back, and he'd take Tressa's father, Crane. But the rest had to continue ahead. None of them were in condition to retrace those last three miles. It'd be broad daylight before they even reached the place.

But how would they find the barn? Jove's slate was in the back of the cart. Tressa had been playing with it earlier. He used his sleeve to brush it clean and drew the road, along with the landmarks.

Chippers shook his head doubtfully. Glory squinted at it and nodded. No need to ask Letty. She couldn't find her way out of a henhouse!

The clouds were billowing in the sky, blotting out the sunrise, when Trojan and Crane started back on the road. In the distance, lightning flashed to the west, and hollow booms of thunder followed.

"Tressa scared of thunder," Crane said, his forehead wrinkling.

They walked faster, but Crane was plainly too tired to keep up Trojan's pace.

"You jus' keep goin' till you gits to where we stops before," Trojan finally said. "If I finds her first off, I meet you on the road."

The wind had risen, and it whipped the roadside trees, swaying some of them double. Then the rain lashed into his face, blinding him. Trojan pulled together his warm fleece coat and thought of the little seven-year-old who'd been a source of both pleasure and annoyance to everyone since the trip had begun.

She'd grow up like Sassie for sure, he reflected. Then his mind went to Zette, and Jove, his son. Zette wasn't what exactly could be called a serious-minded girl, either. But then, Letty hadn't been much that way the time he met her. And look what a good wife Letty had made him.

But Jove was special. Jove wasn't like his pa. Jove had good brains in his head. He was even beginning to talk a little more the way that pleased Miss Poppy.

And take Miss Fannette. She'd been frivolous for sure, almost running away with Mr. Anton, now that he remembered, but nobody could call her frivolous now.

Look how she worried over Junie. How she'd tried to do little things for her. For a dying black woman.

For a smart man, Mr. Jared was a damn fool, Trojan reflected. Well, the white folks had their ways. But it sure wasn't a black man's way.

"Dat Juba," he said to a squirrel that chattered up ahead, "he know how to handle a woman. Sassie, she settle down now for sure."

He'd reached the clump of trees marked by footprints and cart tracks. He cupped his hands to his mouth and shouted out Tressa's name. Then he waited. He shouted again and waited. No answer, except for more thunder, this time closer up.

When Crane, winded and limping, reached the spot, Trojan was still calling.

"We gotta spread out and hunt," Trojan said. "Now mind you don' git lost."

They hunted until nearly noon. They rested awhile and then started in again. Trying not to think of what might have happened to a little girl lost in the rain and terrified of the thunder that was now crashing directly overhead.

VI

It was a subdued group who huddled around a fire in an abandoned barn, waiting for word of Tressa. The barn was a partially demolished structure with the double doors broken and off their hinges. A canvas was strung across the opening against the rain, and a hole in the roof helped to draw off the smoke, but it didn't do much for the breakfast odors. Steam filled the air, coming from the pots where Emma was cooking the morning cornmeal mush. Coffee was boiling on a makeshift stove.

It was warm by the fire that burned on the dirt floor, but the wind found loose boards and whistled through the chinks. By the flapping canvas at the entrance, the air was cold. Fannette shivered as she poised near the crumbling threshold, wondering if her growing nausea would necessitate a dash out into the trees. In any event, food was the last thing she desired.

She shuddered and closed her eyes against the sight of gruel being ladled into outstretched bowls. It seemed incredible that there had been a time when she had looked forward to breakfast.

But never cornmeal mush!

"Drink." The voice wasn't one she recognized. It sounded hoarse from disuse.

Fannette opened her eyes and saw that it was Glory holding a cup of steaming tea. Poppy had mentioned that the old woman was now talking upon occasions, but this was the first word Fannette had ever heard her utter.

And certainly the fragrance of the stewing herbs was about to be her undoing! Fannette shook her head and turned away.

"Drink." Glory's strange, green eyes were as compelling

as her command. Without actually willing it, Fannette found herself downing the brew. Then she hastily pushed the cup back into Glory's hands and rushed outside.

She was protected from the rain by the slanting overhang of the roof. She leaned against the rough boards of the side, wondering if she could make the fringe of trees between showers. As she waited for a lessening in the downpour, the nausea slowly started to ease.

I don't believe it, she thought. Even Glory couldn't brew that potent a tea! But it was true, and a soothing warmth spread through her stomach. Knowing the worst was over, she drew in a deep breath. Still, did she dare reencounter the cooking odors? Might it not undo everything?

A blast of wind determined the issue. She pulled aside the canvas and went back into the barn. Glory was hovering near a pot that steamed on a ledge. She was half surrounded by women. At a little distance, the husbands formed a joking, laughing group.

How could they have forgotten the little lost girl so soon? Then she realized it was a different sort of laughter. A combination of the proud and the sheepish, and each one of the women held a cup of Glory's potion.

Merciful Mother! Did she have that much company? She looked closer, curious to see who was taking the medicine and who wasn't. Not Poppy, of course, nor Emily or Letty; certainly not Abby, Pearl or Sassie. But wait. Juba left his wife to go outside, and Sassie scooted across the floor. Glory already had a cup waiting for her.

Bien, Sassie. And which trip to the woods brought about this? So Jared wasn't the only man due for a surprise! Fannette fingered her crucifix in a rush of guilt. Who was she to feel superior? She who had been Glory's first patient?

Bless you, Glory, in any event! Fannette thought as she took up a bowl, knowing that now she could eat, that she was actually hungry. Even for cornmeal mush.

Then she saw that Jared was watching her. And did he realize this was the first breakfast she'd eaten in over a week?

The rain continued to fall intermittently. Everyone was tired, but no one really rested. Eyes kept turning to the entrance, ears waiting for the sound of the searchers' return. Morning passed. Then it was noon. Then it was well past noon . . .

Jove heard them first. He threw aside the canvas.

"They got her!" he shouted. "They got her!"

He moved out of the way so Trojan could come in. Trojan was carrying Tressa, and she was soaked to the skin. Trojan stood motionless, still holding his limp burden as his eyes accustomed themselves to the dim light and the glow of the fire.

Tressa's mother pushed Jove aside and ran to the doorway.

"She dead!" she wailed. "My baby, she dead!"

Trojan shook his head and set Tressa on her feet.

"I hungry!" Tressa sobbed. "I'se wet an' hungry!"

Meanwhile, over the din, Crane tried to explain what had happened. They'd found her curled into a hollow tree, petrified with terror. It had been the better part of the day before she'd recognized her father's voice through her mounting hysteria. On the way back, she'd stiffened and screamed at each new blast of thunder or flash of lightning.

The women took her close to the fire and stripped her of the dripping clothing. Emily brought her soup, and Poppy spooned it between the chattering teeth.

"She gonna be sick," Glory predicted. "Bad sick."

Jared crossed the floor and looked down on the girl.

"We'll have to stay over the night," he decided. "But I'd feel safer if we can move on tomorrow."

Glory shook her head doubtfully.

Trojan was busy eating. "How you get the chicken?" he asked, chewing on a dumpling. "He sure taste good."

302

"Jove went into town," Jared explained. "He bought some from a farm down the way."

"What he hear?"

"They're still looking in the direction of Louisville. There's a big reward out, so we can be sure every bit of scum that can crawl off a saloon floor will be out with a gun."

"You think we safe if we go by day?"

"We'll try. At least until the end of the week. It's pretty damn slow traveling at night when the moon's behind the clouds."

Trojan handed Emily his bowl for a refill and went to the entrance. He pushed aside the canvas and sniffed at the wind. "What if it snow?"

Jared shrugged. "Nothing we can do but wait it out and trust to luck." He grinnd at Poppy. "Maybe you can make your request and start rattling those beads."

Snow! Down South, at the beginning of the Trace, the greenery would be on all the trees by now, Fannette thought. The birds would be singing mating songs, and the purple of the redbud would mingle with the white of blossoming dogwood. But here it might as well be December!

Tressa's low sobs had reached a pitch of hysteria, and Jove squatted down beside her with his mouth organ. He played a rollicking tune for her, complete with trills. Tressa watched him in silence for the first part, then her cheeks puffed out, and she resumed her keening. A shrill, high sound.

Jove continued to try to divert her, but the combination of the harmonica and the high-pitched howling was completely unnerving. He patted the little girl on the head and got to his feet.

"Haven't you something in that sack of yours to quiet her?" Jared asked Glory.

"She too little. I 'fraid it hurt her."

Surely there must be something someone could do,

Fannette thought. Poppy had fed her, and Letty was comforting the mother. Pearl tried to rock her in her arms, but Tressa struggled like a wild thing.

Fannette knelt beside the child and brushed the tangled hair off the feverish forehead. With her other hand at her throat, she touched the gold crucifix Donna had given her that long-ago morning when she, too, had tossed feverishly. She reached behind her neck and undid the clasp.

"I want you to have this," Fannette said, dangling the chain so that the firelight would reflect on it. "When I was little, I used to reach up and touch it whenever I got scared. It made me feel better."

Tressa opened her eyes wide, tears still trickling down her cheeks. Glory raised the child so Fannette could fasten it around the thin young neck.

"You gib her a good *obeah*," Glory approved. "Mebbe he help."

Tressa looked steadily at Fannette for a minute. Then, timidly, she touched the cross. She smiled, and her fingers closed around it as her eyelids dropped with weariness.

Fannette waited quietly, watching for the hysteria to return, but in her mind she was back at Bijou. Back to when Donna had awakened her from those dreadful voodoo-ridden dreams . . .

Then she became aware of Jared standing over her. Smiling down on her. He reached for her and brought her to her feet. Tressa was sleeping soundly now, and Tressa's mother had quieted. Fannette leaned against Jared, feeling limp, as if some quality of her own had passed to the girl. Jared seemed to understand.

His arm around her shoulders, he led her away to a quiet spot near the barn entrance. He swept aside the canvas so they could look outdoors, and she breathed deeply of the air freshened by the rain. She could feel it sweep away some of the past. The wind had temporarily lessened, and though drops still fell from the sodden tree limbs, the rain had stopped.

304

Jared uptilted a keg, and after she sat on it, he reached down to button her jacket.

"Can't have you catching a cold," he remarked.

She darted a quick, suspicious look at him, but his expression revealed only an ordinary concern. He squatted down on his heels so he could see up into her face, and he took her hands in his.

"The agreement we reached back at Poppy's cottage didn't include riding a horse in the rain or sleeping on the floors of abandoned barns," he told her.

"I haven't complained."

"I know you haven't, but that doesn't alter things. There's a good inn at Elizabethtown. That's a few days' journey ahead. I wish it were closer, but I'd rather leave you and Poppy there than any of the others in between."

"No."

He hesitated, and she dropped her lashes over her eyes, trying to avoid his direct gaze.

"I could arrange to have you put on a boat bound for New Orleans with Poppy. I'd send Letty and Jove along to look after you."

Not even to be permitted the time until Cincinnati? To be dropped off along the way now that her presence was no longer necessary to his plans?

He got to his feet, and drew her up against him, his face close to hers. He kissed her on the forehead.

"Don't you understand, my darling?" his voice was soft, persuasive.

"Darling?" she repeated.

He drew an exasperated breath. "Up until now you've permitted that, at least. Have I no rights?"

She felt her cheeks grow warm in spite of the cold air and the sharpening wind that had risen while they talked.

"Can't you see I'm responsible for you and Poppy? If we're caught, it'll be prison—or worse. When a man's found giving aid to fugitive slaves, the deputies aren't much concerned about capturing him alive."

305

He paused. "A woman might be spared," he added slowly, "but that could be less than a favor."

"I'll not leave of my own accord." She raised her lashes and her long, dark eyes regarded him steadily. "I can't go back to New Orleans. I'd sooner walk in the rain like the others. I'd even prefer to sleep out in the snow."

"After all that's happened, can you still feel that way about Luton?"

She nodded.

"Accepting what life throws at you is a part of the maturing process, my dear." His voice was gentle.

"Then I'm not mature. I caused this touble we're facing now. I'd be less than a person if I ran away and left everyone else to pay for what I started."

His arms tightened, and this time she was ready for his kiss. She put her hands on the back of his neck and pulled his lips down to hers. It was a long, hungry kiss, and when it was over, she buried her face in his chest.

"Let me stay," she pleaded. "Please let me stay."

"Fannette, my darling," he said into her hair, "knowing how much I love you, how can you ask that I expose you to the dangers ahead?"

She drew back. "Love? Since when has that been a consideration on your part?"

"Of course I love you!" Jared said impatiently. Then he stopped and stared down at her.

"Nette, you haven't thought those time when . . . I made love to you were only to . . . to relieve a man's natural inclinations?"

"Was there any reason to think otherwise? Even Anton, who claimed to love me, was willing to put it aside for—for other considerations."

"I think I understand now why you've taken the attitude you took. It never occurred to me—" He started to laugh, suddenly, and drew her back into his arms. "I can't seem to remember you ever mentioning love, either."

"It's not proper for a woman to tell a man she loves him

306

when he's never said he loved her," Fannette replied primly.

Jared laughed harder. It was a moment before he could speak. "Considering what we've been to each other, I hardly think you needed to stand on protocol!"

Then he was whispering the words over and over between kisses. "I love you, Nette. I've loved you from the first. How could you think otherwise? Haven't I been acting like a smitten schoolboy? I love you, do you hear? I love you!"

"And you're not going to send me away," she said as soon as her lips were free. "After what you've just now said, you can't ask me to go!"

Her eyes, shining up at him, were his undoing. "It's against all good judgment," he protested. But she knew she'd won.

They turned back to the group around the fire. All heads faced in the opposite direction, and everyone was making an elaborate pretense of being unaware of the two of them.

Except Anton.

"*Sacre bleu!* If you two are quite finished, would you be so kind as to replace the canvas, *s'il vous plait?* I freeze!"

VII

"That was a good thing you do, Miz McLaury. Givin' that cross to Tressa."

"Miss Fannette," Fannette corrected, realizing that this had become a game. She was certain that Jove had winked at Jared over her shoulder.

The air was frosty and clear, and the path, icy. Tressa had been wrapped in blankets and bundled into the back of the cart Trojan drove. She was sniffling, but even Glory was ready to agree she might not suffer any worse aftereffects than a slight cold.

"If'n she keep carryin' on, she be bad sick," Glory explained, and Fannette realized the old woman was crediting her with the child's recovery. But it still didn't stop her from being annoyed at Glory.

It had happened earlier in the morning, when Glory had replaced her mug of coffee with herb tea.

"If Mr. McLaury should ask you what I'm taking, I want you to tell him it's for a headache," she instructed the old woman.

Glory had stubbornly refused. "I say him ask you." Then she began to chuckle.

"But it's important," Fannette insisted. "He'd not let me stay, if he knew."

"He turn you 'way for dat, he have to turn 'way 'bout half de wimmin here."

Fannette tried not to think of that aspect, as they gathered at the barn's entrance, breaking into groups. How could women in their condition be expected to hike through mud and ice while she rode grandly on a gently paced mare?

"Better than dey work in cotton or cane till der time,"

Glory had said.

That evening she brought the matter up to Poppy.

"They're happy just to be heading for Canada," Poppy explained. "Just to know that is enough."

"While I ride a comfortable sidesaddle."

Poppy's gaminlike appearance continued to disconcert Fannette. The short, curly mass of black hair, the great, wide-spaced golden eyes and the boy's clothing. Poppy poked at a rock with the toe of her boot, furthering the illusion.

"Did you tell Jared?"

"Of course not. He'd insist I go back to New Orleans." She glanced down at her middle. "In a few months, can you imagine?"

"He has the right to know, Nette."

Fannette shook her head.

They stayed in a warm barn that night. Again the floor was a jumble of blanket-wrapped sleepers.

"I can arrange for you and Poppy to stay up at the farmhouse," Jared had offered earlier, but Fannette had shook her head.

"I prefer to stay with the others," she said.

"Aren't you being foolish?"

She'd looked at him coldly, but she really couldn't stay angry with him. As she rode beside him during the day, she told herself that if she were a bird, she'd be trilling out her love from every branch overhead. He loves me! He loves me! The words were never far from her heart and mind.

That he continued to hold himself apart no longer mattered. It was better that way. The day of Tressa's sickness, back in the barn, if he'd told her to climb the broken ladder and wait for him in the mildewed remnants of hay, she'd have gladly done so. But this was no time for lovemaking. And there was no place.

And then there was the darker side of the coin. He loved her, yes. But what did love mean to a man who had tasted

309

danger and adventure? She'd heard of men who were unable to give up that sort of life, not even for the woman they loved. No. She wouldn't trap him. She couldn't. Let the decision be his own. And let it be for no reason other than herself.

"It's no easy thing you're doing," Poppy commented. "And I'm not convinced that it's honest."

After another two days of keeping to the schedule of twelve miles a day, they neared Elizabethtown. They rode past the inn where Jared had wanted her to stay, and Fannette kept her head averted. The others were skirting the town, away from roads and travelers, somewhere up among the trees.

"You're certain?" he asked.

"I'm certain."

The weather was fair that day. She could believe that spring was only two weeks away. The ninth of March. And they'd left New Orleans on January sixth. An eon of time.

And where was Fannette Randolph these days? Was she merely hiding behind Miz McLaury? Or was she gone?

A shack near Boston, Kentucky, and Tressa was again begging for Jove's slate so she could play at making pictures. She still coughed, but she was feeling better each day.

Near Bardstown they spent the night in a barn again. In the middle of the night, Sassie began to scream.

Fannette sat up quickly, and next to her she saw Poppy throwing back her covers. Others rushed to where Sassie lay, and Juba called out for Glory.

"You ain' g'wan die," Glory assured the terrified girl. "You carryin' wrong, dat's all. We gits you clean, and pretty soon you can start ober, if you likes."

For no understandable reason, Fannette started to cry.

Poppy went to her. "Sassie'll be all right," she said. "Shouldn't even be a month. That soon, most women hardly know what's happened."

310

"It was more than a month," Fannette said. "She was taking Glory's tea."

And she couldn't stop the tears. Couldn't stop thinking that it could have been the baby she herself carried. Her baby, draining out of her, onto the dirt floor, the way Sassie's had.

Suddenly she wished Donna were near. Donna who would understand.

Jared brushed past Poppy, his eyes searching Poppy's face. Poppy looked away, avoiding the questions he hadn't asked.

"A woman gets tired," Poppy said, hating herself for the lie. "None of us is used to riding a horse day after day."

"We'll rest here tomorrow," he decided. "It'll be better for Sassie, and it'll make Juba feel easier."

He looked at the group as they returned to their blankets.

"And after tomorrow," he announced, "we'll take up moving by night."

He eased Fannette back into her covers, pulled them around her, and returned to his place by the door.

VIII

Sassie rode in the back of Trojan's cart with Tressa the following evening. But after that, she stood by Juba ready to start out on foot again.

How can she laugh and chatter as if nothing had happened? Poppy wondered. But then, she was very young. And had she even known who'd fathered her baby? Certainly not Juba. And there would have been accusations had she carried the baby the full term and given birth much too early for it to be of Juba's seed. No. Perhaps it all was for the best. And without a doubt, a relief to Sassie.

Trojan's cart rattled down the overgrown path to the road, and his followers disappeared into the darkness of the fields. Some led loaded horses, and some perched in front of the packs, riding part of the way and giving their place to a walker later in the night.

Follow the North Star. But where was the North Star this evening?

Poppy dug her heel into the side of her roan and trotted it to where Anton waited on his gelding. He was handsome in the halflight of a moon that only occasionally came from behind clouds. Proud and elegant, even in clothes that were becoming more shabby each day.

There was a time of decision ahead, Poppy mused. She who had always thought that such a decision would never be hers . . .

Anton was gentle and he was kind. He was patient, and it took much to discourage him. None of Jared's hasty temper. He was courageous, without loving danger. Without, in fact, courting it. He would be an easy man to live with. An indulgent husband.

Jove pulled up his horse alongside of hers. In his saddle-bags was stored the food to be prepared for the midnight lunch.

"Just imagine," Poppy said, sniffing in the freshness of the air, "spring will be here in another week. Spring, and up here in the north, it could be midwinter!"

"And it could snow," Anton added. "I've invoked all the saints, but it still could snow!"

"Hush," Jove said. "You bring it to us, you keep talkin' like that."

They watched the people belonging to their group. Watched them disappear into the night one by one. Then it was their turn to set out. And after them would be Fannette and Jared with their people. All so well organized. And all so easily shattered.

There had been luck thus far. Great good fortune. But for how long? Deep in her heart, she knew it wouldn't continue. There were forebodings.

Oh yes, Fannette, you are not the only one who inherited some of our mother. We are half-sisters, Nette, whether you are pleased to acknowledge it or not!

"You're so quiet," Anton remarked as they started out, keeping their horses to a walk.

"My thoughts are not quiet."

"Nor mine," he agreed.

"Why, then, do you stay with us?"

He shrugged. "I've never left a duel unfinished, nor a game of cards half played."

Was it still Fannette that held him? Or was it herself? It was better not to consider the possibilities.

Jared and Fannette rode quietly for the first half-hour. The beat of the horses' hoofs was muffled by the mud, and they traversed a muted world of unreality. There seemed to be no substance to the bare trees or to the occasional evergreen, nor to the dim lights of a farmhouse

313

tucked into its fields for the night. They moved across gentle slopes and shallow valleys. All remote, all transient . . .

And darkness. Could horses see in the dark like cats?

"After this trip," Fannette asked because she had to ask, "will there be more?"

"No. This is the last." Jared paused in thought. "I was a lawyer, you know, but I've been away a long time. I don't think I want to take up a practice in the East again. It'll be hard to settle into a quiet life."

Impossible, maybe, she thought with a flutter of fear.

"It's bound to be dull," she said aloud.

"I've considered going west. To San Francisco, perhaps. There's room for lawyers out there. The aftermath of the gold discovery, the fights over claims. It could be a challenge."

San Francisco. So far away. The other end of the world. Her world.

"There's bound to be temptation if I remain in the South—or even near it. These last few years have been spent living as if each day might be the last, and up until now I've enjoyed the uncertainties. But this trip's been different."

"Why?"

"Because of you and Poppy. I must have been out of my mind to take the two of you into such danger."

He turned, taking her rein.

"Damn it, Fannette, isn't it time we had some serious words about the future?"

She was silent.

"Do you think—" He suddenly stopped speaking, and his hand covered the hilt of his gun, his eyes straining to see down the slope into the hollow.

The moon had emerged from behind a cloud, and they were bathed in a sudden burst of light. Below them she could see two men sitting over the faintly glowing embers of a fire. One had a bottle tilted to his mouth, head back,

314

but the other had seen their silhouette on the hillside. He jumped to his feet, rifle in hand, swaying slightly.

"Evenin', friends," he called up to them. "Come down and join us in a soshable snort. I'm Bill Ashbury, and my par'ner here is Clem Swift."

"Stay back," Jared said to Fannette, and he trotted down to the campfire.

"You folks out to git the slave stealers, too?" Ashbury wanted to know. "Reckon most the country's lookin' for them killers."

His partner had put down the bottle. He was a fat man, and even in the darkness, he looked unwashed. But his eyes were sharper than those of his companion. He made out Fannette's outline back in the shadows.

"Kind of late to take a lady for a ride, ain't it?" he asked.

"We're strangers in these parts," Jared explained. "We were visiting kin, and got a late start back to where we were staying. Then we took a wrong turn."

"Where you headin'? Mebbe we can help." The fat man's eyes narrowed as he appraised them.

"Oh, we're on the right track now," Jared assured him. "We stopped at that farmhouse back there, and they told us which way to go. We've still got maybe six miles, so I'll pass up your hospitality."

"Better keep a mighty sharp lookout," Ashbury cautioned. "You alone with the little lady, and them killers loose, the devil knows where!"

"I'm handy with a gun," Jared replied. "Had my hand on it the minute I spotted your fire. Thought you might be some of them. But last we heard, they were up Louisville way."

"Not now. Folks are figurin' they might not be goin' by Louisville, after all. My par'ner and me, we thought we'd give a look down here."

"If I were you, I'd build my fire higher so folks can see you aren't a nigger. I came close to taking a potshot, and you're just lucky the moon came out when it did so I could see you were a white man."

"Now that's a idear," Ashbury agreed, and Clem pulled himself to his feet. The two of them set to work heaping brush on the embers.

"Hopefully, that'll keep the others from stumbling onto them," Jared said when they were out of hearing distance. "It's too early for anyone to mistake it for our midnight signal fire."

He thought a minute.

"It might be a good idea to circle back so we can head any stragglers away from this slope."

And that would mean another hour, possibly two more hours, in the cold, Fannette thought wearily. The night wasn't even half gone, and already she felt it would never end.

They rode nearly a quarter of a mile before Jared turned the horses and started to follow the road back. They waited at the junction for a much longer time than seemed reasonable to Fannette. Still, there was no sign of shadowy, plodding figures, nor of laden pack horses.

"They're keeping to cover far better than I dared to hope," Jared remarked with satisfaction.

We came so close, Fannette thought. So terribly close. If she hadn't been wearing a riding habit that still looked stylish in the dim light, and if Jared hadn't used his wits . . .

And if the two men hadn't been nearly blind drunk . . .

How much longer? How much longer before they ran into hunters who would recognize them for what they were? Group by group, traveling separate routes, traveling alone, how, even so, could they hope to outwit men who were hungry to fill their purses with blood money?

They reached the spot that had been marked for the midnight rendezvous, but the fire was extinguished and cold. There was no sign to show that a group of nine people had rested and eaten there.

"They've gone on," Jared decided. "Thank God they got by those men."

Fannette caught his arm. A man stepped out from under an overhanging cliff. For the second time that night, Jared drew his gun.

"Don' you shoot that, Mr. Jared!" George Washington stepped into full view. "We worry half to deaf 'bout you an' Miz McLaury. I stay here to wait."

Jared put back his gun. "You left Pearl to go on alone?"

"Oh, she wid Abe. She stay jus' a little behind him, and he look after her." George Washington chuckled. "Or mebbe de other way 'roun'!"

"We'll catch up with them. Are you rested enough to go at a fast clip?"

"Go as fast as you wants. See how I cares."

So on through the night they went without even the comfort of a cup of coffee or a piece of hoe cake. Fannette thought hungrily of the cabbage Pearl carried. The night before, she had wrapped potatoes and corn pone in the leaves and put them into the ashes to cook. Of course, they could have baked longer, but still they were far better than the usual midnight rations.

Her mind traitorously went back to the heaped breakfast buffet at Bijou when there were guests. Fresh oysters and prawns. Bacon and sausages. Eggs. Preserved meats. English and French delicacies. Jam. Honey. Coffee. Chocolate and tea. Fresh cream . . .

Was this what being pregnant did to a woman? Come, now, Fannette, she told herself, you've always had a disgraceful appetite! Not anymore, though. At least, not until Glory brought her the tea in the morning. But at night she was ravenous.

"I'm hungry," she said to Jared without intending to.

"Yes. I believe you."

From nearby, George Washington spoke up.

"We pass by Miss Poppy and Mr. Anton. Mr. Anton got

317

two turkeys tied back of his saddle. We eats good today."

Turkey! Fannette sat up straighter in her saddle, remembering how deliciously Emily prepared them.

Apparently Jared's thoughts were above food. "Tomorrow night we'll be close to Lexington," he said. "Last fall when I was up this way, I made arrangements for a stop at one of the stations. I figured we'd be pretty weary by the time we reached the place."

"An actual house?" Fannette asked, not really believing it.

He smiled at her, and his voice was softer. Gentle, even tender.

"A barn and a cabin. I dickered for both. The folks who live there plan to go down the line and stay with their married daughter when we take over." Then he added. "We'll need the rest. The worst weather is up ahead."

"But it's spring."

"It is?" He looked at the grim, bare outline of trees in the bright moonlight. "You tell folks up north about spring."

"At least the sky has finally cleared."

But she was thinking about the treat he'd promised. A house and a bed. Perhaps a bath. With luck, she might even be able to wash her hair!

IX

Their stomachs were still content from the evening feast of turkey when they rode out into the night, and they were grateful for the still air. Cold as it was, a wind would have cut through even the heaviest of the fleece-lined coats.

Poppy found herself anticipating the comforts that waited at the end of this night's journey. Two days in a warm cabin with a bed. Hopefully, a soft bed. Warm water off the hob, and a place to sleep away from snores, snorts and Tressa whimpering in the night.

Poor thing. Would she be haunted all of her life by those storm-ridden hours when she'd huddled inside a hollow tree?

"Touch our Lord," Poppy would whisper to the child in the darkness, and the whimpers would subside. It had been good of Fannette to give Tressa that comfort. Certainly, the crucifix was very old and valuable. But then Fannette had absolutely no concern for the value of anything. Money or jewelry. Her upbringing had been very different.

And had Jared noticed how pale Fannette had become? Fannette who had been the reason for the comfortable phaeton and for, yes, for the portable privy? How they missed that now. Poppy sighed. *Bien*, she thought, with the aid of our Blessed Lady, it would soon be over. Perhaps within the next two weeks—providing nothing went wrong.

She murmured a rosary under her breath, using her fingers to count the beads.

Jove trotted up and rode alongside her horse.

"I been worryin' 'bout Zette," he confided.

She noted in her mind that she was on the third decade

319

and turned her attention to him. She took off her hat and brushed her curly hair back off her forehead. Even with her bulky jacket she really didn't look very much like a boy, unless she kept it buttoned. Well, no fear of forgetting in this weather!

"Zette's safe at Bijou. Why worry about her? Worry about us. We need it."

Jove rode silently for a few minutes, his forehead wrinkled, and his usual grin missing.

"Miss Poppy, what if my girl catch? Like Sassie?"

"Catch?"

Jove nodded. "Glory say that Sassie—what she lost—wasn't no one month carrying."

Poppy smiled slightly. "I suspected."

"Well, suppose Zette, she catch?"

"Oh Jove! Jove, you didn't?"

"Course I did," he replied calmly. "If I didn't do it to her, somebody else, he do it. That girl was ready, Miss Poppy. And I mean ready!"

"You're the one should know."

"Oh, I know!" Jove's grin was back. "She a lot of girl, that Zette. But she say she'll wait till I comes back for her. She says no dance, no barbecue, no foolin' around."

After a second, he added, "But I worry anyhow. I worry all the time. If Miss Donna give us the word, we be married now. But Miss Donna say wait till I get back."

They rode in silence, ready to separate at the first glimpse of a stranger.

Anton moved up beside them and they slowed the pace, remembering that the others walked. They wished the moon would shine more brightly, but were grateful it didn't. Above all, they hoped the bed would be soft.

"Holy Mary, full of grace . . ."

Was she on the third or fourth decade in the second round of the imaginary beads? How had she come to leave her rosary in the pocket of her dress back at Bowling Green?

320

And Anton. What of Anton? And what of herself? Had she forgotten what she had always been so certain of? Of what she had always looked forward to with hope? Everything now seemed to be so unclear.

"It's cold enough to snow," Anton commented out of the stillness. "*Diable*! That is not a thought to bring pleasure."

The wind had risen, and Jove put up a finger to test it.

"That wind, he—" He stopped to correct himself. "That wind will bring the clouds and snow. It's too cold to rain."

"Oh, we could have sleet," Poppy observed pleasantly. She turned in her saddle and caught a glimpse of someone walking up near the fringe of trees. Nine people. Nine men and women trudging through the icy darkness. Stumbling, perhaps. Watching for the North Star when they lost their way after circling a farmhouse or town.

But freedom drew closer each day. Canada. A dream that was about to become reality. Let the cold, the wind, the snow come! A few more weeks and they'd look down on the Ohio.

We left on the sixth of January, she mused. And Fannette complained about sleeping on a hard pallet. What innocents! And the date now? Somewhere past mid-March? She must remember to ask Jared, she had lost all count of time.

The moon was high when they reached the spot set aside for the midnight lunch. Jove built a fire to heat water for coffee and to serve as a signal. Poppy sat on the ground, resting her back against a tree trunk.

Jove came over and leaned on the tree as he watched the fire work itself into a subdued blaze.

"I think Zette will be all right," he said, and Poppy realized his mind had never left the subject. "I tell Miss Donna I got good intentions, and Sat'day 'fore we leave, Zette and me, we jump the broomstick backwards."

"That makes everything different," Poppy agreed. She

321

was aware of Anton moving up close, attending what Jove had said.

Jove chuckled. "Zette, she got her foot caught, so I boss for sure!"

Anton looked at Poppy. "I hear this thing about jumping a broom. I've never quite understood.

"That's because you never lived on a plantation," Poppy replied. "If Jove and Zette jumped backwards over a broomstick, that's as binding as if they were married in the big house."

" 'Cept Zette want to be married in the big house. She tell me Miss Donna promise when the time come she give Zette a white dress and gloves and a veil. But if Zette catches, she'll be big when I get back, and Miss Donna'll be mad."

"And you actually jumped a broomstick?" Anton persisted, intrigued.

"Zette have her brother hold it real high. But I think he hold it higher when she jump. He say she a flighty girl and she need a boss."

Anton still looked bemused, so Poppy explained. "They hold the stick a foot or more in the air, and when the bride and groom jump over it backwards, they're married. But if one of them touches the stick, then the other will always be boss."

Anton considered the explanation.

"Poppy," he said, "let's go look for a broomstick."

Poppy leaned back, laughing. Anton had sounded far too serious. When she stopped laughing, she realized both Jove and Anton were staring at her.

"I'm not making a joke," Anton went on. "But perhaps we should delay until we find a priest."

"Can you forget Fannette so soon?"

Anton tapped the toe of his boot with his riding crop.

"An *enciénte* woman holds very little appeal to me. Unless the child were mine. Which it most certainly is not."

It was Poppy's turn to stare.

322

Anton shrugged. "In certain matters, it is difficult to deceive a Frenchman." Then he added truthfully, "Besides, I find it amusing to listen to gossip. It's seldom I miss anything of interest."

The first of the walkers approached the fire, and Jove went to take the night's provisions from his pack. Anton rose lazily to his feet in order to help.

"It's to be hoped that tonight's fare will be more edible than the last," he commented, "If it hadn't been for that wild turkey, I think I'd have gone out of my mind."

"Where are you going once we reach Cincinnati?"

"To the East Coast. I'll take a ship for France from there." He paused. "With you, I hope, Poppy."

"I've no desire to be a mistress. Not even to you, Anton."

"I did not hear myself suggest you go as a mistress. I believe I made it clear I had a wife in mind."

Poppy regarded him steadily, the firelight reflecting the golden depth of her eyes.

"I've had another vocation planned."

Anton bowed slightly. "I've suspected that. But it isn't too late? There've been no vows?"

"Only to myself." Then she added, "And what of your mother? There's more to object to in me than there was in Fannette."

"As long ago as our stay at the Lemmon plantation I'd decided that my happiness meant more than my duty to the deValois name. Perhaps it was being free of the constant reminder. Would you believe that even when I was at the university, Maman sent me weekly letters to impress on me what was expected?"

"But still you didn't tell Fannette of your change of intentions?"

Anton shrugged. "There was much to be considered. Then, just as I was about to speak, we stopped at the shack. After that, marriage was out of the question. Besides, much as it wounded my pride, it became obvious that Fannette had her heart elsewhere."

His voice softened and he smiled down at Poppy. "And at about the same time I became aware of you as more than a very beautiful woman. I found myself going over things you had said, laughing again at a witty remark. Admiring the practical way you face what must be faced. You will be a good wife for a Frenchman, Poppy."

"And does love enter into this?" she asked very quietly.

He had moved closer and he put his arms around her. He turned her face up to his. "I know now that before you I had no real understanding of love. Desire, yes. I very much desired Fannette. But I love you."

His lips were gentle, his kiss tender. She felt cherished, and it was good to feel his lithe body against hers. Good to feel herself a woman. She'd often wondered if she'd been born without a woman's natural reaction to an attractive man, and now she knew she had not. Her mother's blood flowed through her veins, just as it flowed through Fannette's.

She raised her arms, palms against his back, pulling him closer and permitting herself the joy of his embrace, the thrill of the warmth circulating in her body.

Then Jove's voice, slightly disapproving, broke in on them.

"Miss Poppy! The rest of the folks are coming down the hill."

She moved out of Anton's arms, but his eyes remained on her face.

"Yes?" he asked.

She shook her head.

"I've got to think. And I must pray."

"And so will I," he assured her. "But perhaps our prayers will not be for the same thing and will only confuse those who listen." Then he added, "I think you know I'm a patient man."

Patient? Yes, that and more. But was this for her? She who'd always been so certain of what her answer would be, should such a question ever have arisen?

I've been too smug, she thought. Too proud of being above the errors of my sister . . .

She joined the folks who had come from the night to gather around the fire.

"Don't know what hurts the baddest, my bottom or my feets," Wednesday complained as he fell to the ground. So far, he had as yet to land upright when he slid off the back of a pack horse.

Jove turned to Poppy, his eyes worried.

"Nobody's seen Leon," he said.

Leon. A brownish man, broad of shoulder and muscular. A loner. He never danced to Abe's fiddle or sang when Wednesday led a spiritual. And he never sat gossiping. There were times when he and Wednesday became involved in a heated discussion, but other than that he kept to himself. Another of the insurrectionists, she long ago decided.

She asked around. No one had seen him.

"All of you know the way to the station," she said. "We won't be at the next rest, you'll go on alone."

"What you do, Miss Poppy?" Wednesday asked.

"Jove and I will retrace the route on horseback. When you get to the place where we're to stay, tell Mr. Jared what's happened."

"I'll not permit that you ride back in this cold!" Anton exclaimed. "You go on ahead to the shelter and leave this business to Jove and me."

Poppy shook her head. "I've the responsibility. It's really not your concern."

"*Vraiment*," he agreed. "But you, *ma chérie*, are my concern." He paused. "Why should it be necessary for anyone to go back? Why can't he find his own way? How can you expect to discover him in this darkness?"

"He could be hurt," Poppy explained. "There's a storm on the way, and I couldn't rest knowing that one of our people might be lying out in the snow freezing, perhaps."

325

"I'll accompany you, then. I carry a gun and I know how to use it. Let's hope it won't be necessary."

The three of them left the others to put out the fire. They rode together down the hillside, but separated when they came to the road. They crossed, meeting again in the wooded shadows. The wind had sharpened, and now clouds hung low and black.

"This is insane," Anton said as the hours stretched toward dawn. "The horses are exhausted, and we'd have found him by now." He tightened the woolen scarf around his neck. "Most likely he's back and safe while we freeze."

"Snow comin' fast," Jove agreed, pointing to the first splotches that landed on his horse's neck. Poppy held out her hand and watched the crystallized water melt.

"Snow, he don't wait for no one," Jove added.

"We'll have to turn back," Poppy agreed reluctantly. She glanced upward, "It's nearly daylight, so we'll have to ride separately."

"But any one of us could lose our way," Anton protested. "And how would the rest of us know?"

Poppy considered the matter. "I think we should meet at last night's resting place," she said finally. "That way we can keep check on each other before we've gone too far."

Daylight was all around them, struggling through the growing haze of white. A grim, grudging brightness under a black sky.

They had paused at the top of a ridge, and suddenly Anton gave out an exclamation. He pointed down into the valley.

"There's smoke coming from that broken-down shack!" he said. "When we stopped near there last night, it was empty."

Poppy made out the ruins of what once had been a farmhouse. The back portion had fallen in on itself, but

326

the walls of the main room were still intact.

"Leon never come by while we there," Jove put in, his voice rising with excitement. "But Leon, he always travel alone, 'cept for midnight. He like his coffee."

"He must be hurt!" Poppy exclaimed. "He'd never have stayed there if he wasn't!"

She dug her heel into the side of her roan and started down the hill at a gallop.

"*Merde!*" Anton shouted in alarm. "She could be going into trouble!" Both he and Jove spurred after her.

Her voice came back to them, above the sound of the pounding hoofs.

"I can see the pack horse tethered by the door. We've found Leon!"

She came into view again as she rode up to the cabin.

"Leon!" Her voice was sharp and clear in the morning silence. "Leon, are you hurt?"

Anton, followed by Jove, galloped his horse through the stand of pines and drew up beside her.

"Watch out!" Anton exclaimed as he reached for his gun. But he was too late. A shot boomed out, and his horse veered in fright. The bullet lodged in his left shoulder instead of his heart, where it had been aimed. He struggled to steady his mount, while the blood streamed down his arm.

"Put up your hands, all of you," a fat man bellowed from the porch. "Next time I won't just nick a shoulder. You, too, black boy, get them up! My par'ner has his shotgun leveled at your head."

Another man came out of the shadow of the doorway. He staggered slightly, but quickly regained his balance.

"Get that gun, Bill," the fat man said, jerking his head in Anton's direction. "And you! Keep that horse steady, I aim to shoot at the both of you if you try to pull anything funny."

The short man, Bill, wrenched Anton's revolver out of its holster, and the fat man moved closer.

327

"Get off your horses. All of you." His eyes flickered over Poppy, then narrowed. "That's a likely looking boy," he observed, licking his lips. "Real pretty."

Poppy looked down, grateful for her bulky jacket.

"I've a fancy for pretty boys," the fat man elaborated.

"Clem, there ain't no time for that kind of thing," Bill reminded him. "We got that nigger tied up in the cabin, and sooner we get them wrapped up beside him, the sooner we can leave for town. That snow could trap us here before we get help."

"We'll hog tie them, and you can ride to town to let them know what we got out here," Clem replied. "I aim to stay and look out for them."

Bill moved over to Poppy. He reached out a hand and jerked open her jacket.

"You're out of luck, Clem," he snickered. "This ain't no boy! I knew it was too pretty."

"Have you no decency?" Anton exclaimed. "Take your hands off her! Pig!"

"Ain't a boy?" the fat man looked as if he might dissolve into tears. Then he brightened. "Reckon I can use a she like a he." Again anticipation glinted from between his puffy eyelids.

"Then when you're through, I can use a she like a she!" Bill roared with laughter over his own wit.

"Mister," Jove moved toward the fat man, his lean hips swaying just the least bit, "mister, why you make believe with a woman? Us a boy."

Clem's eyes swept over the long, slim frame. "How old?" he asked.

"Sixteen," Jove replied, looking at him boldly. "But us ain't so scrawny everywhere." He snickered. "When ole missy ain' roun', ole massa, he like de boys. He have two of us'uns in the quarters." Jove's diction grew thicker as he went on. "He shore teach us some joyful tricks. Black Ass an' Brown Ass, he call us'uns."

"And you was Black Ass?"

"Sho was! Den dar was Yallar Ass. But we neber see him much. He drive ole Massa 'roun'."

The fat man moved closer, and Bill watched in drunken fascination.

"An' I ain't as tall as I looks," Jove continued. "You jus' look see how short I get when I takes off dese boots."

He bent down and started to untie his laces. Clem bent even closer, swaying. Before any of them realized Jove's intentions, his right hand whipped upward, knife clutched and ready.

Clem stumbled sideways. He made a move to bring up his gun, but Jove's hand had shot backwards. There was a flash of metal, and the knife was buried to the hilt in the fat rolls of the slave hunter's neck. The revolver fell onto the ground, imbedded in the mounting snow, and Clem clutched at his throat. His knees bent under him, and he fell. Bright blood spurted out as he yanked the knife free. Bright red blood against the white snow.

Bill's drink-numbed brain galvanized through the stunned haze that surrounded it. There was an explosion, followed by the sickening *splunk* as a bullet dug deep into flesh. Jove lurched forward and carried Bill to the gound with him.

Bill shook himself free of the boy, and leaned on his elbow, gun leveled. But Anton had caught up the revolver that lay in the snow, and his shot rang out first. The shot of an expert marksman. Bill fell back. Where there had been an eye, there remained only a bloody hole.

Poppy turned away, sickened, and Anton held her to him with his one good arm, pushing her face into his chest, trying to shield her. To keep her from seeing . . .

"Jove!" she screamed, remembering. She pulled herself free and ran to where the boy lay. "Jove!"

The left side of Jove's coat was blood soaked, and there was perspiration on his forehead even though the cold wind was lashing snow around them.

"Miss Poppy," he said. "I sorry I talk dirty."

Poppy ripped back his shirt and tried to plug the wound. Anton was tying his own scarf around his upper arm, one end held between teeth.

"Miss Poppy, you don't think I that kind of boy?"

Poppy shook her head and tried to smile. "You just wait till I tell Zette!" she said.

"She ain't going to believe you." He closed his eyes and she whispered a thankful prayer when she saw he'd fainted.

Anton bent over, his face white from the pain of his own wound.

"*Mort*?" he asked.

Poppy loked up. "It's bad. We need help. And you—?"

"There's Leon," he reminded her, and went to the cabin.

Poppy hesitated by Jove, but there was nothing she could do, and the snow flurry had cleared. She went to the cabin and watched from the doorway, while Anton awkwardly undid the ropes that bound Leon to a post.

"I squattin'," he explained. "Man can't run with his pants down. Fact, a man can't do nothin' time like that. Day headin' back, 'cause dey think he gonna snow. They most fell right over me.'

Poppy's mind wasn't on the explanation, but on the boy lying outside and Anton's bloodless face. A stain was spreading on his improvised bandage.

"You and Leon can get Jove inside between the two of you," she said. "I'll ride back for help."

"You?" Anton asked.

"You can't, and you'll need Leon to watch over things."

"Are you up to it?"

She nodded. There was really no choice. Weeping and grief could come later, but now it was important to clear her mind of everything except the need to ride. And to ride as fast as her weary horse could go.

Leon was carrying Jove into the shelter of the shack as

Poppy mounted a horse. The boy was limp. Still unconscious.

Jove! she thought as she spurred the horse. She was riding Anton's gelding, their most powerful mount. Jove! Where's your harmonica? Where's your Zette?

X

By the time Poppy reached the farmhouse station, the snow had started to fall again. Jared ran out to meet her, followed by the others. She tumbled down into his arms, and he turned, shouting for Abe to see to the winded horse.

"Where are the others?" he asked, looking up the road.

"Back." That was all she could say for the minute. He half carried her into the warmth of the cabin. Fannette ran to her and helped her take off her wet outer clothing.

She paused to give Poppy an unexpected hug. "I've been so afraid for you! I thought you might have been caught!"

"We were." Poppy had recovered her breath and she looked up at Jared. "Get Trojan to hitch the cart as soon as he can. You'll have to go back. Take Glory."

"Back where?" Jared asked as Trojan ran out the door. "Is someone hurt?"

"Badly." Poppy warmed her hands on the hot cup of coffee Emily had brought her, but she made no move to drink it. "Anton in the shoulder, and Jove—" She couldn't go on, the tears welling into her eyes.

Letty screamed and sat on the floor, rocking back and forth, her hands covering her face.

"Where?" Jared demanded. "For God sakes, Poppy, where?"

"I'll have to go with you; you'd miss it in the snow. And there's not that much time." She lowered her voice, eyes on Letty. "I couldn't stop Jove from bleeding. I'm afraid—"

"Drink down that coffee," Jared said. He pulled on his boots and heavy coat and snatched up some blankets.

"The cart's out there," Trojan announced, running up

to the door. Jared carried Poppy outside and put her in the bed of the cart. He threw in the blankets and then climbed up beside Glory, who waited on the seat, kerchief bundle in lap.

"How far before we turn off?" he asked. "I'll wake you then."

She told him, and pulled the covers tightly around her aching, chilled body as she resolved not to sleep. Groggy with weariness, her eyes closed almost immediately.

She awakened to Jared shaking her shoulder.

"You'll have to give us directions from here on," he told her.

She sat up, forcing her eyes open with difficulty. They were at the midnight stop of the night before. She climbed out of the cart and, still bundled in blankets, changed places with Glory.

It was still snowing, but not heavily, a steady fluttering of white that had had already cloaked farms and fences.

It was a little past noon when they reached the fallen gate post next to a hollow tree. Poppy had marked it in her mind that morning when she'd galloped past it.

"Turn to the right of the post," she said, sitting up straighter. "There's a road of sorts."

Let them be in time. Blessed Mother, Blessed Saints, let them be in time!

There was smoke still emerging from the crumbling chimney, and Leon opened the sagging door. He called back into the shack, and Anton appeared at his side.

Jared lifted Glory down, while Trojan rushed inside to his son.

Poppy followed Jared and Glory, but she paused by Anton. He was very white, his dark eyes dark with pain. He put his right arm around her, holding her for a long, comforting minute.

"Jove?" She had to ask, even though she feared the answer.

"Not good. He's never recovered consciousness."

333

She glanced down at the debris-strewn yard, now white and fresh under a cover of snow.

"Leon found a broken spade. He patched the handle and managed to dig a hole in the back part of the shack. The ground was softer there."

She breathed deeply, in relief, realizing for the first time how she'd been dreading the sight of the sprawled bodies.

They moved together into the shack. Jared had brought candles, and aided by their flickering light, Glory busied herself making a poultice. She removed the packing Poppy had made from her shirt and bound the poultice into the hole. Then she looked up into the anxious faces of Trojan and Jared.

"We take him back. No need he die here."

They ripped the door off the post and moved Jove onto it. They placed the improvised stretcher in the back of the cart and Glory climbed in beside it. Trojan took a place at the front, just behind the seat, so he could hold Jove's head in his lap. He hadn't spoken since they'd entered the cabin, but now he crooned softly to his son, as if it were a baby he was cradling.

Somehow the four of them managed to crowd onto the seat. Jared and Leon on the outer sides with Anton and herself in between. Anton lay his head back and closed his eyes. His body slumped, and she put her arm around him, holding him steady, hoping that he'd finally fainted and was spared the throbbing of his arm, at least for awhile.

You're a good man, she thought. And a brave one. But I have a duty. A responsibility to my people. To the *gens de couleur* who aren't as fortunate as I've been . . .

But what of me? Don't I have a responsibility to myself? To the woman of me?

She thought of the joy that filled her when she wore a new gown. Of the soft, rich feeling of satin. The delight she found in color, in tints. The satisfaction of knowing she was pretty. More than pretty, beautiful. Never before had she considered what she would be foresaking. All of those things had mattered very little.

Then, why did they now? Was it being loved by a man that caused a woman to relish all that was feminine? Or was it some mysterious ordeal of decision that had been pressed upon her?

Finally, blissfully, she dozed again. Even in her sleep, she was aware of Anton next to her. Of the creaking of the cart. Trojan's soft, grieving croon. The beat of the horses' hoofs. . . .

"Blessed Mary, full of grace . . . Let Jove live. Please, dear Lord, let Jove live."

And it was her fault. It had been she, Poppy, who had abandoned caution and galloped down to the shack shouting out Leon's name.

But for her, Jove would be laughing. Dreaming of his Zette and playing his harmonica.

But for her.

Leading the three of them into a trap that hadn't even been set!

XI

Letty had a bed prepared for Jove on a broad sleeping bench. There was one on each side of the fireplace, and Poppy stumbled to the other. She curled up and immediately fell asleep.

When Letty saw her son, she shrieked, throwing her skirt over her face, tears washing down her cheeks.

"Shut up, woman!" Trojan shouted at her, misery deep in his own eyes. "You want his ma yelling, the last thing he hear?"

Glory was busy cleaning Anton's wound, muttering to herself as she worked. Fannette stod near, ready to help, and she wondered how long he could continue to sit up straight without flinching. Even his lips were white. He made no sound, his eyes on Poppy's quiet form.

"What you doin' ober there?" Letty screamed at Glory. "Ain't you goin' do nothin' 'bout my boy?"

Jared touched Letty's shoulder gently. "Glory's done all she can. There's nothing more she can do but give him a sleeping potion for his pain, if you wake him up."

Glory finished with Anton, and he lay down on the bed Fannette had prepared in a corner not too far from the fire. She had started to have his bedding taken into the sleeping room, but Glory made it plain she wanted him where she could watch.

"She's worried about him developing a fever," Jared explained.

Glory took possession of a rocking chair and placed it where she could see both patients. She picked up a piece of mending and a darning needle, and Fannette knew everything that could be done had been.

"He be all right," Glory told Fannette, her eyes on

Anton. "But mebbe he neber raise his left arm good."

Fannette started to go to Jove, but Letty caught her shoulder and yanked her back.

"You go way!" she shoulted. "Go out into the snow and don' eber come back! 'Cept for you, my baby be fine, 'cept for you, Lem and Junie be here! 'Cept for you, mebbe we all be in N'Orleans by now!"

Trojan put his big hand across Letty's mouth and pulled her away. He spoke softly, soothingly, pressing her to him.

She's right, Fannette thought. No one else has the courage to say it, but Letty's right.

She pushed aside the curtain that shut off the single bedroom. There was a rag rug on the split timber floor where one could feel its warmth under bare feet on a cold night. A clapboard ceiling resting on round poles sectioned off the loft, and she could hear their people moving around up there, preparing their sleeping places. In addition to the fireplace, there was a lean-to kitchen. Emily had taken charge out there. Already the savory smell of cooking food had spread even as far as the sleeping room.

Everything that was happening was because she'd refused to obey the rules. Only it was others who paid the price. Yes, Letty was right.

And where were the tears that had come so easily since her pregnancy started? Could she only cry for herself? She leaned against the wall, dry-eyed and every part of her crying.

Trojan tapped on the outside, and then put his head through the curtain.

"Jove awake," he said. "He want to talk with you."

"You must mean Poppy."

"No. He ask for you."

She went back into the big room, trying not to see Letty's resentful glare as she crossed to where Jove lay.

His eyes were open in a face more gray than black.

" 'Bout Zette," he said.

Fannette bent lower to save him the straining.

337

"Pa got the money for her."

"I don't want money, Jove. I'll give her freedom. It isn't easy under Louisiana laws, but I'll find a way."

"Zette mighty flighty. I want you keep her till she find a good man."

Fannette nodded. She couldn't manage any words.

"And Miz McLaury, no reason you fuss we call you that." He smiled, his teeth flashing briefly. "Miss Nette . . ."

Letty shoved her away.

"Leave me my boy!" she said fiercely.

Fannette backed away. She was aware of the eyes on her. Pearl, who had just come down from the loft and was still by the ladder. Glory who had risen from her chair to watch the herbs she was simmering on the fireplace hob. Anton, wide-eyed in his corner.

But where was Jared? Where was Trojan? Poppy still slept.

Then everyone except Poppy and Anton were bending over Jove. Letty gave a drawn-out wail.

And Fannette knew why.

She pushed open the outside door and ran down the three stairs to the path.

"Go into de snow!" Letty had screamed. "Go way! Don' eber come back! Leave me my boy!"

XII

Glory watched the door close, knowing that the time had come. She wondered if there was enough strength left in her worn old body for what she knew would be demanded of her.

It had been wise to wait until the weak one surfaced, she reflected. No longer had she the endurance to seek out the hiding places deep inside the mind. It would take all the power she possessed just to force obedience to her command.

Still, it might not be so difficult. The other might welcome freedom. Nearly always it was like that.

Glory reflected on this power of hers with very little pride. Even a snake could hold and hypnotize with the glitter of its eyes. Was she so much greater when by the same means she reached into a mind to sort out a confusion of identity?

She turned to Pearl. "You come," she said, "but not yet."

Yes. It was time to free Miz McLaury.

She went out the door, following the footprints that led away. This that lay ahead would deplete her strength, but it would be even harder for Miz McLaury, a shock of the worse sort. Perhaps an emptiness?

Ahead was the one for whom she searched. Glory drew a deep breath, still wondering what it must be like to lose a part of one's self.

The blinding white haze welcomed her. It reached out to hide her. All she had to do was run, Fannette told herself. Run!

Whiteness and haze. Cold. Falling snow. Drifted snow. What did any of it matter?

Then, green eyes out of the whiteness. Glory's green eyes in a wrinkled black face. Staring, probing. Finding.

Wrenching. Pulling. Wrenching a part deep inside her. Twisting and severing.

A breeze passing in the sharp wind. A soft, lonely little breeze . . .

Peace. Peace—until she heard a voice telling her to follow. Stumbling, falling. Unable to follow any longer. Unable to move. The voice and the eyes no longer compelled her to do what there was no strength to do.

Arms holding her, carrying her. A woman's softness. Then a man's hard chest. Finally the shelter of the farmhouse.

But would she ever be warm again? It was so cold.

Opening her eyes to the lamplight, she saw a hot brew steaming in a cup that Glory held. So old. Glory looked so old, so frail, so tired . . .

Pearl and Jared were standing near. The smell of rum and the fragrance of herbs. Then Jared was holding her up so Glory could give her the drink. A blurring again. Finally sleep. But still cold.

And she was free! The voiceless communication that told her the other was at rest. That now she was she.

Jared holding her. Secure. So very secure.

XIII

Shock as much as exposure, Jared thought, as he helped Glory get the warm drink into Fannette. She shook with passing chills and her skin kept a bluish tint. Pearl brought in more covers and heaped them onto the bed, and Glory massaged her hands and feet.

What terrible thing had happened to Fannette out there in the snow?

Glory straightened up and looked at him. Her meaning was clear. Human warmth was the thing most easily transferred.

He stripped off his heavy clothing, forgetting that Pearl was there. She slipped out of the room.

When he was naked, Glory nodded in approval, and taking the lamp with her, she left them alone.

He cradled Fannette into the curve of his body, running his hands over her cold flesh, trying to restore the warming circulation of her blood. Her teeth had stopped chattering after Glory's brew, and he felt her body began to grow limp, to relax.

The narcotic, for it must have been a sedative of some sort, was finally working. He wondered if Fannette was aware of his nearness, and decided that she wasn't.

Her long, dark eyes had been heavy under their fringe of lashes when Glory had left, and he was certain she slept now. She still experienced spells of uncontrollable trembling, but they were lessening and her flesh was warming to his touch. He rubbed his chin in her hair, thinking of the bright glory of it.

He rested his hand on her abdomen, cupping it to the rounding of his own doing. Just the thought brought on desire for her. A desire that must be curbed.

341

Fannette, he thought, it's no wonder you felt you were treated more like a mistress than a wife. How many times have we had together since you became my wife? That first night in the shack and that afternoon. He tried to blot this from his mind, the time he had crept into her tent to apologize, though they both knew differently.

And now. So pathetically little time in each other's arms.

How did one explain to the woman he loved that these black people must come first? These people who'd put their lives and meager savings into his hands?

"We'll make up for it," he promised her sleeping self. "We'll have to wait until Cincinnati, but then, damn it, we'll make up for it!"

And later, would she understand how much he'd wanted to talk about the child she carried? How happy he was?

He thought back to the morning he'd watched Glory administer her morning tea to certain women. What a shock to find his own wife was the first to be given a cup!

And his talk with Letty.

"I ain' s'posed to say it, Mr. Jared, but Miz McLaury ain' come roun'. Not even one time."

Of course it was the fruit of that night in the shack near Baton Rouge. Certainly it couldn't have been from the afternoon. No, their child could only have been created in love.

How could she imagine that he wouldn't know? Didn't she realize how closely he watched over her?

Headstrong, obstinate Fannette, who thought to hide her condition. Yet, it was better this way. Until Cincinnati. This was her strength. She couldn't let down. She wouldn't dare show weakness for fear he might notice.

And it was his strength as well. He couldn't permit himself the luxury of pampering her. There was a priority. To see the people safely under the protection of the Quakers in Cincinnati. Even though he had to accompany them to

342

Sandusky, the responsibility then would have been passed over to the experts.

But now. Now there was an oasis in the wilderness of self-deprivation. His arms tightened around Fannette, and she stirred. How many hours had they been lying here together?

"Jared?" She spoke drowsily, her words slurred. The sedative was still at work.

"Of course."

"It was cold. I thought I was dying. But now I'm warm."

"I'll have you know," he said, "that I'm a quilt."

She giggled a little. "You don't feel like a quilt. I never knew a quilt to have a—"

"Woman!" he interrupted hastily. "And I say woman because I'm forbidden to say wife. Woman, I've been holding you for hours. Just waiting for you to wake up. And do you realize how long it's been since—"

"Oh, but I do! I do!" she said happily, turning in her arms so she faced him. "Yes, I do!"

"I didn't intend to take advantage of the situation," he lied as his mouth found hers in the darkness. For a minute, with a twinge of guilt, he thought of Jove, of his own resolutions.

But this was an oasis. A time when they both needed each other in a world threatening to fall apart. She would remember soon enough. But now . . .

They came together like thirst-driven travelers in an oasis of deprivation.

"That was dessert without the dinner," he protested when they were back on earth. "There wasn't even time to—"

"There is now," she whispered, taking his hand and putting it on her breast.

"I must say I can feel an improvement," he commented.

"I've always had a good bosom," she said, offended.

"Have I complained? But what became of the girl? You feel like a woman."

"Jared, I love you. You know I love you. Stop!"

"Do you really want me to stop?"

This time they savored each second, moving slowly at first, enjoying the mounting ecstasy.

Suddenly she stiffened in his arms, and he knew awareness had finally returned to her.

"How can we? How can we when Jove's dead out in the next room?"

"Do you think Jove would want to stop us? Maybe it's because of Jove that we must."

She came to him again, holding him as if she feared it might be he who was lost to her, as well as Jove. He felt the dampness on her cheeks when she finally lay still in his arms.

"There are things I feel I should say to you," he ventured after awhile.

"Just tell me you love me. That's all I want to hear."

"You know that already. It's about Jove. About the woman, Tansy. And about her baby."

"I don't think there's much left that can be said about that." There was bitterness in her voice.

"Letty was wrong. All of us had something to do with what's happened. You saw things differently because you hadn't spent months plotting and making plans. You did what you thought was right."

"But it was wrong."

"None of the people hold it against you."

"But Jove—"

"I was the one who thought Jove would be useful. I was the one who asked him to go. Tansy or not, Jove would be alive right now if I hadn't invited him. And Poppy. If Poppy hadn't lost her head, it still might not have happened. You could even reason that if Letty hadn't given birth to Jove, he'd not be out there dead."

"Letty hates me."

"A mother who's lost her son."

He pulled Fannette back into the circle of his body. "Enough has been said."

But still she sobbed softly against him, and he made no move to stop her. This was another release she needed. Finally she slept.

He awakened just before dawn to the awareness of her body next to his. This is true contentment, he reflected. Just being close. Even the delirium of sex failed to bring the fulfillment of awakening to a loved one's nearness. To know that what you hold is a part of yourself.

If only they were in Cincinnati, and the time of sharing was with them . . .

If only Jove hadn't been the one . . .

Out in the main room, he could hear movements. Time to get up and face what lay ahead.

"I can't go out there," she whispered, her face buried in his chest. He wondered how long she'd been awake.

"You must. We must."

She pulled away. "This time, please don't leave me."

"We've got until Cincinnati," he told her, remembering his earlier thoughts. Cincinnati when they'd be free to live their own life.

"After Cincinnati?" Her voice was strained.

"I'll have to go on to Sandusky, to see our people safe on the boat to Canada."

He kissed her, not realizing the meaning she'd read into his words. They had till Cincinnati.

She lay very still, wishing that Pearl hadn't carried her in from the snow. Knowing that the part of her that had run blindly toward self-destruction no longer existed.

XIV

"They crucified my Lord
An' he never say a mumblin' word;
They crucified my Lord
An' he never said a mumblin' word;
Not a word, not a word, not a word.

They nails him to de tree
An' he never say a mumblin' word."

Wednesday's selections might be mournful, Fannette thought, but no one could deny he had a sense of what was fitting. No, neither had anyone ever heard Jove say a mumbling word. Except maybe about Letty's cooking, and that had been understandable!

All morning there had been the sound of sawing and hammering as Chippers worked in a shed with wood Jared had brought back from town. Letty had refused to move from the corner where Jove's body lay. She rocked back and forth, moaning and calling out her bereavement. Trojan stayed next to her, his hand on her shoulder, his face deeply grooved.

After Poppy had recovered from her first burst of grief, she sat on the bench near the fire with Anton beside her. They conversed softly, seriously. Occasionally he reached for one of her hands and covered it with his own.

So? she thought. And what was between the two of them? Poppy with her curly, short hair looking very unboylike, and Anton, with his neat, pointed beard, showing such concern? Anton, elegant still, despite his clothing, but so much older than when he'd followed her from New Orleans.

We're all older, Fannette thought, as she watched Chippers and George Washington carry in the long wooden box. Suddenly she felt frightened at the frailty of her own humanity and knew that the others shared the realization as they gathered together for Wednesday's funeral prayers.

It could have been any one of them. They could be like Junie, Willie, Tansy's baby—and now Jove.

An entire life over before it had really begun.

> "De Angels mourned, and I mourned too,
> Mournin' wid a sword in my hand, Lord,
> Mournin' wid a sword in my hand."

Wednesday finally finished the ceremony, and they all stood with lowered heads. Above them, the sun came out and they knew that for the while, at least, the snow was over.

Jared had called a meeting, and Fannette could not help but remember the last one. It was right after they'd put Junie in the ground.

"We've two weeks at the most before we reach the Quakers," Jared told them. "That's allowing for stopping and the possibility of another snowstorm."

Two weeks. How far to Banbury Cross? Two weeks, my dear! Two weeks in the snow. And then—then she'd know . . .

Oh, my Lord, Fannette thought, am I going out of my mind? She tried to listen. To hear his words. This man who had held her in his arms and made love to her only the night before—and who seemed a stranger now. No intimate look. No special glances.

"We won't need the cart. We can carry food and bedding on the pack horses. Trojan, Letty, and the children can ride ahead on the regular roads. There's no notice out for them. Traveling by day, they should reach Cincinnati well ahead of us."

"What about Glory?" Trojan asked. He made no attempt to hide his relief. Letty was in no condition to continue hiding in barns in the cold nights ahead.

"Glory can ride Jove's horse. We'll put Abe and Chippers on the horses that belonged to those slave hunters."

Then came what she'd been dreading. "There's no reason why Mrs. McLaury and Miss Poppy—or Mr. Anton, for that matter—should have to go with us. They'll be safe enough riding their horses in the daylight and stopping at night in inns."

"No!" Fannette exclaimed. "No! No! No!"

Jared scowled, but she had the feeling he wasn't displeased.

"My obedient wife," he said softly. She saw a smile flicker across Anton's lips. He took Fannette's hand and bent over it, not quite touching his lips to the flesh, with only the warmth of his breath on it.

"*Ma chére* madame!" he said, half humorously.

"Poppy?" Jared asked, ignoring Anton.

"No," she said. "I want to stay."

Anton had released Fannette's hand, and when Jared turned to him, he shrugged.

"I've come this far," he said. "I'm curious to see the end."

"Your arm?" Jared inquired.

Another indifferent shrug. "It mends. Perhaps my dueling days are over. A man appears awkward when he can't lift his left arm."

The meeting over, Jared dispatched George Washington to the barn to get a couple bottles of rum.

"A belated wake," he explained later to Fannette as they listened to the sounds from the loft. "But necessary. Tomorrow night we set out again."

Poppy protested, her eyes on Fannette, but Jared insisted she move into the bedroom. Fannette tried to hide the hurt she felt.

348

"It's not easy for Jared," Poppy attempted to explain later. "But for now he belongs with the people."

Fannette undressed slowly, listening to the voices in the outer room. Trojan was to set out early in the morning, and she could hear Jared as he went over the plans. Explaining where he was to go, what he was to say. Only once did Letty speak, but her voice was dull, as if none of it really mattered.

Poppy paused, brush in hand, her eyes on Fannette's waist.

"I hope Zette catches," she said.

Fannette glanced down, anxiously.

"Do I show?" she asked.

"A little. When you wear a thin nightdress. In the breasts mostly, I think."

Fannette brought up her arms protectively, shielding her breasts. Remembering what Jared had said about them. Savoring the memory.

"When does a woman really begin to show?" she asked. "Hopelessly, I mean."

Poppy smiled. "Depends on the woman."

Only two weeks to go. No worry for so short a time. Two weeks. But she'd have to ease out some of the seams on her skirt if she wanted to continue buttoning it.

The snow had melted rapidly, and the greening had started. Here and there trees began to show new growth. The night was bright with the moon and stars when they passed around Lexington. That dawn they stopped in a barn and slept through the day. Fannette had grown accustomed to the quiet exchanges between Jared and the station masters, or conductors, as they appeared pleased to call themselves. She noted the quick acceptance of a need for shelter, and upon occasions, the even more welcomed contribution of warm bread and hot soup. Word is sent ahead, Jared explained to her.

And who were these people, she marveled, these people who lived in the midst of slave owners and risked their lives, risked everything they possessed, to help black refugees?

Abe now led the group that had been under Trojan's care. Poppy and Anton still had their own following, as had Jared and Fannette.

They conversed very little during those never-ending hours of darkness. The weather continued to be cold, sometimes frosty, but there were no clouds and the paths were well lighted by a full moon.

Mile by mile, night by night, they neared their destination. Jared arranged for a rest stop near Williamsburg, Kentucky. Laundry was piling up, and the women were demanding the time to wash it.

"How can there be so many things dirty when no one has any more than one change of clothing?" he complained.

It was a barn again, and not as clean as most. The men built a fire out in the yard, and Jared arranged for water and boiling tubs.

Fannette apprehensively watched the gathering clouds. When the first drops began to fall, she expected to hear wailing from the women. Instead, they had their lines strung up around the fire that burned in a drum in the barn.

The smell of steaming wool and lye soap permeated the air. Fannette tried to ignore her churning stomach, and she regretted the decision that had led her to refuse Glory's tea that morning.

"Nette, you're green!" Poppy told her. And Fannette could swear there was a glint of laughter in those innocent, golden eyes.

"Nonsense!" Fannette disclaimed, and moved away. But there was very little space left for movement. One was constantly lashed by a wet garment. And there was the need to watch for slumbering bodies. The air was thick

350

with fumes. Too much, she decided. Too much!

She looked around for Glory, but then she realized she'd never be able to hold off until the tea could be brewed. She tried to move toward the door at a sedate pace, but she ended by dashing through it.

When it was over, someone handed her a handkerchief. She used it and looked up into Jared's concerned eyes. He held her until she'd stopped trembling, then he tilted up her chin, so he could look into her face.

"Are you certain there isn't something you should tell me?" he asked. His eyes glinted as humorously as had Poppy's.

Did they consider it laughable that she'd been sick? Beasts! Both of them!

"The smells," she explained.

"Bad," he agreed. "They'd welcome you up at the house."

She shook her head, but when she thought of going back inside, her stomach made threatening heaves. And the rain was thickening into snow.

"My dear," he said, "it's about time you learned to take orders graciously." With a firm grip on her elbow, he started up the path.

"Will you stay with me?" she asked hopefully. Fannette, she thought, where's your pride? Fannette Randolph, you should be ashamed of yourself! But Mrs. McLaury was something else, again. Didn't she have the right to ask this of the man who called himself her husband?

"I'll send Poppy up to stay with you," he said quietly, and she felt it was the tone an adult might have used to an importunate child.

Poppy showed no reluctance to accept the hospitality offered by the farmhouse.

"*Tôt ou tard*," she admitted. "I might have had to run outside myself."

But the people seemed oblivious to the closeness and the

351

fumes. Not since first they'd started on the road had Fannette heard so much laughter among them.

Two days of steady snow. Two days shut in the smoky, odorous barn, and they danced to Abe's fiddle and clapped their hands in time to the song Wednesday led. Fannette suspected that Jared had broken out the last of the rum. Eyes and faces were shining, and the voices were loud.

"When you waits as long as us," Pearl told her, "a day more don't make no difference. We knows for sure we gits to Canada now."

"Not if they hear you over at the next farm," Jared said, joining them. "See if you can hush up the folks a little."

Thirty miles and they'd be at the Ohio. No wonder they felt it was time to celebrate.

Everyone had a reason to be happy. Everyone, that is, but she.

When they started out the next evening, the snow had stopped, but what lay on the ground was over a foot deep. As the night grew colder, a crust of ice formed, and footing became insecure. Sinking, slipping, and sliding, each step a new hardship.

The midnight stop was at a deserted shack. They decided to stay there, though they had only gone seven miles. Jared rode to the other two groups and brought them back with him.

The fire was slow to start, and when it did, there seemed no warmth in the feeble blaze. The only real heat came from human bodies packed closely in the tiny room.

"*Merde*!" Anton muttered, rubbing a foot. "If I don't end with a chilblain, it will be a miracle."

"Shame!" Poppy said, laughing at the miserable sight he made huddled in a corner. "And you on a horse! Think of those who walked!"

352

"They had the good sense to wear warm shoes," Anton protested, looking at his elegant, but worn riding boots. "They make these of paper, I suspect."

The next night they progressed as far as the farmhouse that had been planned for the night before. But during the day the sun beat down, melting the snow, the first real promise that winter was finally loosening its grip.

Three more days and it'll be April, Fannette thought. The fields would be readied for the plow down South. Another month and the corn and cotton would go in. The trees would be in full leaf, and at Bijou it would most likely be raining.

She felt a sense of loss. I'm homesick, she told herself. I never felt I'd ever be homesick.

And in a few more weeks her baby would start its fourth month. She wished she had listened more closely to the conversations at Donna's teas, but it was certain things were becoming quite tight around her middle, even with the seams let out. Maybe if she ate less . . .

They were near! Two more days and they could be as close as Covington. From there, Jared had said he would arrange for skiffs to get them across the Ohio.

Then Cincinnati!

They came to a barn, then a farmhouse. Birds were singing in the trees. At a place near Covington, the conductor and his wife were awakened by Jared's dawn knock.

"We haven't known what to think!" Ken Stanton, a tall, lean man exclaimed. "We heard the rumors and we knew the hunt was on."

"And still is," Jared confirmed. "Will we be able to cross tomorrow night?"

Mrs. Stanton had already thrown on a robe and was leading the people toward the barn, where she had prepared a place to hide them. She had led Poppy and Fannette to a bedroom, but Fannette refused to leave Jared, and sat by quietly while the men worked over maps.

"I trust you will excuse me?" Anton inquired. "My arm has been a bother the last two nights, and I'm looking forward to a comfortable bed."

He left for the room assigned him, and Fannette reflected that it would be the first time he'd slept in a bed since the visit to his friends in Baton Rouge. Jared, of course, would stay in the barn with the others.

And Cincinnati was so close . . .

"The skiffs will be hidden in this cove," their host was telling Jared, his fingertip on the map. "Try to land over here on the north shore. It's lonely, and there's a ravine with a creek running through it. There are caves which will give some sort of shelter until you can get word to the Quakers. They'll have to come by night."

"But we'll be in a Free State!" Fannette interrupted.

Stanton nodded. "You'll be in a Free State, but there's still the Fugitive Slave Law, and it respects no state. There's no safety for a refugee this side of Canada."

Mrs. Stanton had returned from the barn, and she brought them coffee and cake.

"Someone responsible should go in the first skiff," Stanton said, as he sipped at his cup. "Someone to see to the scattering of your people. I suggest it should be you, Mr. McLaury."

"I'll go with them."

"And a white person should be in the last skiff, just in case. Mr. Verdier, perhaps?"

"There's his arm to consider. It's giving him more trouble than he likes to admit. The bullet went too deep for Glory. He'll have to see a physician as soon as we're with the Quakers."

"It still will be better for him to be in the last skiff." Stanton hesitated. "I heard a rumor yesterday that your party was headed this way. I expect they'll be watching the Ohio within the next few days."

354

To have come this far, to have gone through what they'd gone through, only to be caught on the outskirts of their goal! Fannette tried to keep back her exclamation. Mrs. Stanton leaned closer and patted her hand.

"Wouldn't you care to rest, my dear?" she asked.

Fannette shook her head.

"Only four skiffs!" Jared was saying. "But there's twenty-seven of us—and all adults!"

"It's the best I could do. You could go in two relays."

"One crossing holds more danger than I care to consider." Jared swirled his coffee thoughtfully. "And horses? I'll want two, so I can ride into Cincinnati to get word to the Quakers."

"Two?"

"Yes. One with a sidesaddle. I want to take Mrs. McLaury with me."

"I'll stay with the others," Fannette said flatly.

Jared's eyes flashed over her, cold with displeasure. "You will do as I say," he told her.

She felt the color rush to her cheeks, but again Mrs. Stanton patted her hand. "It'll look better," she reasoned. "No one's likely to be suspicious of a man and his wife riding into the city.

"They will be when they see the condition of my best riding skirt. It's been bundled into a budget."

"I can press it, my dear. Do you have a hat?"

That, at least, she had. When the rain had made it necessary to wear her hooded cloak, Letty had put her hat into a clean sack that had been suspended over one of the packs.

"You cum to a town, you needs to look lak a lady," she had insisted.

And there was the problem of her jacket. She hadn't worn it in weeks. She knew it would be tight.

"We'll have the horses tethered by this creek," Stanton was saying, his fingers on the map. "You'll land close by. We've used the place before. Follow the ravine and you'll find some deep caves."

Mrs. Stanton held out Fannette's hat, freshly steamed and brushed. Fannette worked at arranging her scarf so it would hide where her jacket buttons didn't meet.

"The time for riding is past, my dear," Mrs. Stanton remarked, smiling. "It's a good thing tomorrow will end it."

Tomorrow will end it. Tomorrow she'd be in Cincinnati.

XV

Fannette caused a delay that they could ill afford, and Poppy found it difficult to keep out of the argument.

"You most certainly will go with me in the first boat," Jared insisted.

The old Fannette with the flashing eyes and chin held high shook her head.

"I want to stay here until I know they're all safe," she said. "It's my fault, what's happened, and I'm not about to run off and leave everyone on this side." She looked over at Poppy. "Poppy'll be more help to you on the other side, anyway."

Anton stepped between them. "*Ma chére* madame," he interposed. "I have no wish to offend you, but Poppy will be better in the last boat with me. Remember, if anyone sees us, they'll consider her a boy. A man and his son, on their way to Virginia, but too poor to hire a regular boat. Alas, we've fallen on evil days, and we have only a few faithful blacks left to us."

Poppy surpressed a giggle. And "*chére* madame," Anton had said, not the more intimate *chérie!* But it was typical that Anton should have accepted her as Madame McLaury. In her condition, anything else would have been unthinkable!

For some reason, Anton's argument carried more conviction than Jared's. She permitted herself to be helped into the skiff with Sassie and old Chippers. Pearl and Glory shook their heads, preferring to wait, so Crane climbed in with Abby, and Leon took the oarsman seat beside Jared.

The men on the bank pushed them off, and Poppy held her breath as she saw how low the boat sank into the

357

water. She decided the skiff that carried only six would be the one she'd load with Pearl, George Washington, and the heavier of the people. The last boat, and the one in the poorest condition, would carry old Glory, who weighed almost nothing, Abe, Wednesday, Nate and Lillie, beside Anton and herself. It should work out well.

Their lantern shed a small island of light, but all else was darkness. Soon, all they knew of the lead boat was the fading sound of oars dipping into the water.

"Time," Anton said, and the two of them worked together loading the second boat. Then the third. It was important that Wednesday and Nate ride the fourth, because Anton's arm made him useless at the oars.

"We work well together," Anton commented, coming to her side as they watched George Washington push off the third skiff, and then swing over its side into it. The boat sank with his weight.

"Yes, that we do," she agreed.

Such a short way to go, Poppy thought. Please, Blessed Virgin, be with us.

Anton put his right arm around her, and their lips met almost without a conscious intent.

"You will marry me," Anton announced with determination. "Anything else is not to be considered. We think together. We understand together."

"You're fickle and I am not."

"Fickle? You think of Fannette? I realize now that I'd find her wearing in time. Her temperament is not one of submission. There'd always be that battle of the minds. *Bien,* for Jared this is well. But for me, *no.*"

"You think me submissive?"

"Quiet. Soothing. Sympathetic. But with a wit that will always be a delight."

"Time we start the last boat," Wednesday announced.

"I gittin' jitters jus' thinkin' I hears people," Nate agreed.

Anton put Poppy in the narrow prow seat. Glory squatted on the bottom, Nate and Wednesday on the rowing bench, Lillie on the bottom behind the oarsmen, and Abe with Anton squeezed into the rear bench.

Nate and Wednesday shoved the boat free of the bank and jumped inside. It sank alarmingly.

How could she have been so stupid as to save this, the worst of the skiffs, for the last? Poppy wondered. No boat to follow them, to help them in case of trouble. Stupid! And she'd been so pleased with her own efficiency!

"He leak!" Glory said suddenly. Poppy leaned forward and found a can under her seat. She gave it to Glory, who was in the best position to bail.

"There's another bailer over on this side," Anton said in the darkness. He gave it to Lillie. "*Sacre bleu!* This wreck must be riddled with holes!"

If they started to sink, how would those on the other bank even know they were in trouble? They had put out their lantern, and it was very dark out on the river. She could feel her feet becoming wet. Could feel the water rising inside the boat.

"Bail faster!" Anton exclaimed. "We'll drown inside the skiff if you don't!" He took off his hat and used it to scoop out water. Abe was using his cap, but without much success.

Poppy reached over the edge in an attempt to judge how low they rode, but the prow was higher than the beam. She could hear the sobbing intake of the oarsmen's breath as they strained to speed up the rowing.

Thank the Merciful Mother that the river wasn't unreasonably wide at this point. But how far to the bank? Were they near, or barely in the middle?

She could hear Glory muttering as she worked. Probably, Poppy decided, a prayer to some forgotten god. She was certain Wednesday would have started one of his spirituals, but he had no breath left for it.

If only she had the comfort of her rosary. Well, she had her fingers. Twice on one hand was a decade . . .

The moon edged out of the clouds and they could see the shore. Before anyone could stop him, Anton climbed over the edge.

"I can pull it in," he said. "We're near enough for me to touch bottom."

The water came to just below his chin, and he worked himself around to the prow. He took the mooring rope in his right hand and loped it over his shoulder and pulled.

Then, suddenly, his head went under. Poppy screamed, but he managed to surface again and grasped the side of the boat.

"It draws!" he gasped. "The sand draws. It sucks me down!"

"Lawd, hear us like Jonah in the whale an' Moses in the Red Sea," Wednesday droned as he pulled on the oars.

There was a shout from the shore. They were seen! Blessed Mother be thanked, they were seen!

Jared yelled out to them and threw a length of rope. It fell short, and so did the next throw. On the third cast, Nate dropped his oar and caught it. He secured the end around his bench. On shore, the men lined up, and began pulling.

They were all nearly as wet as Anton by then. The boat sank completely just short of the land, and they waded to the high bank, grasping at vegetation to pull themselves up.

Anton threw himself face down on the dry earth. He lay there, shivering and gasping for breath.

Poppy picked up the lantern and rushed with it to Anton's side.

"His wound's broken open!" she exclaimed, and moved away so Glory could examine it.

"Hurry!" Jared called. "We can't stay here any longer. We've got to get back into the ravine."

Poppy saw, then, that the women had already been sent ahead. She gave Glory her scarf, and together they bound Anton's shoulder as tightly as they could. Then Juba and

360

George Washington supported Anton between them.

They had only gone a short distance when they met Pearl coming back for them.

"We find a cave!" she told them breathlessly.

It was a good, deep cave, and they were even able to build a small fire. The packs were already heaped inside, and Poppy found the one containing Anton's change of clothing. She left Anton in George Washington's care while she looked for her own things.

"The horses are tethered by the creek," Jared said. "I'll go get them now, and at first light, Fannette and I will ride into Cincinnati.

Poppy looked around for Fannette and saw her sitting away from the others.

"We've done it!" Poppy exclaimed, hugging her. "We'll all be in Cincinnati tonight!"

Fannette looked pale in the firelight.

"I know," she replied. "Oh, I know!"

XVI

They rode at a steady pace, but Fannette fretted at the slowness.

"Shouldn't we go faster?" she asked, thinking of the huddled people they'd left behind. Thinking of Anton who was still shaking with a chill, despite his rising fever. Of the fact that there was no food in the cave. It had gone down with the last skiff.

"It doesn't matter how soon we get there," Jared explained. "The wagons can't go after them until late tonight."

Fannette thought of the women who like herself were pregnant.

"This is the last hardship," Jared told her gently. "They've made it, Fannette, that's the important thing. Tomorrow they'll sleep in comfortable beds with full stomachs. In a few days they'll be on their way to Sandusky. Then the boat to Canada."

It sounded splendid, the way he put it. But what of those cold, hungry women who prayed that what they carried would be born in freedom? Was it really worth all they'd gone through? The lives that had been lost along the way?

At the boarding house they were greeted warmly. Jared led Fannette up the outside steps, his arm around her shoulders half supporting her.

"Aunt Katy will have you fed and resting in no time," he assured her. He brushed back her hat and looked into her face. "You're a pale little ghost."

"Just cold," she whispered. "Cold and damp."

A young girl in gray answered the door. Her pretty face lit up at the sight of Jared.

362

"Jared!" she exclaimed. "Jared, we've worried much about thee!"

"And you, Hope! How you've grown this last year!" He picked her up and kissed her cheek.

"Jared! Thou knowest that isn't proper!" Hope scolded happily. "Oh, 'tis so good to see thee!"

Jared drew Fannette forward, his arm back on her shoulder.

"Hope, this is Fannette. She's in need of food and a warm bed."

Hope took Fannette by the hand. "How cold thou art," she scolded anxiously. "Come to my room and I'll find some night clothes for thee. Aunt Katy will put on the soup pot, and we'll make thee up a bed and put a warming pan in it."

Just as she started to drift off to sleep, fed and blessedly warm, Fannette had a disquieting thought. This was the first time since leaving New Orleans that Jared had failed to introduce her as his wife . . .

"We have a wounded man," Jared said over a bowl of thick soup in the kitchen.

"A fugitive?"

"No. A white man. And there's a girl who's white—or nearly."

"Free?"

"Yes."

"Then thou canst take me there when thou hast eaten. We'll go in a small conveyance. Tonight we'll take the large spring wagons for the others. Wounded? Have I not told thee the Lord does not love guns?"

"Perhaps not," Jared agreed. "But without them, we'd be dead."

They arrived with food and blankets, but Poppy was only concerned with Anton as they lifted him into the back of the small covered wagon. She climbed in after him and cradled his head in her lap.

And wished she didn't remember Trojan doing the same for Jove.

Anton was delirious. Had been since morning. Delirious, and explaining his unsuitable marriage to *maman*.

"She is one to make the deValois proud," he kept repeating in his delirium. "If you must find fault, *maman*, then you'll do me the favor not to write."

And she had her own, private debate. What would she tell the mother superior? It was expected that on her return she would become a postulant.

And did she want marriage? Was it really for her? There was such a hunger in her to teach. But there was also a woman's hunger for a man and children. Which was the stronger? For which did God intend her?

A doctor was waiting when they reached the big boarding house. Anton was put to bed and the bullet probed out of his shoulder. Poppy stood by, feeling helpless.

"The wound's been well cared for and it'll heal," the physician told her. "But his lungs are congested and they're responsible for the fever." He looked at Poppy. "You'll keep a close watch on him? Or are you too tired? I can call Hope."

"I'll watch over him," she said.

She sat by him, preparing what she would say when he was well enough to hear.

"It was a beautiful dream, Anton. But it's not for either of us."

BOOK FOUR

The Sound of Baying Hounds

"Go blow them ram horns, Joshua cried,
Cause the battle is in my hand."

(Traditional spiritual)

"I heard de angels mourning on de hill,
Purtiest mourning I ever hear."

(Traditional spiritual)

I

Late in the night, Fannette was awakened by the muffled sound of the wagons setting out for the ravine. Just before dawn the wagons pulled up to the house and unloaded a hushed cargo. Stifled voices, scurrying feet, sounds in the attic. The smell of food carried past her door and on up the stairs to secret rooms kept ready under the eaves.

Fannette threw back her covers and lit a lamp. She found clothes ready, hanging over a chair. They fit too tightly in some places, and too loosely in others. The style was hardly what she'd have chosen, but they smelled fresh and clean. Starched and ironed to a faultless degree.

When Fannette entered the kitchen, Aunt Katy glanced up from her cooking. "Thou lookest well this morning," she said. "Jared has been much concerned."

"I heard the wagons. How is Anton?"

"We brought him here earlier yesterday while thou slept. He is much improved this morning, and the physician says the fever has left him."

"And Trojan and the children?"

"The children are united with their parents. The big black man has gone with Jared to sell the pack horses in Covington. Later Trojan will take the mare and return to Kentucky where I understand the wagons and carriage were left. The wagons will be sold and Trojan will ship the phaeton back to New Orleans."

"And Jared?"

"On his return tonight, he sets out with Levi. Levi will return in the morning, but Jared will go on to Sandusky."

"Oh." Fannette moved the food around on her plate.

Aunt Katy watched her, her eyes kindly peering from

367

behind her glasses.

"Jared has instructed me to take care of his wife who is in a family way."

Fannette dropped her spoon and stared at the woman.

"He said that?" she exclaimed.

"Also that I was to see she rested. He won't be back until it's time to leave again. But he says he'll see thee then."

"He might have stopped long enough to see me before he left!" The words were wrenched out of her.

"He wouldn't have thee disturbed."

Fannette was silent for a minute, but there was another question that had to be asked.

"And Letty?"

"She stays with neighbors. She's not a fugitive, and Jared thought it best."

Later, Fannette found the room where Anton was recovering. He was sitting up, but still alarmingly pale. Poppy sat across the room. She set down the volume of poems she'd been reading aloud when Fannette came through the open door.

Fannette went to Anton's side, and he raised her hands to his lips.

"*Regardez,*" he said. "The two of you are my destruction. You send me to France but the shell of a man. I, who always was considered irresistible to the ladies."

"You're recovering very rapidly," Poppy remarked. "By the time you arrive, you'll be ready for the wife you'll find. A woman who can see no one but you—and the new baby that'll arrive each year.

"And you give me no mistress?"

"There won't be time. And you'll become a great vintner. If it travels well, maybe someday we may taste your wine."

"You see?" Anton appealed to Fannette.

"But consider your mother," Fannette reminded him. "Think how happy she'll be with the fine French girl you honor."

"You're bitter," he said accusingly. "And Maman said such nice things about you . . ."

Fannette left the two of them and went down the hall to the room given her. She hesitated, glancing toward the attic stairs.

It was a miracle of organization, she reflected. No one would dream there were twenty-three adults up there and two children. Hope had told her that none of the boarders whom she'd seen breakfasting at the long dining table had any idea that fugitives were harbored there. Even she wouldn't have known of their arrival if she hadn't occupied the room closest to the attic entrance.

She put her hand onto the rail and went up the steps. The door was unlocked and she went down the narrow hallway. Faces appeared at the entrances to the rooms and the sounds of muffled greetings met her ears.

"I had to wish you well," she said.

"We leavin' tonight, Miz McLaury," Pearl told her, teeth flashing and eyes shining. "I glad you cum!" She patted her abdomen. "George Washington and me, we want to ast you can we name him Fannette if he a girl?"

"But Pearl! I never saw you take any of Glory's tea!"

"He jus' too glad to be in there to give trouble. But you ain't the only one with more in your belly than when we starts."

"You knew?"

"We all knows. Somethin' 'bout keepin' a woman an' her man apart like we had to jus' seem to make more things happen."

So, Fannette mused, this secret of mine. The only secret was that I thought it one . . .

"Letty and I are leaving in the morning for New Orleans," Poppy announced at dinner, her eyes sparkling. "Just imagine! Three months it took for us to get here—and only eight days back!"

New Orleans. Bijou. Donna. Breel. All part of the past.

Everyone knew what lay ahead. Everyone's life was resolving and branching out in different directions.

But what was ahead for her? It wasn't fair of Jared to keep her in this state of uncertainty. Jared who cared so little about the child she carried that he hadn't even mentioned it! Who claimed to love her, but who hadn't come near her since their arrival at the boarding house.

She went up to her room and sat down in a chair to wait for Jared. He wouldn't have left the message with Aunt Katy if he hadn't some intention of stopping to see her before he left, she told herself.

And what would his words be? I enjoyed our "adventure," Miss Randolph, she heard him saying. I really do love you. I want you to know that. My lawyer will see you in the morning.

Only he was a lawyer so he'd be spared that bother.

She fell asleep, her head against the high backboard. She had no idea of the time when the door opened and Jared came into the room. He was dressed for travel, a great coat slung over his arm. The lamplight reflected on his short beard.

He ran his fingers over it. "I'll see a barber when I come back. There hasn't been time since I got here. There hasn't been time for anything, including sleep."

"Nor for me," she replied. "But then, this is Cincinnati."

He had set aside his coat and was taking off his jacket. He paused. "Is that supposed to mean something?"

"You said we had until Cincinnati."

He knelt down beside her. He tried to take her hand, but she pulled it away.

"I meant until our people were safe. Until we could find a priest so you'd feel right about us."

"Because of what Anton said? That wasn't why I didn't believe in our marriage."

He had recaught her hand and twisted the ring on her finger.

370

"You treated me like—like a fancy piece."

His eyes widened and he laughed. "God almighty, where'd you learn that?"

"I listen," she said sulkily.

"Why do you consider yourself of such little value? Where's the girl who ordered me out of the garden at Bijou?"

"That was Fannette Randolph, and she never really existed."

"Nor does she now," he said softly. "There's only Fannette McLaury." He took her hungrily into his arms. "There isn't time for talk," he said, his lips on hers. "We leave at midnight."

She lay on the bed, watching him take off his clothes. He had undressed her first, pausing to kiss each newly bared stretch of soft flesh. The warm ache of desire made her reach out to touch him.

"Hurry," she whispered. "Oh, Jared, I think being pregnant makes me even more shameless."

He paused and leaned over her, caressing her taunt breasts and kissing the rounded abdomen. She shivered with delight.

He pulled off his underclothes and their lips clung as he moved over her.

There was a loud knocking at the door. Jared swore softly, but the knocking grew louder.

"I'm sorry!" It was Hope's voice. "Word just came that this house is to be watched! They're loading everyone into the wagons right now."

"Oh hell!" Jared muttered. He dropped a quick kiss on Fannette's forehead and sat up reaching for his clothing. "I'll be right down!" he called out.

"You're not going to leave?" Fannette exclaimed. "We haven't had any time together since we came here!"

"You heard her," Jared said, pulling on his shirt. "There's not a second to spare."

It was absolutely the last straw. Fannette caught his

371

arm. "Isn't it time you considered me? Considered my feelings?"

"There isn't a moment when I don't. When I come back all of this will be behind us. The job'll be done."

Fannette spoke coldly. "When you come back I won't be here."

"Would you have me let our people down? Would you ask that?"

"Yes!" she replied. "Yes, yes, yes!"

He pulled her up and held her firmly in his arms, but she struggled to free herself.

"You be here when I come back," he said quietly, and went out, closing the door behind him.

"Why should I be?" she called after him. "Why should I be?"

From outside in the hallway came his reply.

"Because if you aren't, I promise you all hell will break loose!"

II

Fannette kissed Poppy goodbye the next morning and then went to where Levi worked over his accounts.

"How long before he comes back?" she asked.

Levi looked over his glasses at her. "The way will be slow. The wagons must travel by night on dark, muddy roads."

"How many days? How many?"

He smiled the kindly, humorous smile that transformed his stern features.

"Thou art as impatient as a new bride."

Yes. And once she might have been. But not any longer. Not the new Fannette.

"I'll not torture thee," he went on. "It could well be ten or eleven days before the wagons reach Sandusky. And perhaps there might be a wait for the boat."

"And the way back?"

"It is my thought thy husband will travel fast. Eight days? Perhaps less."

Eighteen or twenty days. Practically into May. Then there was time. Hope had told her that morning that Jared had left money for clothing. Though it hurt her pride, Fannette resolved to accept it. She'd need what little she had in her reticule for boat fare. It was well enough for Poppy to travel in donated gowns, but Poppy wasn't pregnant.

She found Hope working in the kitchen. "When you're free," she said, "I would like you to take me to the place you mentioned. The place where there are ready-made gowns that can be altered to drape instead of fit."

It wasn't that she showed so badly, only that these things might have to do her for awhile. Once in New Orleans she'd find a dressmaker, but it would all take time. The new, cold Fannette was adept at making plans, at sensing the pitfalls. And at resenting. There would be no further chance for Jared to humble her, to reduce her to begging.

It was all very clear what she must do. First register at a small decent hotel. Then the visit to Donna's solicitor.

Her plans weren't clear on just where she'd go. But someplace. Some place where Jared would never find her. Some place away from New Orleans and Bijou.

"You can't run away!" Hope wept as she rode in the buggy to where the New Orleans sidewheeler was docked. "Jared will be out of his mind!"

But she could and did. She stood on the deck watching Cincinnati disappear.

And she told herself she was glad. She brushed away the tears with a gloved hand and told herself to smile.

III

She tried to think back, to coldly sort her thoughts until she found the time when resentment replaced love. She found it, finally. It was when Aunt Katy revealed that Jared knew of their child. When she was forced to realize that all those months he had stood silently by knowing and remaining detached. Letting her fend for herself at a time when a woman most needed the support of the man she loved.

And the final insult. When he had left after that brief, disastrous visit to her bedroom, still without an acknowledgement.

But hadn't he touched her with particular tenderness? Hadn't his lips caressed the growing roundness of her abdomen?

She pushed aside those weakening reflections. Just as it had been and still was dangerous to think back on Breel and Bijou, it was foolhardy to remember those moments she and Jared had shared.

Now her thoughts had to be for the future. For the home she'd make for the child.

And there were other matters. Other guilts that must be resolved before she could be free to start a new life.

She wished she could talk to Father Pierre, but that would mean visiting the little church that served the bayou around Bijou. She couldn't chance that. She'd made the old solicitor promise against his will not to let the Lutons know she was in New Orleans. But if she visited Father Pierre the truth could not be withheld.

Instead, she went to the cathedral, to an old priest who did not know her name.

"I need to talk to you, Father. About a thing I did. A

matter of guilt . . ."

While she talked, his age-twisted fingers stroked the large crucifix that fell over his breast. When she had finished, he touched her forehead and gave his blessing.

"Guilt isn't a bad thing," he said, "even though you might find many who say it is. It's a guideline to show where we've erred and a Godgiven incentive toward ultimate perfection."

He touched his crucifix again, his eyes troubled. "I find those who lash themselves with guilt use it as an excuse for every sort of excess instead of as a spur toward improvement. They decide guilt is bad, something to be abandoned. But to discard guilt is to discard shame, and to discard shame is to set aside one's conscience."

He paused thoughtfully. "A soul without a conscience is a soul in anarchy." He smiled down at her. "Now I've given a sermon and not really answered your question. You say there were those that died because of your act. That's a burden you must learn to bear. But you must also remember that you were ignorant of what might happen and that you thought you were doing a good thing."

For a few minutes he searched her face, his wise old eyes missing little. "Are you certain there isn't more that's troubling you, my child?"

She avoided his gaze. After all, there were things one must resolve for oneself. And she couldn't trust herself to speak of Jared yet. Someday, maybe. But not yet. And this wasn't the confessional.

When she returned to the hotel, her door opened without needing a key. Her first thought was that the maid had come to clean, but the room was still in the state she'd left it, except that Jared was waiting in the single uncomfortable chair.

She closed the door behind her and leaned against it, fear draining her strength. She'd seen Jared angry before, but never like this.

"How did you find me?" she asked. Her lips felt dry

and her tongue adhered to the roof of her mouth.

"I wore out my horses and went without sleep and food to get back to you as fast as possible," he told her, his eyes burning into hers. "Then I found you'd run away. I took a boat for New Orleans that same day and went to Bijou."

"You should have known I wouldn't be there," she said lifelessly.

"Donna was hurt, more hurt than you can imagine, that you hadn't cared to see her. Your father—"

"Breel."

"Your father has aged. He feels very deeply about you."

"It's a little late for that." Suddenly she felt a renewal of life, a blinding flash of resentment. "It's a little late for everything!"

"Including me, I suppose?" His eyes were mocking her.

"Yes."

"Fannette, my exasperating love, when are you going to learn that there are things that must be faced? Do you intend to spend the rest of your life running? Dragging our child with you?"

"It's my child. Your interest is a bit tardy. I'm the one carrying it."

"And who put it there? Who gave it to you?"

Her cheeks flamed. "Must you be so crude?"

"You didn't find it under a cabbage bush. Haven't I some say in its future?"

"Why? Why, when until now it's meant so little to you?"

"There was hardly a moment when I wasn't watching over you. When I wasn't aware of your every need."

"But you weren't willing to share it with me."

"It seems that goes both ways. I don't know your reason, but I know mine. Your attempt to conceal your condition gave you the strength to keep going—even when the going wasn't easy."

Fannette stripped off her gloves. A slow, deliberate motion. "My reasons were obvious. But I'm no longer the lovesick girl who followed you almost the length of the United States. Who begged for what crumbs of affection you might find time to offer. That's over. Through."

"It is? After everything we've been to each other?"

She tried to keep her voice steady. "And just what have we been to each other? You said once I was making our being together a rut in the hay. Well, wasn't it? When did you talk to me, share your thoughts? When? Not even the night you left me in Cincinnati."

"I had a duty that night. You knew that."

"I knew Levi was going with the wagons, that you could join them the next morning and take over after that. He would have understood."

Jared looked at her blankly. "Will you believe me when I say it didn't come to my mind? I was so in the habit of—"

"Of sacrificing your wife to anything and everything! It wasn't just the lovemaking, it was my need to talk to you. To find out what was ahead. I'd been nearly crazy with worry all that time in Cincinnati. I lived for the moment I could find out what the future held, and then you left without even a mention of our child."

The anger was leaving his face and he moved toward her, but she backed away.

"I'll scream for help if you touch me," she warned him. "I know the danger there, your way of stopping our arguments."

He smiled, it was his old, amused smile and it did almost as much damage as his touch would have done.

"As I remember it," he remarked, "our arguments were usually after, not before."

She bit her lip, trying to hold onto her dignity, to remember her resolutions. Things were being said that needed airing, but it was disconcerting to have him agree. It took the power from her resolutions.

"I've no intention of going through life in cold fear every time I hear a hound bay in pursuit. Of being second to

378

whatever adventure you might have involved yourself in like some half-grown boy who hasn't realized the responsibility of being an adult. No, the glamour has worn thin."

"As has your love?"

"I can't say that," she admitted. "But it doesn't change anything." She felt the beginning of tears, and she moved over to the long, narrow window. She drew aside the drapes, pretending to look out, but seeing only a blur.

She didn't hear him come up to her, but she felt his arms turning her to face him. He kissed her gently. "It's my time to beg," he said. "I'm nothing without you."

She shook her head.

"You have my promise."

Still she hesitated, but he pulled her closer to him.

"Once you told me you loved the thrill of danger," she reminded him.

"The talk of someone who hadn't outgrown the dream world of high adventure," he murmured as contritely as she could have wished.

"Not entirely." She was surprised to find herself defending him against himself. "I'm glad you were there to help our people."

She pulled herself away, distrusting her own weakness. "How did you find me?"

"Donna gave me the address of her solicitors. We both knew you'd need money. You'd forbidden them to tell the Lutons you were in New Orleans, but a husband was another matter."

He was at her side again, and this time she found herself leaning against him. He took out a handkerchief and wiped her cheek. "While I was at Bijou I called on Father Pierre. There's no impediment now to making our very legal marriage acceptable to your church."

"But—"

"Poppy was a good teacher. And do you know she's with the Ursulines? A postulant?"

"Poppy? Oh no!"

"And that your cousin—or is Ted your half-brother?"

"Half-brother," Fannette said reluctantly.

"He's to be married this Saturday. Donna expects us."

"No!"

"Yes." His hands were moving over the buttons down the back of her dress.

"Jared! It's barely past noon!"

"Do you object to adding half a day to the night? I've had almost no sleep since I left Sandusky. I've been out of my head with worry."

"Are you sure it's sleep you have in mind? Do you think you can win me back that easily?"

She felt the blood rush up into her cheeks under his steady gaze.

There was a knock at the door.

"Goddamn it!" he exclaimed. He lifted his head.

"Whoever it is, go away!" he bellowed.

"The chambermaid!" Fannette whispered. "She's such a gossip! And I've given the impression that I'm a widow."

He chuckled, looking at the black dress that lay on the floor at their feet. "When I take you out to dinner tonight, you'd better wear a veil to hide your blushes. You won't have to worry about the morning. We're leaving early for Bijou."

"I told you I will not go. Not even for—"

He silenced her the way he knew best . . .

When the phaeton rolled through the gate the next afternoon, Donna, Breel, and their son waited to greet Fannette and Jared.

Ted helped Fannette to the ground and Donna stepped forward to embrace her, but Fannette was looking past the woman she'd once thought was her aunt. She was looking into another pair of stormy dark eyes, and in them she saw love, concern, and resignation.

She ran to him. At last she had come home. There would always be those ghosts she'd never be able to completely lay aside: Willie, Junie, Anton's useless left arm, and Jove. The suffering, the cold, the fatigue, all of that which need not have been.

But at least she was at peace with her father.

EPILOGUE

Ted's wedding was splendid, Fannette reflected. His bride was no longer the scrawny, half-grown girl she'd remembered, and her half-brother was almost as handsome as their father. The reception would be discussed along the bayous and in New Orleans for months to come.

But for her it had none of the beauty of the quiet ceremony she had in the little bayou church.

"We have this ring," Jared told her. He held out a man's wedding band with an inset of braided gold.

"Abe gave it to me just before the boat left Sandusky. The people had taken up a collection—most likely everything they had. Hope brought the materials to Abe, and this was their gift to us."

Jared wore it now, and Fannette found herself looking at it. Their joyous people. Now truly joyous. The ring would always bind them to their memory.

And now was the time to relax. To make plans. They sat on the balcony overlooking Bijou's gardens.

"We'll settle briefly in Indiana," Jared was telling Breel. "By Indiana law, Zette will automatically be free when we take up residence. It's just too damn complicated to attempt to get a writ from the legislature, and chances are it wouldn't be granted."

Fannette drew in the scents rising from the gardens below. In two more days they'd be on a river boat headed north. Bijou would be left behind, perhaps forever.

"Then?" Breel was asking Jared.

"Then we'll go east so I can wind up details. Eventually, we'll go west. To San Francisco."

Fannette returned to the present. "By ship!" she exclaimed, her eyes flashing excitement. "Just as soon as the baby's old enough!"

"Well," Jared said evasively, "maybe not quite that soon."

Fannette moved over to the ornamental iron railing that encircled the balcony. She couldn't look at the others, she knew her eyes would reflect the apprehension that gripped her.

"It'll be so quiet here," Donna said, "with Ted married and on his honeymoon, you two heading west. And Fannette, did you know Poppy's joined the Ursulines? That she's a postulant?"

Breel chuckled softly, and they all turned to him.

"Nothing," he said. "My mind was back in the past."

Fannette glanced at Donna and saw that she, too, was smiling reflectively.

Bien, she thought, everyone has his secret.

Jared left his chair and stood beside her, his arm around her shoulder.

"Trojan tells me there are three men who've just reached the Settlement. It's important to get them out of Louisiana as soon as possible."

There it was. The chill tingling down her spine. The sound of hounds baying.

Only, of course, it was all in her own ears.

"You promised!" she whispered.

He smiled down at her. "Yes, I promised. That's why I told Trojan it was time I considered my responsibility to my family."

His arms pulled her to him, and as their lips met, she remembered Poppy's laughing comment: "How two people can so completely forget there's anyone else in the world . . ."

She glanced surreptitiously at her father and saw the amused glint in his eyes as he lifted his brandy glass in a silent toast to the two of them.

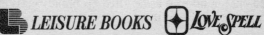